WHO WILL HEAR ME WHEN I CRY

By

David Johnson

1

Books in the Tucker series

Tucker's Way

An Unexpected Frost

April's Rain

March On

Who Will Hear Me When I Cry

ISBN-13: 978-1514803295

ISBN-10: 1514803291

Chapter One

Sitting on the edge of his mother's bed, thirteen-year-old Benjamin Trevathan carefully lifts a spoonful of chicken noodle soup to his mother's thin lips. There is a loud slurping sound as she sips the soup off the spoon.

"Thank you, Bennie," Joyce Trevathan says weakly. "That tastes mighty good."

"T-t-t-take some m-m-m-more," he says, offering another spoonful of soup. He watches her shake her head and feels a familiar sinking feeling in the pit of his stomach. "You ain't gonna g-g-get no better if you d-d-don't eat."

"I'm too tired right now, Baby. Maybe later." She closes her eyes and Benjamin thinks she's fallen back to sleep, but, keeping her eyes closed, she says, "Have the kids eat and got their homework?"

"Th-th-they're finishing up supper, then they'll d-d-d-do their homework."

Opening her eyes, his mother's skinny arm slips out from under the covers and strokes the side of his face. Her fingers feel cold and boney. "You're a good boy, Bennie. You know that don't you?"

"Y-y-yes ma'am." Avoiding his mother's gaze, Benjamin looks over her shoulder.

His mother gives his face a gentle shake. "Look at me when I'm talking, Bennie. Remember, you got that Asperger's disease. Teachers say you got to do a better job giving people eye contact."

Glancing directly at his mother, then averting his eyes again, Benjamin says, "Y-y-y-yes, Mama."

"I'm sorry things is the way they is with you, with me, with all of us," Joyce says. "But I can't do nothing about it."

"It's okay, Mama." Reaching toward her face, he wipes a solitary tear from the side of her sunken cheek. The greenish-yellow tint of her skin contrasts against her blackened and yellow teeth as she smiles at him. In another context she might be laughed at as the sad-looking clown in the circus. But this is no circus. "D-d-d-do you need anything else?" he asks.

"Put me one of them Elvis movies in the VCR."

Benjamin looks at the row of video cassettes, their labels barely legible – they've been used so often. "Which one, Mama?"

"It don't matter. I love 'em all. I can't wait to see Elvis in heaven when I die. I hope there's a special room reserved for Elvis fans there."

Picking out one of the movies and sliding it into the VCR, Benjamin turns on the TV and adjusts the volume. He pulls the covers up to mother's chin, turns off the bedside lamp, and leaves her room.

As he walks into the living room he feels the rotting floor of the house trailer bend under his weight.

"Bennie, I'm hungry," his six-year-old step-sister, Maria, says. "What's for supper?"

"Yeah, me, too," Benjamin's eight-year-old step-brother, Alexander, echoes.

Benjamin thinks about the lie he just told his mother, because he is anything but "okay" with how things are, but he reasons that the lie was justifiable under the circumstances. When the truth will hurt the feelings of someone you love, telling a lie suddenly becomes a reasonable option. "L-l-l-let me see what's in th-th-the kitchen," he tells his siblings.

Opening the refrigerator door, he takes in the two-thirds empty milk jug, the three eggs in their clear, plastic container, two cheese slices (one of which has been previously unwrapped and rewrapped, it's edges having turned dark and hard), an empty pickle jar, bottles of ketchup and of mustard, and eight cans of beer. It's as if the interior of the refrigerator is a mirror of the emptiness Benjamin feels. Sliding open a drawer, he spies a package of baloney and counts six pieces. "How about baloney?" he calls out.

Unbeknownst to him, Maria has followed him into the kitchen and is standing right behind him. "I'm tired of baloney," she says.

Benjamin jumps. "Y-y-y-you s-s-s-scared me! D-d-d-don't sneak up on me!"

"I'm sorry," Maria replies, her bottom lip turning out.

From the doorway, Alexander says, "Not baloney again. I'm tired of baloney."

Blinking rapidly, Benjamin looks from one sibling to the other. "I'm going to f-f-f-fix baloney." He shuts the refrigerator door and makes his way to the counter. Opening a cabinet, he takes out a partial loaf of bread. After he pulls out a handful of slices he notices green mold on one corner of each of them. "I need a knife," he says to no one in particular.

"I'll get it," Maria says.

"You can't get it," Alexander says, "you're not big enough to handle a knife. I'll get it."

"No!" Maria says. "I'll get it."

They both grab for the drawer and fight each other for control of it. Alexander shoves her and Maria slaps at him.

Benjamin ignores them and pinches off the ruined corners from the slices of bread. Taking two mangled bread slices, he slips a piece of baloney between them. "Here," he says, holding it out toward his siblings.

Alexander and Maria stop their jostling. Alexander grabs the sandwich and starts eating.

"I want a sandwich, too!" Maria wails.

Her ear-piercing voice causes Benjamin to wince. He leans his head over and raises his shoulder to his ear to block out the sound. "Stop it!" he snaps and quickly makes another sandwich. "Here."

Maria eagerly grabs the sandwich and joins her brother at the kitchen table.

After he's made himself a sandwich, Benjamin joins them.

"I'm thirsty," Alexander says.

Benjamin looks at him. Taking a bite of his own sandwich, he gets up and goes to the cabinet. Hiding inside are seven empty jars – a tall and skinny olive jar, a small mayonnaise jar, a pickle jar, three jelly jars, and a quart-size Mason jar.

"I want a jelly jar," Alexander says.

"I know wh-wh-wh-which one you want," Benjamin replies. "What about you, Maria? Which one d-d-d-do you want?"

"I want the big, fat one."

Benjamin reaches for the Mason jar and stops. "You can't have that one, Maria. It's D-D-D-Daddy's. Y-y-y-you know what will happen if he f-f-f-finds out we used it."

"Where is he?" Alexander asks.

Benjamin shrugs. "H-h-h-he always says he was away on a job. I g-g-g-guess it's the same this time." Taking out the three jelly jars, he leaves the cabinet door standing open and fills the glasses with water.

"When's he coming back?" Maria asks.

Setting the glasses on the table, then returning to his chair, Benjamin says, "M-m-m-maybe soon. He's been gone for three weeks th-th-this time."

They eat in silence for a few minutes. The strains of Elvis singing "Blue Suede Shoes" drift through the thin walls of the trailer.

"Why doesn't Mama eat with us anymore?" Maria asks.

"How many times do we have to tell you," Alexander answers, "she's got the cancer."

"What's cancer?"

"It's a disease that kills people," Benjamin says.

Maria starts to cry.

"Ya'll finish your s-s-s-sandwiches and then get your homework," Benjamin orders them. "M-m-m-maybe Mama will let you watch part of her Elvis m-m-m-movie with her."

Using the back of her hand, Maria wipes her runny nose then rubs her fist in her tear-stained eyes. She tries to stuff the rest of her sandwich into her mouth but only manages to get half of it in before she chokes.

"It's n-n-n-not good to eat fast," Benjamin says. He, however, consumes his sandwich in three large bites. He knows he'll be hungry later. At five-feet-five-inches tall and 180 pounds he feels like he's always in the kitchen trying to find something to eat.

Hopping off of her chair, Maria scurries out of the kitchen and returns in a moment carrying a book. "I'm supposed to read this story to somebody."

"Read it t-t-t-to me," Benjamin says.

As his sister is climbing onto Benjamin's lap, Alexander exits the kitchen.

In halting fashion Maria calls out the words in her book.

Alexander returns carrying some loose papers. Holding them up, he says, "These are my math worksheets, but I can't find my pencil."

Benjamin sets his sister down from his lap and walks to the kitchen counter. "M-M-M-Maybe there's one in the j-j-j-junk drawer." Opening a drawer, he sifts through a jumble of odds and ends – a brass-colored ring from a Mason jar, an instruction book for a Hoover vacuum cleaner, some pennies, a pot holder whose edges have been burned, a lid to a jar of Bama jelly, five or six ink pens, the thin and outdated 1990 edition phone book for Carroll County, Tennessee, a screwdriver, a measuring spoon, a star-shaped cookie cutter. Finally he spies a pencil hiding along the back edge of the drawer. Taking it out, he sees the point is broken off. From another drawer he extracts a paring knife and whittles a crudely-shaped point onto the pencil. "Here," he says, handing it to Alexander.

Twenty minutes later, Benjamin escorts his siblings to the door of his mother's bedroom. "Wait here," he says. Easing himself into the bedroom and closing the door behind him, he lets his eyes adjust to the flickering light from the TV in the darkened room. "Mama?"

His mother's eyes are open but she doesn't respond.

Walking over to her bed, he touches her shoulder.

She jumps and turns to look at him. "Is that you, B.J.?"

"N-n-n-no, it's just me, Mama."

Turning back to the TV, Joyce says, "Ain't nobody as good as Elvis, are they, Bennie?"

"I don't know, Mama. C-C-C-Can Maria and Alexander come in here and w-w-w-watch TV with you?"

"I guess so. Light me a cigarette, will you?"

"Yes ma'am." Benjamin takes a cigarette out of the package, places it between his lips and flicks the lighter to the tip of it. He draws a breath through his tightened lips and the end of the cigarette responds with a red glow. He places it between his mother's lips then goes to let his siblings in. "She says it's okay. But ya'll g-g-g-gotta be good."

As the two younger children slip through the door, Benjamin steps out, closing the door behind him. In the living room he gets on his knees in front of the tattered couch, reaches underneath, and pulls out a wooden box. The contents rattle as he sets it on the coffee table.

Looking over his shoulder toward his mother's room to make sure he's alone, he opens the lid and takes out a red Camaro Matchbox car. His stubby fingers trace the lines and open and close the hood and doors. He places it on the coffee table with the front of the car facing him. One at a time he takes out eleven more Matchbox cars of varied makes and models, some with peeling paint. After carefully feeling each one, he sets them side by side.

Satisfied with the arrangement, he sits back against the front of the couch and picks up the wooden box. Reaching inside he takes out a worn, dog-eared spiral notebook and an ink pen with an advertisement on its side that says "Vote for Collins for Sheriff." He flips through several pages until he arrives at a blank one. After a moment's pause he begins writing.

This morning I heard a cat outside that sounded like it was crying.

When I looked around I saw that it was a Mockingbird.

Why would someone want to sound like they are crying?

Sometimes I hear Maria crying. She's loud.

Mama makes soft sounds when she cries. But I still hear her.

I wonder if I cried would anybody hear me?

Chapter Two

Benjamin jerks awake. Sitting up on the edge of the couch, which doubles as his bed, he tries to figure out what woke him up. The dim, gray light of dawn creates ghostly shadows in the room. There is heavy pounding on the front door of the trailer. He jumps to his feet.

"I know you're in there, Trevathan!" an angry man shouts. Once again there's loud banging on the front door. "Open up, or I'm coming in!"

Rubbing his eyes, Benjamin walks cautiously to the door. Through the thin curtains Benjamin sees bright headlights and the silhouette of a man with his hands on his hips. He opens the door halfway.

Before the door clears the jamb, the man with the angry voice says, "Where's my rent money?!" When he sees Benjamin his tone changes. "Oh, I thought you was your Daddy. Where's B.J. at?"

"I d-d-d-don't know."

"Is that what he told you to say? Is he hiding inside like a little girl or something?"

"N-n-n-no sir."

The man tugs at the bill of his weathered cap.

Benjamin takes a quick, direct look at his face and sees his flaming red cheeks.

"Then tell your Mama to come out here so I can talk to her."

Benjamin turns his head and looks toward the end of the trailer, "She's in b-b-b-bed."

The man turns to see what Benjamin is looking at. Seeing nothing of interest, he says, ""I don't care. Go tell her to come out here."

Benjamin doesn't move. His eyes dart in multiple directions as he tries to avoid eye contact.

"Is there something wrong with you?" the man asks. "Are you retarded or something?"

Looking to his left, Benjamin says, "N-n-n-no sir. I got that Asperger's d-d-d-disease."

Taking a step back, the man covers his mouth and nose with the crook of his arm. "The what? Is it catching? Who else in there has it? Is that what's wrong with your Mama?"

Benjamin shakes his head. "N-n-n-no, I'm the only one. Mama, she's got the c-c-c-cancer."

The man drops his arm from his face. "Oh…well…uh…I'm sorry about that." Pushing his cap to the back of his head, he says, "What's your name?"

"B-B-B-Benjamin."

Taking his cap off, the man scratches his head. He slaps his thigh with the cap and then jerks it back onto his head. "Well look here, Benjamin, this is the problem. Your Daddy ain't paid the rent in three months. And ya'll have only lived here five months. All he give me was the first and last month's rent when you moved in. So he's into my pocketbook for three months. I ain't running some kind of charity here. These trailers all have to be kept up. You tell your old man that if I don't get my money in seven days, I'm kicking you all out. You got that?"

Benjamin's eyes dart from left to right, down at the ground and up at the lightening sky. "I've got t-t-t-twelve Matchbox cars. My f-f-f-favorite one is the Camaro."

"You what?" Waving his hand in disgust, the man turns, disappears behind his headlights and gets inside his truck.

Benjamin blinks rapidly as gravel flies out from under the spinning tires of the departing truck. Closing the front door and locking it, he turns around and finds Alexander and Maria standing in the living room holding hands. A blanket is draped across their shoulders.

"Do we got to move again?" Maria asks.

"I'm tired of moving!" Alexander says.

"What was all the shouting about?" The three children turn to see their mother leaning against the door frame of her bedroom. Her loose-fitting cotton nightgown is falling off one shoulder. Her thinning hair is mashed flat against one side of her head while the other side looks as if it is jet propelled from the roots.

"Mama, you're up!" Maria exclaims. Letting go of Alexander's hand, she scurries toward her mother. "You're feeling better, aren't you?"

Benjamin yells, "Be careful!"

Too late for the warning, Maria stumbles and falls against her mother. Joyce collapses like a Jenga tower.

The entire house trailer shakes as Benjamin runs to his mother.

Alexander gets there first and scolds their sister. "What are you trying to do?! Mama is sick! You're so clumsy!"

Lying on her side, Joyce has Maria cradled into her midsection. With a weak laugh she says, "Maria's not the clumsy one, I am. I was supposed to catch her and lost my balance. Don't be fussing at her. I'm okay."

Benjamin kneels down beside them. "Y-y-y-your elbow is b-b-b-bleeding, Mama. I'll g-g-g-go get a wet rag." Grunting, he gets to his feet and goes to the bathroom. In a moment he returns.

"Let me have that," Joyce says as she takes the damp washcloth. Dabbing at her injury, she says, "It's nothing but a scratch. All the medicine I've taken has made my skin so thin that it doesn't take much of anything for me to start bleeding."

Through her tears Maria says, "I'm sorry, Mama."

"You should have been more careful!" Alexander says.

"Hush, Alex," his mother says. "Elvis said, 'Don't criticize what you don't understand, son.' Maria didn't mean to hurt me. She was just overly excited." Looking at Benjamin, she asks, "What was all the shouting about?"

"W-w-w-we're going to have to m-m-m-move."

"Move? What are you talking about?"

"The m-m-m-man says he wants his money."

"Bennie, slow down and tell me what happened."

"He c-c-c-called me retarded and said h-h-h-he didn't care if you were s-s-s-sick or not. B.J. owes him m-m-m-money. Three m-m-m-months' worth."

Getting to her hands and knees first, Joyce stands up. Benjamin notices her lips moving silently and reads the swear words. "I don't know if I'm better off with him or without him. I just know that without him we'd have to live in the Projects somewhere, and I don't want that for you kids."

Tugging her mother's hand, Maria asks, "Do we really have to move?"

"If your Daddy don't come home with some money, we will," Joyce answers.

"I'm sick of moving!" Alexander complains.

"I know you are," his mother answers, "but we got to do what we got to do. What day of the week is this?"

"It's M-M-M-Monday," Benjamin replies.

"Goodness! You kids need to get ready for school. Bennie, make sure your brother and sister get something for breakfast. I think there's some pop-tarts in one of the cabinets. I'm going to go back to bed."

"W-w-w-we need some more f-f-f-food."

"I know, but our food stamps don't get filled for another four days, and I don't have no money."

"I want to stay home with you," Maria says.

"Me, too," Alexander echoes.

Turning toward her bed, Joyce says, "We're going to be moving anyway. I don't guess it matters if you go or stay home. Suit yourselves."

"Yea!" Maria and Alexander cheer.

When their mother closes her bedroom door, they turn to Benjamin. "We're hungry."

Turning toward the kitchen, Benjamin lumbers across the floor of the trailer while his siblings follow in his wake. He opens a kitchen cabinet. There is a squeak as a mouse darts to the dark corner of the cabinet and disappears through a hole. Shredded bits of cardboard lie beside the box of pop-tarts. Benjamin reaches inside and pulls out the lone package. It has already been opened and only one pop-tart is left. Taking it out, he breaks it in half. He offers the halves to Alexander and Maria. "H-h-h-here's your breakfast."

They snatch the proffered sustenance out of his hands and greedily gobble it up.

Suddenly there is the sound of someone trying to open the front door. The three children stare at the doorknob and watch it resist the efforts of the person on the other side to turn it. The entire door shudders as the potential intruder gives the doorknob a violent shake.

A raspy, agitated voice outside the door demands, "Open the door!"

"It's Daddy!" Alexander says as he rushes to the door, unlocks it, and flings it open.

B.J. Trevathan steps inside. Each of his hands is gripping multiple, loaded plastic Walmart bags. "Daddy brung you some food," he announces. Lifting one of his hands toward Benjamin, he says, "Here, Bennie, take one of these."

Benjamin walks toward his step-father and takes the bags. Turning around, he heads toward the kitchen.

"What? Ain't you even gonna say, 'Hi'?"

Benjamin stops and faces him. He tries to swallow the lump in his throat, but his mouth is suddenly so dry that he can't swallow. After a moment he says, "Hi."

"Hi, what?" B.J. prompts him.

Benjamin tries to find an object in the room to focus on, but his eyes keep jumping from one item to another.

"And look at me when I'm talking," B.J. growls.

Doing a quick scan of his father's face, Benjamin sees his eyes are bloodshot and he hasn't shaved in several days. There is a dark bruise above one eye. The smell of liquor reaches Benjamin's nostrils. "Hi, d-d-d-d-d-d-d."

"Quit your stuttering! It makes you sound stupid."

Torn between feeling sorry for her brother and happy that her dad has returned, Maria emits a quiet, mewing sound.

There are a couple of beats of silence as B.J.'s inebriated brain processes this new stimulus. Just as he turns his attention toward Maria, Alexander grabs his dad's hand while Benjamin moves to stand in front of his sister.

Pulling on his dad, Alexander says, "Come on, Daddy. I'm hungry. Show me what you bought."

B.J. stumbles forward following Alexander while at the same time his head stays turned toward where Maria is standing behind Benjamin. Just as he is about to pass through the doorway, he turns his head to see where he is going and smacks his forehead against the door facing. The three children watch as he falls and hits the floor face first. Several bags of groceries slide across the floor scattering their contents.

The children stare at his inert form. Alexander and Maria look up at Benjamin. "What should we do?" Alexander asks.

"L-L-L-Let's eat," Benjamin replies, and he strides into the kitchen.

Chapter Three

Benjamin sets his bags on the table as Alexander gathers up the spilled groceries off the floor.

Maria begins exploring the contents on the table. "Ooooo, doughnuts," she says. When she is unable to manage the well-taped box, Benjamin tears it open for her. She stuffs her mouth full of the sugary treat.

Reaching into the box, Benjamin takes out a doughnut. One bite, two bites, and it disappears. He takes out another one and dispatches it as quickly as the first.

Alexander joins them and hungrily devours one as well. With his mouth stuffed full, he says, "Thirsty."

Benjamin looks through some more bags until he finds a 2-liter bottle of Mountain Dew and pours all three of them a drink.

Once the dozen doughnuts are gone, the children scrounge through the rest of the bags to see what treasures they might find.

"M-m-m-macaroni and cheese," Benjamin says with a smile.

"And cookies and marshmallows," Maria adds.

One at a time, Alexander slaps five packages of baloney onto the table. With a disgusted tone, he says, "And more baloney. We're going to turn into baloney. I hate baloney."

"B-b-b-baloney is g-g-g-good for you. Mama says that's what Elvis ate wh-wh-wh-when he was growing up." Reaching in another bag, Benjamin takes out a can of beanie weenies. "Ya'll want s-s-s-some of these?"

Maria makes a face and turns her attention to opening the marshmallows.

"I'll take some," Alexander says. "They're better than baloney."

Benjamin pulls the ringed top off the can and hands it to his brother, then gets another can out and opens it. "We n-n-n-need spoons." Obeying his own suggestion, he retrieves two spoons from a drawer, hands one to Alexander and empties his can.

"Are we going to get in trouble?" Alexander asks.

"F-F-F-For what?"

"For not going to school. My teacher sent home a letter that she said was a warning about me missing so much school. I showed it to Mama, but I don't think she read it."

"N-N-N-Nobody hardly even knows we exist. They don't c-c-c-care if we're there or not. Besides, we'll be living s-s-s-somewhere else by the t-t-t-time anyone gets around to doing anything about it."

With her cheeks distended with marshmallows, Maria mumbles something.

"M-m-m-Mama says don't t-t-t-talk with your mouth full," Benjamin chides her.

It takes several moments for Maria to chew and swallow enough to try to speak again. "My teacher likes me. She knows my name. She'll miss me."

"I don't want to move," Alexander says.

"W-W-W-We have to. That mad man is going to come b-b-b-back here and throw us out."

"Daddy won't let him," Maria argues.

They all turn and look at B.J.'s form as if expecting him to speak up and offer his two cents worth to the discussion.

Benjamin speaks into the silence, "H-H-H-He can't stop him. He's spent up all his m-m-m-money. He's not a g-g-g-good Daddy."

"You don't like him because he's not your Daddy," Alexander says. "He's your stepfather. But he's my and Maria's real Daddy. He will too take care of us."

"H-h-h-he gets drunk a lot and stays away from home instead of t-t-t-taking care of us and Mama. M-M-M-Mama says so."

Caught between the force of truth and the desire of his fairy tale thinking that his father will suddenly be transformed into an adoring parent, Alexander offers no reply.

As if Benjamin's stinging words of condemnation have registered, B.J. stirs and rolls onto his side. Blood is smeared on his lips and chin. His nose is mashed unnaturally to one side.

"Y-y-y-you two g-g-g-get out of here. H-H-H-He's going to be m-m-m-mad."

Having learned to heed their brother's advice, the young ones grab a bag of cookies each and head to their shared bedroom.

As they leave the kitchen, Benjamin adds, "And d-d-d-don't come out until I c-c-c-come and get you."

Maria hesitates and looks over her shoulder at him. Pity tilts the outside edges of her eyes downward and pushes her eyebrows up.

Alexander grabs her arm. "Come on. Do what he said."

A low groan escapes from B.J.. Swearing and spitting blood, he pushes himself to a sitting position. "What happened? Who hit me?" His bleary eyes remain unfocused. As more consciousness comes to him, so does more pain. He reaches for his nose and howls when he touches it.

Benjamin hurries to the freezer, takes out an ice tray and breaks it open in the sink. Finding a dish towel, he wets it and places two handfuls of ice in the middle. Lifting the four corners, he ties them in a knot then carries the homemade ice pack to his stepfather.

B.J. takes it and gingerly places on the side of his broken nose. Wincing, he says, "What happened, Ben?"

Benjamin examines the truth and a lie and decides to choose the latter. "I th-th-th-think you must have b-b-b-been in a fight last night. You p-p-p-passed out in the floor when you got home."

"I think my nose is broke again. Man, I'm getting tired of this. I'm going to start carrying me a pistol and killing me some wise-ass rednecks." Taking a corner of the damp towel, he wipes at the drying blood on his face. "You put a little liquor in someone and he thinks he is Sheriff Buford Pusser back from the dead."

"W-w-w-we have to m-m-m-move again."

"What do you mean?"

"A man came this m-m-m-morning and said if he didn't get his m-m-m-money, he'd throw us out."

"Man, don't nothing ever work out for me. Ever since I left my first wife, Tara, my life has been in the toilet. She was my first true love. I was a fool to leave her. Always remember, Ben, the candle of your first love never goes out. She was the sweetest, kindest, most loving thing I've ever known." The stinging tears of regret begin flowing out of his closed eyelids and running down his cheeks. Through his sobs he says, "Listen to me, Ben. If you ever find a good woman who wants you, grab her and don't let go." Opening his eyes, he looks at Ben and shakes his head. "What am I saying? Ain't nobody ever going to want you. Your Mama lied to me about you or I wouldn't never have taken you and her on." He closes his eyes again and tries pressing the ice pack a little tighter on his wounds. "How she doing, anyway?"

Time has dulled the stings from B.J. that used to make him cry. Instead, Benjamin clenches his fists. "Sh-sh-sh-she's asleep."

Getting to his feet, B.J. says, "That's about all she's good for anymore. She's certainly not taking care of my needs. And I got needs, boy. You hear me? And I'll get them taken care of wherever I can. That's my right."

It's a speech Benjamin has heard several times, often delivered in loud tones from his mother's bedroom. He squares himself to B.J. and says, "She's a g-g-g-good Mama."

His stepfather swings the icepack at him, striking him on the side of the head. "Don't give me none of your sass, Boy! Especially that stuttering like a baby stuff."

Benjamin leans forward to take a step toward B.J. but stops himself. He refuses to give any indication that the blow or the words have had an effect on him.

Having been denied the satisfaction of seeing his stepson cringing from him, B.J. says, "You're just stupid, aren't you? Get out of my way." He shoves past Benjamin and heads toward the front door. "You kids start packing. I've got to find somebody who'll give me some gas for my truck. I ran out a couple of miles up the road."

Watching his father through the front door window to be sure he's left, Benjamin then goes to his siblings' room. He opens the door. "Start packing. We're mov – " He notices they've already started the process.

Going to the couch, Benjamin takes out his box from underneath. It's the Camaro he wants to hold. He rolls it across his cheek and down his neck, noticing the smooth feel of the tires. Returning it to the box, he takes out his journal and pencil. He turns to the back page and reads:

Places I've Lived

1978-1983, Bardwell, Kentucky

1984-1986, Palmersville, Tennessee

1987, Hickman, Kentucky

1988-1989, Ridgley, Tennessee

1990, Rives, Tennessee

1991, Gibson, Tennessee

1992, Union City, Tennessee, Henry, Tennessee,

1993, Trezevant, Tennessee, McKenzie, Tennessee

Flipping back toward the front of the journal, he finds a blank page and writes:

Birds always know where to go at night.

They spread their wings and take flight

Happy to be home.

I sometimes wish I was a bird.

Chapter Four

"I'm gonna win! I'm gonna win!" Maria stands up and dances in triumph while her brothers remain sitting on the floor with the Candyland game board lying between them.

"You don't know," Alexander says, "you might draw the Gingerbread card and have to go way back to the beginning."

Maria stops her dancing and a frown sweeps away her mask of glee. "I want to win. I don't ever win." She lowers herself to the floor and sits cross-legged.

As Alexander and Maria banter about who is going to win, Benjamin sneaks a look at the stack of playing cards that are bent and creased with age. He sees that Alexander is a prophet, or perhaps a cheat. Maria is about to draw the Gingerbread card. With the skill of a card shark, Benjamin slips another card to the top of the deck. "Y-y-you need to draw and see who's right," he says to Maria.

Fear of disappointment and of losing her argument causes Maria to be hesitant. Staring at the deck of cards, she says, "I don't want to go all the way back and have to start over," she pleads.

Sitting up on his knees, Alexander rubs his hands together. "Maria's going back. Maria's going back. Come on, draw the card."

As if she were reaching for the tarot card of a fortune teller, Maria's small hand slowly descends on the stack of cards. With dread etched on her face, she turns the card face up. When she sees the double blue blocks, she squeals and jumps to her feet. "I win! I win! I win!" She jumps onto Benjamin's broad back and throws her arms around his neck. "Ride me around the room."

Like an obedient steed, Benjamin rises to his feet and prances around the living room in his best horse imitation. Maria bounces on his back like a rag doll. Her high-pitched squeals and his tenor laughter create a duet of delight that a composer would be hard pressed to put on paper.

Though he was proven wrong, Alexander cannot remain sulking on the sidelines of his siblings's merriment. "I want to ride, too," he exclaims, grabbing his brother's arm.

Benjamin pauses and lifts his brother onto his back. With his brother and sister riding side by side and their two sets of arms around his thick neck, he returns to the parade of triumph, bouncing from one foot to the other like a Tennessee Walking horse.

The rotting floor joists of the old farm house bend under the combined weight and force of the children's play causing the large velvet painting of Elvis to rattle against the wall. Without warning the hook on the back of the frame comes loose and Elvis falls to the floor in a loud crash.

Benjamin wheels around to find the source of the crash. Before he can react, the sound of his stepfather swearing emanates from inside his parent's bedroom down the short hallway. All three of the children stiffen in anticipation of the verbal maelstrom that is approaching. The doorknob bangs against the wall as the door is flung open.

"What's going on in here?!" B.J. Trevathan yells. His eyes are puffy with sleep and his hair is pushed up on both sides of his head giving it the appearance of a Mohawk cut. Sleep lines cut across his face like scars from a knife fight. "What do you kids think you're doing?! Your mother and I are trying to sleep!" Jabbing his finger into Benjamin's chest, he says, "What are you doing to your brother and sister, you dumb ox? And don't give me any of that stuttering crap. I'm not in the mood for it."

Benjamin relaxes his hold on his siblings' legs. They respond by letting go of his neck and sliding off of him like firemen down a fire pole. He nudges them to stand behind him. Words come easily to him, but he doesn't share them for fear his stuttering tongue will trigger another barrage from his stepfather.

"I asked you a question, Bennie. Answer me!" His stepfather's nose, now permanently askew, glows red with anger and his eyes are wide.

Benjamin decides to try a single word, hoping it will both come out smoothly and will pacify the raging dragon in front of him. "Playing."

Maria peeks out just enough to see her dad and says, "Yeah, we were just playing."

The tiny voice of his daughter finds its way through B.J.'s adrenalin-charged brain and gives him pause. Looking around like a man trying to gain his bearings, he says, "What day is this, anyway? Shouldn't ya'll be in school?" His eyes finally light on the Carroll Insurance Company calendar pinned to the wall. The year, 1994 and the month, September, are large enough for him to easily see, but the numbers are blurry.

Alexander sees an opening that offers hope for directing his father's attention off their recent behavior. He runs to the calendar and points. "It's Tuesday, the twenty-seventh."

B.J. runs his hand through his hair and sits on the threadbare couch. Lighting a cigarette, he says, "Go fix me some coffee, Bennie, and make sure it's strong like I like it."

Benjamin goes to the kitchen and opens the can of coffee. There is barely a tablespoon of grounds scattered at the bottom. His heart races. Opening the other cabinets, his eyes sweep the shelves to be sure there isn't an unopened can hiding somewhere. Having no luck, his eyes fall on a box of tea bags. He takes out a bag and tears it open, emptying its contents into the coffee can. After examining the mixture he adds two more tea bags into the can. He pours the entire contents into the coffee maker's filter. Once he adds water he turns it on.

Back in the living room Benjamin hears his stepfather persist in interrogating Alexander and Maria. "Why ain't ya'll in school?"

Alexander replies, "Daddy, we haven't gone to school in Huntingdon since we moved here back in April."

"Lord! Do I have to do everything around here?" his dad complains. "It takes all my time to be out working trying to provide for all of us. I ain't got time to be a nursemaid to all of you, too. That's your Mama's job."

Even fear of retribution won't keep Benjamin silent when his mother is being attacked. "She's s-s-s-sick."

"Well I'm sick of you kids. Ya'll get dressed. I'm taking you to school."

Standing with his back facing the red-brick school building, Benjamin watches his dad drive away. His heart feels like a racing rabbit, and his legs are trembling so badly he is afraid they may collapse under him. It is a familiar feeling. He has lost count of how many schools he has attended, but the first day is always the same – fear, uncertainty, aloneness, embarrassment, and frustration shadow his every step.

The thought of running away flits through his mind but is quickly discarded as he has no idea where he would go. Besides, who would watch after Alexander and Maria? And who would take care of his mother? Therefore he slowly turns and walks toward the glass front doors. Just as he reaches them, two boys exit the building. One of them glances at Benjamin and gives the door an extra push open, allowing Benjamin to enter without touching it.

As soon as he's inside, the sound of a ringing bell echoes in the empty hallway. Before the bell stops ringing classroom doors open and allow the classrooms to empty themselves of restless teenagers. A cacophony of voices fills the air. The colors and fabrics of clothes are almost too much for Benjamin to distinguish but rather create the impression of a Jackson Pollack canvas. The scurrying students pass close enough to him to create a breeze, but no one pays him any mind, which is fine with him.

In a matter of a few minutes, the tide of students in the hallway subsides as the classrooms refill themselves. Benjamin remains a solitary figure. Glancing around, he spies a door with the word "Office" above it. He makes his way there and steps inside.

A gray-haired lady with a bulbous nose and a pleasant smile looks up at him. "Can I help you?"

Benjamin focuses on the countertop between them. "I'm s-s-s-supposed to be in school here."

"You mean you aren't a student here already?"

"N-n-n-no m-m-m-ma'am."

Looking past him through the glass-walled office and into the hallway, the secretary asks, "Where are your parents?"

Benjamin glances over his shoulder, then back at the countertop, eventually settling his eyes on his tattered tennis shoes. "My m-m-m-Mama is sick."

"What about your father? Is he here with you?"

He shakes his head.

"Just one moment," the secretary says, and she disappears through a doorway. Presently she returns with another lady who is tall and angular. Her gray eyes lock on Benjamin's and won't let them go. He tries to look away but finds it impossible.

"I understand you are here to enroll in school," the woman says. "Is that true?"

Benjamin nods.

"My name is Miss Westin. I'm the Guidance Counselor. What's your name?"

"B-B-B-Benjamin Trevathan."

"Well, Benjamin, why don't you come with me?"

Following behind her, Benjamin can predict what her questions will be: Where do you live? Where did you last attend school? Do you have any school records for us? How old are you? What grade are you supposed to be in? Eventually she will learn how many schools he's attended which will trigger another series of questions, none of which can be easily answered. Then she will try to find a way to ask him about his stuttering without using the word stutter and will ask if he's ever been in "special" classes.

This initial interrogation always concludes with someone saying, "We are going to have to have one of your parents come to the school in order to register you." Miss Westin is no exception. She adds, "But I'm going to go ahead and let you attend classes today. No sense in wasting your time in having come here and then me sending you home. Let me take you to Mr. Thom's English class."

Dread twists Benjamin's stomach into a knot. Walking into a classroom that has already started is the worst possible thing to ask a new student to do. Having twenty-five or so sets of eyes staring at you, picking apart every flaw, can make you feel like an unarmed knight facing the fire-breathing dragon. His fate is doomed.

Miss Westin taps on the classroom door and then opens it. "Mr. Thom, excuse me for interrupting your class, but we have a new student in our school. This is Benjamin Trevathan." She puts her hand in the small of Benjamin's back and pushes him gently into the room.

"Welcome, Mr. Trevathan." The English teacher's voice has the quality that must have belonged to town criers long ago. It's a loud, tenor voice with lots of resonance on the "m" of "welcome" and the "n" of "Trevathan." "Find you an empty desk and have a seat," Mr. Thom continues. "You have entered in the middle of our discussion of the poetry of Wordsworth, Shelley, and Keats."

Benjamin's lifetime diet of junk food and heavy starches has made his hips so wide it is difficult to walk between the row of desks without bumping people's books or shoulders.

"Watch it!" someone whispers harshly.

"Fat ox!" is another comment that reaches his ears.

Keeping his head down, he finally reaches the empty desk and squeezes into it.

"Are you a fan of poetry Mr. Trevathan?" Mr. Thom's voice has the effect of a hand underneath Benjamin's chin, jerking it up in shock.

Please don't make me answer you. Not out loud in front of everyone. Please.

Unfortunately for Benjamin, Mr. Thom is not a mind reader. His eyebrows are peaked in anticipation of Benjamin's reply.

Benjamin nods his head.

"Excellent!" Mr. Thom says with some excitement at having found a male high school student who might share his enthusiasm for poetry. "And who is your favorite poet?"

His mind is swirling so fast that Benjamin fears he is going to fall out of his chair from feeling dizzy. He half expects his face to burst into flames at any moment he is so embarrassed. Recognizing he has no choice but to verbalize a response, he says, "E-E-E-Elvis P-P-P-Presley."

There is a one beat moment of dead silence in the room as everyone processes the absurd reply. Then everyone bursts into riotous laughter. One boy stands up and strikes an Elvis in Las

Vegas stance. His pose serves the purpose of gas being poured on the flame of laughter in the classroom, carrying it to ridiculous heights.

Benjamin tries to get up from his desk but his girth has him wedged in so that when he stands, the desk comes off the floor with him. Grabbing the desk with both hands, he pries it off and drops it on its side onto the floor. He runs from the room with the sound of derisive laughter ringing in his ears.

Chapter Five

Maria stands looking at the December 1995 calendar. "Bennie, is today Christmas?"

Benjamin finishes unwrapping a honeybun and takes a bite. He considers how best to answer his sister. The truth will resurrect hope in her heart; hope that will not be fulfilled. But telling her a lie will result in him having to tell her more lies. And he and his two siblings have heard enough lies in their brief lifetimes to both kill and bury hope.

Before Benjamin can formulate a reply, Alexander comes out of the bathroom and joins them. "It's Christmas Day," Alexander says, "and another year with no presents, huh?"

Tears immediately spring up in Maria's eyes. Hope dies hardest in the hearts of the youngest.

Benjamin resists the urge to hit his brother for causing sadness in their sister, but he realizes that Alexander has simply told the truth. "I-I-I-I've g-g-got something for you t-t-two."

Blinking away her tears, Maria turns around. A smile creases her face.

"What is it?" Alexander asks.

"Let me g-g-g-go get it." Benjamin finds his treasure box, opens it and takes out two folded pieces of paper. On the front of one of them is a hand-drawn star colored yellow, with Maria's name underneath. On the other are dozens of hand-drawn snowflakes dropping onto a primitive looking snowman below. Getting down on his knees, he hands Maria's homemade card to her and gives the other to Alexander.

"It's got my name on it," Maria announces. Her eyes dance with delight. She opens it and reads aloud:

On this day a long time ago

A special baby was born

Into a world that had lost its glow

And where hearts were tattered and torn.

My heart has felt better

Since another baby was born.

It's my own sweet sister –

Maria.

Merry Christmas!

Squeezing the card to her chest, Maria runs to Benjamin and tries to throw her short arms around him. "I love you," she says.

"My card has a poem, too," Alexander says. He, too, reads aloud.

Today is Jesus' birthday.

He made the world a better place.

My brother makes my world okay

Because he has a smiling face.

Merry Christmas Alexander!

Alexander moves beside his brother and sister and puts his arm around Benjamin's neck. "Bennie's the best brother in the world, isn't he, Maria?"

"Uh-huh," Maria agrees. "Can we sing a Christmas carol?"

Benjamin looks over his shoulder toward his parents' bedroom door. "We d-d-d-don't want t-t-t-to wake them up."

"We can sing it quiet," Maria urges.

"I g-g-g-guess we can. B-B-B-But we've got to be quiet."

"Let's do Silent Night," Alexander says.

Benjamin starts them off, and the two younger ones take over as they sing the two verses they know from memory.

A knock at the front door grabs their attention. They stare at the door and then at their parents' bedroom door to see if the knock stirred them awake. When they hear nothing from the bedroom, they return their gaze to the front door.

"Is somebody here to make us move again?" Maria whispers.

"Shhh! Be quiet!" Alexander whispers. "Let's act like no one is home. Maybe they'll go away."

When there isn't another knock on the door, or an angry voice outside, or someone rattling the doorknob to get in, Benjamin slowly stands up. "Stay here," he whispers. After making sure his siblings heard his warning, he tiptoes to the front door and puts his ear to it. When he's confident no one is outside waiting, he opens the door.

Sitting on the porch are four large cardboard boxes brimming with brightly wrapped packages. A white van is pulling away from the house.

Benjamin stares in disbelief at the boxes. Leaving the door open, he steps outside into the cold December air. As he looks into the first box, he sees name tags on the packages. Opening one, he says Alexander's name aloud.

From the open door, Alexander says, "What is it, Bennie?"

Benjamin turns and sees his brother and sister watching him. "It's Christmas p-p-p-presents."

Still dressed in the t-shirt and shorts she slept in, Maria scoots outside to join Benjamin. Taking his hand, she says, "Presents? From who?"

"S-S-S-Santa Claus, I think."

Alexander, who has joined them, says, "Ain't no such thing."

"Is too!" Maria snaps back.

"Is not!" Alexander retorts.

"What's going on here?!" B.J.'s angry voice startles them. They turn and see him standing in the door way in his underwear. His hair is tousled and his eyes are red-rimmed. "Are ya'll trying to heat the whole outdoors? Who pays the electric bill around here? Me, that's who. I'll bet that meter is spinning faster than a pinwheel in a windstorm. And what's all that stuff in them boxes? Where'd all that come from?"

"Santa Claus, Daddy," Maria says with a smile. "Santa Claus came. Come look." Though a part of her wants to go grab his hand and bring him outside with them, she chooses to stay with Benjamin where she feels more secure.

B.J. swears. "Santa Claus. Don't tell me you still believe in that crap." Ignoring the fact that he's dressed only in his underwear, B.J. steps out and looks in the boxes. "You kids bring all this inside. We'll see what this is all about."

Benjamin picks up a box and carries it inside while his siblings begin dragging a box each toward the door. Once all four boxes are in, the kids sit on the floor waiting to see what B.J. will do.

Suddenly the sound of Elvis singing Bossa Nova Baby can be heard as their mother opens the door to the bedroom. "B.J., I feel sick," she calls out feebly.

"When don't you feel sick?" B.J. answers. "Go see about her, Bennie."

Reluctant to leave his younger brother and sister with their father, Benjamin hesitates.

B.J. kicks him in the shoulder.

The blow rocks Benjamin to one side, but he prevents himself from falling over.

"Boy, did you hear me?! Get up and see about your mother."

Benjamin gets up and sees to his mother. He finds her holding onto the doorknob of her bedroom. Her eyes are closed, and she is swaying. At first he thinks she is swaying to the sounds of Elvis singing, but he suddenly realizes she's about to faint. Gripping her hand, he leads her toward the bed with its rumpled covers. "You need t-t-t-to lay down, Mama."

Joyce allows herself to be led without comment. When she gets in bed, she says, "I think the cancer is back, Bennie. Them doctors said I was cured last year. But they lied. I think it's back this time real bad. Give me one of my pain pills and light me a cigarette, will you, Bennie?"

Benjamin dutifully obeys. But by the time he's got the cigarette lit, his mother has fallen asleep. He extinguishes it among the pile of butts in the ashtray. A sudden squeal from his sister sets off alarm bells in his head. He quickly returns to the living room and finds Maria and Alexander surrounded by torn wrapping paper and open packages.

"I got a baby doll!" Maria says excitedly when she sees Benjamin.

"And I got a giant Transformer!" Alexander says.

B.J. is reaching inside a box that has canned vegetables and fresh fruit sitting beside it. "Well here it is. Here's who your Santa Claus is." He lifts out a pamphlet. "These gifts," he reads from the pamphlet, "are from your friends at New Bethel Missionary Baptist

Church. Peace and good tidings to earth." He flips the pamphlet in the air. "Is that that bunch up the road you kids have been going to church with?"

"Yes sir," Benjamin answers.

"So, they see us as some kind of charity case? Like I can't take care of my own? Well, ya'll can just forget about them people because we're not going to be here much longer anyway. We have to be moved out of here by January first, a week from today. I found us a place just outside Dresden we're going to move to. I got a job at a sawmill over there. Maybe a change of scenery is what we need to change our luck."

Chapter Six

"I jest love Th' Price Is Right, don't you?" Tucker asks.

"I don't know," Smiley Carter replies. "Seems to me it's just a bunch of foolishness. It's all probably rigged anyway."

"It ain't done it! That Bob Barker is a honest man. He wouldn't have nothin' t' do with a show that was crooked."

"You don't think he's had more than one fling with those pretty girls that stand by the merchandise showing off their wares?"

"Just 'cause you couldn't keep yore pants zipped when you was younger don't mean ever' man is like that. You're jest jealous 'cause y' can't run 'round like y' used to."

Grabbing his cane, Smiley gets up off the couch. "There ain't no need in talking ugly about me, Tucker. I was just talking about what I've read. I saw his picture on the front page one of them papers when I was standing in line at the grocery store. The headline said he had a child by one of those models."

Tucker drops the foot rest of her recliner and stands up. "Where do y' think you're headed to? Sit back down an' quit carryin' yore feelin's on yore sleeve. I'll go git us a piece o' pie. Besides, them papers in the grocery store also says they's aliens walkin' 'round on th' earth. Do y' believe that's true?" She heads to the kitchen.

Smiley sits back down and calls to Tucker's retreating form, "If the good Lord wanted to make aliens, he could. And if He wanted them here on earth, He'd put them here. I know I've seen some folks in my time that looked like they were aliens." He decides to get back up and join Tucker in the kitchen. As he's walking in he says, "You're walking around pretty good since you got that cast off your leg. Your Achilles tendon has healed up real good, hasn't it?"

"I think I surprised that doctor with how quickly I healed," Tucker answers. "He prob'ly thought, 'That old woman won't heal for three months.' I can tell it's prob'ly gonna hurt me some on those days when th' weather changes." She slices two pieces of pie, slips them on separate paper towels, and sets them on the table.

Smiley pulls out a chair and sits down in front of one of the pieces of pie. Picking it up with his hand, he takes a bite that consumes a third of the piece. His eyes close. "Mmmm," he moans.

Sitting down in front of her piece of pie, Tucker says, "I'll say one thing 'bout you, Smiley, y' ain't never met a piece o' pie y' didn't like."

Smiley nods and takes another bite.

Once he's finished his piece of pie, Smiley takes the paper towel and wipes his mouth. "Mighty fine, mighty fine. You do have a way with making pies, Tucker."

Tucker ignores the compliment and takes a bite of her piece of pie.

"Have you heard from the kids in Knoxville lately?"

Shaking her head, Tucker says, "Seems like when they got back there from March an' Debbie's wedding they all got busy with school an' work. I ain't heard a peep out o' any of 'em.

"Maybe what people say is true: No news is good news. We just need to be happy that they all seem to be doing fine."

Getting up from the table, Tucker goes to the refrigerator. "Y' want somethin' t' drink?"

"Sure. Some milk would taste good."

She pours them both a glass of milk. As she turns to go back to the table, she glances out the window toward the McDaniel place. "Somethin' don't seem right down there."

"Huh? Down where? What are you talking about?"

"Down at th' McDaniel place."

Smiley nods his head. "I can't believe anybody moved into that old house. It's been abandoned since Miss Ella died. Last time I was in there it looked like it was ready to crumble to the ground. Isn't there a hole in the roof?"

"Yep. Th' day those folks moved in somebody was up on th' roof nailin' a blue tarp over th' hole. But there ain't no way that keeps all th' water out."

"Do you ever see or talk to any of them?"

"I sometimes see them three kids gittin' on th' school bus. But they don't do that regular like they's s'posed to. An' except for th' day they moved in I ain't seen th' man nor th' woman. Their pickup truck ain't never there."

"Do you think we need to go down there and check out what's going on?"

Tucker pauses before answering. "Sometimes I do think 'bout that. Then other times I think, what business is it o' mine? People used t' think all sorts o' stuff 'bout me an' Maisy's kids. I ain't one fer medlin' in other people's business."

Suddenly there is a knock at the door.

"I didn't hear nobody drive up. Did you?" Tucker asks.

"No," Smiley replies.

Getting up from the table and going to the door, Tucker opens it to discover an overweight, pimple-faced teenager standing outside. Though the morning is brisk, he is in a short-sleeved shirt. His tennis shoes are untied.

Without looking in her direction, he says, "W-W-W-We live d-d-d-down the road from you. D-D-D-Do you have any f-f-f-food we can borrow?" The boy holds out a yellow toy car. "I've got this c-c-c-car I can trade f-f-f-for the food."

Tucker stares at the boy and blinks rapidly. She looks around to see if anyone brought him or if anyone is with him. A movement at the corner of the house catches her eye. "Are y' by yoreself? Or did somebody come with y'?"

"I t-t-t-told them n-n-n-not to come."

Stepping out onto the porch, Tucker calls out, "Whoever that is at th' end of th' house, step on out an' come up here."

A frail looking little girl with scraggly hair, dressed in a t-shirt and sweat pants, slowly steps out from the end of the house. A dark haired, dark-eyed little boy, dressed in jeans and shirt that are too small for him, joins her.

"What in th' world?" Tucker exclaims.

"What's going on, Tucker?" Smiley appears in the doorway.

"It's th' kids from down at th' McDaniel place." Waving her hand at the two at the end of the house, she says, "Come on up here like I said."

Holding each other's hand, the small children join the older boy.

Tucker looks at Smiley. "They's hungry. An' from th' looks of 'em, cold, too."

"Well bring them in the house," Smiley says. "Let's fix them something to eat."

Looking back at the three children huddled together, Tucker says, "Well y' heard what he said. Git inside where it's warm. We'll see what we can find fer y' t' eat."

Maria and Alexander look up at Benjamin. "It's o-o-o-okay," he says, and he leads them into Tucker's house.

As the children step inside, Smiley says, "Come sit at the table and let's eat. I'm so glad to finally meet you. Good neighbors ought to do a better job of getting acquainted than we have, don't you think?"

Ignoring his question, the children pull out chairs and scoot up to the table.

"What'll it be?" Tucker asks. "Are y' ready fer breakfast? Or do y' want t' eat lunch?"

"Do you have any pop-tarts?" Maria asks in a small voice.

Tucker and Smiley exchange a glance.

"I think we can do better than that, don't you, Smiley?"

"For certain!" he says emphatically. "What about French toast, syrup, and sausage? How does that sound?"

"Well, it sounds delicious t' me," Tucker replies, "but what about you kids? Would that hit th' spot?"

"What's French toast?" Alexander asks.

"Lord have mercy," Tucker says. "You ain't never ate French toast? Well, git ready, 'cause me an' Smiley's gonna fix y' some. It'll make y' lick yore lips."

Smiling, Maria says, "You talk funny."

"Now there's a little girl with a sharp ear," Smiley says, suppressing a laugh.

"Oh hush up an' make yoreself useful," Tucker says to Smiley. Hand me th' eggs, milk, an' sausage."

As Tucker slices the sausage and places it in the skillet, Smiley joins the kids at the table.

"You're black," Alexander says.

"Now there's y' a boy with a sharp eye," Tucker says over her shoulder.

Ignoring Tucker's comment, Smiley says, "You've got me there son. Yes I am."

"But she's white," Alexander says while pointing at Tucker.

"Right again," Smiley says.

"My Daddy says its abundation for a black and a white to live together."

"It's a what?"

"An ab-b-b-bomin-n-n-nation," Benjamin corrects his brother.

"Could be yore Pa don't know nothin'," Tucker says. She turns from frying the sausage to look the children. She notices their dirty hands and fingernails. "Smiley, you done fergot t' wash yore hands. Why don't y' take th' kids with y' t' th' bathroom an' let 'em wash up, too?"

Smiley starts to protest, then glances at the children's hands. He says to them, "You know, she's right. And Tucker there is a stickler for clean hands at the table. You all come with me."

Chapter Seven

In the bathroom, Smiley turns on the water in the sink then points to Maria and says, "Ladies first."

Maria holds her hands under the water briefly and then reaches for the towel.

"Whoa there," Smiley says. "That won't never do for Tucker. Let me show you." Picking up the bar of soap, he washes his hands thoroughly. After drying them, he holds them up and says, "Now see? That's clean." Looking at Maria, he says, "Why don't you try again?"

Once all three of the children have completed the task sufficiently to satisfy him, Smiley leads them back to the kitchen.

The air is thick with the smell of sausage.

"Smells g-g-g-good!" Benjamin says enthusiastically.

"Git 'em all a plate an' a fork," Tucker says to Smiley.

Smiley slides the Melamine plates across the table like he's dealing cards. They clatter to a stop just before falling off the edge.

Tucker places a platter of steaming sausage in the middle of the table. The children's eyes grow wide. They pause for just a second and then each grab a piece and start eating it with their fingers. Benjamin finishes his piece in two bites and reaches for another.

Smiley stands staring at them and holding forks in his hand. He and Tucker exchange a look. Tucker shakes her head and turns back to the skillet to cook the French toast. Smiley sets the forks on the table and pours three glasses of milk.

The only sound in the kitchen is the sizzle of the French toast in the skillet as Tucker and Smiley wonder about the living condition of these children, and the children focus on filling their empty bellies.

When Tucker finishes the French toast, she sets it on the table, sits down in a chair, and motions Smiley to sit, as well. There are only two sausage patties left out of the pound of sausage she cooked. "I surely do like t' see people who enjoy eatin'," she says. "If'n y' want more sausage, I'll fix more, but first I want y' t' try this French toast." She forks a piece onto each of their plates and then pours maple syrup on them.

Alexander picks up the piece of bread as if it were a sandwich and takes bite of it. Syrup drips onto his arms and chin. As soon as the sweet tasting treat hits his tongue, his eyes dance with glee and he takes another quick bite.

"Whoa, whoa there," Tucker says. "You'll end up with more syrup on y' than in y' if y' eat it like that." She retrieves a damp wash rag from the sink and wipes Alexander clean. "Here's how y' do it." She takes a fork and cuts the bread into bite-size pieces, then hands the fork to Alexander. "Now dig in."

After watching the demonstration, Benjamin quickly cuts his bread into large pieces. He notices Maria trying to cut her bread. Stopping what he's doing, he takes her fork and says, "L-L-L-Let me do it f-f-f-for you."

For a few moments Tucker and Smiley watch them devour the French toast.

"I think it's time for introductions," Smiley says. "Don't you?"

The children look briefly at him, then return to eating. Benjamin is eating the last bite of his piece. He looks at the plate that is stacked with more slices of French toast, then he glances quickly at Tucker.

"Go ahead," Tucker says. "Eat all y' want. There's more where that come from."

Benjamin greedily forks two pieces and places them in the pool of syrup on his plate.

Looking at Smiley, Tucker says, "Go ahead with yore introductions."

"My name is Smiley Carter. That's cause I've got the biggest and easiest smile in the county. See here?"

The heads of the children bob up to look. Smiley rewards them with an exaggerated, toothy grin.

Maria chuckles.

"And this," he says as he points to Tucker, "is Tucker. That's her first and last name. We all call her Tucker."

When the children don't reciprocate Smiley's move, he says, "So tell us, what are your names?"

"I'm Maria." Some of the loose flying hairs from her head have gotten stuck to her syrupy cheeks.

"And I'm Alexander. Some people call me Alex. But I like Alexander. He was famous."

"Nice to meet you, Maria," Smiley says. "And nice to meet you, Alexander the Great."

Alexander beams.

Benjamin's eyes dart around the room for something to focus on. He spies a calendar on the wall and locks his eyes on the snow scene depicted above it. "M-M-M-My name is B-B-B-Benjamin. But I'm called different n-n-n-names sometimes."

"We call him Bennie," Maria comments. "He doesn't like to talk to strangers because they make fun of him."

"He's got Ashburglars disease," Alexander says.

"He's got what?" Tucker says.

"It's c-c-c-called Asperger's," Benjamin corrects his brother.

Frowning, Tucker says, "I ain't never heard o' nothin' like that."

"T-T-T-Teachers tell me I don't have good p-p-p-people skills. Sometimes I s-s-s-say the wrong thing."

Tucker laughs out loud. "So that's what it's called! I guess I've suffered from that Asperger's disease most of my life. Don't you agree, Smiley?"

"I've never been one to argue with the truth," Smiley says with a slight grin.

"Don't y' worry, Ben. Ain't nobody in this house gonna make fun o' y'. I spent most o' my childhood being made fun of, an' I won't tolerate it bein' done to nobody."

Benjamin glances at Tucker and holds eye contact for a few seconds, then returns to eating his French toast.

"Seems like I don't never see ya'll's mom and dad outside very much. They must be gone at their work, I guess."

"Mama's sick," Maria says.

"She's got the cancer," Alexander adds.

The words cancer pushes Tucker back in her chair. A fleeting image of Ella McDade lying in her bed, dying with cancer, rises from her memory.

Smiley sees that Tucker has lost some of her wind. "How long has your mother been sick?" he asks.

"Several years," Benjamin says. "It g-g-g-goes away but keeps coming b-b-b-back. She likes Elvis. I like M-M-M-Matchbox cars. I've got t-t-t-twelve of them. The Red Camaro is my favorite." He stops suddenly and reaches in his pants pocket. "Here's m-m-m-my yellow car for the f-f-f-food. It was really good." He lays the car on the table and looks at it like Arliss did at Old Yeller when his mother told him he couldn't keep him.

Smiley picks up the toy car and looks at it admiringly. "Mmm-mmm, that is a fine looking car. But to tell you the truth I don't think it would be a fair trade. Your car is worth a lot more than this food. Why don't you just keep it? Let's just say that this meal today was our gift to you kids, our way of getting to know you. Is that okay?"

A satisfied look spreads across Tucker's face as she listens to Smiley's balancing act between returning the gift and not offending the gesture.

Benjamin snatches the car out of Smiley's hand and returns it to his pocket. "Th-Th-Thank you."

Tucker begins taking up the plates from the table. "What about ya'll's Pa? Ain't he never at home?"

"He works at the sawmill," Alexander says.

"He said it's easier to spend the night there and work than it is to come home," Maria says.

"But he comes home sometimes and brings food with him," Alexander adds.

Benjamin listens to them trying to find ways to present their Daddy in a positive light. He wants to tell the truth but doesn't want to hurt their feelings, so he chooses a two word depiction. "He drinks."

In that two-word, understated description Tucker and Smiley hear everything that Benjamin chose not to say about his dad: the walking on eggshells around him, the unpredictability of his mood and behavior, his neglect of his family.

Tucker shakes her head, remembering how difficult it was for August, March, and April to deal with their mother Maisy's unpredictable behavior. "How come ya'll ain't got no food in yore house? And how long've y' been out?"

Benjamin speaks up, "He used n-n-n-nearly all of last month's f-f-f-food stamps on steaks."

"Steaks?!" Smiley exclaims. "Why in Sam Hill would he do that?"

"He said he was tired of Hamburger Helper," Alexander answers. "He said we deserved steak every once in a while."

"I didn't like it," Maria says. "It was bloody."

Under her breath Tucker says, "Bloody hell!"

Chapter Eight

Rolling over in bed, April Tucker looks at the glowing red numbers of the clock on the bedside table. 6:30 a.m. The smell of cooking bacon from the kitchen of her brother August's apartment slips under the door to her bedroom and fills her nostrils. Her stomach immediately roils. Throwing back the covers, she moves to a sitting position on the side of her bed, hoping the wave of nausea will pass. It doesn't.

Darting out of the bedroom and into the bathroom, April kneels in front of the toilet. Tiny drops of sweat appear on her face. Suddenly her stomach convulses and she throws up. She pushes down on the chrome-plated handle and the toilet flushes. Though there is nothing left in her stomach, it still wrenches a series of involuntary dry heaves.

Exhausted from the effort, April sits in the floor and lays the side of her face against the cool, porcelain bowl. Once she is convinced her stomach is finished torturing her, she gets up and splashes cool water from the nearby sink onto her face. Looking into the mirror, she notices dark circles under her eyes. *What do you think you're doing? What is going on with you?* She slaps the mirror with her open hand and holds it there, covering her reflection.

Her head snaps to the left at the sound of two taps on the bathroom door.

"April," August says from the other side of the door, "are you okay?"

Taking a hand towel, April dries her face and hands. She walks to the door and opens it. "Sure I am," she says to her concerned brother.

August's dark eyes scan her face carefully. "You look tired. What time did you come in last night? I went to bed around midnight and you weren't home yet. Where were you?"

Pushing past him, she says, "Who are you, the zookeeper?"

August follows her as she heads toward the kitchen.

"I was over at March and Debbie's and fell asleep on the couch. I woke up around two this morning and came back here." Opening a cabinet door, she pulls out a box of saltine crackers.

"You don't want any breakfast?" August asks. "I was making some bacon and French toast."

"I'm not that hungry," April replies. "I'm just going to eat a few crackers and get ready for class."

August turns to the stove and places two milk-and-egg soaked pieces of bread into the hot skillet. The clash of temperatures produces an even sssss sound. Keeping his back to April, he says, "It sounded like you were throwing up in the bathroom a moment ago. You didn't go to a bar and get drunk last night, did you?"

"Honestly, August," April snaps, "you are worse than Tucker used to be. First of all, I don't have to answer to you. And secondly, I already told you where I was last night."

Turning around to face her, August says, "Look, I'm just concerned about you. You went through a heck of a lot two months ago. You never went to any counseling after you....you know." His voice trails off.

"After I was raped? Is that the phrase you were looking for? It's really okay to say it out loud. I know I was raped. You know I was raped. I'm not going to freak out if you say the word rape. Why do I need to go to counseling? You're forgetting that I got plenty of counseling when I was at Spirit Lake. It's not that I'm opposed to counseling. It's just that I think I'm doing fine."

"March told me that he thinks you should go to counseling whether you think you should or not."

April opens and slams a cabinet door. "So you two have been talking about me?! Look, if you all have something to say, say it to my face not behind my back. That infuriates me! I thought we were a closer family than that." Pointing at the stove behind August, she says, "You need to pay more attention to your own stuff. Your French toast is burning." She walks away, leaving him scrambling to scrape his burnt toast out of the skillet.

A few minutes later she walks back in the kitchen dressed and with her book bag. "Have you got twenty dollars I can borrow? I don't have time to go by the bank and get any cash."

Reaching for the billfold in his back pocket, August says, "Sure, Sis." He takes out a twenty dollar bill and hands it to her.

April grabs it out of his hand and leaves, slamming the door behind her.

August reaches for the phone on the wall and dials a number. March answers.

"Well, I talked to our sister about counseling," August says.

"How did it go?" March asks.

"Not well at all. She got mad about it, especially when I told her you thought she should go."

"Why did that make her mad?"

"She said we were talking about her behind her back."

"Hmmm, well I guess she's right. I just didn't think of it in that way."

"Why didn't you bring up counseling to her when she was at your place last night?" August asks.

"What do you mean? She wasn't here last night."

Furrows appear across August's forehead. "But she told me she fell asleep on your couch last night. I never heard her come in, but she said it was two o'clock in the morning when she woke up and drove back here."

"Why would she say she was over here?" March asks.

"The only reason I can think of is in order to give herself a cover story for where she really was. Has she mentioned to you anything about dating someone? Maybe she's just out late on a date."

"I overheard Debbie asking her about that recently and April said she didn't want anything to do with guys. Debbie has told me that April doesn't look well. That she's losing weight."

"Yeah, I agree. This morning she had these dark circles under her eyes."

"Here's something that's odd to me," March says. "She's been asking me for money lately. Nothing big, just like twenty dollars. I don't know why she would need money. We've all three got trust money set up from what Ella left Tucker."

"Right before she stormed out of here five minutes ago she asked me for twenty dollars."

There is silence as both of them ponder the picture they have painted of their sister.

August finally speaks. "I don't know what's going on with April, but I'm afraid she's in trouble. Not like she's in trouble with the law but like she's in trouble mentally. You don't endure the kind of trauma that happened to her without there being some kind of residual psychological effects."

"I couldn't agree more," March says. "I've got a bad feeling about all of this, a really bad feeling."

Chapter Nine

After a full day of classes, August arrives at his apartment at 6:30 p.m. Opening the door, he is greeted with the aromas of tomatoes, oregano, and freshly-baked bread. His empty stomach reacts immediately by growling.

"Is that you, August?" April calls from the kitchen.

"Yeah," August replies. "What is that wonderful smell?" He crosses the small living room and walks into the kitchen.

Imitating an Italian accent, April says, "It's my famous spaghetti sauce, a family recipe handed down for generations. Don't ask me how it is made because it is a tightly held secret." Unable to maintain the personae, she breaks into laughter.

Giving her a hug, August says, "Somebody's in a good mood this evening."

When he releases her, April stirs the sauce and peeks into the oven. "I'm just trying to make up for being so snippy this morning. I guess I woke up on the wrong side of the bed. I'm sorry I bit your head off."

"And I apologize for sticking my nose into your business," August replies. "It's just that you're the only baby sister I've got, and I still feel the need to protect you like I did when we rode the school bus."

Turning to face August, April says, "You were always my Sir Lancelot, charging in to rescue me. Do you remember the day you told Jeremy Powell that you were going to throw him out of the bus window? You freaked him out."

"He was a bully and needed to be taken down a notch. If he'd said one more word, I think I really would have tried to shove him through the window."

"And do you remember when his dad showed up at the house that evening? He thought he was going to make you apologize."

August laughs. "Yeah, but that was before he met Tucker face to face."

Imitating Tucker's high-pitched voice, April crosses her arms and says, "You an' yore snot-nosed kid is jest alike. You think if y' blow enough hot air, ever'body'll let y' have yore way. But my kids an' I ain't like ever'body else. You an' yore kid need t' grow up. Now git b'fore I take my axe handle to you."

By the time she finishes, August is bent double laughing. Gasping for air, he says, "Oh my gosh, you sound just like Tucker! And I do remember when that happened. Ol' mister Powell scooted backward toward the door like a crawfish after Tucker gave him what for."

"That's the one thing you could always count on about Tucker; she always took up for us when we were in the right."

"I agree," August says. "But lord, look out if we were in the wrong. What was her expression?"

"I'll show you how the cow ate the cabbage," they say in unison and burst into laughter.

Suddenly the doorbell rings.

"You expecting someone?" August asks.

"Not me," April answers. "I'll fix our plates while you go check who's at the door."

August walks to the door and opens it.

James Davis says, "Hi August. It's James. Remember me?"

"Of course I do. April was your children's nanny. What can I do for you?"

"It's taken me quite a while to track down where you live. I've been wanting to speak to April and was hoping she might be living with you."

August makes no move to invite James in. "Why do you want to see her?"

"Can I come in for a minute?"

"That depends on what – "

"Who is it?" April calls as she walks into the living room. Peering past August, she stops in her tracks. She soundlessly mouths James's name.

"April?" James says.

Turning to April, August notices her normally porcelain complexion has turned even paler. "Do you want me to let him in?"

April hesitates for a moment then says, "Let's let him join us for supper. I'll fix another plate." Without waiting for August's reaction she turns and goes back to the kitchen.

Stepping away from the open door, August says to James, "Looks like you'll be eating supper with us."

James steps inside the apartment. "This may not be a good time. I can come back later, if I need to. I don't want to barge in on your meal."

"Look," August says, "I'm not crazy about you being here, but if April says it's okay, then it's okay. And if she says you'll eat with us, then you'll eat." Walking away from James, he goes to join his sister and finds there are three plates of spaghetti on the table. He whispers to April, "Should I go get lost for a little while so you two can talk."

Her eyes wide, April whispers, "No! I need you to be here. Where is he?"

August nods toward the living room.

"Show him in here," April whispers.

Without moving, August calls out, "Come on in, James. Supper's ready."

April frowns at August.

Walking into the kitchen, James says, "That is a familiar aroma. Must be your homemade spaghetti, April."

April gives him a nervous smile. "It is." Motioning to a chair, she says, "Let's all sit down and eat."

For the next few minutes they eat in silence. Then James says, "I've wanted to talk to you for months, but I wasn't sure if you would let me. You have no idea how guilt ridden I've been over what happened to you. So the first thing I want to say to you is I'm sorry. I'm sorry for how I handled everything that happened between us, but especially for that night."

"What do you mean by everything that happened between you two?" August asks.

James opens his mouth to speak, but April interjects, "That's none of your business. That's between me and James."

Frowning, August chews on his lip to keep from saying anything back to her.

"I'm glad to hear you say you're sorry," April says to James. "But what happened to me after I left your house that night was not your fault. I just happened to be at the wrong place at the wrong time. Don't worry, the ones responsible for what happened to me will pay, and they'll pay dearly."

"How can you say that?" August asks. "The police haven't done one thing about it. When's the last time anyone from there contacted you?"

In an icy tone, April says, "There are more ways for people to be punished than just by what the law can do to them." Standing up, she says, "Who wants some more tea?"

Both August and James hold up their glasses to the pitcher of tea as she offers it to them.

Setting his refilled glass on the table, James twirls a forkful of spaghetti and raises it to his mouth. "You still make a mean plate of spaghetti," he says with a nod toward April.

April and August follow James's lead and return to eating. After a few moments April asks, "How are Christopher and Michael?"

"They're doing okay, but just okay. I have an older lady who is helping with them, but they don't like her. 'She's not any fun,' is what the boys say to me about her." Setting his fork down and wiping his mouth with a napkin, James says, "Which brings me to the other reason I've wanted to talk to you. I want you to come back and live with us. The boys miss you terribly."

April's fork falls out of her hand, bounces off the rim of her plate, and lands on the floor.

August looks at his sister and notices her neck becoming flushed. Leaning down, he picks her fork up off the floor and sets it on the table. "So let me get this straight," he says. "You kick my sister out on her ear like she's nothing. She subsequently endures a horrific rape and now you want to try to make it all better by asking her to move back in with you? Sounds to me like you're just trying to ease your own guilty conscience."

"August," April says sharply, "can you leave us alone for a bit?"

"But I thought you wanted me – "

"I know what I told you. But now I'm telling you I need some time in private with James."

August looks from April to James and back to April. "I hope you know what you're doing." Rising from his chair, he says, "I guess I'll go take a walk." Lifting his jacket off a hook on the wall, he walks out the front door.

Chapter Ten

Once she hears August leaving the apartment, April turns her attention to James. "I've wondered how I would feel if I ever saw you again or if I ever would see you again. Now that you're sitting here in front of me I'm flooded with all sorts of emotions: surprise, anger, resentment, love, attraction, hatred." She pauses. "And curiosity."

Tears well up in James's eyes. "I'm a therapist. I'm supposed to be in tune with and in control of my emotions. Honestly, right now I feel like a kid. My palms are sweaty. My heart is racing. I'm about to jump out of my skin."

"Was it something that I made up in my head?" April asks.

"What do you mean?"

"Weren't we attracted to each other? Didn't you feel something for me other than I was just your nanny?"

Looking down at the table, James replies, "It wasn't all in your head. It was true." Raising his eyes to look at her, he adds, "It is true."

April feels heat pushing through every cell in her body. Her skin feels like it is on fire. She fears she may suddenly spontaneously combust and disappear in a puff of smoke.

"It's hard to explain," James says. "My fear was that I was just rebounding from the loss of Susan and what I was feeling for you was a selfish longing for someone to hold me."

"But how can that be a selfish thing? Isn't that what everyone wants; someone to hold them tenderly and lovingly?"

Nodding, James says, "You are wise beyond your years, April. Yes, you're right. It is what humanity craves. My therapist had to help me see that truth."

"You were in therapy?"

"I am in therapy. Every therapist needs a therapist or trusted confidant to help them keep their equilibrium. I've been talking to Mary about us. You remember her from Spirit Lake?"

"How could I forget Mary," April says. "Such a wonderful woman."

"I even had some sessions with Dr. Sydney, the psychiatrist who helped your brother March."

"So, what have you gotten out of all your therapy?"

"First of all, that there is nothing wrong with me, that my feelings are valid. Secondly, that I was letting myself be blocked by social constraints and my fear of what other people might say."

"I understand the first part of that, but I'm not sure what you mean by the second part."

Sliding his hand across the table and placing it over April's hand, James says, "It's the difference in our ages. I was afraid people would accuse me of robbing the cradle."

Frowning, April says, "Robbing the cradle?"

"It's an old expression that basically means an older person marrying a child."

"But I'm not a child," April protests.

"I understand that now. And it really doesn't matter what people think. They're entitled to their opinion. But I shouldn't live my life based on what other people may or may not think. That's part of my own codependency that used to control my life. I thought I was past all that until I spent some time talking to Mary and Dr. Sydney and heard myself talking it outside my head. Things started coalescing, and I saw things more clearly. That's what set me out on my quest to find you again and try to make things right between us."

April feels her heart beating in her ears like a big bass drum. *If this is a dream, please don't let me wake up.* When she speaks her voice sounds far away to her, "So what are you saying, James?"

"My excuse in coming here is the boys want you to come back and live with us. But the truth is I want you to come live with me."

The next sensation April has is of someone patting her cheeks and calling her name. She opens her eyes and sees James's face above her. His expression is frantic. "April," he says, "are you okay?" She becomes more aware of her surroundings and realizes she is lying on the floor. "What happened?" she asks.

"You fainted," James replies. "I'm going to run to the bathroom and get a cold wash cloth, okay?"

"Sure," she replies feebly.

After a moment, James returns.

The cold, moist cloth sharpens her senses. "Help me up," she says.

"Just wait a minute. Let's make sure you didn't hurt yourself when you fell out of the chair. Your head hit the floor like a melon. You could have a mild concussion."

At that moment the front door of the apartment opens and August calls out, "I forgot something."

As he comes through the opening into the kitchen, August sees April on the floor and James hovering over her body. "What the - ! " he cries and catapults across the floor, crashing into James. They roll across the small room. August's hands find James's neck, and he begins choking him. "What have you done?!" he yells.

"August, stop!" April screams. But her voice cannot pierce the adrenalin-charged fury that has taken control of her brother. Darting over to the wrestling men, she grabs August's wrists and tries to pry them off of James. "August, I'm okay!" she yells in his ear. "I had only fainted!"

Somehow April's message finds its way to a sane part of August's brain, and he releases his grip on James, shoving him away as he does so.

James crawls to a sitting position on the floor holding his throat and coughing. April kneels beside him. "Are you okay?" she asks.

Nodding his head, James says hoarsely, "Water."

Jumping up, April dashes to the sink and fills a glass with water. She offers the glass of water to James who eagerly drinks it.

August uses the wall for support as he stands up.

April closes the distance between them, draws her arm back, and slaps him hard across the face. "Have you lost your ever-loving mind? What is the matter with you?"

Scowling, August says, "I thought he had hurt you. You were lying on the floor, and he was – "

"He was trying to help me because I had fainted," April says. "You have got to quit treating me like I'm your child or something."

Looking at James, August says, "I'm sorry."

With a wave of his hand, James says, "It's all right. No serious harm done." Standing up, he hands the empty glass back to April.

Suddenly, April's stomach roils again. "I'm going to be sick," she says and bolts to the bathroom, slamming the locked door behind her. Falling to her knees in front of the toilet, she lifts the ring just as her supper comes flying out of her mouth. Twice more her stomach heaves before she flushes the toilet.

The doorknob to the bathroom rattles and August says, "April, it's me. Let me in."

"Go away. I'll be out in a minute." Using the sink to aid her, April rises off the floor, splashes cold water on her face and rinses her mouth out. Then she carefully lifts the lid of the tank off the back of the toilet and sets it on the floor. Reaching her hand in the tank, she takes a small plastic ziploc bag out. She towel dries the outside of the bag and looks at the white pills inside. Opening the bag she pours the pills into her hand. *Crap! Only five? I thought I had more than that. I've got to get some more tonight.* Opening her mouth, she tosses all five pills in and chews them up. The bitter taste that used to make her gag no longer fazes her. She swallows, then swishes a mouthful of water and swallows again. After putting the lid to the tank back in place, she checks her reflection in the mirror, brushes her hair back, and walks out of the bathroom.

Halfway rising out of his chair as April walks into the living room, James says, "Are you all right?"

"Sure. I'm fine. My stomach has been giving me trouble lately."

"I guess I'll be going," James says. Looking directly at April, he says, "Maybe we can talk again – soon."

"Yes," April says. "And I'll be thinking about what we said. Why don't I walk you to your car?"

"You don't have to do – "

"I want to," April insists.

When they get to James's car, he opens the door to get in. "James," April says, "this is a little embarrassing, but could you loan me twenty dollars? I'm running a little short this week. I promise to pay you back."

Reaching for his billfold, James says, "Sure you can. And don't worry about paying me back." He presses two twenties into her hand. "Take this."

April's eyes shine as she looks at the money. "Thank you so much. I'll call you later, okay?"

"Yes, please do."

April hurries back in the apartment and grabs her jacket and the car keys.

August watches her rushed movements and says, "Where are you going?"

"I'm going to run to the grocery store and pick up some eggs and bacon for breakfast in the morning. I noticed we were all out." She hurries out the door before he can respond.

Walking into the kitchen, August takes the tea pitcher to the refrigerator. He notices an unopened package of bacon on the shelf and a full carton of eggs beside it.

Chapter Eleven

As she drives down North Broadway toward the campus of the University of Tennessee, her left knee bobs up and down with the speed of a rabbit scratching its ear. As she steers with her left hand, the fingers of her right hand tap a rapid, uneven cadence on the console. So focused is she on her mission that she barely notices the other cars in the lanes beside her. She turns on her blinker and takes the exit onto Cumberland Avenue. After a few blocks she pulls into the parking lot of Hess Hall, one of the dormitories.

Bouncing out of her car, April hurries into the lobby and pushes the button for the elevator. When the doors don't open within a few seconds, she stabs the button repeatedly. Once the doors begin to open, she quickly charges forward but has to stop and back up to let others off the elevator. She taps the floor impatiently with her foot.

As soon as the last person exits the elevator, April slips inside and pushes the button for the fifth floor. Sticking her hand in the pocket of her jeans, she feels the two twenty dollar bills James gave her and smiles. As she exits onto the fifth floor she turns down the hallway to her right, stops at the third door and knocks.

From the other side of the door someone calls out, "Who is it?"

Looking left and right, April puts her mouth closer to the door and says, "It's me. I need to come in." She listens as the deadbolt clicks open.

The door opens just wide enough to reveal a young coed's face. The bloodshot whites of her eyes look like the lines on a roadmap. A strong smell of marijuana floats out the door opening and envelopes April. "What do you want?" the coed asks.

"You know what I want," April answers testily. "Where's Candice?"

"She's not here."

"What do you mean, she's not here? She has to be here!"

The girl blinks slowly at April as her mind tries to filter April's words through her marijuana haze. Finally she says, "Well she's not here."

April puts her face closer to the girl's face. "Listen, Monica, I know you are stoned, but I need some pills. Why don't you look where Candice keeps her stash and sell me some? She won't mind. As a matter of fact she'll probably thank you for helping her not miss a sale. Candice does like her money, you know."

Monica looks at her stupidly. "Look where she keeps her stash? Sell you some?" She giggles. "You look funny."

Putting her hand on the door, April shoves hard. The corner of the door cracks Monica on the forehead and she stumbles backward. April steps inside the apartment and quickly shuts and locks the door.

"Ouch!" Monica cries, putting her hand on her forehead. "You hurt me."

"Oh put a bag of frozen peas on it!" April says as she walks past her. She goes directly to Candice's bedroom.

"Hey, you can't come in here," Monica says as she comes up behind her.

"I've been here lots of times, you idiot. Candice won't care." She scans the room. "I've just got to find her stash." Going to the dresser, she rummages through each drawer, tossing the contents over her shoulder. As each drawer fails to reveal the prize she seeks, April's panic increases. She jerks the last empty drawer out of the dresser and tosses it across the room.

Next, she attacks Candice's bed, stripping it down to the mattress. Slipping her hands underneath the mattress, she lifts it off the box springs and pushes it into the floor on the other side. The blank surface of the box springs glares back at her.

"Candice is not going to be happy about this," Monica says.

Whirling around, April slaps Monica. "Tell me where it is!" She grabs the front of Monica's shirt. "Listen to me! I'm out of medicine. If I don't have something to take in the morning when I get up, I'm going to be sick. Just tell me where she keeps the pills, and I'll leave you alone."

"Hey," Monica says as her senses begin to clear, "cut it out! You need to leave, or I'm calling the campus police."

"Okay, okay," April says softly, "I'm sorry. I shouldn't have done that. I'm just a little on edge. But I need you to help me."

Monica pulls away from April and grabs the phone and punches in a number.

"Okay," April says, "I'm leaving. You can hang up the phone. There's no need to report this." Swearing, she hurries past Monica and leaves the apartment.

After she boards the elevator to go back downstairs, fear, anger and panic press tears into her eyes. On the bottom floor, she exits into the bright lights of the lobby of the dorm. With her vision blurred from the lights passing through the prisms of her tears, she finds her way to her car. Inside, she pounds the steering wheel with palms of her hands. *What am I going to do?! Where else can I find some?*

She cranks her car. With no destination in mind she pulls out of the parking lot onto the street.

With the force of a locomotive, a car slams into the rear passenger door of April's car sending it spinning across the street. The initial impact causes her head to bang hard against her window. The effect is like having a thousand stars showering down on her.

She sees trees, buildings and cars in a single stream as her car spins out of control. The spinning stops abruptly as the front of her car smashes into a telephone pole. There is a loud explosion as the airbag deploys and shoves April back.

The next thing April is aware of is a man's voice to the left of her.

"Ma'am, can you talk to me? Are you hurting anywhere?"

April opens her eyes. Flashing blue and red lights fill the night sky and bounce off of buildings and cars. Dazed, she says, "What happened?"

"You were in a car wreck," the man says. "My name is Keith. I'm a paramedic. What's your name?"

"April."

"April, can you tell me if you're hurting anywhere?"

"My head hurts."

"Okay. That's probably because it hit your window during the impact. Anything else hurting?"

"I don't think so."

"Great. Some of the firemen are going to have to come open your door further so we can get you out. Then we'll check you more closely in the ambulance. Is that okay?" He turns his head and hollers at someone.

"What happened?" April asks.

"The best I can tell, you pulled out in front of someone."

"Really? Was anyone hurt?"

"We need to get you out of your car, April. I'm going to step back out of the way so these guys can do their job. But I'll be right back."

April feels her car shaking as the men try to force open her bent door. There is the sound of metal groaning and then a loud pop as the door gives in to the combined efforts of the firefighters.

"Okay, April," Keith says as he leans into the door opening, "I'm going to shine my light in your eyes before we try moving you."

April winces as the bright penlight strikes her pupils.

"Everything looks good," Keith says. "Have you noticed if you're hurting anywhere else?"

"I think my foot and leg are hurting some."

Keith takes his flashlight and shines it in the floorboard. "Looks like it might have jammed your leg when the firewall got shoved backward. What we'll do is put you on a gurney right here so you don't have to walk."

Lying on her back while strapped to the gurney, April watches the flashing colored emergency lights create a kaleidoscope on the bare branches of the trees overhead. She squints as she is slid into the brightly lit interior of the ambulance. Keith listens to her chest with his stethoscope then slips a blood pressure cuff onto her arm. The other paramedic is slipping something on her leg. She tries to raise up to see what he's doing, but the straps prevent her.

Keith lays his hand on her shoulder and eases her back down. "He's putting an inflatable cast on there to keep it immobile. I don't know if it's fractured or not, but it's best to keep it stabilized until the doctor at the hospital takes a look at it."

"Hospital? I don't need to go to the hospital. I'm fine. Just a bump on my head, that's all." As she speaks she feels the ambulance beginning to move. She struggles against the straps. "Let me up! Let me out of here!"

Keith shifts positions so that his face is above and parallel to April's. "April, we want to make sure that there aren't any internal injuries. Sometimes those kinds of injuries can become life threatening. Let's do the safe thing, don't you think? I'm sure you have loved ones who would want us to be extra cautious with you and take the best care of you. Why don't you try to rest and let us do that?"

April studies Keith's face for the first time. *He has kind eyes, sort of like James's.* "Okay," she says to Keith, "I'll let you do what you think is best."

Squeezing her hand, Keith says, "That's a good girl."

When Keith and the other paramedic roll April into the emergency room of the hospital, April feels like she is flying on a magic carpet. The panels of overhead florescent lights that she sweeps past remind her of clouds.

For the next hour April has multiple vials of blood drawn and x-rays taken of her foot and leg. But much of that time she lies still, waiting for the next step in the process. Someone asks her if there's someone she wants called. April hesitates then gives them March's name and number.

Finally, the curtain surrounding her opens and a woman steps inside. She has a stethoscope hanging around her neck and is wearing a white lab coat. Approaching April's bed, she looks at her and recognition dawns on her face. "April? Is that you?"

April looks more closely at the woman but fails to place her face. "My name is April. Do I know you?"

"We met a few months ago. I'm Doctor Oliver. I took care of you when you were raped."

Turning her face away, April says, "Oh." Then turning back to look at the doctor, she says, "Am I okay? Can I go now?"

"Well, the good news is there are no fractures in your foot or leg. However, you have a minor concussion. I think it's best if you stay here overnight. Besides, I want to make sure that baby you're carrying is all right."

Chapter Twelve

"Baby?!" April exclaims. "I'm not carrying a baby."

Dr. Oliver looks back at the lab reports. "It says here that you are."

"But I can't be. I'm not even dating anyone, much less having sex with someone."

"When is the last time you had sex?"

April looks toward the ceiling. "Gosh, it's been a long time. No one's even been close to – " Suddenly she stops speaking. Slowly her head turns. She looks at Dr. Oliver. Her eyes grow wide with alarm, and their eyes lock.

"The last sexual contact you had was the rape, wasn't it?" Dr. Oliver asks.

Tears spring up in April's eyes and quickly begin rolling down her cheeks. She finds it hard to get her breath.

Stepping closer, Dr. Oliver takes April's hand in hers.

"Please," April says through her tears, "tell me it's not possible."

The doctor's eyes glaze over with a film of tears. Swallowing hard, she says, "I'm afraid it is possible. It's rare, only about five percent of the time, but it does happen."

"No, no, no!" April cries. "This can't be happening to me! Why are things always happening to me? Do I have some kind of curse on me? Oh my god, what am I going to do? What are people going to say? How will I tell my family?"

"Hold on," Dr. Oliver says, "let's not get ahead of ourselves. You have options."

"Options? What do you mean?"

"You don't have to keep this baby. You can have an abortion, if you want to."

"An abortion? I've always thought of that as wrong, like you're taking the life of a child."

"I understand where you're coming from, but there is an alternative view, you know. It's only a bunch of cells at this point, not a fully developed human. It's not murder, or it would be against the law. Besides that, there is no way of knowing who the father is. You'd be raising a fatherless child on your own, with no child support. I'm just thinking of how hard your life will be if you choose not to keep it. Because you got pregnant as a result of rape no one's going to fault you for having an abortion. Let me get me get you the phone number of the local Planned Parenthood facility."

Without waiting for a reply, Dr. Oliver exits the room.

April slams her fist onto the mattress. *Pregnant! I can't believe I'm pregnant!* She grits her teeth so hard the grinding is audible. *No one has the kind of luck I have. But now what? Abortion? Give birth and raise the child by myself?*

As April is ruminating, Dr. Oliver returns. Handing a card to April, she says, "Here is the contact information I told you about. Is there anyone you'd like me to call to come spend the night with you? One of your brothers perhaps?"

April considers the question then says, "Somebody is supposed to have called my brother March."

"Okay then. Is there anything else I can do for you?"

"What about some medicine for pain? I'm probably going to be pretty sore from this wreck, don't you think?"

Dr. Oliver fixes her with a gaze. Holding up April's chart, she says, "You realize that I got a complete lab on you, don't you? It shows me everything that was in your system at the time of the wreck."

April looks away. She feels herself break into a sweat.

"If you have a prescription for everything that was in your body, then there isn't a problem. However, if…"

April's eyes dart to the doctor's face. A quick list of excuses flies through her mind in a nanosecond. Selecting one, she says, "I borrowed a hydrocodone from my brother August yesterday. That may have showed up in the labs. My back has been hurting me periodically since the rape. I think my spine may have been damaged."

"Mmm hmmm." Doctor Oliver purses her lips. "Well now that you're pregnant I'm not going to give you any opiates. I've left an order for prescription strength ibuprofen. You can have that if you start hurting badly enough."

April finds it impossible to prevent her facial muscles from trembling as she forces a smile. "Sure, that'll be fine. Thanks."

"I'll see you in the morning. If you have no complications, like spotting or bleeding, you can go home then."

After the doctor leaves, April reaches for the phone and starts to punch in numbers. Just before she hits the last number the door to her room opens. Debbie and March walk in.

"April!" Debbie exclaims as she rushes to her bedside. "Are you all right?"

March joins them and finds April's hand. "What happened? Are you all right?"

"I'm fine," April says. "I pulled out in front of someone and they hit me broadside. Lucky for me nothing was broken."

Debbie leans over and kisses her forehead. "Bless your heart. You seem to have the worst luck."

"I know," April agrees. "Can you believe this?"

"Are you sure you're okay?" March asks.

Squeezing his hand, she says, "Yes, big brother. I'm fine. Just some bruises from the impact of the other car and from when I hit the telephone pole."

"Telephone pole?" Debbie says.

"When the car hit me, it sent me spinning in circles until the front of my car hit a telephone pole. Thank goodness for airbags."

Turning to Debbie, March says, "You said she had the worst luck, but I'd say she's extremely lucky to even be alive after the wreck, much less not have any serious injuries."

"You're right," Debbie says. "I was just thinking about all that's happened to her in the past few months. You know the…uh…"

"You mean the rape," April finishes her sentence. "It's okay. I've told you all you can refer to it for what it was. It's not going to freak me out. But you know what a weird coincidence is? My doctor tonight is the same one that treated me when I was raped. She even remembered me."

"If there are no serious injuries," March says, "I guess they're going to let you leave in a little bit?"

April hesitates a moment, searching for a way to explain why she's being kept overnight without mentioning the pregnancy. "You know how cautious hospitals are nowadays, afraid of being sued. So they are going to keep me overnight just as a precaution. Then I'll go home in the morning."

"That's probably a good idea," Debbie says.

Thankful that Debbie accepted her excuse, April says, "The truth is, there wasn't any reason for you to go to all the trouble to come here. I mean, I appreciate it and all, but I'm fine. Actually I'm feeling tired and sleepy. Why don't you all go on back home? I'm just going to sleep the night away and then call August in the morning to come pick me up."

"We'll just spend the night with you," March says. "I don't want you to be all alone."

April feels her leg muscles cramping and her bowels wanting to move. She recognizes these familiar symptoms of withdrawal from the pain pills and knows they are only going to get worse if she doesn't get some more pills. "That's sweet," she says, "but I'll be fine. Besides, if you stay all night, you all will be worse off than me tomorrow. You know how impossible it is to sleep in a hospital when you're the visitor."

March's eyebrows furrow. "You sound like you're trying to get rid of us."

April forces herself to laugh. "Will you quit being such a mother hen? Debbie, you know what I'm saying makes sense. Take this worry wart with you, go home, and get a good night's rest."

"Your advice is practical," Debbie says. "It just feels wrong. But if you insist - "

"I insist. Now give me a kiss and be on your way. Thank you for coming."

Debbie and March kiss her and head out of the room.

As soon as the door to her room clicks shut, April reaches for the bedside phone. She punches in a number and waits. "Kyle, this is April. I need you to bring me some, and to bring it now…I don't care what you've got going on. I'm out. I'm in the hospital and can't afford to be sick from withdrawals…I had a fender bender and they're just keeping me overnight to be safe…Yes, I've got money."

She gives him the address of the hospital and her room number, then hangs up.

Thirty minutes later there is a single knock on her door. It slowly opens. A young man with stringy hair and wearing sunglasses sticks his head in.

"Kyle!" April gushes. "Thank god you're here. Come in and shut the door."

Kyle's nasal voice precedes his entrance, "Has ol' Kyle ever let you down?" A sideways smirk creases one side of his face as he approaches her bed.

"Did you bring me anything?" April asks.

He sticks his hand in the outside pocket of his black leather jacket and gives it a shake. The unmistakable sound of pills rattling in a plastic bottle can be heard. Laughing, he says, "But don't you think it's a little ironic that you are in a hospital full of pills and have to call me to bring you something?"

Ignoring his comment and pointing to a chair, April says, "Look in the pocket of my jeans over there and bring me my money."

"What, no small talk? What's your hurry?"

April punches him in the chest. "Just give me what I want and get out of here. I don't want them to catch you or me in the middle of a deal."

Kyle scowls at her and rubs his chest. Walking over to the chair, he rifles through her pockets until he finds the money. He counts it as he returns to the bedside. He stuffs the money into his pocket and then takes out the pill bottle. "I'm feeling generous tonight. I'm going to let you have all of them, but you'll still owe me some money."

Snatching the bottle out of his hand, April says, "Fine. You know where you can find me. Now get out."

"No 'thank you'? Wow, April, you make me feel like you're just using me."

"We both know who is using who. We're done. Leave."

Kyle pushes his hair behind his ear, makes a kissing sound, and exits her room.

April's hands are trembling as she opens the bottle. She shakes three pills into her hand, pitches them into her mouth and chews. The bitter taste contorts her smile of relief.

Chapter Thirteen

Strains of Elvis singing "Hard Headed Woman" find their way into Benjamin's dream and begin pulling him toward consciousness. The two worlds meet when he reaches out to shake Elvis' hand and someone shakes his arm. Startled, Benjamin sits up on the couch.

Maria is standing in front of him rubbing sleep from her eyes. "Mama said she needs you."

Benjamin locates the clock. "It's s-s-s-six thirty. Time to get ready for the school b-b-b-bus. Wake Alexander and ya'll g-g-g-get dressed. I'll see about Mama."

"Why do we have to go to school again today? We went yesterday."

"Remember what T-T-T-Tucker told us yesterday? She promised to g-g-g-give us food when we need it as long as we g-g-g-go to school every day. Now go d-d-d-do what I said." He walks away from his sister and heads to his mother's bedroom.

Once inside her bedroom he looks at the grainy images on the television.

"Is that you, Bennie?" His mother asks.

"Yes ma'am."

"Nobody can sing it like the King, can they, Bennie?"

"Elvis is the b-b-b-best," he replies.

"I hope I can see Graceland before I die. That's my wish, to see Graceland."

Benjamin doesn't know how to respond to this statement, so he remains quiet.

"How long has it been since your stepdad has been home? I lose track of time."

"N-N-N-Nineteen days."

"Are we out of food yet?"

"No ma'am."

"Why not? Usually it's been all eat up by now."

Unsure that his mother would approve of them getting food from someone she doesn't know, Benjamin decides to dodge the question. "D-D-D-Do you want a Pop-Tart?"

"Have we got strawberry flavored?" Joyce asks.

"I think so."

"Yeah, get me one of those and something to drink. I'm thirsty this morning. And tell the two little ones to come in here and see me. We can watch the rest of this movie together."

Benjamin hesitates between what he's been asked to do by Tucker and what his mother has asked of him. "They're g-g-g-getting ready for the school b-b-b-bus."

In slow motion, his mother sits up. Benjamin notices lumps of hair on her pillow, the result of chemotherapy.

Joyce tears her attention away from the TV screen and looks at Benjamin. "School? Again? Didn't ya'll go yesterday?"

Shifting nervously, Benjamin nods. He snaps his fingers. "One P-P-P-Pop-Tart on the way." He turns to leave the room.

"Bennie." His mother's voice acts like the crook of a shepherd's staff, stopping him and turning him around.

"Yes, ma'am?"

"Ya'll are going to school again today?"

Benjamin nods.

"How come? You could stay home with me and watch Elvis, if you want to. Besides, I don't like being home alone. What if I have a spell of some kind and need help? I depend on you, Bennie. You're good to me."

The conflicting feelings of guilt and resentment play tug-of-war with Benjamin's heart. He knows his mother leans on him and truly needs him, but he is tired of playing the role of husband to her and father to his brother and sister. He struggles to find a way to do what he wants to do while at the same time placating his mother. He says, "I'll l-l-l-let you play with my M-M-M-Matchbox cars while we're at school. I w-w-w-want to go to school."

It looks as if his mother is about to question him further, but her red-rimmed and tired eyes turn away from him and back to the TV She lays back down. "Bring me that Pop-Tart and something to drink, too."

Thankful that his mother is too fatigued to argue with him, Benjamin exits her bedroom and heads to the kitchen. He is careful to walk around the rotted hole in the floor. Just as he does so, a large drop of water falls from the sagging sheetrock overhead and splatters on the edge of the hole. He finds the box of Pop-tarts, checks to be sure the mice haven't eaten into it, and takes out enough for himself, his siblings and his mother. He places four into the dented and rusted toaster.

Opening the refrigerator, Benjamin looks to see what there is to drink. He selects an unopened bottle of Juicy Juice.

"I don't want Pop-tarts for breakfast." Alexander has found his way into the kitchen. "I want Fruit Loops."

Benjamin ignores him and pours the juice into empty jars of various sizes. When he turns to look at his brother, he says, "Z-Z-Z-

Zip your pants and t-t-t-tie your shoes. There's no m-m-m-milk for cereal. You'll have to eat PopTarts. Where's M-M-M-Maria?"

"I don't know," Alexander says. He pulls out a chair to the kitchen table and sits down hard, a pouting expression on his face. He folds his arms on the table and rests his chin on them. "I don't want to go to school."

The toaster ejects the warm Pop-tarts so violently that two of them land on the counter. Benjamin picks up one of them, grabs a jar of juice, and says, "I'm t-t-t-taking this to Mama. G-G-G-Go get Maria and ya'll eat. The b-b-b-bus will b-b-b-be here soon."

Benjamin walks into his mother's bedroom and sees that he has arrived at the point in the movie where Elvis is being stabbed. He's seen this scene scores of times. His mother, however, is crying as if this is the first time she's ever seen the movie and doesn't know that the stabbing is not fatal.

"They ought not done that to him," Joyce says as she wipes tears from her sallow cheeks.

Benjamin first thinks she is talking to him but realizes she hasn't even noticed he walked in. He sets the Pop-Tart and drink on the table beside her bed and leaves the room.

By the time he eats his pop-tart and Alexander and Maria finish theirs, the school bus driver is honking his horn, impatient to be finished with his morning rounds.

Benjamin ushers his reluctant siblings out the door. When they arrive at the open door of the bus, the driver scolds them, "You're supposed to be out here waiting on me. I'm very punctual and expect you to do the same. Tell your folks to get you ready on time." As they file onto the bus one at a time, the driver continues his diatribe, "And I'm not going to keep stopping here if you're not going to be consistent about riding to school."

Alexander and Maria sit down on the second seat. Benjamin makes his way past the younger children towards the back of the bus.

"Is that B-B-B-Bennie the b-b-b-bowling b-b-b-ball?"

Several kids laugh at the mocking voice of Mark O'Riley.

"That's enough of that," the voice of the bus driver carries over the laughter.

Benjamin grins at the older kids and sits in an empty seat. "Good m-m-m-morning."

Mark snickers. Keeping his voice lower so the bus driver won't hear him, he says, "Bennie, you're so stupid you can't tell when somebody's making fun of you. I called you a bowling ball. Don't you get it? Your body has no shape to it, just like a bowling ball."

This is a pin prick that Benjamin can't ignore. He's looked at himself in the mirror and seen his pimpled face and large nose. And he's noticed the difference in the size of his stomach and the stomach of his peers. He hates looking at himself and wishes he looked more like Elvis.

As the bus drives past Tucker's, Benjamin looks to see if he can see her or Smiley. But no one is stirring outside. A few miles further the bus makes a stop that he doesn't remember it making before. It is a brick house that has appeared empty, but now there are boxes out by the road, vehicles in the driveway, and curtains on the windows.

The bus slows to a stop and waits. Everyone is looking out the windows to see what new rider is going to join them. When the door of the house doesn't open, the bus driver honks three times.

Immediately there is a response from inside. The door opens and a girl appears, along with what looks to be her mother and father. They exchange hugs and the girl proceeds to the bus.

The closer she gets to the bus, the older she appears to Benjamin. *She looks like she's my age.* As she climbs the steps of the bus her chestnut hair bounces on her shoulders while wisps of hair hang across her face. Benjamin cannot keep from staring at her. *I've never seen eyes that green.* Her nose is tiny compared to his, but is the perfect size for her face. When she smiles at the bus driver, dimples frame the corners of her mouth.

So mesmerized is he by her face that Benjamin's eyes travel no further and therefore don't notice what Mark O'Riley has noticed – the curves of her body. As the girl passes the full seats and moves toward the back, Mark pushes his companion out of his seat and calls to her, "Hey, I've got a seat for you right here."

The girl looks at him, then looks around. Seeing an empty seat in front of Benjamin, she says, "Thanks anyway. I'll just sit here."

When she sits down, her perfume washes over Benjamin. He's never smelled anything so sweet and tantalizing. He feels as if it is lifting him off his seat, like in a cartoon he once saw. Her hair hangs over the back of the seat and barely brushes his hand.

The girl turns around and says to him, "Hi, my name is Cassie Armour."

Her move and directness catches Benjamin off guard. He says, "I'm B-B-B-Benjamin. You smell."

Cassie makes a face and turns back around while the kids sitting close by burst into howls of laughter.

Throughout his first period class Benjamin tries to sort out what he was feeling, what he was thinking, and what he said relative to Cassie Armour that resulted in her making a face at him and the others laughing. It is familiar ground for him, often confused over people's reaction to his reaction. *It's that stupid Asperger's! I can spell it, but I can't figure it out.*

Between first and second period he goes to his locker. As he's looking for his book, someone opens the empty locker beside him. He steals a look from the corner of his eye and can't believe what he sees. Cassie Armour is putting books into the locker.

When he closes his locker, she notices him. "Oh no, not you," she says.

Even though he's not positive what he did wrong earlier, Benjamin decides to use a technique one of his past teachers taught him. "I-I-I-I'm sorry for what I s-s-s-said. I like how y-y-y-you smell."

Cassie's expression softens. She smiles. "That's okay. Maybe I had my feelings on my sleeve. I should have given you a chance to explain. It's Benjamin, right?"

He tries to maintain eye contact with her direct gaze but finds himself having to keep redirecting his line of sight. He nods his head.

"Well," Cassie says, "I need to get to class." Closing her locker, she leaves him standing speechless.

That night, before he lies down to sleep, Benjamin takes his journal out of his treasure box and writes:

I've seen a bright yellow sunrise

And a red and orange sunset.

I've seen a white, full moon

And twinkling stars, too many to count.

But I've never seen anything that compares to you.

Chapter Fourteen

The door to April's hospital room opens and Dr. Oliver walks in. "So, how are you feeling this morning?"

"Not as bad as I expected," April replies, "but I can tell I'm going to be sore."

"Most definitely. Probably more sore tomorrow and the next day than today. The night shift said you didn't have any incidents last night, so I'm going to turn you loose. Have you called anyone to pick you up? One of your brothers, perhaps?"

"I've got a friend who's standing by waiting for my call."

"Okay then. You should go ahead and call because it will take some time to get the paperwork done for your discharge. Have you decided what you're going to do about the fetus you're carrying?"

April chews on her bottom lip. "I'm not sure."

"That's understandable. Just keep in mind that there is a limit on how far along you can be when they do an abortion. The people at Planned Parenthood will tell you all about that. Good-bye, April. And good luck."

They shake hands. Dr. Oliver holds April's hand until April looks her in the eye. Giving her one more firm shake, she releases her hand and leaves the room.

Once she's alone, April picks up the phone and makes a call. "James? It's April. I'm ready for you to come pick me up."

Half an hour later, James walks through the open door of April's room. "Are you okay?" he asks.

Before April can answer, a nurse appears in the doorway with a wheelchair. Smiling, the nurse says, "We're ready to kick you out, if you're ready to leave, girl."

April stands up and winces as she puts her weight on her ankle. "You all have taken good care of me, but I'm definitely ready to go."

James looks at the nurse. "Are you sure she's okay to leave?"

"Her ankle is just bruised and slightly sprained. She needs to put ice on it for a couple more days. But she'll be fine."

April backs into the wheelchair.

James lifts her feet and folds the foot rests in place.

When James gets in the car after making sure April is buckled in the passenger seat, he says, "The boys are going to be so excited to see you. I told them I was coming here to get you. You should have seen them jumping up and down and yelling your name."

April smiles at the mental picture. "And I can't wait to see them. Who's watching them now?"

"Miss Scarlett. She's who I hired after you left."

"Miss Scarlett? Are you serious? And are you her Rhett Butler?"

"Hardly. Let's just say that I'm being kind when I describe her as rather matronly."

"Old?"

"While that is a relative term," James answers, "in her case it is an accurate term. And she doesn't really know how to deal with boys and all their energy. She expects them to be little gentlemen."

"No wonder they've been so unhappy," April says.

James pulls out of the parking lot. "I was a little surprised when you called so soon after our visit. I thought you might want to think some more about what you wanted to do."

"I guess this car wreck just sped things up. Truthfully though, I had pretty much made up my mind to accept your offer the instant it was given. Are you sure this is what you want to do? Me live with you? The two of us a couple?"

"Like I told you, April, I thought it through as thoroughly as a person can. And the longer I thought about what life with you might be like, the more I saw it was the right choice, not only for me, but for the boys as well. Family is important to me, and I know family is important to you, too." He reaches across the console and takes her hand.

"And we will have the perfect family, won't we?" April says.

Laughing, James says, "I don't believe I would use the word 'perfect'. There's no such thing. But whatever imperfections our family has, we will work through them. That's my commitment to you."

April is quiet as she absorbs the truth that a dream she'd lost is about to be fulfilled. But in the far corner of her mind truth holds up a placard reminding her of secrets she's keeping from James. She squeezes her eyes shut, trying to block out the message.

"Are you hurting?" James asks.

April opens her eyes. "No. Why do you ask?"

"You looked like you were wincing in pain."

"If there was any kind of pain, it might be hunger pains. I'm starving. You know what they say about hospital food."

"I'll take care of that as soon as I get you home. I'll fix us a big breakfast – eggs, waffles and pancakes. How does that sound?"

There is an audible growl from April's stomach. She laughs. "Does that answer your question?"

They drive in silence for a few minutes.

James says, "I've been so focused on having you with me I haven't even asked you about the wreck. What in the world happened?"

April relates the details to him, but omits the conversation she had with Dr. Oliver.

Shaking his head, James says, "Wow, April, you were lucky you weren't killed."

"That's what everybody says. I'm probably going to get a ticket for it though. I was careless and pulled right in front of the other car."

After a few moments of silence, James says, "Have you told your brothers and Tucker about your decision to move in with me?"

April's conscience plucks a string that resonates in her heart. "Not really," she replies. "I probably should have but didn't really want to get into a long discussion about it. You know how they would have given me the third degree, especially from March."

"Well, that's your decision. But you did let them know about the wreck, didn't you?"

"I had the hospital call March last night, and he and Debbie came to the hospital. So I'm sure the word has been spread."

When James finally pulls into his driveway, the front door of the house bursts open and Christopher and Michael explode out of the house like they've been shot from a cannon. It reminds April of the first time she came to James's house and was bowled over by them on the front steps.

As soon as the car stops, the boys pull her door open and start climbing onto her.

"Michael! Christopher!" James scolds them. "Be careful. April was hurt in a car wreck."

"Please don't stop them," April says looking at their disappointed and concerned expressions. "Any pain I feel is going to easily be swallowed up by the excitement in seeing them again." She throws her arms around the boys. "I've missed you all so much."

"And we've missed you," Michael says.

"I don't like Miss Scarlett," Christopher says.

"Now boys," James says, "you know we've talked about this, and we're not going to talk bad about Miss Scarlett. She's just trying to help."

"But she's leaving now, since April's here. Right?" Michael asks. He looks April in the eye. "You've come home to us, haven't you?"

Tears well up in April's eyes. "Home. It's the most beautiful word in the English language. Yes, I've come home."

Unbuckling his seatbelt, James says, "Then why don't we all go inside instead of sitting out here in the driveway?"

"Good idea," April says, as she unbuckles her seatbelt.

Inside the house, April meets a tall, thin, gray-headed lady with a stern expression. Without smiling, the woman says, "You must be April. I didn't realize you were so young."

April feels her cheeks burning. She resists the urge to slap the woman. Instead, she says, "And I didn't realize you were so old."

James cuts in, "Miss Scarlett, you may leave now. Thank you for staying with the boys until I got back."

"Whatever you say, Mr. Sullivan. They're your children, and you can do as you please with them. But – "

"No 'but' is needed," James interrupts her. "Good day."

Scarlett turns and leaves.

"That woman is worse than a cold front on a sunny beach," April says. "I don't know how you all have stood her."

"Let's forget about her," James says. "Who's ready for a big breakfast?"

April and the boys yell in unison, "Me!"

Chapter Fifteen

"I didn't hardly sleep a wink last night after gettin' th' call 'bout April's wreck." Tucker scoops coffee into the coffee maker as Smiley takes a seat at the table.

"I know what you mean," Smiley says. "Between that phone call and meeting those children earlier in the day, my mind would not shut down. I'm really concerned about those kids. The oldest one seems like he's in charge, but I'm not sure he's playing with a full deck, if you know what I mean."

"He seemed t' me like he has a head full o' sense but may have trouble gittin' it out, or at least gettin' it out in a way that makes sense t' anybody but him. If he's attended school all these years as irregular as he has since moving here, it's a wonder he ain't flunked out already. Only a really smart kid could miss that much school an' still pass."

"You make a good point," Smiley says. "That Asperger's thing he was telling us about. That must have something to do with it. I've never heard of that. Have you?"

"No. But that don't mean nothin' 'cause there's lots o' stuff I ain't never heard of." After pouring water into the coffee maker and turning it on, she opens a cabinet. "I feel like a bowl o' oatmeal this mornin'. How's that sound t' you?"

"One thing you should have learned about Smiley Carter by now," he replies, "is that when it comes to food, I'm not hard to please. Anything you fix, I'll eat. And oatmeal does sound good."

Bending over, Tucker pulls a pot out of the stove drawer and sets it on the stove. As she begins making the oatmeal, she says, "I keep expectin' one of th' boys t' call this mornin' an' update us on April. Trouble just can't seem t' leave her alone. It's one thing after another."

"You spoke the truth there, Tucker. Bless her heart, she's had a difficult life, and it doesn't seem to be getting any easier. Satan must want her really bad."

"What makes y' say that?" Tucker asks.

"Well, I believe that the bad things that happen to us, providing it's not just the result of our own foolish choices, come from Satan. He thinks if he makes us hurt enough then we'll begin to doubt if there is such a thing as God. And once he gets us to doubt, he has a foothold in our heart that he can build on. That's what he was trying to do long ago to Job in the Bible."

Tucker stirs the oats into the boiling water and sets a timer. Sitting down at the table, she says, "They'll be ready in a little bit." Idly she draws circles on the table with her finger. After several moments, she says, "I sure hope God'll protect April's heart an' not let 'er git discouraged an' turn 'er back on Him. That's one lesson I wish I'd learned early in life, instead of when I'm toward th' end o' life. Hold on t' Him an' He'll hold on t' you."

"Beautifully said, Tucker," Smiley says. "Watching this part of you grow over the last several years has been a thing to behold. It's warmed my heart to see it."

"That's 'cause yore such a sentimental ol' fool. I ain't never knowed a man who was as emotional as you are."

Smiley laughs. "Truth be told, Tucker, you haven't known that many men."

Cocking her head to one side, Tucker says, "Well, I guess y' got me there."

The timer interrupts them and Tucker fixes them a bowl of oatmeal. "Brown sugar an' cinnamon in yore's?"

"Definitely," Smiley says. "Even a tad of maple syrup would taste good, too."

"You an' yore sweet tooth. Diabetes is gonna git y' sooner or later, if'n y' ain't more careful."

"I said 'a tad.' I didn't ask for you to empty the bottle in it. Don't deny a poor, old, crippled man the simple pleasure of something sweet to eat."

Tucker rolls her eyes. "I ain't gonna even make a reply t' that nonsense."

They dig into their warm breakfast and eat in silence.

When she's finished her oats, Tucker drops her spoon into the empty bowl. "I think we need t' go down t' th' McDaniel place an' see what's going on with these Trevathans. I'm worried them kids is bein' mistreated."

Smiley looks up at her. "You mean to tell me that Tucker, the woman who doesn't want anyone sticking their nose into her business unless they want to risk getting it cut off, wants to go stick her nose into somebody else's business?"

"I'm serious."

"I am, too. I've never known you to get involved in anybody's business except yours and your family's. What's come over you?"

"Maybe I had a dream last night 'bout a little girl who was cold an' hungry an' didn't have nobody she could turn to fer help. Maybe I got t' thinkin' 'bout what a difference it might've made in 'er life if somebody had've stepped in an' done somethin' t' take care of her or rescue her. Maybe that's what's become wrong with this world. People see people all th' time that they know is in need of help, but they don't want t' git involved, don't want t' git their hands dirty. I can't change th' world, Smiley, but I can change me. I can try t' do somethin' when I have a chance to. I ain't got many years left on this ol' earth, an' I want t' do what I can t' help others. I'm tellin' y', them kids need help."

97

A single tear makes its way down Smiley's cheek. "My Lord in heaven, what a woman you have become. You're a force, Tucker. I'm amazed at you. If you think we need to go down there and check things out, then let's go. The kids being at school right now might make it a good time to go there."

"But don't mention that th' kids come up here yesterday. That might not go over too well."

After getting their coats, the two of them load up into Tucker's truck and drive the short distance to the McDaniel place. A hundred feet from the house, Tucker cuts off the engine and coasts up to the front of it.

They get out of the truck and make their way toward the front door.

"Don't look like there's any signs o' life around," Tucker says.

When they get to the door, Smiley says, "What's that sound?"

"Sounds like somebody singin', don't it?"

They turn their heads to try and pick up the sound more clearly.

"Sounds like Elvis singing Jailhouse Rock," Smiley says.

"My lord, somebody's got th' volume turned all th' way up, if we can hear it out here. They prob'ly won't even hear us knock on th' door. Maybe we ought t' go on in."

Smiley grabs her arm. "Whoa there. We don't know anything about these people except what the kids told us. They may sit around holding guns across their laps all day. They might not shoot you, but they might shoot a black man who barges in. Let's try knocking."

"Suit yoreself," Tucker says with a tone of exasperation. She slams her fist twice against the door, making the windows rattle.

"This place is gonna fall down one o' these days, an' sooner than later."

"You won't hear any disagreements from me on that point," Smiley says.

Suddenly the singing from inside stops abruptly.

"Somebody heard you knock," Smiley says.

After a moment, the door opens a crack. But it's so dark inside the house, nothing can be seen. A thread-like voice says, "Yes? Who is it?"

Tucker looks at Smiley. He whispers, "This is your show, not mine."

Looking back at the door, Tucker says, "My name's Tucker. I'm yore neighbor up th' road. We come t' see 'bout y'."

The door opens a little more and a pale, rail-thin face appears. The woman squints and says, "You're who?"

"Th' name's Tucker. This here's m' friend, Smiley."

When the woman's gaze lights upon Smiley, her eyes pop open as if she'd been stuck with a cattle prod. She closes the door a bit. "What do you all want?"

Tucker folds her arms across her chest. "We just come over t' be neighborly. Y' know. That's what neighbors do. They see 'bout each other an' help out if'n there's a need." She places her hand on the door and pushes lightly. "Can we come in?"

A look of panic overtakes the woman's features. "Oh, I don't know. Things are a mess. I'm sick…"

As the woman is speaking, Tucker pushes the door all the way open and walks in. "Thank y'. Come on in, Smiley."

As their eyes adjust to the dim light, they see that the woman is dressed in a thin t-shirt that has holes in it, sweat pants with stains on them and dingy white socks. She backs up against the wall, looking like a rabbit who's suddenly found itself face-to-face with a wolf.

"Quit lookin' so scared," Tucker says. "Relax. We ain't gonna hurt y'. Like I told y', my name is Tucker and this here is Smiley Carter."

"My name is Joyce. Joyce Trevathan."

Tucker looks around the room, remembering it as it was when Ella lived there. "Who owns this place now? They sure have let it run down."

"I really don't know. My husband handles all those things. I've been sick and can't do much to fix things up like I used to." She pulls at her t-shirt, trying to straighten it on her bony frame.

"What's wrong with y'?" Tucker asks.

"The cancer. I've been battling cancer off and on for over four years. It'll go into remission for a while and then it comes back again. I'm not sure I've got enough strength to fight it off this time."

"I've seen kids come an' go out yore door. Is them yores?"

"I got two boys and a girl. The oldest one has a different father but he hasn't never been involved in the boy's life. B.J. took him on to raise just like he was his own when we got married."

"Y' look like y' might need t' sit down," Tucker says, motioning to the couch. "Why don't I go make us some coffee?" She starts walking toward the kitchen.

"I don't know if we have any or not," Joyce says. "And watch out for that hole in the floor. B.J. said he's going to fix it, that the landlord said he'd take some of the rent off if he'd fix it."

Tucker takes a quick look in the refrigerator then moves to the cabinets to inspect them. She returns to the living room where Joyce is sitting on the sofa staring at Smiley. "You was right. There ain't no coffee in there. Tell me something, do y' need any help? Is yore ol' man mistreatin' you or th' kids? You can tell us. We ain't tryin' t' cause no trouble. We just wanna help, if'n there's a need."

The scared look runs across Joyce's face again, but she tries to reshape it into relaxed features. "B.J.? Mistreating us? No way. He's good to us and takes care of us. He works really hard. Sometimes he's gone for weeks at a time he works so hard."

"Hmmm," Tucker reacts to the story. "Well, let me tell y' somethin'. I know what it's like t' need help an' not know where t' turn. If'n there's ever a time when y' need anythin', send one o' yore kids up t' th' house an' fetch me. I ain't that far away. Will y' promise me t' do that?"

Joyce looks from Tucker to Smiley and back to Tucker. Nodding her head, she says, "Yes. I promise."

"We best be on our way, Smiley," Tucker says to him. To Joyce she says, "Thanks fer lettin' us drop in."

When they get back in the truck, Tucker says, "There's trouble here, Smiley. I can smell it."

Chapter Sixteen

Debbie leads the way as she and March and August approach the nurses' station. When a nurse acknowledges them by looking up from her computer screen, Debbie says, "We came to see the patient in room 103, but no one's there. Has she been moved to another room or been discharged? The patient's name is April Tucker."

"How do you know the patient?" the nurse asks.

"We're her brothers," March replies. Nodding toward Debbie, he says, "She and I were here with her last night."

The nurse types a few keys and looks at the computer monitor. "She was discharged this morning."

"With who?" August asks. "Her car was totaled. Someone had to pick her up."

"I don't have that kind of information," the nurse replies.

The three of them turn away from the nurse and walk a few paces. "What the hell is going on?" March says, agitation tinting his voice.

Debbie places her hand on his arm. "Easy, March. We need to take a moment and think this through."

"Why didn't she call one of us to pick her up?" August asks.

"And where is she right now?" Debbie asks.

"The only reason I can think of as to why she didn't call us," March says, "is because she's trying to hide something. But what that is, I have no idea."

"Let's all go to my apartment," August suggests. "Maybe she'll show up there or at least call."

When they are in the car and heading toward August's, he says, "Let me tell you something that happened yesterday that doesn't add up. Last night when April left the house, she said she was going to the store to buy us some eggs and bacon so we could have some for breakfast. A little bit later, I opened the refrigerator to get some tea and noticed that we had plenty of eggs and bacon."

"Really?" Debbie exclaims. "That doesn't make any sense."

"Exactly my point. Why would she lie about where she was going? And where was she really going?"

"And does that have anything to do with why she had a wreck?" March asks. "Remember, you and I were just talking recently about her going out late and always asking for money."

For the rest of the ride to August's the group silently sifts through theories that would explain their loved one's behavior.

When they get inside the apartment, August snaps his fingers. "James!"

"James?" March and Debbie echo.

"In all this it slipped my mind that James was here yesterday."

"Are we talking about *the* James?" Debbie says. "The James she was a nanny for and the one who fired her?"

"Yes. That James."

"What was he doing here?" March asks.

"I wish I knew. He just showed up and wanted to speak to April."

Debbie asks, "Did she act like she was expecting him? Like maybe they'd talked earlier and his dropping by was planned?"

"Not at all," August replies. "She was clearly as shocked as I was. As a matter of fact, she fainted. But she made me leave so they could talk in private. Afterwards was when she said she had to leave to go to the store."

"So maybe she actually went to meet James somewhere," March offers. "A clandestine meeting of some kind. Maybe James is who picked her up from the hospital this morning. Does anyone know his phone number?"

"No," August says, "but I remember where he lives. Let's go over there."

"Wait a minute. Wait a minute," Debbie says. "Listen to me. If April is there, she's there by her own choice. She's not in any kind of danger or trouble. But I know how you two will be if we go over there. You'll charge in like the cavalry, ready for a fight. April will get furious at you. I've heard her say several times that she gets tired of you two trying to control her life for her. If you go over there, it will just make things worse."

"But I think she's in trouble," March counters. "I just have a sixth sense that something's not right with April."

"And I agree with March," August says.

"So if you go over there," Debbie says, "what's your plan? What are you going to do and say?"

Neither brother responds.

"Exactly," Debbie says. "You don't have a clue what you'd do. I know what you want to do. You want to swoop in and bring her back here so you can keep her under your thumb. You all have got to give your sister room to make her own choices and decisions. Let her grow up."

"But you don't understand," March says, "April has a history of making bad choices. She needs our help."

"And you and August and I have never made bad choices? Choices that have cost us dearly? Choices that we regret?"

August and March drop their heads. After a moment, March turns to August, "I hate it when she's right."

August looks at Debbie. "So what do you suggest we do?"

"Don't do anything. When April wants to let you know what's going on with her, she'll do so. In the meantime, I'm going to pray for her."

August sighs. "I don't like it, but I guess that's all we can do. But someone is going to have to call Tucker to let her know what's going on. I called her last night and told her about the wreck, so I know she's going to want an update. I'm surprised she hasn't called here already."

As if on cue, the phone rings. They all jump.

"Maybe that's April," March says hopefully.

"More than likely, it's Tucker," August says. "Either of you want to answer it?"

March holds up his hands. "Not me."

Debbie shakes her head. "It's your phone. You answer it."

Taking a deep breath, August reaches for the phone and answers, "Hello." He listens for a moment. "Yes ma'am. I was just talking to March and Debbie and said I need to call you." He pauses again. "Well, I really don't know how April's doing because when we got to the hospital this morning she wasn't there." He jerks the receiver away from his ear and Tucker's high pitched voice can be heard yelling. When he returns the receiver to his ear, August says, "Someone had to have picked her up. And she had to have been well enough to leave, or the hospital would have kept her. That's the good part." He closes his eyes as Tucker talks. "Yes ma'am, we know she's our little sister and we're supposed to take care of her.

But she's old enough to make her own decisions." Again he has to jerk the phone away from his ear to keep from being deafened by Tucker's loud response. He gives a pleading look at Debbie and offers her the phone.

Debbie sighs and rescues August by taking the phone. "Tucker, this is Debbie." She pauses. "No ma'am, we're not pregnant yet." She rolls her eyes.

March whispers to August, "She asks that every time we talk."

"Here are my thoughts about April," Debbie says. "Wherever she is right at this moment, she's there because she wants to be. When she feels the time is right, she'll call one of us and let us know. Right now she knows we're all worried about her, and she won't wait long before contacting someone. The other thing is that if March and August try to find her and barge in on her, she will hate them for it. And it may drive her away from all of you. I know you don't want that to happen." There is a long pause as she listens. "I know you're worried about her. We are, too. I think the best thing we can do is just wait and pray." She waits for Tucker's reply. "I love you, too, Tucker. Whoever she calls first, if it's you or one of us, we'll immediately let each other know. Bye bye." She hangs up the phone.

Chapter Seventeen

When the bell rings, ending the school day, Benjamin Trevathan files out of class and enters the hallway that is choked with students eager to leave the building. With the teachers and principal just as eager for the students to be gone, they no longer try to keep the noise down in the hallway. Loud voices, banging locker doors, and laughter fill the air.

Benjamin keeps his head down and walks as quickly as he can to school bus number four. Climbing up the steps, he finds that he is one of the first on board. He makes his way down the aisle, his hips bumping the edges of the backs of the seats, finds his usual seat, and slides in. He anxiously looks as the other kids begin loading onto the bus. Alexander and Maria take their seat close behind the bus driver. When someone starts to sit in the seat in front of him, he jumps to his feet, grabs their arm, and says, "No!"

The young student looks at him with eyes wide with fear. Jerking away from Benjamin, he quickly finds another seat.

"Is there trouble back there?" The voice of the bus driver can be heard over the rising din of boarding students.

Benjamin's quick eyes dart toward the driver and see his concerned expression in the wide, rearview mirror. "N-N-N-No sir," Benjamin says.

"Keep your hands to yourself," the driver warns.

Benjamin starts to reply but stops when he sees Cassie Armour getting on the bus. Her red cheeks are impossible to ignore. With a frown on her face, she walks purposefully down the aisle. When she gets to the seat in front of Benjamin, she throws her backpack in and flops down beside it. "People!" The word explodes from her mouth.

Uncertain of whether she is talking to him or not, Benjamin decides to say nothing.

"Hey there, Stutter Boy. How was your day?" The taunting voice of Mark O'Riley is unmistakable.

Benjamin looks up at him and grins.

"Wipe that stupid grin off your face, you idiot," Mark says.

Without warning, Cassie shoots out of her seat and shoves Mark. He loses his balance and falls to one knee. "You're the idiot!" Cassie exclaims. "Why do you get off making fun of other people?"

Mark gets up and faces her. His expression is a mixture of surprise and confusion. "What the – ?"

"Have you got some kind of inferiority complex that makes your self-esteem so low that you have to make fun of people just to feel good about yourself? Do you know how pathetic that makes you look?"

The bus is suddenly as quiet as when the last student gets off and the driver is returning home. All heads are turned and looking at Cassie and Mark. The bus driver, too, is watching via the mirror but choosing to say nothing so far.

Benjamin's body has quickly become so full of adrenalin that he feels like he could rip one of the bus seats from the floor, yet he feels paralyzed. It's a familiar feeling for him, the same one he feels when his stepfather is launching into a tirade at him or his brother or sister. He grips the back of the seat and looks from Cassie to Mark.

Mark looks around at everyone staring at him then looks at Cassie. "You're the one who's crazy!" He points at Benjamin but keeps his eyes on her. "What's going on between you and the retard? Are you and him getting it on?"

Quick as a flash of lightning, Cassie slaps Mark.

He draws back his fist. Whatever he intends to do with that fist is never revealed because Benjamin comes out of his seat, hitting

Mark in the stomach with his shoulder and takes him down to the floor.

Mark cries out in surprise and rage. He struggles to get up, but Benjamin's weight is too much for him.

"No, no, Benjamin," Cassie cries. "Stop. It's okay." She grabs his shoulders and tugs.

Benjamin barely notices her cries and tugs. He's never been in this position before. He looks down and sees that Mark is helpless against him. A loud roar escapes from Benjamin. Then he feels himself being forcefully pulled up and off of Mark.

"Okay, that's enough," the bus driver says into his ear. "You need to calm down."

From behind the driver, Cassie says, "Mark's the one that started it. People are tired of him being a bully."

Mark struggles to his feet and backs up a few feet. He hears snickering behind him. He whirls around toward the group of boys he usually rides with. "Shut up! Or you're going to get it!"

"I saw the whole thing," the driver says. "Mark, I'd say you got what you deserved, but that's not for me to say. I'll have to report all of this to the principal tomorrow. What you are going to do now is to come sit on the front seat with the other little boys and girls."

This is met with howls of laughter from Mark's compatriots and cheers from the younger boys and girls. Mark's face turns crimson as he follows the bus driver to the front.

As Benjamin and Cassie return to their seats, she sits sideways with her feet toward the aisle and her back against the side of the bus. Looking at Benjamin, she says, "See? That is exactly what I'm talking about. People like Mark O'Riley make me sick. I'm so tired of it! The last few times my family has moved, and I became the new girl in school, I've gone through the same kind of torture. The boys like me, which makes the girls hate me. They think I'm going to steal their boyfriend. They make fun of me, write me nasty notes, and spread rumors about me. My dad has always told me to turn the other cheek to these people. Well my cheeks are getting sore! I'm tired of taking it without defending myself. Don't you get tired of it?"

Uncharacteristically, Benjamin never took his eyes off of Cassie during her tirade. He is amazed at having someone so beautiful talk to him so passionately and so directly. But now that she's become silent and is expecting him to speak, his eyes flit erratically, like a butterfly trying to find just the right flower to alight upon. "Y-Y-Y-You mean p-p-p-people make fun of you?"

"The guys don't. But the girls do. My mother says it's because they're jealous of how pretty I am."

"Your m-m-m-mother is right. Y-Y-Y-You are pretty."

"Thank you, Ben. Can I call you Ben?"

Benjamin nods.

"I'm sorry. I haven't thanked you for jumping into my fight with Mark. But you didn't have to do that."

"H-H-H-He was going to hit you."

"I don't think so. I think he wanted to hit me, but I don't think he would have. He's full of hot air."

Benjamin thinks of a hot air balloon and of Mark blown up like one of them and floating in the air with a gondola hanging underneath him. He laughs out loud at the image. When Cassie frowns, he knows he's done something inappropriate. He wipes the smile off his face. Cassie continues looking at him but says nothing. Benjamin squirms in his seat.

Eventually, Cassie says, "Don't you get tired of people making fun of you? I never see you get mad about it, either on the bus or in school."

"My m-m-m-Mama says 'it is what it is.' She t-t-t-tells me 'you can't change people.' She tells me that b-b-b-because I've got that Asperger's disease I d-d-d-don't always notice when people make f-f-f-f-fun of me."

"Asperger's? What's that?"

"My t-t-t-teachers tell me it's that I s-s-s-sometimes do or say inappropriate things. It m-m-m-makes people think I'm weird. And I g-g-g-guess I am."

"Is that also why you stutter?"

Benjamin shakes his head. "Th-Th-Th-That's because I g-g-g-get nervous."

Cassie stares at him for a moment. "But you're actually pretty smart, aren't you? I mean, you're not retarded like people say you are."

"No. I m-m-m-make good grades."

"What was it you said your mother tells you?"

Benjamin pauses to remember his part in this conversation with Cassie. "She said I've g-g-g-got Asperger's and – "

"No, not that," Cassie interrupts him. "What was the other thing she said?"

"Oh," Benjamin answers. "She said 'it is what it is' and 'y-y-y-you can't change people.'"

"Yes, that's it," Cassie says. "That's so simple but so profound, too. I'm going to try to remember that."

That night, after putting his brother and sister to bed and checking on his mother, Benjamin takes his treasure box out from under the couch. One by one he removes his Matchbox cars, lining them up side by side facing him. A relaxed smile spreads across his face. Using his thick index finger, he rolls each one backward and forward a few times, enjoying the smooth, fluid feel. Then he takes out his journal, leans back against the front of the couch, and writes:

Anger, Happiness, Love, Sadness, and Fear

Are words I can define.

But the feelings sometimes confuse me when they appear.

My Mama = love

Maria = love

Alexander = love

B.J. = anger? Fear?

Cassie = ???

Chapter Eighteen

April awakens. It's still dark in the bedroom. James's arm is draped across her waist. He is sound asleep. April turns her head to look at the alarm clock: 4:12 AM.

What am I going to do? I've been here for three days and haven't called my family to let them know where I am. When I do call, I'm going to get an earful from all of them. I haven't told anyone about being pregnant. I've got to decide something. I just don't want to do anything to burst this beautiful dream of the past three days – being in James's home, sleeping with him, seeing the boys. Everything is perfect.

Ha! Who am I kidding? Perfect? This pregnancy is going to mess everything up. I've never thought I could be the kind of person who had an abortion. But I never imagined I would be raped and end up pregnant. Even Doctor Oliver said no one will blame me for aborting it. I can't keep putting it off. I need to go to the clinic today and just talk with them to find out more about what's involved in an abortion.

A wave of nausea sweeps over her. Slipping out of the bed, she pads quickly to the bathroom and gets on her knees beside the toilet. Perspiration beads up on her forehead and above her upper lip. For a moment she believes the feeling has passed. But abruptly it hits her with the force of a punch in her belly. Bowing her head into the toilet, she heaves.

When she's finished, she goes to the sink and wets a washcloth with cold water. She swabs her face, then leans over and rinses out her mouth. Looking into the mirror, she notices the dark circles under her eyes. *I've got to quit taking pills! But I'll get sick if I do, and how will I explain that to James? He'll know it's not just morning sickness. If he finds out I'm an addict, he'll kick me out again. I can't let that happen. First things first though. Today I go to the clinic and make a decision about this baby I'm carrying.*

Once James has left for work and the boys for school, April calls a cab and starts getting dressed.

When she gets into the cab she gives the driver the Planned Parenthood card Doctor Oliver gave her. He looks at the card then at her via his rearview mirror. He starts his meter and pulls away from James's house. After a few minutes, he says, "You been to this place before?"

The question catches April off guard. "Huh? Well, no." When the driver falls silent, she asks, "Why would you ask me that?"

"I've carried lots of women there. I just wondered if you knew what to expect."

"'To expect'?"

"Oh, I don't mean inside the clinic. I'm talking about what to expect outside the clinic."

"I don't understand what you're talking about. What is there outside the clinic that I should be interested in or concerned about?"

"Protesters, that's what."

"Protesters? Seriously? I mean, I've heard about that kind of stuff in the news, but thought it was only in the big cities."

"And I don't know about anywhere else, but they are here in Knoxville. And they can be pretty mean and intimidating. If you want me to, I'll walk with you from the cab to the front door."

Uncertainty climbs onto April's shoulders and sits heavily. She watches out both sides of the car as if she is already at the clinic and is about to be attacked. "Has anyone ever been hurt outside the clinic?"

"None that I've ever heard of. You just relax. I'll get you inside and the staff there will take care of you."

Relax? You think I can relax? I was already a little nervous, but now am a little freaked out.

Fifteen minutes later, April sees three or four people on the sidewalk up ahead holding up handmade signs. "Is that it?"

"That's it," the driver answers.

As they pull up to the curb the messages on the signs are clearer:

ABORTION IS MURDER!

IT'S NOT A FETUS. IT'S A BABY.

HELL WON'T BE HOT ENOUGH FOR BABY KILLERS

WHAT WOULD JESUS DO?

"Oh my gosh," April whispers. "I can't do this."

"Hey," the driver says, "I told you I would take care of you. Nobody's going to touch you." He gets out and opens her door. "Come on. Don't let these fanatics stop you from doing what you have a right to do."

Slowly, April emerges from the cab. As she and the driver walk up the sidewalk, the protesters cry out:

"Don't kill your baby!"

"Life is sacred!"

"Only God has the right to take a life."

"Murderer!"

By the time April has made it through that verbal gauntlet and arrives at the front door, she is gripping the cab driver's arm. Her heart is beating against her chest with enough force that she's surprised the front of her shirt isn't vibrating in rhythm.

The driver opens the door and says, "You're okay now."

April steps inside and looks around. She is in a waiting area. There are eight or nine other women sitting in chairs. None of them looks up at her. On one wall are a series of brochures. April walks over to it and selects one title: *What Happens During an In-Clinic Abortion?*

She sits beside two women who are engaged in conversation. Though she doesn't want to, she can't help overhearing them.

"I wish that doctor would hurry up," one of them says. "I've got to go buy some groceries before the kids get home."

"I know what you mean," the other one says. "They're in a hurry for you to give them your business but in no hurry to take care of your business."

"How many is this for you, anyway?"

"This is my fourth one. What about you?"

"Lord, I don't know. I lost count after six."

They both laugh.

"Do you remember the first time you had an abortion?"

"Scared to death, that's what I was."

They both stop talking. April looks up and they are looking at her.

"Your first time?" one of them asks.

April nods.

"Listen, honey," the other one says, "there ain't nothing to it. You'll be in and out before you know it. Nice and clean and tidy."

April smiles at them weakly and looks down at the brochure which is shaking in her trembling hand. *Over six abortions?! How can someone do that? I never dreamed of such a thing. And they act likes it's no big deal.*

Opening the brochure, her eyes alight on a paragraph titled, D&E – DILATION AND EVACUATION. As she reads the detailed account of what happens during this procedure, she freezes at the phrase "you may also need a shot through your abdomen to make sure the fetus's heart stops before the procedure." A feeling of horror mixed with revulsion sweeps through April. *They have to kill it? They admit it's alive?* Tears fill her eyes at the thought of a doctor putting a needle into her, searching for her baby in order to kill it.

She suddenly throws the brochure away from her as if it was contaminated with a deadly disease. She rushes from the waiting room and out the door of the clinic. Blinded by her tears and the bright sunlight, she bumps into someone. Without looking at them, she mutters, "I'm sorry."

"That's okay. I was waiting for you."

April squints against the sunlight and sees the cab driver who brought her to the clinic.

"Want me to take you back home?"

Nodding, April says, "Yes, please."

Once she is safely inside the cab, April asks, "Why were you waiting for me?"

"I've been doing this a long time and am a pretty good judge of people. I don't know what your story is, but you for sure have one. You're twisted up inside, pulled in every direction, and uncertain what to do. Am I right?"

April hesitates. *I don't even know this man. Why should I even be talking to him?* Yet she says, "You're right."

"Why don't you tell me what's going on? We're just two strangers who will never see each other again. Talking about it might help you figure some things out."

"You sound like a counselor."

"I used to be one."

"You mean like a professional counselor?

"Yep. But I let alcohol ruin my career. Between multiple DUI's and crossing some ethical boundaries while under the influence, I lost my license."

"Ethical boundaries?"

"I had affairs with a couple of my patients."

"Wow."

"Yeah, hard to believe, isn't it? So that's my story. What's yours?"

With this prompt April has a memory of sitting in Mary's office at Spirit Lake and their intimate conversations. She folds her legs Indian-style, sits back and says, "I was raped back in December and just found out a couple of days ago that I'm pregnant from the incident. I've also just gotten back with my boyfriend. He knows about the rape, but I haven't told him I'm pregnant."

"And so you want to get rid of the problem because you're afraid to tell him?"

"I don't know what I want to do. I just went to that clinic because . . ." her voice trails off.

When she doesn't finish her sentence, the driver says, "'Because'?"

"I'm not sure of the answer to that. I thought I was going there to have an abortion. But between those protesters, the conversation I heard between two women at the clinic, and the information I read in a brochure telling what happens when they perform an abortion, I got rattled. Now I'm uncertain what I should do." She searches the features of the cab driver by way of his rearview mirror. "What do you think I should do?"

"Sounds to me like you're at a crossroads. What you do next is going to be life changing. When I'm faced with those kinds of situations, I talk with people I love and trust because I know they are going to be honest with me."

April chews on this piece of advice. The faces of James, August, March and Debbie appear one at a time then fade away. Then the image of Tucker appears. Immediately, April starts to cry. "I need to talk to Tucker," she says aloud.

Chapter Nineteen

April takes the lid off of the pot of steaming green beans. After tasting them, she sprinkles in some more salt. Opening the oven door, she bends down and checks on the parmesan-coated chicken breasts. She hears the front door open and James dropping his keys on the hall table.

"Something sure smells good," he calls.

From the other end of the house Christopher and Michael holler, "Daddy!" They rush past the kitchen doorway. April pictures James bending down and the boys running into his open arms. In a moment, James walks into the kitchen smiling and with a wriggling boy under each arm.

"I found these hooligans running loose in the house. I'm thinking about throwing them out the back door or putting them in the garbage can. What do you think?"

April folds her arms across her chest and purses her lips. "Maybe they're just a couple of strays. Isn't there a place similar to the dog pound where we could drop them off? Maybe someone would like to adopt them."

"You're not going to get rid of us," Michael says to April.

"Yeah," Christopher agrees, "you like us. We're going to adopt you."

James looks at April with raised eyebrows. "That's certainly a novel idea. Your idea?"

April laughs. "Not me. They came up with that one on their own."

James lowers the boys to the floor. Looking at April, he says, "Supper about ready?"

"Ten minutes," she replies.

"You boys go wash up," he says to his sons. As they leave the kitchen, he asks, "What can I do?"

"Fix everyone something to drink. I'll set the table."

He moves in front of April and puts his hands on her waist. "What about a 'hello kiss' first?"

April looks up into his eyes. "That sounds good."

He kisses her lightly on the lips and is about to pull away when she puts her arms around his neck and pulls him into her, kissing him hard. She breaks off the kiss gasping and presses her cheek tightly against his. "Oh James . . ."

"Hey, hey there, what's wrong?" Gripping her wrists, he unwraps her arms and pulls back to look at her. "You're crying! April, what's wrong?"

Just then the boys return to the kitchen.

"All clean," Christopher says, holding up his hands.

"I'm hungry," Michael says.

Frowning, James continues looking at April.

She wipes her tears and mouths the word "later." "I better get the chicken out of the oven before it burns," she says. Grabbing a potholder, she opens the oven and retrieves the dish of sizzling, bronze-colored chicken. The aroma of parmesan and rosemary fills the air.

After everyone is seated at the table, they hold hands. "Michael," James says, "do you want to say the prayer?"

"Yes," Michael answers. As they bow their heads, Michael says, "Dear God, Thank you for our food. Thank you for our house. Thank you for my pet turtle. But most of all, thank you for bringing April back home. Amen."

When they release each other's hand, April reaches for her tea and tries to drown the lump that is in her throat. She sniffs back her tears. She clears her throat and says, "Thank you, Michael. That was a sweet prayer."

As she dips a spoonful of green beans onto Christopher's plate, he says, "Daddy said you left because he said some things that hurt your feelings. But he's sorry now." Looking at James he says, "You told her you're sorry, didn't you?"

April feels her face getting red. "Did you tell them – "

"I told them I said some things that were hurtful," James cuts her question off. "And that I was wrong to have done that." To Christopher, he says, "Yes, I told her how very sorry I was."

"Did you forgive him?" Michael asks April.

"Yes, Michael, I forgave him. Forgiving people is something that's very important. You must always remember that."

The boys beam as they look from April to James.

Christopher blurts out, "When are you going to get married?"

The question hits April square in the chest. Her heart immediately responds, striking her chest like a drummer in a marching band.

James says, "I think that's enough questions for now. Let's eat our supper."

After everyone finishes eating, April says, "I'll give the boys a bath and put them to bed, if you'll take care of the kitchen."

"Agreed," James replies.

While walking the boys toward the bathroom, Michael says, "Will you sing us a song with your Autoharp after our baths?"

"Yeah," Christopher says, "I missed hearing you sing."

With her heart so full of emotions, April finds it impossible to prevent tears from leaking from her eyes following the boys' tender request.

Once they are in the bright lights of the bathroom, Christopher touches her wet cheeks as she kneels down to help him undress. "Daddy says there are lots of kinds of tears. What kind are these?"

April pauses and looks at the boys. She throws her arms around them and hugs them tightly. "Oh, boys, they are tears of love. I love you both so much." When she releases them, she smiles and says, "But one day, when you are older, you will learn that girls don't always need a reason to cry. We just cry sometimes."

Later, while sitting in a chair beside the boys' beds, April gives her Autoharp one final, light strum as she ends a song. Rising from the chair, she leans over and gives Michael a light kiss on his forehead. When she does the same to Christopher, his eyes open halfway and he gives her a cherubic smile. "Go back to sleep," April whispers. Leaving their room, she gently closes the door.

Walking down the hallway, she's pleased to see that the kitchen is as clean as if she did it herself. She pauses before entering the living room. *God, give me strength to do this. Help me choose my words.*

As she steps into the room, James looks up from reading the newspaper. He quickly folds it and lays it on the floor. "Come in here and sit with me. We need to talk."

A bit startled that James has served the first volley, April says, "Talk? Talk about what?" She sits beside him and he turns to face her.

Taking her hands, James says, "Christopher asked a good question at the supper table. When are we going to get married? As far as I'm concerned, there's no point in delaying it. I want you to

123

be with me forever. I know there will be challenges to be faced and questioning looks from people who think our age difference is a problem, but we can deal with all that. We can face anything as long as we do it together. The boys will be thrilled when – "

April places her finger on James's lips and stops him in mid-sentence. "James . . ." her throat chokes off her voice. She coughs to clear it. "There's something I've got to tell you."

Concern etches every inch of James's face. "I'm feeling a little scared," he says. "What do you need to tell me?"

"This is not going to be easy because I don't know how you're going to react. But I want you to be honest. If this changes how you feel about me, then I'll understand."

"Okay, now I'm really scared. April, there is nothing you can tell me that will change how I feel about you. You can tell me anything. Just put it out there and then we can deal with it together."

April locks her eyes on James's and holds them there. Without blinking, she says, "I'm pregnant."

James's head moves back a bit, and he blinks several times. "You're what?"

"Yes. I'm pregnant."

He takes a deep breath and lets it out. "You mean you've been seeing someone else?"

April can no longer look him in the eye. She looks down at her lap. "No, that's not it. It gets worse. I'm pregnant from the rape back in December." She hears James take a quick breath. She looks back at him and sees his confused expression but also sees something else in his eyes. They seem more distant, as if he'd taken a step back from her. "It's okay. I know this changes everything."

"No, no, just hold on. I'm just trying to process this. Becoming pregnant during a rape is so rare, I never thought about that."

"Yeah, me either. But the doctor says it's definite."

"So tell me, how are you doing with the news?"

April shakes her head. "I don't know, James. My mind is all over the place."

"When did you find out?"

"In the hospital after my wreck."

Suddenly James's eyes brighten. "You are still early in your pregnancy. You don't have to keep it. It's just a fetus, not a living, breathing person. We can find a clinic that can do an abortion. No one will ever know. This doesn't have to stop us from our plans."

Like an iceberg tearing the hull of the Titanic, a shaft of disappointment slices through April, leaving her feeling lost in her ocean of emotions. "I see. So that's what you think I should do?"

"April, even avid anti-abortionists recognize that in the case of incest or rape, abortion is an understandable option. No one is going to fault you for your decision. Besides that, who will even know? Have you told anyone else that you're pregnant?"

April shakes her head, not so much in reply to James's question as in response to the sadness filling her heart.

"Then if you haven't told anyone, what's keeping you from having an abortion?"

"It's not that simple, James. You can't fully understand. You're not a woman and you're not pregnant."

He puts his hand on her shoulder. "You're absolutely right. I'm sorry. And I'm sorry that you're having to deal with this. It's just not fair."

"If there's one thing I've learned about life, it's that life's not fair."

James folds her into his arms and lies back with her head on his chest. "Just tell me what you want to do and what I can do to help."

"I want to go see Tucker. But my car is wrecked. I don't want to ask my brothers for help because they'll want to know why I'm going home. I'm not ready to tell them about being pregnant."

"Then this is something I can fix for you. Susan's car is still in the garage just collecting dust. I've been meaning to sell it but just haven't gotten around to it. Why don't you take it and drive yourself home? That is, if you think you're up to it."

April shifts to where she can look at his face. "Oh James, would you let me do that?"

"Sure. I still love you, April. Nothing you've told me has changed that and nothing ever will."

She kisses him. "You don't know how much better you've made me feel. If it's okay, I'll leave tomorrow after the boys go to school."

Chapter Twenty

Sitting outside the principal's office beside Mark O'Riley, Benjamin tries to listen to what is being said inside the office between Cassie and the principal. The only thing he can tell is when each one is speaking, but then only by the change in pitch from the muffled tones of Cassie's high voice and Principal Clelland's bass voice.

"Worried about your girlfriend?" Mark says in a voice that can only be heard by Benjamin.

Benjamin glances at the secretary's desk fifteen feet away. Ms. Collins' head is bent over as she studies something on her desk. She reaches up and removes an ink pen from the bun on the back of her head.

"You really think she likes you?" Mark continues in low tones. "She just feels sorry for you like she would a stray dog or something. But I don't feel sorry for you. The world would be better off without people like you in it. We don't need your kind contributing to the gene pool."

Benjamin's knee begins bouncing and he grips the arms of the wooden chair.

"Did you say something, Mark?" Ms. Collins' voice draws their attention. She arches the eyebrow over one eye and squints with the other eye.

"No ma'am," Mark replies. "I'm just waiting my turn so we can get this misunderstanding cleared up. Is that a new sweater you're wearing?"

Ms. Collins' expression remains unchanged. "Mark, do you know how long I've been secretary at this high school?"

"No ma'am. But it couldn't have been long for such a young woman as you are."

"I was here," Ms. Collins says, "when your father would sit in that very same place, waiting for his punishment for being a troublemaker. Clearly, the apple doesn't fall far from the tree. Just keep your mouth shut until Mr. Clelland comes out and gets you."

Just then the door to the principal's office opens and Cassie walks out. Mr. Clelland follows her. "Thank you, Cassie," he says.

Cassie looks neither left nor right but strides directly out of the office area and disappears into the hallway.

"Your turn, Mr. O'Riley," the principal says.

"Yes sir," Mark replies and walks into the office as Mr. Clelland closes the door behind him.

Benjamin wrings his hands. *Cassie hates me. It's my fault she got into trouble and got called to the office. She's probably never been to the office before meeting me. It's like my stepdad says, I've got a curse on me, that's why people don't like me. I'm just stupid.*

Suddenly the sound of a loud smack coming from inside Mr. Clelland's office jerks Benjamin out of his ruminations. Two more loud smacks follow the first. The door jerks open and Mark walks out red-faced and rubbing his backside. Mr. Clelland appears in the doorway gripping a wooden paddle. "I don't want to see you in my office again," he says to the retreating Mark. Looking at Benjamin, he says, "Your turn. Come in."

Benjamin bolts out of his chair as if it were spring loaded. He rushes into the office and sits in one of the two chairs across from the principal's desk.

Mr. Clelland closes the door and takes his seat behind the desk. "Your name is Benjamin Trevathan. I don't believe we've ever – "

"M-M-M-My mom loves Elvis," Benjamin blurts out. "I like M-M-M-Matchbox cars. I've got t-t-t-twelve of them. I c-c-c-could bring them to school sometime if y-y-y-you want to s-s-s-see them." His eyes dart about the room trying to find something to focus on.

Mr. Clelland looks at him for a moment. "I see. I looked at your record, Benjamin, and see that you've recently started attending school here. From the looks of things you've changed schools quite a lot through the years."

When the principal ignores his comments, Benjamin is unsure how to proceed, so he remains silent. However, his knee returns to its nervous bobbing up and down.

Mr. Clelland says, "Cassie told me what happened on the bus. Then Mark told me his version of what happened. Why don't you tell me what happened?"

For a brief moment Benjamin looks in the principal's eyes, but then looks away. "H-H-H-He was going to hurt C-C-C-Cassie."

"Mark was?"

Benjamin nods.

"Has Mark been making fun of you or calling you names?"

"He c-c-c-calls me names. M-M-M-My stepdad c-c-c-calls me n-n-n-names, too." Now both of Benjamin's knees are bouncing.

"Benjamin, you are not in trouble here. Just relax for a moment. I want to tell you something."

Benjamin places his open palms on his knees and presses against them. His legs slow and finally stop their frenetic dance.

"I understand why you did what you did to Mark. And quite honestly I don't blame you. Mark's a bully and a trouble maker. But, and this is an important 'but,' you cannot assault another student on school property. You should have let the bus driver take care of matters on the bus. That's not your job. Do you understand?"

Benjamin turns the principal's words over in his mind. "B-B-B-But he was g-g-g-going to hurt Cassie."

"I realize that's what you believed was going to happen. But you don't know that for sure. Cassie might have taken care of things by herself. She seems quite capable to me."

Pressed between what he believes and what the principal is telling him triggers Benjamin's bouncing knee again. He looks at Mr. Clelland. "I u-u-u-understand what you're s-s-s-saying. I j-j-j-just think you are wrong." A second later he adds, "Sir."

The principal surprises Benjamin by laughing. "Well, Benjamin, I appreciate your honesty. I like it when people tell me what they think. One of my heroes growing up was John Wayne. He had a saying that I think fits here – 'A man's got to do what a man's got to do.' I'm confident that that is what you will do, Benjamin. I just want you to understand that if something like this happens again, I won't be able to ignore it. You will be punished. Is that okay with you?"

Suddenly feeling like a weight has been lifted from him, Benjamin jumps up. Smiling, he holds out his hand and says, "Y-Y-Y-Yes sir."

Later, when the last bell of the day rings, Benjamin hurries out to the bus and sits in his regular seat. He rests his folded arms on the back of the seat in front of him and eagerly watches the door as students young and old board. But he hardly notices any of them, even his brother and sister. When Mark O'Riley walks by him and covertly flips him off, the gesture doesn't even register with Benjamin. It's when he sees Cassie boarding the bus that his eyes brighten and he breaks into a smile.

Sitting back in his seat, he waits for her to claim the seat in front of him. Her normally pleasant face is twisted into a frown. She looks at no one as she walks down the aisle. Then she sits in an empty seat on the opposite side of the bus and three rows in front of Benjamin.

Benjamin cocks his head to one side. *Did she forget where she usually sits? Didn't she see me saving her seat for her?* He starts to call out to her but knows his stuttering cry will only trigger laughter from the kids on the bus. *Maybe I should pass a note to her.* He sighs. *But everyone who passed it would read it. I wouldn't want anyone else to read it.*

As the bus begins its stop-and-go route of dropping off kids, Benjamin racks his brain for a reason for Cassie's action. When the bus stops to let off Mark, Mark shoves a folded piece of paper in Benjamin's lap as he passes by him. Benjamin slowly unfolds the note and reads:

What did I tell you, you stupid idiot. Did you really think she liked you? She's a winner. You're a loser. It'll never work. It's time for you to quit thinking you're normal like everyone else. Grow up!!!

Benjamin reads and rereads the note. He feels a pain in his chest and rubs it with the heel of his hand. Reaching inside his backpack, he takes out a handful of papers that are turned in every direction as if they were leaves blown in his backpack by an October wind. He shuffles through the papers and stops when he gets to one with the title "Feelings" at the top. It is a fill-in-the-blank exercise. Benjamin takes a pen out of his pocket and fills in some of the blanks.

- I felt happy when

_____.

- I felt sad when *Cassie didn't sit in front of me on the bus*.
- I felt confused when *on the bus after school Cassie sat in a different seat*.
- I felt afraid when

_____.

- I felt angry when *I read a note someone wrote that told me I was stupid*.
- I felt like giving up when *I realized Cassie and I would never be friends again*.

"Bennie!" Maria's shrill voice grabs Benjamin's attention. "Come on! We're home."

Benjamin looks around and is surprised that they are at his house and that he didn't even notice when Cassie got off at her house. Stuffing his papers inside his backpack, he stands up and then makes his way to the front and exits.

"Benjamin," the bus driver speaks to him just as he steps off the last step.

Benjamin turns around to look at him.

"It'll be okay," the driver says. Rather than the sharp, eagle-like expression his eyes normally have, they look sad. "You'll get over her." The driver closes the door without waiting for a reply and drives off, leaving Benjamin standing by the side of the road.

That evening, after he has finished putting Maria and Alexander to bed and giving his mother her medicine, Benjamin sits in the floor between the couch and the coffee table. He reaches under the couch and takes out his treasure box, but doesn't open it immediately. He stares at the box and runs his hand along the edges and corners. His chest is hurting again, just like it did on the bus this afternoon. He holds the box tight against his chest and closes his eyes. A lone tear escapes and travels slowly down his round, pimpled cheek. His nose runs, and he wipes it on his sleeve.

Laying the box on the table, he releases the catch and opens it. One by one, he takes out his Matchbox cars. When he gets to the red Camaro, he rubs it against his cheek. The action has the effect of the locks on a dam being opened. Benjamin cries uncontrollably.

After several minutes, his crying subsides, and he takes out his journal and pen.

I used to wonder what feelings are

If they were something other people kept in a jar

Then, reaching in, they would choose whatever feeling they wished.

Today I learned the truth about feelings –

You don't choose them; they choose you.

They grab you, HARD, and don't let go until they decide to.

I think I liked it better when I didn't know what feelings are.

Chapter Twenty-one

April turns on her blinker, slows, and turns off the state highway onto the county road that leads to Tucker's. As she passes by familiar houses, trees, and fields, her body becomes more relaxed. Even though it's a brisk February morning, she rolls down her window to take in the fresh air. As she gets closer to Tucker's house, her mind braces for the news she is about to deliver.

Rounding the last curve before the straight stretch to Tucker's, she sees a school bus approaching with its yellow caution lights flashing. In front of the McDaniel place the bus stops and the stop sign swings out from its side. April stops and watches as two young children step off the bus followed by a teenager. She looks at the McDaniel house and then back at the children. *Surely they don't live there. No one has lived there for years. It's ready to be bulldozed down.* As she muses, the kids walk through the front door and disappear. April shakes her head.

The bus passes her, and she proceeds to home. Scenes of the old shack she grew up in drift across the movie screen of her memory. She pictures the old wash tub that she used to take baths in and the wood-burning stove that she used to warm herself by in the winter.

She pulls in the driveway and coasts to a stop. Getting out, she stretches to relieve the tension of the long trip from Knoxville. A sound catches her ear and she looks toward the barn. Tucker's truck is parked there and a tractor is working up the garden spot while two people stand by looking. April laughs. "It's time to plant potatoes!"

She decides to walk over and surprise them. Having been used to always seeing Smiley Carter drive the tractor and Tucker standing by critiquing him, she's curious to see who the third person is. However, as she gets closer she can see Smiley leaning on his cane beside Tucker. The only question remaining is who is driving the tractor.

So intent are Smiley and Tucker on watching the tractor, they don't see April coming up behind them. She stops within a couple of feet of them and says, "It's awful late in the year to be planting taters."

Tucker whirls around and yells, "April!" She grabs her in a bear hug and lifts her off the ground. "What in the world are you doing here? And where is everybody else?"

April buries her face in Tucker's neck and smells the familiar. Memories are triggered so fast that they barely register before another jumps up. "Put me down before you hurt yourself." As soon as her feet touch the ground she reaches for Smiley and hugs him tightly.

"Sweet baby girl," Smiley coos, "you warm an old man's heart."

The tractor has turned around at the end of the garden and is coming toward them, its engine laboring from pulling the disc through the rich dirt. As it gets closer, April exclaims, "It's Preacher!" She is surprised by a sudden rush of emotions. Tears appear.

Preacher stops the tractor a few feet from the group and shuts off the engine. He steps off and opens his arms to receive the onrushing April. As they embrace, he says, "Well lookee here! What a nice surprise. How in the world are you, April?"

April is careful to wipe her tears on Preacher before releasing her hold on him. "What in the world are you doing driving Smiley's tractor? I didn't think anyone was allowed to do that." Before he can reply, she turns to Tucker, "And what are you all doing planting potatoes after February fourteenth? Growing up, that date never passed without us being out in the cold planting potatoes."

"See what I toldja?" Tucker says to Smiley. "Even April knows when t' plant taters." She motions toward the garden. "These taters ain't gonna make. They should o' done been in th' ground. But no, you said it was too cold an' wet."

Smiley rolls his eyes. Looking at April, he says, "You just had to bring that up, didn't you? She has been impossible ever since Valentine's Day. You'd think the fate of the civilized world hinged on us getting our potatoes in the ground."

April laughs. To Preacher, she says, "Nothing has changed here, has it?"

A grin skirts across Preacher's features. He shakes his head. "I've told them they need to get their own TV sitcom because they are quite hilarious."

There's a pause in the conversation and everyone looks at April. "I know you all have lots of questions, and I'll answer them all. But first, why don't we finish planting the potatoes so Tucker will get off Smiley's back about it."

"Thank you, thank you," Smiley says. "I was hoping you weren't going to become a reason to delay the planting."

As April drops the last piece of seed potato into the ground, Tucker uses her hoe to quickly cover it with dirt.

Tucker leans on the hoe handle and says, "Now we'll have t' jest wait an' see if'n they make taters 'r not."

"I'd be willing to bet they turn out to be one of the best crop of potatoes you ever raised," Smiley says.

"Hmpf," Tucker replies. "We'll see. Now come on an' git in th' truck. Let's all go git a cup o' coffee an' maybe a piece o' pie."

"That sounds wonderful," April says. "Your pies are to die for."

"I'm going to have to take a rain check," Preacher says. "I've got some things I've got to go take care of. But I'll take you up on your offer soon."

"You can come by anytime, Preacher," Tucker says. "An' thank y' fer comin' an' workin' up th' garden fer us."

"No problem. I was glad to do it." He nods at Smiley. "And thank you for sharing with me all your secrets about how best to work up a garden spot. Don't be surprised if some of your tips turn up in one of my sermons. I think there's some real application to people's hearts."

With a broad smile, Smiley says, "You hear that, Tucker? Preacher's gonna be quoting me from the pulpit."

This time it's Tucker who rolls her eyes. "Come on an' let me help y' git in th' truck."

April starts to move toward the passenger side of the truck to help, but Preacher stops her.

In a low voice, he says, "They've got their own way of doing this. I've offered to help in the past, and it's not received very well."

"Where's your motorcycle?" April asks.

"It's parked behind Tucker's house."

As Tucker closes Smiley's door, she says, "Ya'll jump in th' back o' th' truck."

Preacher waves her off. "I'll just walk. Thanks anyway."

April says, "And I'm going to walk with him. We'll be right there."

She and Preacher walk in silence for a bit. Then she says, "I think you're the calmest man I've ever met. I can feel it just walking beside you."

"Well thank you," Preacher replies. "It's certainly not something that has come easy for me. I used to be anything but calm. I work on it daily. Tell me about you. I hear you had a wreck."

"Yeah. It was my fault. I wasn't paying attention and pulled into the path of another car. I'm really lucky that I wasn't severely injured."

"'Lucky' probably wouldn't be the word I would use."

"You'd say it was God, wouldn't you?"

"Yep."

"I'm still trying to sort through all of that. It's hard to make sense of it all."

"Maybe that's what you need to quit trying to do."

"What?"

"Make sense of it all. Maybe we can't make sense out of everything because we aren't God. Maybe we're not supposed to make sense of it all. Practicing acceptance is something else I've been working on lately. I just try to accept things as they are."

They arrive at the house as Tucker and Smiley are walking inside.

"We can talk about this more later, if you want to sometime," Preacher says.

"I'd like that," April replies.

"Just give me call." Preacher steps astride his Harley and fires up the engine.

April watches him drive away, then goes inside the house. As soon as she enters, Tucker begins peppering her with questions.

"Come in here an' tell me 'bout yore wreck. Are y' okay? An' why did y' leave th' hospital without tellin' no one where y' was going? Where did y' go? Why are y' here?"

"Tucker, Tucker," Smiley says gently, "give the girl a chance to answer one question before you fire another at her. Let's sit down together at the table, drink some coffee, and eat some pie. I'm sure April will tell us her story in her own way, if we'll give her half a chance."

"I'm sorry," Tucker apologizes. "You're right. I just don't understand what all's been happenin' with m' April."

April lays her head on Tucker's shoulder. "And I'm sorry, too, for worrying everyone. But Smiley's right, I've got some things to tell you in my own way. Right now coffee sounds really good."

Tucker takes April's face in her large hands and looks deeply into her eyes. "You're troubled. Sit down at th' table, and I'll get the coffee going. Smiley, get us some plates an' serve this girl a piece o' pie."

Smiley claps his hands and rubs them together. "Now you're talking!"

"I need to go to the bathroom," April says. "I'll be right back." Once she's inside the bathroom, she reaches in her pocket and takes out a square of folded tissue. Opening it, she picks out two pills, then stuffs the rest back in her pocket. She tosses the pills in her mouth and chews them up. After using the bathroom, she gets a swallow of water out of the faucet.

When April exits the bathroom, the smell of coffee brewing greets her. She has a memory of the first time Tucker let her drink some of her coffee when she was little. It tasted so bitter she spewed it out. She laughs at the memory.

"What's s' funny?" Tucker asks.

"Do you remember the first time you let me drink coffee?"

"My lord, yes. Y' spit it out like it was poison 'r somethin'. But March an' August done th' same thing when they was little."

When April sits down, Smiley slides a plate with a piece of pie on it. "Cherry!" she exclaims. "My favorite."

Tucker pours them all some coffee and sets the mugs on the table. "Watch Smiley," she says. "I've taught him t' drink out of a cup like reg'lar people does."

Smiley picks up his cup and in an exaggerated manner sticks out his pinky. He stops with the cup an inch from his lips. "I've got culture." Then he slurps the hot, black liquid.

April laughs. "Preacher's right. You two are like a comedy team." She eats a forkful of pie and washes it down with the coffee. Setting her mug down, she says, "I've got some things to tell you all."

Tucker and Smiley stop and give her their full attention.

"Let me start with my wreck. It was my fault. I wasn't paying attention and pulled out in front of someone. It totaled my car, and an ambulance carried me to the ER. Earlier that day James came to August's and he and I talked about things."

"You talkin' 'bout that sorry man that fired y' when y' was keepin' his kids?" Tucker interrupts.

"Yes. I know that doesn't make any sense to anyone but me, but my heart said it was the right thing to do. So during that night in the hospital I found myself thinking about James and how things had been between us," April says. "The next morning I called him and he came and picked me up. I've been at his house since then. I didn't tell anyone because I didn't want to deal with all the objections I figured I'd hear, especially from March and August.

Those two have turned into a pair of watchdogs when it comes to me, and I'm very tired of it."

She pauses and everyone picks up their coffee and takes a sip.

"But April," Tucker begins.

April holds up her hand. "Don't. Not yet. Let me get all of this said, then I'll listen to anything you've got to say."

"Tell your story, child," Smiley says. "We're listening."

"James apologized for everything he did, saying he was wrong and only acting out of fear of what other people might say about us. He told me he wants to marry me and I told him I want to marry him."

This news pushes Tucker away from the table, and she sags against the back of her chair. She opens her mouth to speak but closes it. She looks at Smiley who is gazing steadfastly at April.

After she has let them absorb this bit of news, April says, "But there's more I have to tell you." She swallows, trying to get rid of the lump in her throat created by the double-barreled bombshell she's about to deliver. "While I was in the ER getting checked out, they discovered that I am pregnant. I got pregnant when I was raped."

"O dear God," Tucker's voice is a whisper. Her eyes close, and she leans to one side like a sinking ship. Unconscious, she falls out of her chair.

Chapter Twenty-two

"Tucker!" April cries.

"Sweet Jesus!" Smiley exclaims.

They kneel down beside Tucker. April pats her cheek. "Tucker, can you hear me?"

Tucker stirs.

"She just fainted," Smiley says. "Get a wet rag."

April hops up and runs cold water over one of the dish cloths. She wrings it out, kneels back down, and places it on Tucker's pale face.

Tucker's eyes flutter open. "What happened?"

"You fainted," Smiley says. "Let's try sitting you up." He and April assist Tucker to a sitting position. "Scoot yourself back against the cabinets," he says to Tucker.

Tucker obeys and rests against the cabinets.

"I'm sorry," April says. "I know I threw a lot of shocking news at you at once. I didn't mean for it to upset you so much."

The color begins returning to Tucker's face. She says, "Me faintin' didn't have nothing t' do with y'. I been havin' these spells pretty reg'lar lately. Ain't I Smiley?"

Smiley looks perplexed for a moment, then says, "Yes, that is so." To April he says, "She's turned into one of those fainting goats. Sometimes I'll slip up behind her and clap my hands just to see her faint."

April studies his face, then looks at Tucker. "Nice try, you two. I don't believe a word of it."

Tucker lays her hand on the side of April's face. "You're gonna have a baby?"

April places her hand on top of Tucker's. "I'm for sure pregnant. Do you want to try to stand up and go to your recliner?"

"I'm fine," Tucker replies. "Ya'll scoot back an' give me room t' git up." Tucker struggles to her feet and leans against the counter, catching her breath.

"You okay?" Smiley asks.

Tucker nods. "Let's go in th' livin' room where it's more comfortable. Bring m' coffee, April."

"Yes, ma'am," April replies. She carries the cup and sets it on the end table beside Tucker's recliner.

Smiley sits on the couch and April sits on the floor facing both of them.

Rubbing the back of his hand, Smiley looks at April with sad eyes and says, "I don't know whether to be happy for you that you're pregnant or sad that you're pregnant. That's just the truth of it."

"I know," April says.

"How do you feel 'bout it, April?" Tucker asks.

"My emotions have been all over the place once I got over the shock of it. I had no idea I was pregnant. I was stupid for not thinking about the possibility of getting pregnant during a rape. It just never crossed my mind."

Tucker blinks rapidly. "It does happen sometimes."

"I've been scared, a little excited, and a whole lot nervous. Here's the thing I need to ask ya'll's advice about." She looks down at the floor. "I don't have to keep the baby."

"You mean give it up for adoption?" Smiley asks.

April nods slowly. She draws small circles in the carpet with her index finger. "That's one option. But there is another option that used to not be readily available to women years ago." She gives them a moment to think, hoping they will say the word before she does. When neither of them says anything, she looks up and sees a puzzled look on Smiley's face while Tucker's face is impossible to read. "Abortion," she says quietly.

Smiley's expression doesn't change, but she sees his eyes reddening.

Tucker is weeping openly.

"I know," April says. "It's hard to even say the word. It's a subject that's never been part of our family. But nobody in our family has ever been raped and had to face this situation. I know what it's like to grow up without knowing who your Daddy is and without having one in your life. I don't want that for any child."

Smiley cuts his eyes toward Tucker and she looks at him. "Time to tell the story," he says to her.

"Story?" April says. "What story?"

Tucker draws a big breath and says, "I'm gonna tell y' somethin' that don't nobody livin' know, except Smiley here. I told it t' Ella afore she died, an' she took the secret with 'er t' her grave."

"A secret?" April asks. "What kind of secret?"

"I knowed how hard it was fer you kids t' grow up without no Daddy, without knowin' who y' Daddy was. It was hard fer me, too. I tried t' do right, but nobody can be both Mama and Daddy to a child. But before you three kids come along, I seen how it affected yore Mama, Maisy. Maisy never knowed who her Daddy was, though she asked me lots o' times. I promised m'self I'd never tell 'er."

"But why?" April asks.

"'Cause th' truth would o' been worse."

April feels like an approaching storm is coming, a storm of such magnitude that it may destroy her. Her heart is in her throat. She sits quietly, waiting for Tucker to tell the rest.

"You kids heared things 'bout my Pa. I told y' some of 'em, and y' heard it from people 'round town. Whatever y' heard, it was true, except it was ten times worse. He was like Lucifer himself. Th' most depraved person I ever knowed. I can't remember a time in m' life that he wasn't usin' me fer sex."

The thunder of Tucker's story releases a shower of tears from April. She reaches up, holds her grandmother's hand, and silently mouths her name.

"The last time he had sex with me was on m' sixteenth birthday. He wasn't never seen after that an' I thought I was finally rid o' that nightmare. What I didn't know was that this time he left somethin' inside me. It was yore Mama, Maisy."

April feels as if she has been struck by a bolt of lightning. Shock and disbelief, the twins that accompany traumatic news or events, briefly cauterize the wound that Tucker's story has created, and April suddenly stops crying. Shaking her head, she says, "That can't be true. That would mean Mama's grandDaddy was also her Daddy. You and she would have the same Daddy. No, I don't believe it."

Tucker ignores April's statements of disbelief. "Back in those days, abortion wasn't somethin' that was legal. Women did all sorts o' things t' git rid o' their babies. I didn't want the baby that was growin' inside o' me. T' have somethin' inside o' me that was part o' m' Pa made me sick t' m' stomach. I hated him, an' I hated that baby inside o'me. So I decided t' git rid o' it."

The raw honesty of Tucker's story pulls April back in. It was too unbelievable not to be true. In a childlike voice, April asks, "What did you do?"

"I was scared. An' I was all alone, livin' by m'self. What was I gonna do with a baby when I wasn't but sixteen years old?" She grips April's hand tightly. "I found m' Mama's crochet needle." Tucker's voice begins to tremble. "I didn't know nothin' 'bout what I was doin'. It was just somethin' I'd heard o' people doin' t' git rid o' their babies."

April hears Smiley sniffing. Through her own newly tear-filled eyes she sees his cheeks are shiny from tears. He pulls out his red bandana and wipes his face. Looking back at Tucker, April says, "But you didn't do it, did you?"

Tucker shakes her head. "I couldn't. It made me mad at m'self that I couldn't do it, like I was weak or somethin'. So I went t' see th' only person I knew who might could do it. She was a black midwife named Mama Mattie."

"Mama Mattie," Smiley echoes her name. But his voice rattles, having been shredded by the sharp edges of Tucker's painful story.

"But Mama Mattie wouldn't do it," Tucker continues. "She said she saved babies, not killed them."

"So all of this is why you and Mama had such a stormy relationship, isn' it?" April asks.

"It makes me ashamed now t' think how I treated yore Mama. It wasn't her fault that we shared th' same Pa. But," Tucker pauses and cradles April's face in her large hands, "if I hadn't had yore Mama, I wouldn't o' had you, an' March, an August."

April climbs into Tucker's lap and puts her arms around her neck. "Oh Tucker, I love you. You're the most amazing woman I've ever known."

"An' I love you, too," Tucker says. "Always have an' always will."

"I wish I had me a camera," Smiley says. "Ya'll are the perfect picture of love."

April sits up and looks at Tucker. "So are you telling me I don't need to have an abortion?"

"Sweet April, this ain't mine t' tell. It's yore body, yore life that's gonna be changed forever by what y' decide t' do. I just felt like I oughta tell y' my story. Maybe I shouldn't have."

"No, I'm glad you did. It actually helps me understand things about growing up that I never could make sense out of."

"What does this fella, James, say 'bout it? Does he know you is pregnant?"

"Yes, I told him. He thinks I should get an abortion. He's says no one will fault me since it was the result of a rape."

"An' what would he say if'n y' decided to have th' baby?"

April drops her head. "I honestly don't know."

"Mmm hmmm," Tucker says with tight lips.

April turns to look at Smiley. "What do you think I should do?"

"Oh my little angel, I'm an old man with old ways. I don't look at things the way most people do. So I don't think I should say."

"But I want you to say. The reason I came home was not only to tell you all this news but to get some advice from you."

"The only advice I can give you," Smiley says, "is that you ought to do what you think God would want you to do. 'Cause if you do that, you won't go wrong."

Turning back to Tucker, April says, "And what do you say I should do?"

"Darlin', I think Smiley has done give y' th' best advice a person can git."

"I had already had the thought of doing something, but you all have helped me see the need even more," April says.

"Thought of doing what?" Smiley asks.

"I need to have a talk with Preacher."

Chapter Twenty-three

The morning after his trip to the principal's office, Benjamin is awakened by someone tugging on his hand. Opening his eyes, he sees Maria.

"It's time to get up," Maria says. "You slept late. I want something to eat for breakfast. The bus will be here soon. Hurry up."

Benjamin rolls over, turning his face to the back of the couch. "I d-d-d-don't want to g-g-g-go to school. F-F-F-Find your own breakfast. Let Alexander help."

"Are you sick?"

"L-L-L-Leave me alone."

"What's wrong?" Alexander says as he joins Maria beside the couch.

"Bennie doesn't want to go to school," Maria replies.

"Neither do I," Alexander says, "but if we don't, Tucker said she won't give us any food when we run out." He shakes Benjamin's shoulder. "Get up, Bennie."

"N-N-N-No."

"You have to," Alexander pleads. "Remember what Tucker said."

"I d-d-d-don't care."

"You will when you get hungry," Alexander reasons with him.

As if adding an exclamation point to Alexander's statement, Benjamin's stomach growls. He rolls over and sits up. "N-N-N-Now you've made m-m-m-me hungry." Walking toward the kitchen, he says, "You t-t-t-two finish getting ready. I'll f-f-f-find something for us to eat."

Benjamin opens the cabinet and sees a package of Oreo cookies. He grabs them and heads back to the living room. He looks for and finds his shoes. After slipping them on, he stuffs the shirt-tail of his wrinkled shirt into his even more wrinkled pants. He combs his fingers through his tousled hair. "Hurry up!" he calls to his brother and sister.

"Bennie." The thin, frail voice of his mother comes from inside her bedroom.

Clutching the bag of cookies in one hand, Benjamin moves quickly to her door, opens it and sticks his head inside. "I-I-I-I'm sorry, Mama. We're going t-t-t-to miss the bus. B-B-B-Bye." Without waiting for her to reply, he shuts the door and finds his siblings waiting for him.

The three of them respond to the honking horn of the bus like Pavlov's dogs and head out the front door. As they walk to the bus, Benjamin reaches in the package of cookies and says, "H-H-H-Here, eat these on the w-w-w-way to school." He gives each of them four cookies.

He makes his way to his regular seat and sits down. Opening the bag of cookies, he looks inside and counts three cookies. He takes one out and, holding it where no one can see, separates the two halves. The half with the most cream on it, he pops into his mouth, relishing its sweetness. Once it's gone, he eats the other half of the cookie. He continues eating the next one in similar fashion, all the while conscious of the fact the bus is drawing closer to Cassie's house. He feels the bus slowing to a stop but keeps his head down, refusing to look at this most recent source of pain.

Benjamin waits for the bus to start moving forward once Cassie has taken a seat. Suddenly he feels the back of the seat in front of him push back against his knees and hears someone sitting down. Then comes the smell of perfume.

"Hi."

It is Cassie's voice, but Benjamin refuses to look up, fearing it might be a dream.

"I'm really sorry," Cassie says. "I wouldn't blame you if you don't want to talk to me."

Hope slips its tender fingers under Benjamin's chin and slowly lifts his head to look at Cassie. He suddenly wishes he had changed clothes and combed his hair this morning. He tries hard to maintain eye contact with Cassie but finds it impossible. Words race through his mind, but they are so jumbled up that he can find nothing to say.

"Listen, Benjamin," she says, "I was upset yesterday, but not with you. I didn't mean to hurt your feelings by not sitting in front of you on the bus. It was just a bad day for me. I'm not mad at you. Do you understand?"

Benjamin feels pressure in his chest again, but this time it feels different than yesterday's pain. It is a sense of excitement. He looks at her. "Are we f-f-f-friends?"

Cassie smiles. "Yes, Benjamin. We're friends."

Even if he wanted to, Benjamin could not have prevented the broad smile that spreads across his face. He looks at the last Oreo cookie that he has just halved. Holding up toward Cassie the half with the icing on it, he says, "Y-Y-Y-You can have this."

A series of changes in her expression flit across Cassie's face in quick succession. Finally she smiles. Taking the cookie, she says, "Thank you. I'll put it in my backpack and save it for later."

Hardly anything that happens the rest of that school day registers with Benjamin. All he can think about is Cassie's smile and her words, "Yes, Benjamin. We're friends." He cannot recall the last time someone called him "friend." His family's nomadic life has not been conducive to making lasting connections with people.

That plus his own shortcomings with reading social cues and knowing how to make friends have produced a solitary life.

When the school bus returns him and his siblings home that afternoon, he sends Alexander and Maria inside while he stands in the yard looking at the house. He feels as if he's seeing it for the first time. All its flaws stand out – the sagging roof with the blue tarp covering the hole, rotting porch posts and rails, chipped and peeling paint, plastic covering broken window panes. The ebullient mood that has boosted his spirits all day begins leaving him like helium from a leaky balloon. *Why do we always have to live in such trashy places? Why can't we have a nice house to live in like other people? Why are we always running out of food? I'll bet Cassie never goes hungry.*

"Bennie!" Alexander's sharp cry jerks Benjamin out of his ruminations. "Mama wants you. And me and Maria are hungry. What is there to eat?"

The last few molecules of air leak out of Benjamin's spirit. His shoulders slump. "I'm c-c-c-coming."

As soon as he walks in the front door, Maria says, "I'm thirsty."

"D-D-D-Drink some m-m-m-milk," Benjamin says.

"I tried, but it tastes nasty."

"You'll j-j-j-just have to wait until I check on M-M-M-Mama." He enters her dark, shadowy bedroom, pausing to give his eyes time to adjust to the light. The ever present, flickering light from the TV is absent.

"Bennie!" His mother screams his name.

The sharp edge of his mother's cry startles Benjamin so badly that his feet clear the floor when he jumps. His heart starts galloping like a runaway horse. "I-I-I-I here, M-M-M-Mama."

The thin, pale arm of his mother slips out from under the cover and extends toward him. She turns her head to look in his direction. Her eyes look like small pieces of charcoal, black with no sign of life. "My sweet, Bennie." Her voice is soft and placating. "Where have you been? I've needed you."

Benjamin walks toward the bed and steps into his mother's web of helplessness. He takes her offered hand. And though a large part of him wants to run out of her room and out of the house and never stop running, he feels trapped, unable to move. "What d-d-d-do you need?"

"I can't get the TV to come on. And I need a drink of water."

Benjamin turns this over in his mind. "B-B-B-But you can g-g-g-get a drink of water f-f-f-from the bathroom."

"I know, Bennie, but I just like it better when you get it for me. It's time for me to take some medicine."

Like an obedient drone, Benjamin lets go of his mother's hand, goes to the bathroom and returns with a glass of water.

"You're such a good boy, Bennie," Joyce says. "I don't know what I'd do without you. Now hand me a couple of those pills from that tallest pill bottle."

Benjamin looks at the clutter of pill bottles on top of the bedside table, all of which are within easy reach of his mother. "B-B-B-But . . ." His protest goes no further, shut down by his obedient, golden retriever nature.

"But what?" his mother asks.

"N-N-N-Never mind." He shakes two capsules from the pill bottle and places them in his mother's hand.

Joyce pauses before taking them. "I think the TV just needs a hard smack on the side. See if you can get it going."

Benjamin turns the set on and waits a few seconds. When nothing happens, he strikes the side with his open hand. The TV responds with a bright flicker then goes dark again. Benjamin strikes it again and the TV decides coming on will be less painful than staying off. The screen gives off a soft, gray light.

"There's already a movie in the VCR," his mother says excitedly. "Turn it on and push play."

Benjamin does as he is told, and the screen comes to life. Elvis is singing "Mean Woman Blues." Having been exposed to Elvis on a constant basis all his life, Benjamin has become an Elvis savant. He gives the movie title. "That's "L-L-L-Loving You.""

"Yes," his mother agrees. "He plays Deke Rivers in this one."

Satisfied that his mother no longer needs him, Benjamin leaves the room. When he does, Alexander and Maria are waiting for him.

"Now can you get something for us to eat?" Alexander asks.

Again the urge to run away strikes Benjamin. Instead, he sighs and walks into the kitchen. Opening the cabinets, he sees a lone package of ramen noodles. "I'll f-f-f-fix some noodles."

"Not again," Maria whines. "We've had it every day. I'm tired of noodles."

Though he knows it's wasted movement, Benjamin walks to the refrigerator and opens the door. He closes it and says, "There's n-n-n-nothing else to eat."

"We need to go see that Tucker lady," Alexander says.

Chapter Twenty-four

April hangs up the phone. "I've called Preacher's house several times today and no one answers."

"Well, th' man has got a life, y' know," Tucker says.

"Why doesn't his answering machine pick up?"

"Maybe he ain't got one."

"Tucker, everyone has an answering machine, even you."

"That don't mean nothin'. Maybe he don't like being bothered by phone calls. Maybe he just answers when he wants to. I don't know. You'll git holt o' him eventually. Quit stewin' 'bout it."

"Speaking of stew," Smiley says, "wouldn't that be good for supper?"

"Oh my lord," Tucker exclaims. "Is that all y' think about, what's t' eat?"

"That does sound good, Smiley," April agrees. "That and some of Tucker's homemade hoecake. Mmmm."

A knock on the door interrupts them.

"Will you answer it, April?" Tucker asks.

"Who could it be?" April asks.

"I ain't got no idea. That's why y' got t' open th' door an' see." Tucker shakes her head.

April opens the door. Voices can be heard. She shuts the door and comes back to the living room. "It's some kids that say they need some food."

Tucker drops the foot rest of her recliner and stands up. "Is one o' them a fat teenage boy an' th' other two a couple o' smaller kids?"

"Yes, exactly," April says.

"Well let 'em in. Where's yore manners?"

April frowns. "I didn't know you were running some kind of soup kitchen."

When April doesn't move toward the door, Tucker bustles past her. "They's from down at th' McDaniel place. It's a pitiful situation." She opens the door. "Hello. Ya'll come on in."

Benjamin steps inside, followed by Alexander and Maria. Their walk through the crisp air has tinged the ends of their noses and tops of their ears with rouge. Benjamin's wrinkled flannel shirt has a hole at one of the shoulder seams. Alexander's shoes are untied and he has no socks on. Maria's tangled hair appears to be alive as its loose ends fly at random angles.

"I been watchin' ya'll git on th' bus ever' mornin' since we had our talk," Tucker says to them. "I'm really proud of y'."

Maria beams, walks over to Tucker, and hugs her leg.

Tucker notices Benjamin stealing glances at April. "Look here," she says as she takes hold of April's arm. "This is m' granddaughter, April. She come fer a visit. She lives in Knoxville."

"P-P-P-Pretty as m-m-m-my Camaro," Benjamin says.

"Well thank you," April says with a smile. "I'd love to see your Camaro sometime."

Quick as his bulk will let him, Benjamin spins around and leaves the house.

"What in the world – ?" April says.

Alexander looks at Tucker and says, "Do we have to go, too?"

"Not less'n y' want to. Benjamin done thought o' somethin'. He's lible t' be back. Are ya'll hungry?" Her question is met with bright eyes, big smiles, and nodding heads. "Let's go in th' kitchen an' see what we can find." The children follow in Tucker's wake.

April sits beside Smiley on the couch and in a low voice says, "What's going on with them?"

Smiley looks toward the kitchen to be sure no one is listening. "It's a sad picture, April. Them kids is living worse than you all did when you was little. That McDaniel place should have been torn down years ago."

"I know," April says. "I saw it yesterday and couldn't believe someone was actually living in it."

"Tucker and I went down there and met the mother. She looks like a scarecrow. She has or has had cancer, or both. I'm guessing she lies in bed all the time taking her pain medicine."

Reflexively, April puts her hand on her pocket containing the rest of her hydrocodone. Trying to cover her actions, she quickly asks, "What about the dad?"

"He's hardly ever there, that either one of us can tell. The kids claim he's off working somewhere. But if he's working steady, how come there's often no food in the house? Tucker is mighty suspicious something's not right."

"Sounds like she has reason to think that," April says. "What's up with that kid who just bolted out of here? Does he have mental issues?"

"His name is Benjamin. He told us he has . . . let me see . . . what was it he called it? Something like Actionberger or Aspenbur, or something like that."

"Do you mean Asperger's?"

"Yes, that's it. You heard of it before?"

"I've read about it in one of my psychology classes. It's sort of like autism, but there are varying degrees of severity of symptoms, from mild to severe. Oftentimes they are very bright. They just have trouble knowing how to relate to people."

Smiley laughs. "He told us that he sometimes says things and does things that are inappropriate. Tucker told him that that sounded like her, that maybe she has Asperger's."

April cackles. "That is hilarious. It certainly is an apt description of Tucker."

Just then there is a knock at the door.

April looks at Smiley. He says, "I bet you it's Benjamin."

April goes and opens the door. "Come in, Benjamin," she says.

Benjamin steps inside. His head darts from side to side, unable to look directly at April. He stands with his fists at his side and looks at his feet.

"Do you want to come in the kitchen and eat?" April asks.

Benjamin shuffles his feet. Then he sticks his fist in front of her. Opening it, he reveals his red Camaro Matchbox car.

Tucker has joined them and smiles. "That there is Benjamin's Camaro. Ain't it purty, April?"

April says, "You mean his car is a – "

Tucker shoves April with her shoulder and cuts in before she finishes her question, "It's as fine a lookin' Camaro as you is likely t' see in these parts. He's mighty proud of it."

April looks at Tucker and searches her features. Looking back at the car in Benjamin's hand, she smiles. "Can I look at it? I don't think I've ever seen one exactly like this one."

Benjamin lifts his head to reveal a nervous smile. "Y-Y-Y-You can l-l-l-look at it, if y-y-y-you want to. I d-d-d-don't mind."

April lifts the prize possession off of Benjamin's palm. She gives a low whistle. "It's really special. You should be really proud of having something like it."

"I-I-I-I've got eleven m-m-m-more Matchbox cars. M-M-M-Mama likes Elvis. C-C-C-Cassie is my new friend. I-I-I-I got in trouble on the b-b-b-bus."

"Whoa there, Benjamin," Tucker says. "That's a lot o' information at one time. Let's go in th' kitchen so's you can eat. Then we'll talk about what's been goin' on."

As they arrive in the kitchen Alexander and Maria are each busy devouring one of Tucker's leftover biscuits with a slice of fried tenderloin tucked inside.

"Goodness gracious," Tucker exclaims. "Ya'll is gonna choke t' death. I got interrupted an' fergot t' git y' somethin' t' drink. What about some orange juice?"

With breadcrumbs framing their smiles, the children nod.

"Here's a tenderloin an' biscuit fer you, Benjamin," Tucker says as she hands him one.

Benjamin eagerly grabs the offered food and sits down at the table.

April watches him spread his elbows and lower his head as he eats, reminding her of how a dog will guard his dish while he eats.

With his cheek stuffed full of the biscuit and tenderloin, Benjamin turns and looks at Tucker.

"I ain't got another one," she says. "What about a peanut butter an' jelly san'ich?"

Benjamin says something, but between his mouth full of food and his stuttering no one can make it out.

"Let me make it for him, Tucker," April says. "That way you can get started on that pot of stew." She gives Smiley a wink.

"Now we're talking serious business," Smiley says. "I'll help hasten things along by pouring the kids something to drink."

"Oh brother," Tucker says. "These kids may think you two is bein' nice, but I know better. You two is only interested in yore own bellies."

Benjamin looks at Tucker and then at April.

April smiles and winks. "Don't pay any attention to her. She just likes to fuss and carry on."

Soon the sound of meat sizzling in the cast iron skillet can be heard and the aroma of onions, garlic, and pepper fills the air. After a few minutes, Tucker says, "I'm gonna put th' lid on here an' let it simmer afore I add th' vegetables." She pulls out a chair and joins everyone else at the table. "How's yore Mama doin'?"

"I don't hardly ever see her," Alexander says. "She stays in her bed most the time."

"She's got the cancer," Maria says, looking at April.

April looks at her and thinks about the time that she lived with Ella and Ella got cancer. Reaching for Maria, she takes her hand and says, "I'm sorry. That must make you very sad."

Maria drops her head.

"Ya'll run out of food again?" Tucker asks.

"All we got is noodles," Alexander says. "We're tired of eating noodles all the time."

April notices Smiley clenching his fists and a furrow gathers between his eyebrows. A hard look comes over him that April has never seen. A chill runs through her.

"Where's your Pa?" Smiley asks with an edge in his voice.

The younger ones look at Benjamin. "H-H-H-He's busy w-w-w-working," Benjamin says.

"Hmph!" Smiley snorts. "If you ask me – "

"I don't think I heard nobody askin' you," Tucker cuts in. She and Smiley stare at each other for a moment.

The momentary tension makes April uneasy. "Hey, Benjamin," she says, "you said you got in trouble on the bus. What happened?"

"He beat up Mark O'Riley!" Alexander says excitedly.

"He picks on Bennie," Maria adds.

This second piece of information April can readily believe, remembering her own experience of being taunted as a child, but the assertion by Alexander hardly seems plausible. "You beat a boy up?" April asks Benjamin.

Having everyone focusing their attention on him triggers Benjamin's bouncing knee. The floor of the kitchen shakes and the table vibrates.

Recognizing the signs of Benjamin's increasing anxiety, April says, "We don't have to talk about that. I want to see your collection of Matchbox cars. Do you think we could go look at them while the stew is cooking and then come back here and eat supper?"

Benjamin jumps up, knocking his chair over backwards. He sets it upright and then leaves the house.

April looks at Smiley and then Tucker. "I guess that means yes." Nodding at Alexander and Maria, she says, "You want me to take them with me?"

"Naw. They'll be fine here with me an' Smiley. You go on. The stew'll be ready in 'bout an hour."

Chapter Twenty-five

April stands outside the McDaniel house taking in the tired structure that was once her and Ella's home. Images of the house she lived in with Tucker and her brothers while growing up flash forward from her memory. The similarities between the two are striking. She suddenly feels like a little girl, hesitant and unsure.

The door to the house opens and Benjamin stands in the doorway. "M-M-M-My cars are in h-h-h-here."

April is stirred from her journey down memory lane. "Yes," she says. "I'm coming." She steps cautiously on the rotting boards of the steps and porch. When she walks into the living room, her senses are assaulted. She hears the voice of Elvis Presley singing "Can't Help Falling In Love" coming from the bedroom that used to be her grandmother Ella's. The smell of mold and mildew overwhelm her. And there is another smell, a smell she remembers from when she and Ella lived here. It is the smell of death. As her eyes sweep the room, she is shocked at the amount of trash and clothes on the floor. The walls are dingy and stained, and the carpet on the floor lies flat, having lost its nap.

Benjamin gets on his knees in front of a sagging couch. He reaches under it and pulls out a box. Turning around, he sits in front of a coffee table. "Th-Th-Th-They're in here," he says, tapping the box.

Realizing he means for her to join him, April feels uncertain. She sees a mouse skirt along a baseboard and disappear into a hole in the corner. She shudders. *Suck it up and get over yourself! Anything that will rub off on me will wash off of me.* Listening to her inner voice, she walks over and kneels beside Benjamin. Though he is not looking at her, she can see his eyes are dancing with delight.

As if he were opening the lid to Davey Jones' locker, Benjamin slowly opens his treasure box. Silently, he takes his cars out one at a time, handing them to April to look at, then taking them back and lining them up beside each other on the coffee table. After the eleventh one is in place, he reaches in his pocket and brings out the red Camaro and places it in line with the others.

April follows his lead and decides not to comment on the cars, thinking he might find it disrespectful in some way.

Benjamin picks up the Camaro and rolls it up and down April's arm.

It takes all her self-control not to jerk away.

"I l-l-l-like the way if f-f-f-feels," he says.

"It does feel smooth, doesn't it," April replies. She notices a notebook in his box. Reaching for it, she says, "What's that?"

Benjamin quickly slaps the lid shut. "N-N-N-Nothing."

April jerks her hand back, thankful to still have all her fingers.

Benjamin clutches the box to his chest and says nothing.

"Did you know I used to live here?" April asks.

Benjamin frowns and relaxes his grip on his treasure box. "H-H-H-Here?"

"Sure did. Lived here with my other grandmother. She died here." As soon as she adds that Ella died in the house, April wishes she could retract the words.

Benjamin turns and looks her directly in the eye. His eyes are full of panic. "Is this h-h-h-house cursed? A b-b-b-boy on my b-b-b-bus said it was cursed. Is m-m-m-my Mama g-g-g-going to d-d-d-die?!"

April feels her heart go out to Benjamin as she hears in him the same fears she had when she lived in the house and Ella got so sick. Forgetting her earlier trepidation, she impulsively hugs Benjamin. "It's going to be okay, Benjamin. This house is not cursed." She lets go of him and sits back. "Look at me. I'm fine. You'll be fine, too."

"S-S-S-So you used to s-s-s-sleep here?"

"I sure did."

"Y-Y-Y-You can come s-s-s-sleep with me sometime."

April opens her mouth to voice a strong objection, but just then, Benjamin's mother calls out, "Bennie! Is that you? I need you."

"That's your mom, isn't it?" April asks.

Benjamin nods his head. Standing up, he says, "C-C-C-Come with me."

A movement on the floor just to her left catches April's attention. She looks and sees a roach walking across the floor. It disappears underneath some clothes. All the excuses she was going to give Benjamin about not going with him to his mother's bedroom evaporate. She gladly jumps up off the floor.

Benjamin is already walking to his mother's room. April follows him.

He pauses at the door, then opens it and walk in.

April enters the dim room. The only artificial light comes from the television. She glances at it and sees Elvis Presley with a surfboard, the ocean behind him. Benjamin's voice draws her attention to the bed where Joyce lies.

"It's me, M-M-M-Mama. What do you w-w-w-want?"

April moves to where she can see Joyce, but keeps to the shadows.

"Can you fix me some ramen noodles? I'm hungry."

As her eyes adjust to the room's lack of light, April notices the bedside table and its collection of pill bottles on top.

Without a word to his mother, Benjamin turns and walks out of the room, leaving April behind.

Like a moth to the flame, April is drawn to the pill bottles. Stepping silently, she makes her way to the bedside table. She looks at Joyce and sees that her eyes are locked on the television screen. One by one, she picks up the bottles and squints to read the name of the drug. Finally, she sees what she's looking for – hydrocodone. She feels a rush of excitement. Taking off the cap, she pours the contents into the palm of her hand. Only two pills tumble out. She bites her lip to keep from swearing out loud. *Just my luck!*

April checks to be sure Joyce is still hypnotized by her movie, then slips the pills in her pocket. Putting the cap back on, she returns it to where she found it. She decides to go join Benjamin and tiptoes out of the bedroom

When she arrives in the kitchen, she is stunned to see a hole in the floor. Some of the cabinet doors hang cockeyed, one of their hinges having pulled loose.

Standing at the stove, Benjamin is calmly stirring a steaming pot.

April walks to the refrigerator and, using her forefinger and thumb, opens the door. Another dismal picture greets her. When she checks the cabinets, she says, "Benjamin, where is all your food?"

"It's all g-g-g-gone. We always r-r-r-run out before our d-d-d-dad brings us more."

"This is just all wrong. People aren't supposed to be living like this nowadays. Something needs to be done."

Benjamin turns off the eye of the stove, lifts the pot off the eye, and turns around. "B-B-B-But what c-c-c-can be done? What d-d-d-do you mean?" He walks to the sink and picks up a bowl that has some dried ramen noodles stuck to the inside and pours the hot noodles in.

"Benjamin!" April says. "That bowl's dirty!"

He cocks his head to one side and frowns. "The p-p-p-pot's too hot to eat out of."

April closes her eyes. "I know that, but you need to wash the bowl first."

"N-N-N-No soap."

The incredulity of his statement causes April's head to push back. "No soap? You mean to tell me there's no soap in this house?"

"N-N-N-No soap," Benjamin repeats. He picks up a dirty spoon out of the sink and drops it into the bowl. Turning, he heads toward his mother's bedroom.

April trails him through the living room. She is about to speak to him when the front door slams open.

A bleary-eyed man with several days' growth of beard on his face stumbles inside. He reels to his left, then sees Benjamin and April frozen in their steps. With effort, he rights himself. B.J. says, "What the hell is going on here?!"

Chapter Twenty-six

Benjamin drops the bowl of hot noodles. They splatter across the grimy carpet.

April is immediately in fight or flight mode. She quickly surmises this is Benjamin's step-father. Though he has the front exit blocked, April sees that she has an open lane to the back door, if needed.

B.J. staggers toward them. He looks at April, then at Benjamin, then back at April. "Who the hell are you? And what are you doing in my house?"

The smell of alcohol reaches April. She has a sudden urge to vomit.

Benjamin says, "Th-Th-Th-This is A-A-A-April."

"Quit your stuttering! Can you not open your mouth without stuttering? I'm getting sick of it."

There is a sudden shift in April. Rather than feeling like potential prey, she feels like a protective mother bear for her cub. Without thinking, she says, "Shut up talking to him like that! What's your problem?"

B.J. stares at her dumbly. He blinks slowly, his alcohol-numbed brain trying to assess April's challenge. Suddenly, a lascivious grin spreads across his face. "So, Bennie, you finally find a girl who'll give you some?"

Quick as sabre in the hand of an Olympic fencer, April slaps B.J.

The sting awakens his dulled senses. His expression quickly morphs from surprise to rage. "You little whore!" He grabs for her but his body bends in half and flies backward as the charging Benjamin hits him in the midsection with his shoulder. Benjamin's legs don't stop churning until the two of them crash into the wall beside the front door. All the air in B.J.'s lungs escapes in a whoosh. The house shudders as if experiencing an earthquake.

Benjamin releases his grip on his step-dad and steps back.

B.J. collapses in a heap onto the floor. His face is pale and his eyes are wide as he tries to not only regain his breath but also as he tries to comprehend the shift in the tectonic plates that has just occurred in his house in the last few seconds.

April stands with her hand over her open mouth.

The door to Joyce's bedroom opens. Standing in the door way, she says, "What's going on out here?" She frowns when she sees April. "Who are you?" When B.J. moans, she turns and sees him on the floor. Her expression quickly turns to one of a frightened deer. "Bennie," she says, looking at her son, "what happened?"

Benjamin backs away a few steps and then goes to his mother. "H-H-H-He was g-g-g-going to hurt her." He points at April.

"And who are you?" Joyce repeats to April.

"My name is April Tucker. My grandmother, Tucker, is your neighbor up the road. I'm visiting her. Benjamin came by and wanted to show me his car collection. So I came here to see it."

Using the wall to support himself, B.J. rises from the floor. He clutches his stomach. "You talking about that old woman who lives over there with that nigger?"

Anger spreads through April as quickly as an Oklahoma grassfire. "If anyone is a nigger around here, you are! Look at this house your family is living in. It's not fit for animals to live in. There's no food here. All because you are useless and worthless, out drinking up what little money you earn. You ought to be ashamed of yourself, but I know you're not. People like you never are. All you can think about is yourself. As long as you have what you want, you don't care about other people, not even your family. You're not worth anything to anybody. All you are is a lazy piece of scum! If you were a hunting dog, Tucker would take you out and put a bullet in your head." By the time April finishes her diatribe, spittle is flying from her mouth. She stands with her fists clenched and nostrils flared. Even she is shocked at her vicious verbal assault.

Silence fills the small living room like black coffee being poured in a cup. The only sound that can be heard is April's heavy breathing. All eyes are on B.J. He tries to stare at April but blinks in the heat of her laser-like glare. He turns his focus on Benjamin and Joyce. "What are you two doing letting someone like this in my home? I told you you wasn't supposed to have nothing to do with those people up there. And by the way, where are my real kids at? Where's Alexander and Maria?"

Joyce gathers the neck of her t-shirt in her fist. "I've been sick in bed all day, B.J. It's been a bad day for me. I don't know where the kids is."

Finding strength in the face of his wife's weakness, B.J. walks over to her. "When was the last time you didn't have a bad day? And don't throw out the word 'cancer' at me. I've heard that for so many years that I'm not sure it's even true anymore. It's just your excuse for being lazy. When's the last time you tried to clean up around here?"

Joyce appears to shrink like a slug that's had salt poured on it. In an even more timid voice, she says, "Bennie, where are your brother and sister? Didn't ya'll ride the bus home from school?"

The truth dances to the front of Benjamin's tongue but pauses like a child on the end of a diving board as he thinks about his step-dad's response. "W-W-W-We were hungry," he says.

This change in the direction of the conversation seems to please B.J. He waves toward the door. "Well go outside and bring the groceries in out of the truck. Don't I always take care of ya'll?" He gives April a smirk. "And you, 'Miss Smarty-Pants', you get on out of here. We don't want your kind around. And tell the rest of your people to stay away, if they don't want trouble."

April thinks about arguing with him but doesn't want to make things more difficult than they already are for Benjamin and his mom. She looks B.J. squarely in the eye. "Just to be clear, I'm leaving because I want to, not because you're telling me to." She strides purposefully out the door and carefully makes her way off the porch.

She meets Benjamin as he approaches the house with his hands full of plastic bags heavy with food. They pause facing each other. "Listen to me, Benjamin," she says. "If he ever, and I mean ever, hurts any of you, you go straight to Tucker's and tell her what happened. She'll know what to do. You can trust her. You understand?"

Benjamin nods.

"I'm going to get your brother and sister back down here without anyone seeing me. Just tell your parents they've been outside playing. That's what I'm going to tell them to say. That's the plan, okay?"

Again, Benjamin nods.

Without another word, April strikes out in a jog toward Tucker's.

By the time she arrives there, she is out of breath. When she walks in Tucker is dipping stew out of the pot into bowls. Alexander and Maria are sitting at the table looking eagerly at the approaching feast. "You all have got to get up and come with me," she says to the children.

"They ain't even eat yet," Tucker says. "Where's Benjamin at? An' why are y' so out of breath?"

Before April can answer, Smiley says, "There's been trouble, hasn't there?"

"Yes," April replies, "but I don't have time to explain right now. I've got to get these two back to the house. Don't worry, there's food there now. Their dad brought some."

"Daddy's home?" Alexander asks.

"Yes, he is," April replies. "Now come on, both of you." She takes their hands and ushers them quickly out the door. On the way to their house, she tells them, "Normally I wouldn't encourage anyone to tell a story, but I don't want your dad to know that you've been at Tucker's. It will make him mad, and I don't want you to get into trouble. So I want you to go on inside your house and if he asks you where you've been, just tell him you've been playing outside. Okay?"

Both the children nod assent.

April gives them a gentle push toward their house and heads back to Tucker's.

As soon as she walks in the door, she meets Tucker who has on her denim jacket and is brandishing an empty axe handle.

"Is ever'thin' all right?" Tucker asks. "Do I need t' go down there with y' an' set some things right?"

April holds up both hands. "No, you don't! You've got to quit thinking that you and your famous axe handle are the answer to every problem. If you go down there, it will just make things worse."

"I tried to tell her the same thing," Smiley says. "But you can guess how far I got."

"I ain't gonna stand by an' let no child be mistreated, I don't care what anybody says. Them would be good kids if someone was t' give 'em half a chance. An' if I can be part of that half a chance, then I'll do it."

April sits down at the table. Her body starts shaking now that all the adrenalin has drained out of her.

Tucker sets her axe handle down and takes off her jacket. She sits beside April and puts her arm around her shoulders.

April puts her face into Tucker's chest and begins to cry. Between her sobs she says, "It's awful the way those people are living down there. It's filthy and nasty. Until their drunk sorry excuse for a father showed up today, there wasn't any food in the house. I really wanted to hurt him – bad."

"If you wanted to hurt him," Smiley said, "then he must have deserved it."

April sits up and wipes her face. "There's no excuse for his behavior. He's an ignorant, racist, sack of you know what. Why can't people just live right?"

"I don't know th' answer t' that," Tucker says. "Why don't y' ask Preacher that question when y' see him t'morrow?"

"What do you mean?"

"We forgot to tell you," Smiley says. "Preacher called while you were down at the McDaniel place. He said he could tell by something called a 'caller i.d.' that someone from here had been trying to call him. I told him it was you. He said to tell you he was sorry he missed your call but that he'd been out of pocket. He said if you'd come by sometime in the morning, he promised he'd be there."

April gives a weak smile. "That makes me very happy." Looking at Tucker, she sighs and says, "Why don't the three of us enjoy a quiet supper?"

Tucker pats April's face, then stands. "Three bowls o' warm stew, comin' up."

Chapter Twenty-seven

Alexander and Maria approach their house cautiously.

"Remember," Alexander says, "we don't tell Daddy that we've been at Tucker's house, or we'll get in big trouble. Okay?"

"Why doesn't he like us to go there?" Maria asks.

"Because Smiley Carter lives with her."

"But I like Smiley. He's a nice man."

"I do, too, but don't say that to Daddy. You know he doesn't like black people."

"How come?"

"I don't know. And you better not ask, either. Just do what April said and don't talk about Tucker or Smiley. You hear me?"

"Okay," Maria finally agrees.

Once they are at the door. They hear yelling inside.

"It's Daddy," Maria whispers.

Alexander slowly turns the doorknob and opens the door.

"I make the rules! And I expect you to carry them out!" B.J.'s voice spills through the open door and onto the porch. "I don't care how sick you think you are. You better do what I say."

Joyce stands with her back pressed against the wall. All the blood has left her face. Her arms are crossed over her chest and her fists are closed in a self-protective stance. Her entire body flinches at every punctuation in B.J.'s delivery as if every time he emphasizes a word he shocks her with a cattle prod.

Benjamin's body lies in a heap on the floor.

Holding each other's hand, Alexander and Maria stand transfixed by the scene. Maria makes a mewing sound like a lost kitten.

At the sound, B.J. turns and faces them. Pleased to see even weaker targets for his rage, he walks toward them, yelling, "And where the hell have you two been?!"

The children take small steps backward from the approaching danger.

"We were outside playing," Alexander says.

B.J.'s impaired brain takes a moment to process this information. "Then how come I didn't see you when I drove up?"

Not having been coached on how to respond to this question, Alexander stares silently at his dad.

"I asked you a question, Boy!" B.J.'s voice rises even higher in volume.

Unable to keep her inner tension held in check any longer, Maria begins to cry. "Don't hurt us, Daddy," she begs.

Tentatively, Alexander asks, "What's wrong with Bennie?"

B.J. glances over at Benjamin's still form. "He's taking himself a nap," B.J. says sarcastically. He looks from his cringing wife to his cowering children. "I don't know what I did to deserve such pitiful people. Ya'll have the backbone of a jellyfish. At least Bennie there put up a fight. Not that it did him any good."

As if she were walking onto the edge of a frozen pond, unsure how thick the ice is, Joyce walks tentatively toward B.J. She slips her arms around his waist. "Why don't you come to bed with me? I haven't seen you in so long. I've missed you."

Having discharged the majority of the steam from his rage, B.J.'s energy starts to wane. He looks down at his scarecrow of a wife and grins. "Now you're talking." He turns with her and they walk toward their bedroom. Over his shoulder he says, "You kids keep it down out here and don't bother us."

Once the door to their parents' bedroom closes, Alexander and Maria rush to Benjamin's inert body. They shake him.

"Bennie," Alexander says, "are you okay?"

"Wake up, Bennie," Maria pleads.

Benjamin stirs, and a groan works its way out of him. He rolls onto his back and blinks with one eye at the faces of his siblings hovering above him. His other eye is swollen shut. Its puffy eyelid is dark pink.

"He's hurt!" Maria cries.

"Shhh!" Alexander cautions. "Keep it down, or Daddy will come back out here. Go to the bathroom and wet a wash rag and bring it here."

Eager to be helpful, Maria scurries away on her mission.

Slowly, Benjamin comes to a sitting position. He reaches up and touches his eye. Wincing, he says, "What happened?"

"Daddy," Alexander says simply.

The one-word answer is all the explanation Benjamin needs to remind him of the drama that has unfolded this evening. "Oh, yeah."

Maria returns to them carrying a dripping washcloth.

"You're supposed to wring it out first!" Alexander says in a harsh whisper.

"You said to wet it," Maria replies.

Benjamin takes the soaked cloth and says, "It's o-o-o-okay." Gingerly, he holds it up against his swelling face. Water drips down his hand and his neck. Looking around the room with his good eye, he says, "Wh-Wh-Wh-Where is he?"

"He and Mama went to their bedroom," Alexander informs him.

Benjamin's focus turns to his siblings. "D-D-D-Did you tell him you were at T-T-T-Tucker's?"

"No," Maria says. "Alexander told him we had been outside playing."

"I don't think he believed me," Alexander adds.

"D-D-D-Did he hurt you?"

Both of them shake their heads.

Benjamin gets to his knees, then stands up. "Are y-y-y-you hungry?"

"Yes," they say together.

"Let's go in the kitchen and see what he brought home."

Like marauding Huns, they enter the kitchen and begin pillaging the plastic sacks of food, opening boxes and cans at random, eating a spoonful of Beanie-Weenies, a bite out of a pop-tart, a confectioner sugar-coated mini doughnut, a slice of cheese.

With their bellies full and the chaos of the night apparently over, Benjamin eventually puts his young siblings to bed. Strains of Elvis come drifting through the house.

"Which one is that?" Alexander asks his brother.

Benjamin listens closely for a moment. "Th-Th-Th-That's 'Clean Up Your Own B-B-B-Backyard' from the movie 'The T-T-T-Trouble With G-G-G-Girls.'"

"How do you always know?" Maria asks.

"'Cause he's heard them forever," Alexander says scornfully, as if the question were ridiculous.

"You all g-g-g-go to sleep now. Everything's all right." Benjamin says.

After Alexander and Maria say their goodnights, Benjamin goes to the couch that doubles as his bed. He retrieves his treasure box from underneath. Opening it, he only takes out his journal and pen. He closes his good eye and sits in silence for several minutes. When he opens his eye, he writes:

Who is the strong man in a house?

The one with the biggest fists?

The one who's the tallest or heaviest?

I don't think so.

It's the one who can stand tall in his heart

Even though his body has been defeated.

When fear takes a back seat

And courage to say or do the right thing moves to the front

That man will never be overcome.

But will anyone see him?

Will anyone know the war he has won?

Who will pin a medal on his chest?

The next morning, Benjamin goes into the bathroom to start getting dressed for school. He looks into the mirror and is shocked to see the multi-colored bruising on and around the eye that is still swollen shut.

He gets Alexander and Maria up and brushes aside their questions of concern about his injury. After they've gotten dressed and had breakfast, the school bus horn prompts them to head outside.

Just as Benjamin is about to head out the door, B.J. calls his name. "Hold up, Bennie."

Benjamin stops and turns slowly around.

B.J. approaches and looks at Benjamin's eye. He reaches out and grabs a handful of Benjamin's shirt and jerks him forward. "Listen carefully to what I'm about to tell you. You're going to get all sorts of questions about how you got that little black eye. I don't care what lie you tell them, but you are not going to mention me or my name to anyone. Because if you do, I'll kill your mother. You hear me? I will gut her like a deer right in front of you and make you watch her bleed out. Do you understand?"

Benjamin nods.

"Good." B.J. releases his grip on Benjamin's shirt. "Now get on out of here."

Chapter Twenty-eight

The morning after her confrontation with B.J., April awakens with the now-familiar feelings of withdrawal from the opiates she takes regularly. Her leg muscles twitch, and her back hurts. Sweat gives her face a sheen even though she feels chilled. Getting out of bed, she finds her jeans, reaches in the pocket and retrieves her stash of pills. She pops two in her mouth and chews them up. Making her way to the bathroom, she starts the shower, then gets in. The combination of the opiate she's taken and the warm water running over her body causes a wave of pleasure to run through her.

She glances down at her belly that has yet to reveal to the outside world the life that is growing inside her. *What will I do with you, or with it? Why aren't answers more clear?* She closes her eyes. *Preacher will help me find the answers.*

After April gets dressed and puts her makeup on, she joins Tucker and Smiley for breakfast.

"How come you're just pickin' at yore breakfast?" Tucker asks her.

"I'm not very hungry this morning," April replies. "But this coffee is really good."

"Y' know how t' git t' Preacher's place?"

"Yes, I believe so. The way you and Smiley described it last night makes it sound like he lives off to himself."

"He does indeed," Smiley says. "I think that's the way he prefers it. I've seen other men who spent time in prison that wanted to get away from people once they got out. I guess after being cooped up for years, they need room to stretch and breathe."

"I still find it hard to believe that Preacher used to be in prison for a violent crime," April says. "He's such a kind and gentle spirit. I can't imagine him any other way."

"I bet people thinks th' same thing 'bout me," Tucker says. "They hear all them rumors 'bout me, and it don't mesh with the sweet an' kind person I am t'day."

April and Smiley stare at her in disbelief.

There is a twinkle in Tucker's eye and a repressed smile tugs at the corners of her mouth.

Suddenly all three of them burst into laughter.

"April," Smiley says, "we'd better jump back away from this table because somebody's fixing to get struck by lightning."

"Sweet?" April laughs. "You might be accused of many things, Tucker, but being sweet won't be one of them."

Tucker puts her hand on her heart. "M' own granddaughter! That hurts." She tries to hold a serious expression on her face but the humor of the moment proves stronger and she laughs again.

Standing up, April says to Smiley, "I'm going to leave you with this sweet, kind lady. But I'm going to warn you – keep your eye on her axe handle."

The laughter in the room sweeps April out the front door. She gets in the car she borrowed from James and heads toward Preacher's. The morning frost hides in the shadows of fields that she passes, trying to avoid execution by the sun's rays.

After a few miles, April eases the car into Preacher's driveway and slows to a stop behind his motorcycle. The morning sun is filtered by the tall, leafless trees surrounding his singlewide mobile home. Looking in the rearview mirror, April checks her hair and makeup and steps out of the car.

Almost simultaneously, the door to Preacher's trailer opens. "Good morning. I don't know which is prettier, this morning's sunrise or you. You look great."

April reciprocates his offered hug and says, "Thank you. It's good to see you, too." She presses her face against his soft, flannel shirt and smells a mixture of aftershave, bacon, and the outdoors.

"Come on in," Preacher says.

Inside, April looks around the Spartan interior.

Preacher points at a loveseat. "Have a seat." He sits in a ladder back, cane-bottom chair.

"You live pretty simply, don't you?" April says.

Preacher glances around. "Yeah, I guess I do. In prison I learned how to live without. You know what I mean? So once I got out, I didn't see the need to clutter my life with things. But tell me how you've been. And how are August, and March and Debbie doing?"

"They're all doing good. August is awfully busy in school. March and Debbie are still in love and all smiles when you see them together."

"That's good to hear. And what about you? How are you doing?"

Up to this point April has been able to return Preacher's gaze, but now she looks away.

In the moment of silence that follows, Preacher says, "What's wrong, April?"

"There's something I need to talk to you about."

When she doesn't continue, Preacher says, "Take your time. I've got nowhere I have to be. Do you want some coffee or water? Sorry, but that's all I've got to offer."

April shakes her head. "No thanks." She takes a deep breath and says, "You remember that I got raped back in December. Well, just the other day I had a car accident and was taken to the ER as a precaution. They ran all sorts of tests and lab work on me. When the doctor came to talk to me, she told me I was pregnant."

She looks up to see Preacher's reaction, but his expression doesn't change. Looking down at her hands folded in her lap, she squeezes them so tightly the knuckles turn white. "I haven't been with any man since my rape. So . . . " She doesn't finish her sentence. She lifts her face to look at Preacher.

"So you got pregnant when you were raped," he says.

April nods. She feels her face getting warm and her eyes blur with tears.

Preacher reaches across and puts his hand on her wrist. "April, I'm sorry life has to be so difficult for you."

The effect of his physical touch combined with his comment that pricks the very complaint she has about her life is more than April can withstand. She bursts into loud sobs. "Why, why, why, why, why?!" she cries. "Nothing ever works out for me! What's wrong with me?! Why does God hate me?!"

Like a farmer trying to halter-break a young calf, Preacher keeps a tight grip on April's arm until her crying subsides. After several minutes, he lets go, gets up, and walks the few feet to his kitchen. He returns with a glass of water and some paper towels. "Here, take a drink, wipe your face, and blow your nose."

April complies like an obedient child. After she blows her nose loudly, she takes a deep breath and lets it out.

"Better?" Preacher asks.

"Yes. Thank you."

"April, there's nothing wrong with being upset, even with being upset at God. He's a big boy. He can take it. But when you look at everything that's happened to you in your life, you need to be sure you factor in the Prince of Darkness."

"Huh? The Prince of Darkness."

"That's one of the names of Satan. I believe that his mission is to destroy us, not physically, but spiritually by causing us to doubt God and eventually to turn away from him. Just like a wolf, he goes for our soft underbelly, that vulnerable place in us. He's vicious and sadistic. Because of the fact that he has put so much energy into destroying you, it makes me believe that you must be destined for greatness, for some grand purpose in God's plan."

"Me? What can I do?"

"I don't know. But I have no other explanation for all you've had to go through. Look, here you are, sitting across from me. I mean, you're still here. God has brought you through 'the valley of the shadow of death' many times. It amazes me that you haven't given up."

April eases back into the couch, trying to absorb everything Preacher has said. After several moments, she places her palm on her abdomen. "What about this? What am I supposed to do about this?"

Preacher looks at the back of her hand and slowly shakes his head. "That's a difficult one, April. Have you talked with Tucker about it?"

"Yes, yesterday."

"And what did she say?"

"She said I needed to come talk with you."

This time Preacher leans back, lifting the two front legs of his chair off the floor. "Trust me, child, I am not the answer man."

"I know that. But I want to know what you think. I believe you are wise and that you try to do the right thing, the thing God wants you to do."

"Thank you, April. I do try, but I often fail. I've concluded that's the way it will always be for me."

"What do you think God would want me to do about this?" she nods toward her belly.

"I guess, for me, the first thing we need to decide is what 'this' is. I mean is it a living being or is it just a collection of tissues?"

"I went to an abortion clinic and looked at one of their brochures describing what happens in an abortion. In one of the procedures they actually do something to stop its heart from beating. Doesn't that mean they are admitting it is alive?"

"You'll have to ask them that question," Preacher replies. "But it sounds to me like it is. There is also a verse in the Bible that makes me believe that God's involved in a baby's life from the moment of conception." He reaches over to a small table and retrieves a well-worn Bible. "It's in the book of Psalms." He flips through some pages before he begins reading. 'For you created my inmost being; you knit me together in my mother's womb.' Now I'm not a Bible scholar or anything like that, April, but in my simple mind it sounds like God has a hand in things right from the start."

"So you think abortion is murder, like the protesters say?" April asks.

"I just don't think it's our place to decide when to end a life."

"But what about capital punishment? Isn't that an example of people deciding to end a person's life?"

"You bring up a really good point. And you may be right. Maybe we need to re-evaluate the death penalty. But I'm going to give you the opinion of someone who lived with people who were on death row. Sometimes a person can do something so bad that they forfeit the right to continue living. I know not everyone is going to agree with me on that, and maybe even most won't, but that's what I believe."

They both sit in silence for a bit, considering everything that they've shared.

Finally, April says, "So you think I should keep this baby?"

"April, this is a hard, hard matter. The baby wasn't yours by choice. It was conceived in violence. If you keep it, it will grow up never knowing who its father is. You won't have the aid of a husband helping you raise it. My convictions say you should keep it, but my heart says if you decide to abort it, I will stand by you and hold your hand, if you ask me to."

April swallows the lump in her throat. "I don't know if I should say this or not, but I love you. You are an awesome man. I'm so glad you came into my family's life."

"And I thank you, April, for being one of my heroes."

"Hero? Me?"

"Absolutely. You have not given up the fight. There are a dozen reasons why you could have given up on life, even taken your own life. But you have a tenacity that is unmatched. I stand in amazement at you."

"Wow, I never thought of myself in those ways."

"You should."

April takes a deep breath and says, "Well, here's what I intend to do. You've heard us talk about James, the man whose children I worked for as a nanny?"

"Yes."

"I'm going to keep this baby. James will help me raise this child and be a father to it. We have talked about getting married and he is eager for us to be together."

Preacher's eyebrows rise. "He knows you're pregnant and that it was due to the rape?"

"Yes, he knows everything about it."

"And he's told you he's willing to help you raise the child?"

"We didn't exactly talk about that decision. But I know he'll support me in whatever I choose to do. He's that committed to me."

"Then that will be a wonderful thing. I'm happy for you. Can I ask you one other thing?"

"Sure."

"How long have you been abusing pills?"

Chapter Twenty-nine

Throughout her drive back to Knoxville, April replays her last exchange with Preacher. His question about her using pills bowled her over. *How in the world could he know? Nobody in my family knows, so he didn't learn from them. And he couldn't know anyone in Knoxville who knows about it.*

She did her best job to act shocked at his question, which wasn't that hard to do. She just hoped it didn't look like the fake shock of someone who is guilty but trying to cover up. *I'm not even sure what I actually said to him. Something like I didn't know what he was talking about.* Whatever it was, it seemed to satisfy Preacher because he didn't pursue the topic.

As she reaches the western edge of Knoxville, she brushes thoughts of Preacher aside and turns to her anticipated reunion with James. *Things are going to be so perfect! We will raise this baby just like it is ours, and it will never know the difference. At last, all the shattered pieces of my life are going to come together.*

A twinge of guilt reverberates through her when she thinks about how long it's been since she talked to her brothers. But being able to think things through without them pressuring her one way or the other has been time well spent.

Telling them that I'm pregnant won't be easy, and I'm hoping they'll be happy that James and I – Suddenly a thought startles her so much that she swerves in the road. A driver in a car in the lane beside her sets down on his horn. April jerks the wheel back and looks in the rearview mirror for signs of a police car or state trooper.

I don't have to say that I got pregnant in the rape! I can say that James is the father. He and I were together the same night as the rape. Who's to know we didn't have sex? That's what we can tell everyone. She breaks into a broad smile and her heart soars, now that it's unburdened from having to tell the truth.

It is late afternoon when April pulls into the driveway of James's house. Cumulus clouds are backlit by the setting sun. Sunbeams shoot through the clouds. One of them lights up the front of the house. April shuts off the engine and sits quietly, remembering the first time she came to this house. Michael and Christopher knocking her to the ground as they ran pell-mell out of the house. James kneeling down to see if she was okay. Their eyes meeting and recognition dawning for both of them.

She blinks and twin tears of happiness are pushed out of her eyes and roll down her cheeks. Swiping them away, she gets out of the car and heads inside the house.

As she opens the door, loud voices from deep inside the house can be heard. She pauses to listen.

"We want April back here with us!" one of the twins shouts.

"I've told you," James forcefully, "she's going to be with us. She just had to run back home for something important. But I promise you, she is coming back."

Newly triggered tears of joy make April's cheeks shine as she walks up on the three new men that will be a permanent part of her life. She gets down on her knees. In a choked voice, she says, "And here I am."

Michael and Christopher whirl around. "April!" they squeal. Rushing into her open arms, they throw their arms around her neck.

April squeezes them tightly.

"You did come back," Michael says.

"I knew she would," Christopher says.

"You did not."

"Did so."

"Did not. Did he Daddy?" Michael turns and looks at James.

James smiles at the reunion scene in front of him. "It really doesn't matter now, does it? April is here." He takes her hand as she rises to greet him. He folds her into his arms and says, "April is home."

At that moment, any shred of uncertainty and hesitancy that April had been having about returning to James evaporates in the warmth of his embrace and his words."

She whispers to him, "Yes, I'm home where I belong."

The two boys join them and wrap their arms around their legs.

"We're a family, aren't we Daddy?" Christopher says.

"Yes we are," James replies. "A beautiful, loving family. But a family who is hungry. Who wants to go out to eat?"

Christopher and Michael begin jumping up and down. "Yes, yes, yes!" they sing enthusiastically.

"I'll be glad to fix something," April offers.

"No," James says. "This is a special night. We need to do something special. I know a great little mom and pop restaurant, Mama Lucia's. It's just the right atmosphere for us. How does that sound?"

The boys stop jumping. "I want to go to McDonald's," Michael says.

"You always want to go to McDonald's," Christopher counters. "I want to go to Steak and Shake. It's fancier than McDonald's."

James and April laugh.

"I think we can do better than that, boys," James says. "Let's take April to a really nice place."

Reluctantly, the boys relinquish their wishes.

"Well," April says, "if it's going to be some place special, then you all are going to have to give me a little time to take a quick shower and change."

"No problem," James says. "We men will get ourselves looking sharp and wait until you're ready."

After returning from the meal at Mama Lucia's, April says to James, "I'll put the boys to bed. You go ahead and relax in the living room."

"You'll get no argument from me," James replies.

"Will you sing us a song?" Christopher asks April.

She tousles his hair. "You know I will. You all get your pajamas on while I get my Autoharp."

Going to her bedroom, April takes the case out from under her bed and opens it. Memories of Ella float out of the case and find their way into April's musical memory, humming and strumming familiar tunes. She rests her hands on the strings, as if that will stop the music. *I still miss you, Ella. I wish you could see me now.*

Lifting the Autoharp from its case, April carries it into the boys' bedroom. They are already in place under the covers like sandwich meat between two pieces of bread.

She sits on the edge of Michael's bed and strums for a while as she searches for a song to sing to them. After a few minutes she sings:

> *Lord, keep us safe this night,*
> *Secure from all our fears;*
> *May angels guard us while we sleep,*
> *Till morning light appears.*

And when our days are past,
And we from time remove,
Oh may we in Thy bosom rest,
The bosom of Thy love,
So death will soon disrobe us all
Of what we here possess.

When she concludes, she gives both them a kiss. "You all sleep tight," she says.

They send her on her way with a duet of, "Goodnight."

She makes her way into the living room where she finds James lying on the couch with his shoes off and his eyes closed. Crouching silently beside his head, she watches him breathe. She smiles, then says, "You couldn't stay awake so we can talk? How's that supposed to make a girl feel?"

James's eyes flutter open. Without looking at her, he says, "I think I heard an angel's voice. Is that really possible?"

She grabs his arm. "An angel that's going to give you the devil if you don't talk to me," she says jokingly.

James turns on his side. His eyes drift slowly over every facet of her face. "It sure looks like an angel," he says in a low voice.

April leans in to kiss him on the lips, but when their lips are millimeters apart, the static electricity that has built up from her walking on the carpet jumps from her lips to his.

"Ouch!" they both cry at the same time as they rub their lips. Then they laugh.

When they stop laughing, James sits up while April remains sitting on the floor in front of him. "How was your trip to Dresden?" James asks. "How are Tucker and Smiley?"

"Tucker and Smiley are good, except I can see age really taking a toll on Smiley. That makes me sad. But my trip was good. I also visited with Preacher. Everything they all had to say helped me figure out what I want to do."

"I'm glad you've got them in your life," James says. "We all need people who work as compasses to keep us from drifting off course."

"That's a perfect way to describe what they do for me. They help keep me grounded, reminding me of my roots. All of them are really happy for me and you and excited about our plans to get married."

"What about August and March? What do they say about that?"

"I haven't talked to them about it yet. But I will tomorrow." She scoots forward and grasps his hands. "Here's what I've figured out. And it only struck me on the way here. We don't have to tell anybody about my being pregnant from the rape. We'll just tell people the baby is yours. We were here together that same night. Who's to know that we didn't have sex and I got pregnant then? See how simple that makes everything? That makes the baby truly our baby."

As she finishes speaking, she feels James's grip on her hands loosen ever so slightly and his eyes dart away from hers for an instant. She pulls away from him. "What? What's wrong?"

"You've decided to keep the baby?" James asks. "I thought you were going to have an abortion."

April feels like an icy hand has surrounded her heart and is slowly squeezing it. "I went to Dresden to help me figure out what I wanted to do with the baby. And I want to keep it. I want to raise it with you." But the energy and excitement have left her voice.

James reaches for her. "April," he begins, but April blocks his hands.

"April what?" she says. When he doesn't say anything, she says, "You don't want this baby, do you?"

"I want us to be together. And I want you to be my boys' new mother."

Tears sting April's eyes. "So you want me but not my baby."

"I just think it will be easier on you," James says. "Going through a pregnancy and delivery is not an easy thing. You've never — "

"Just shut up!" April snaps at him as she stands up. "Don't try and say this is about me, because this is all about you. This is a side of you I've never seen. I didn't know you were selfish. You don't want to raise a bastard child. It's too much of an inconvenience."

"April, please," James says. "You, me, Michael, Christopher, we can have a beautiful life together. It's all we need. Another child is an extra stress we don't need."

April grabs her abdomen with both hands. "This is my baby! I now see that I don't want you to help me raise it. You don't deserve to. I do love you, James, but I'm leaving and going back to Dresden."

James stands up and tries to put his arms around her, but April pushes them away. "No!" she says. "I'm done with you. This is the second time I've let you break my heart. I don't ever want to see you again. Who I will miss the most will be Michael and Christopher."

"They're going to be heartbroken," James says. "They're not going to understand."

"I agree, but that's all on you. You'll have to figure out what to tell them." When he doesn't say anything, she says, "I've got to pack up my things." She turns and walks away from the dream she'd coveted for years.

Chapter Thirty

Cassie Armour closes her locker and looks at Benjamin. "I don't care what you said this morning on the bus, I don't believe you fell and did that to your eye. Do you promise me Mark O'Riley didn't do it? Because if he did, I'm going to take matters into my own hands."

"I p-p-p-promise he didn't d-d-d-do it," Benjamin says.

"Well, have you been to see a doctor about it?"

Benjamin shifts nervously. "N-N-N-No. Only M-M-M-Mama goes to the d-d-d-doctor."

Frowning, Cassie says, "What is that supposed to mean?"

"B.J. says that d-d-d-doctors are what made M-M-M-Mama sick, and they're going to have to f-f-f-fix her."

"I'm not even going to comment on how ignorant that is. But what about you and your brother and sister?"

"B.J. s-s-s-says he's going t-t-t-to protect us from doctors."

"Well that's the stupidest, most backward thinking thing I've ever heard of! When's the last time you saw a doctor?"

Benjamin thinks for a minute. "C-C-C-Can't remember."

"But you've at least had to get vaccinations for school."

"We g-g-g-go to the health department f-f-f-for those."

Cassie shakes her head. "I don't even know what to say, Benjamin. I mean, this is not right. For one thing, you could have damage to your eye, damage that could affect your ability to see. It needs to be seen about. I'm going to tell the school nurse about it. At least she can have a look."

Panic seizes Benjamin. He grabs Cassie's arm and squeezes.

"Ouch, Benjamin! That hurts!"

"Y-Y-Y-You c-c-c-can't t-t-t-tell anybody."

"I can if it's going to help you."

"No!" Benjamin shakes her.

Cassie jerks away. "You're hurting me! What's wrong?"

"S-S-S-Somebody will g-g-g-get hurt."

Cassie looks at him for a moment. Suddenly her eyes widen. "You've been threatened, haven't you? That's what's wrong. Someone has threatened you if you tell. Is that what it is?"

Suddenly Blake Barker, the captain of the football team, shoves Benjamin against his locker. "What's going on here? Why don't you pick on somebody your own size?" He turns to Cassie. "Are you all right?"

Cassie slaps him. "What is your problem?! Did I ask for your help?"

"Whoa," Blake says. "I'm just trying to help. I saw Stutter-Boy here look like he was hurting you. I guess it's true what they say about the police. The most dangerous calls are the ones involving domestic violence."

"Well I'm fine," Cassie says. "I don't need rescuing by some Prince Charming. But I will apologize. I shouldn't have slapped you."

Blake rubs his reddening cheek and smiles. "You've got a pretty strong right hook."

"Huh?"

"You know, like in boxing."

"I don't know anything about boxing."

"Okay. Never mind. I'll just say I'm surprised at how hard you can hit."

As Cassie and Blake engage in their repartee, Benjamin inches away from them.

Blake turns to him and extends his hand. "Look, I'm sorry I shoved you."

Benjamin hesitates, then, ignoring Blake's offered handshake, says, "Late for class." He turns and walks down the hallway.

"But this is lunch period," Cassie calls after him.

After lunch, Benjamin is walking to his next class when the principal, Mr. Clelland, calls out, "Benjamin Trevathan."

Benjamin stops and turns toward the sound of the principal's voice behind him. As Mr. Clelland approaches him, other students on the way to classes give them a wide berth like cars on a busy highway trying to avoid a shredded piece of tire off of an eighteen-wheeler.

"Can we talk for a moment, Benjamin?" the principal asks.

"L-L-L-Late for class." Benjamin replies.

"I'll take care of that. Let's go step inside my office."

Benjamin hesitates and entertains the thought of running out of the school building. Instead, he follows in Mr. Clelland's wake.

Once they are behind the closed door of his office, Mr. Clelland says, "First of all, Benjamin, you're not in trouble. You haven't done anything wrong. So I want you to relax about that. Okay?"

Benjamin's leg bounces. His eye darts around the room. "Uh-huh."

"That's a pretty serious looking black eye you've got there. Must have hurt pretty bad when it happened."

Benjamin's hand moves involuntarily up to his closed and swollen eye. "It's o-o-o-okay."

The principal gives him a steady gaze. "Do you mind telling me how it happened?"

"I-I-I-I ran into a d-d-d-door."

"Really? I had heard that you fell and hit it on a table or something like that."

Benjamin gives him an inquisitive look.

"Didn't you tell Cassie Armour that you fell?"

Benjamin's eye grows wide and his chest feels tight. Both legs start bouncing. Not used to lying, he tries to remember what he has told others about what happened. "I-I-I-I forgot. I did f-f-f-fall."

"So then, why did you tell me you ran into a door."

Benjamin is silent a moment, then says, "M-M-M-My Mama likes Elvis."

Mr. Clelland comes out from behind his desk and pulls a chair up close to Benjamin. When he sits down, their knees are nearly touching. "Listen to me, Benjamin. I've come to really like you. I think you are a student who tries to do the right thing. I know that you don't really know me, but I'm telling you that you can trust me. I want to help you. When I look at your eye, I believe someone hit you. If you're not safe in your home, if there is someone there who is hurting you or hurting anyone else, you can be protected from them. If you will tell me who it is, I can call someone who will make sure that person is put in jail and won't bother your family anymore. Whoever did this needs to be punished for what they've done."

Benjamin's eye locks onto Mr. Clelland's face. They sit staring at each other, the rescuer and the victim, one with a heart full of compassion and the other with a heart full of fear. Though their bodies are inches apart, there is a gulf between them as wide as the Grand Canyon.

His voice barely above a whisper, Mr. Clelland says, "Is it your stepdad?"

Unable to continue sitting between the sharp edges of Mr. Clelland's on-the-mark question and B.J.'s threat to kill his mother if he tells, Benjamin jumps out of his chair, knocking it backwards, and bolts out of the office.

Chapter Thirty-one

With a suitcase in each hand, April steps out onto the landing in front of James's house. She sets one suitcase down and shuts the door behind her. Turning around, she spies the waiting car. As she does so, three doors of the car open and August, March, and Debbie appear.

As April walks toward them, March opens his arms and says, "That's the sound of my baby sister."

April steps into him and lays the side of her face on his chest. She wraps her arms around his waist.

March kisses the top of her head. "We're all here for you, April. No matter what has happened, no matter what you may think, we'll always love you."

August and Debbie join them and create a group hug.

"It's good to see you, April," August says.

"We've been worried," Debbie adds.

"I know," April says. "I'm sorry you all had to worry so. I'll tell you everything. But first, let's get away from here."

August puts April's suitcases in the trunk, then they all pile inside the car.

April lays her head back against the headrest and closes her eyes, enjoying the feeling of security from being surrounded by her family. Like a three-ring binder that has fallen on the floor and popped open, allowing all the paper to fly helter-skelter, April's thoughts fly randomly through her mind. She tries to organize them in order to tell her story to her brothers and Debbie.

They ride in silence to March and Debbie's apartment.

When April feels the car stop and the engine shut off, she opens her eyes. "We're here?"

"Come on," Debbie says as she opens her door, "let's go inside and fix us something to drink. Just bring her suitcases inside."

"Just wait about that," April says. "Let's talk first." She feels everyone shooting her a questioning look, but she chooses to ignore it.

Debbie unlocks the apartment door and lets them in. "Who wants coffee?" she asks.

"I do," August says.

"I'm in," March agrees.

When April doesn't say anything, Debbie says, "What about you, April? Coffee? Or a glass of tea?"

"I just want to get this over with," April says. "Can we all sit down at your table?"

"Uh, well, sure," Debbie hesitates. "Ya'll come on and let's sit together."

The four of them sit on each side of the small dinette table, April and Debbie on opposite sides and August sitting across from March.

March places both his large hands, palms up, on the table. "Let's hold hands. I want to hear this, but I also want to feel it."

Debbie takes March's hand and gives her other hand to August.

April slowly extends her hands toward her brothers, placing one in March's hand.

March lifts it and kisses it. "This is going to be okay, Sis."

August squeezes her other hand. "We're family, April."

April feels a strong surge of emotion pushing up from her chest and into her throat. She swallows hard and blinks rapidly to hold her tears at bay. "There are things I need to tell you that will be hard for you to hear and hard for me to say. But especially after what happened at James's house tonight, I've decided I have to start living an honest life, a life of truth. I'm tired of pretending." She takes a deep breath. "The first thing is that I've been abusing pain pills." She looks at everyone's face, expecting looks of shock, disappointment, and disapproval. But no one's expression changes.

"I'm ashamed," April continues, "so very ashamed." The burning tears that shame brings begin streaming down her cheeks. "I never meant to get into the habit. They just gave me energy and made me forget about things." As her heart, that she has kept sealed for so long, opens up, the gall that she has felt toward herself is emptied out. She begins to sob. Between the sobs she says, "I have lied to you all. I have stolen money from you. I don't deserve you." She jerks her hands away from March and August's grip and covers her face as she bows her head.

Debbie bursts into tears. "Oh, April!"

Suddenly March slams his fist onto the table. "Stop it! Stop it right now!"

Everyone stops and stares at him.

He looks toward April. "Do you know how many years I spent hating myself? Despising myself? Not being able to look myself in the eye? It's hell, that's what it is. Everyone in this room has done things they are ashamed of, things they regret. Everyone on earth has. I am not going to let you beat yourself up like this. I'm not going to listen to it. You hear me? You've told what you've done. And the way you've told it says to me you're sorry for what you've done. God's forgiven you. Now you work on forgiving yourself."

"How can God forgive me?" April asks.

August says, "One of the great blessings of my life was learning Smiley Carter was my father and getting to live with him and learning so many things from him. What a wise man he is. Here is one thing he said to me, 'You can't out-sin God's forgiveness, August.' He told me that God's got more forgiveness than we have sin. That's how God can forgive you, April, or anybody."

April gives a weak smile and looks at each of them. "I really don't deserve you all."

"You may not," Debbie says with a smile, "but you've got us."

April puts her hands on August and March's. "There's more to tell. You know I had a wreck the other night, but you don't know the reason. I was out hunting for pills. I was upset and pulled right out in front of someone. It should have killed me. The paramedic said I was lucky. At the ER, the doctor on call was the same doctor who took care of me when I was raped. Of course they did all kinds of tests to be sure I was okay. When the doctor came to me with all the reports, she told me I was pregnant."

The shocked looks she'd expected from them earlier now appear.

"Yeah," April says, "that's exactly what my face looked like when she told me. I told her there was no way I was pregnant. I haven't been dating or had sex with anyone." She pauses to see if they will be able to piece together the truth.

All the blood empties from Debbie's face. "No, April. Don't tell me."

"Yes," April says.

"Yes what?" March says.

"What are you all talking about?" August asks.

April looks down at the table. "The last sexual contact I had with anyone was the night I was raped."

March makes a sound like someone has punched him in the stomach.

"Oh my God," August says slowly. "I just never, ever considered that possibility when it happened."

"Neither did I," April agrees. "The doctor said it is rare, but it does happen."

"So how far along are you?" Debbie asks.

"I'm nearly three months."

While her brothers and Debbie are still trying to assimilate her bombshell, April decides to continue her story. "So I'm in the hospital, trying to process what Dr. Oliver has told me, plus thinking about James's plea for forgiveness and wanting me to come back to him. And I'm thinking about what to do with this baby. That's when I decide not to call any of you." She looks at August. "I knew you and March would immediately start telling me what to do. And that's not what I needed right then. I decided to go home with James. In spite of how things ended with him, I've always loved him. He told me he wanted us to marry and be a family. I can't tell you how much joy I felt at seeing his boys, Christopher and Michael, again."

April pauses to look at her abdomen. Placing her hands on it, she says, "The doctor recommended I get an abortion. And even James encouraged it. So I went to an abortion clinic." She looks up and sees the tension in everyone's expression. "I listened to women talking about getting their third and fourth abortion. I read a brochure about what happens when they do an abortion. I was suddenly unsure what to do. I realized what I really needed to do was go home and talk to Tucker."

Nodding his head, March says, "Tucker."

August says, "If anyone ever needs an honest opinion on something, Tucker is the person to see. What did she tell you?"

April has unintentionally led herself on a path that takes her to Tucker's own bombshell that she dropped on April. She hesitates for a moment, considering if she should tell, then decides it's not fair to keep this from her brothers. "Tucker told me that she got pregnant with our mother because of a rape, a rape at the hands of her own father."

The bottom jaws of all three of her listeners drop open, and they stare, gaping.

April connects the dots for them. "Yes, Maisy's grandfather was also her father."

"That explains so many things," August says.

"No wonder Mama and Tucker never got along," March says.

"Exactly," April says. "Tucker said she wanted to abort our mother but couldn't bring herself to do it. She said she's glad she didn't because if she had, she wouldn't have ended up with all of us. It's a bittersweet tale."

"Wow," Debbie says solemnly. "What a remarkable woman Tucker is. I have a whole new level of respect and admiration for her."

"So that's why you decided to keep the baby?" August asks.

"That, plus a conversation I had with Preacher about what he thought God would want me to do."

Like the lawyer in training he is, August presses forward with his questions, "And you came back to Knoxville, to James, so you all could get married and raise his boys and your baby, right?"

April's shoulders sag. "Right. What I hadn't counted on was discovering how selfish a man James is. He wanted me, but not my baby."

"I never did like him or trust him," March says through his gritted teeth.

"What a scumbag," Debbie says.

"Now what are you going to do?" August asks.

April looks at them. "If Tucker will let me, and I know she will, I'm going to move back home and have my baby."

Chapter Thirty-two

"Why ain't they here yet?" Tucker asks while looking out the front window of her house into the coming of night.

"'Cause it's a long drive, that's why," Smiley Carter answers. "They'll be here when they get here. You've worked yourself up into a tizzy ever since April called last night. Just relax and calm down."

"Don't try t' tell me what t' do. If I wanna be in a tizzy, I'll be in a tizzy. I just can't believe m' April is comin' home t' live here an' t' have 'er baby. It's a true blessin' from God."

"A new generation being born," Smiley says. "I remember when I used to pitch April up in the air like she was nothing and then catch her. You do realize you're going to be a great-great-grandmother."

"I've always been great," Tucker says with a slight smile. "I ain't never felt like I was Grandma 'cause I raised 'em their whole life. I wish luck on anybody that tries t' draw this family's family tree. All they'll end up doin' is scratchin' their head an' sayin', 'Really?'"

Smiley laughs. "You told the truth on that. I just feel sorry for kids that have the same kind of complicated life but don't have someone like you to help rescue them."

Tucker waves off his compliment. "Pshaw! I just done th' best I could. Wish I'd've known how t' do better, but it's hard t' know how t' make biscuits if y' ain't never seen it done or had nobody t' show y' how, if y' know what I mean."

"You're just spouting off one truth after another today," Smiley says. "Somebody ought to be writing these down. I will say this, I'm so glad April decided not to have an abortion. I wish I could have been a fly on the wall and heard what she and Preacher had to say to each other. He must have told her something that helped settle her mind about it."

"I know what y' mean. I guess I can see why some women do it. Sometimes they're just selfish. But then they's situations like April's when carryin' an' havin' a baby will forever more be a reminder o' th' horrible event that created th' baby. That's how it was with me an' Maisy. 'Specially 'cause she looked so much like m' Pa."

Smiley shakes his head. "Goodness, goodness, Tucker. That was a story within a story, twisting and turning like honeysuckle on a woven-wire fence. There wasn't no way to sort it out. Once again you did the best you knew how to do."

Tucker has a faraway look in her eye. "Y' just don't know how much regret I have 'bout how I done Maisy. She'd've been better off if somebody would've took 'er from me an' give 'er t' somebody else t' raise. I try t' lay down m' regret an' give t' th' Lord, like Preacher says we ought to, but I keep pickin' it back up. It's like a tick that's burrowed so deep in yore skin that y' can't git holt of it t' pull it out."

Smiley sucks his teeth. "Forgiving yourself, that's the hardest thing in the world to do."

They sit quietly for a few minutes, digesting this mutual sharing of intimate thoughts and feelings.

Suddenly, bright light fills the living room as headlights shine through the open-curtain picture window.

Clapping her hands together, Tucker says, "They's here!"

Smiley rises with her, and they go out onto the porch.

April gets out of the passenger side of August's car and August steps out from behind the steering wheel.

"April!" Tucker exclaims.

April rushes to her, and they embrace. April kisses her cheek. "Oh, Tucker, what would I do without you? You've been there for me my whole life, through difficult times and good times. I love you so much."

"Oh hush yore carryin' on," Tucker says as she starts to cry. "You're gonna break an' old woman's heart."

August sets April's suitcases on the porch and walks to Smiley. "Hey, Dad." They share a hug.

Smiley whispers in his ear, "You're a good boy, August, for bringing her here. How's she doing?"

"Actually, I think she's doing better than she has in a long time," August whispers back.

They relinquish their hold on each other. Smiley says to April, "Come here and give ol' Smiley Carter a hug, too."

April beams. "Oh Smiley!" She throws her arms around his neck. "I wish you could still throw me up in the air and catch me like you used to."

"Me and Tucker were just reminiscing about that," Smiley says. "That seems like a long time ago, and it seems just like yesterday."

"Well if'n y' need any reminder that it wasn't yesterday, just try an' pick 'er up," Tucker says.

They all laugh.

August steps over to Tucker and puts his arm around her. "Tucker has a way of cutting through all the bull and getting to the truth, doesn't she?"

A spontaneous "amen" comes from Smiley and April.

"Well come on inside," Tucker says, "an' let's git y' settled in."

As they file inside, August says, "I'll put these suitcases in the spare bedroom."

"No," Tucker says. "Put 'em in April's old room at th' end of th' hall."

"But that's Smiley's room," April says.

"Not anymore," Smiley says. "You're going to need more room, especially when the baby gets here. Plus having your own bathroom will be important. I'm moving into the spare room."

"You didn't have to do that," April says. "I'll be fine in the other room."

"We done sorted all that out," Tucker says. "Puttin' you back in yore ol' room is what's best."

April kisses Smiley's cheek. "Thank you."

"You kids want some pie an' coffee?" Tucker asks.

Heading down the hallway with April's suitcases, August calls over his shoulder, "I'll take a cup of your coffee and a piece of your pie anytime, anywhere."

As they take a seat at the kitchen table, Tucker pours thick, black coffee into everyone's cup as Smiley sets the fresh pie in the middle of the table.

"You know," April says, "I've gotten pretty good at making apple pie using your recipe. James used to say. . . " Her voice trails off. In a more subdued tone, she says, "I haven't gotten used to this new life. I do know this: I'm weary of change."

"You're better off without that man," Smiley says. "Just close the door on that one."

"I intend to. I'm tired of making bad choices about people who I can trust and who I can give my heart to. You people right here and March and Debbie, that's who I can trust. I need to be content with that. I don't need anyone else in my life." She pauses and smiles at her abdomen. "Except for this precious baby that's growing inside me."

Tucker reaches over and puts her hand on April's abdomen. "Listen t' me. This child is goin' t' bring more of them changes you say you're tired of. But if you let us, yore family is gonna be here t' see y' through all of 'em."

April puts her hand on top of Tucker's. "I don't know how you did it all by yourself."

"Grit, that's how she did it," Smiley says. "Tucker's always had more grit than anybody I've ever known."

"Grit an' Mama Mattie," Tucker says. "That woman was a saint."

"Sweet Jesus, she was that," Smiley agrees.

"I've heard so many stories about her," August says. "I wish I could have known her."

"Me, too," April says.

"Here's what I want to know," Smiley says. "Are we all going to sit here and stare at this fresh pie, or is somebody going to serve it?"

They all laugh.

Later, as everyone is settling in for the night, August goes to April's room and taps on her door.

"Come in," April says.

August steps inside. "I'll be leaving in the morning. I can't afford to miss any more classes than absolutely necessary."

April hugs him. "Thank you so much for bringing me here. I know it complicated things for you."

"I was glad to do it. It makes me feel good to know you are here where you are safe." He pauses.

"Is there something else?" April asks.

"We haven't really talked about it, but I've got to ask, what are you going to do about your pill addiction?"

"I don't know. I want to quit and have tried to. But every time I do, I go into withdrawals. I can't stand the pain, so I go back to the pills. I'm going to talk to Preacher about it. Maybe he'll know what to do."

Chapter Thirty-three

Benjamin follows Alexander and Maria out of the house to board the morning bus to school. Strains of Elvis singing "Charro" echo in his head. "Oh no! Charro, don't go! Charro, don't go!"

As he walks past the tree in the front yard, he notices buttercups pushing up through the leaves as they try to hasten the coming of spring. Unconsciously, he's humming Charro to himself as he boards the bus.

"What's that, Ben?" the bus driver speaks to him.

Benjamin stops and looks at the driver. The question doesn't make any sense to him. "S-S-S-Sir?"

"I thought you were saying something."

"N-N-N-No sir."

"Okay then." The driver releases his brake, turns off the flashers and eases forward as Benjamin takes his usual seat. A wadded up piece of notebook paper bounces off his head and lands in the floor at his feet. It is a morning ritual that Benjamin has come to expect and chooses to ignore.

Someone in the back of the bus laughs. Benjamin hears the word "retard."

He focuses his attention on the pending stop at Cassie's house. All the ridicule of the bus ride evaporates when he sees her come out of her house and board the bus.

She finds her way to the seat in front of him. As soon as she sits down, she turns in her seat and says, "Did you hear about what happened in England?"

Benjamin tries to remember if he heard anything at school yesterday about England. Recalling nothing, he says, "N-N-N-No."

"It was in a place called Dunblane Elementary School. A man walked in and shot and killed sixteen children and a teacher. Then he shot and killed himself."

"H-H-H-He killed kids?"

"Yes! Sixteen of them! How awful is that?"

"In a s-s-s-school?"

"I know. Scary, isn't it?"

"Why d-d-d-did he d-d-d-do it?"

"I guess no one will ever know for sure, since he killed himself. Maybe he had a grudge against the school for something that happened to him when he was a kid. Or maybe he thought God told him to do it. Or maybe he was just crazy."

Benjamin thinks about Alexander and Maria sitting in class and a man walking in and starting shooting. A sense of panic takes over him. "D-D-D-Do you think that c-c-c-could happen at the elementary s-s-s-school here?"

"Gosh, I don't know. It's a crazy world nowadays. I guess anything is possible."

"R-R-R-Really?"

The bus drives past Mark O'Riley's house without stopping. Cassie points at the house. "He's the kind of person who would do something like this. Ever since he got his driver's license and started driving himself to school, he's gotten weirder. Have you seen how different he looks?"

Benjamin nods. "Flat black."

Cassie frowns. "Huh?"

Benjamin puts his hand on his head.

"Oh yes," Cassie says, "his hair. He did dye it black and plastered it flat on his head."

"J-J-J-Johnny Cash," Benjamin says.

"Benjamin, you've got to do a better job of giving a complete thought rather than just a word or two. What are you talking about, Johnny Cash?"

"Johnny Cash, m-m-m-man in black," Benjamin replies.

"Now I got it. Mark has changed his wardrobe, hasn't he? Black jeans, black shirts. Someone told me he even painted his fingernails black."

"H-H-H-He uses a ch-ch-ch-chain for a belt."

"I haven't seen that. He's really gone off the deep end. I think it's called 'Goth'. Does he ever bother you at school?"

"S-S-S-Sometimes. I j-j-j-just ignore him."

"Oooo that makes me so mad! I hate to see people picked on."

Benjamin shrugs. "I-I-I-I'm used to it. It's always b-b-b-been that way for m-m-m-me."

"Maybe that's why we're friends," Cassie says, "because that's the way it's often been for me, too. We move every two or three years. I'm always the new girl in class. You know what the scariest thing in the world is? It's when you walk into a school and everyone knows where they are supposed to go except you."

Benjamin cocks his head to one side. "B-B-B-But you're pretty and smart. Why p-p-p-pick on you?"

"Yeah, it's ironic, isn't it? But that's exactly why I'm picked on by other girls. My mom says it's because they're jealous and threatened by me. It would mean so much to me if I could finally have a group of girls accept me, that we could be friends and do things together."

A new feeling stirs in Benjamin's chest. He feels the urge to put his hand on Cassie's shoulder, but hesitates, unsure if it would be a personal space issue like his teachers have talked to him about through the years. He decides to try to put his feelings into words. "I saw a d-d-d-dog one time standing on the s-s-s-side of the road. S-S-S-Skinny. With puppies. It's eyes were s-s-s-sad. It m-m-m-made me want to c-c-c-cry."

Cassie looks at him intently. "It was a stray dog, wasn't it?"

Benjamin nods. "I know how it f-f-f-felt."

Tears well up in Cassie's eyes. "What happened to the dog?"

Benjamin looks away. He blinks rapidly at the memory. There is a lump in his throat. "M-M-M-M-My stepdad t-t-t-turned the car around and went b-b-b-back and – " Benjamin's words are cut off by the pain he feels in his chest.

Cassie's eyes widen. "What did he do, Benjamin?"

"He ran o-o-o-over her and k-k-k-killed her. H-H-H-He said it w-w-w-was the Christian th-th-th-thing to do."

Cassie cups her hands over her mouth to muffle her cry. It is several moments before she speaks. "He is a monster, your stepfather. At least I have a loving mother and father who are there for me and try to raise me right. I don't know how you do it, Benjamin."

"Do it?"

"How you cope with all you have to cope with. It's just a lot. I really admire you."

Benjamin puts his hand on her shoulder. "Friends."

Cassie smiles and says, "Friends."

Benjamin has difficulty paying attention in class the rest of the day. He imagines graphic images of his brother and sister being shot by a gun-wielding Mark O'Riley. He replays his conversation that morning with Cassie on the bus, focusing on her words "really admire you" and "friends." Searching his memory, he tries to find any other instance in his life when anyone told him he was admired. His search comes up empty.

He puzzles over why his mother has never told him that and why he's just now realizing it. To suddenly see a chink in the armor of the one person you've put on a pedestal your whole life is a disturbing thing. A wave of guilt washes over him for even considering that his hero might be flawed. *If I deserved being admired, she would have told me. I just have to try harder to make her proud.*

That evening, after he has helped Alexander and Maria with their homework, fed them supper, given them baths, and put them to bed, an exhausted Benjamin slumps to the floor in front of the couch that doubles as his bed. The house is quiet except for Elvis singing "You Don't Know Me" in his mother's bedroom.

Benjamin reaches under the couch and pulls out his treasure box. Opening it, he looks at his Matchbox car collection. He commences his nightly ritual, setting them out one at a time, lined up side by side. But the exercise fails to make him feel settled like it usually does. By the time he gets to his prized red Camaro he feels as if his chest is going to cave in. Tears sting his eyes.

Suddenly he rakes his arm across the top of the table, sending his car collection flying across the room. He folds his legs and rests his forehead on his knees. For several minutes he weeps.

Once he has emptied himself of tears, Benjamin picks up his journal and pen and turns to a blank page.

Who am I? And why am I here?

Would anyone care if I disappeared?

What I want, I never get.

Even a stray dog deserves to be someone's pet.

Son, Brother, Friend, are titles that I wear.

Having and being a friend is something rare.

Being a brother is really a chore.

What I want is something more.

To be taken care of,

to know I matter

to my mother.

Chapter Thirty-four

Walking down the hallway, April says, "I saw my first buttercup blooming this morning." The aroma of bacon cooking has acted like the fingers of a magic genie, lifting her out of bed and toward the kitchen.

"I've always heard it said," Tucker says, "that th' older the buttercup bulbs are th' earlier they bloom. Them buttercups in th' yard have been 'round at least as long as I have. That's why they's usually th' first ones t' bloom 'round here."

"First day of spring is next week," Smiley says. "Then things will sure enough start busting out."

"I just love spring," April says. "Everything is waking up from its winter slumber. It all looks so fresh, like starting all over again. That's what I want to do, start all over again. I've screwed my life up so many times, I want to get it right this time."

Pushing a chair out from under the kitchen table with his foot, Smiley says, "Have a seat here and let me tell you about 'getting it right.'"

April takes a seat as Tucker sets a cup of coffee in front of her.

"Y' want yore eggs fried or scrambled?"

"Fried sounds good," April replies.

Smiley taps his finger on the table. "Now listen to what I'm going to tell you. I've been trying for years to do things the right way. Everybody wants to get life right. But they make mistakes, fall down, and get up and try again. Especially me."

"You?" April sounds incredulous. "But you're so kind and good-hearted."

"Maybe, but you've only known me during your lifetime which is just a small portion of my entire lifetime. And I'm glad you've only known me now because this has been the best part of my life."

Tucker hands April a plate of eggs and bacon. "I'll tell y' why this is th' best part of his life. It's 'cause he come here t' live with me."

"Lord, this woman!" Smiley exclaims. "April, I'd like you to meet the Good Shepherd Tucker. Want to know what to do with your life? Ask her and she'll tell you. Actually, you don't even have to ask her. She'll stick her nose right in your business and tell you anyway."

Tucker gives him a small slap on the back of his head.

"Ow!" Smiley howls. "Did you see that April? She's assaulted me. You're my witness."

"Oh hush," Tucker says. "You're lucky I didn't smack y' with m' axe handle."

April smiles inside at the banter, but on the outside plays her part in the drama by keeping a straight face. As she's cutting up her eggs, she says, "I know what you mean, Smiley. It's like Tucker thinks she's the Great Oz and has all the answers."

"Okay, now y' done it. Y' done turned m' own granddaughter against me. I'm half a mind t' put y' out, except y' couldn't survive on yore own. You'd turn right back into th' stray y' was when I took y' in. Even I ain't that mean."

"I'll tell you both what the truth is," April says. "The truth is that the best thing either of you ever did was moving in with each other. Me and August and March have talked about it several times. You two need each other. You're good company for each other. Each of you keeps the other going because neither of you is going to let the other quit and become sedentary like so many people do when they get older. You should be happy you have each other." She takes a bite of eggs and bacon, then washes it down with coffee.

Neither Tucker nor Smiley has a rebuttal to April's on-the-mark assessment of their relationship.

"Well someone needs to write this date down," April says smiling. "Because on this date both Smiley Carter and Tucker had nothing to say. I may have to call August and March and tell them about this."

"Now don't start gittin' smart, little miss too-big-for-her-britches," Tucker says.

April quickly eats a few more bites of her breakfast and gulps some coffee. Rising from the table, she says, "That was delicious. I'm going to run over to Preacher's for a little while."

"Again?" Tucker asks. "Seems like y' been over there nearly ever' day since y' moved back. What's goin' on?"

April feels her face flush. "Going on? Well . . . we're only . . . uh . . . we're just studying the Bible together. I've never really studied it before and Preacher makes it so simple and easy to understand."

"Praise Jesus," Smiley says. "There's always something to be learned from the Good Book."

April notices Tucker looking at her with one eyebrow raised. "What?"

"You know what," Tucker answers.

"No I don't. What's bothering you?"

"Lookee here, April. You're a good lookin' young woman an' Preacher is a man what's been single fer some time."

"My gosh, Tucker! He's old enough to be my father."

Tucker's expression doesn't change. "That don't mean nothin'. Th' birds an' th' bees don't pay no attention t' birth certificates. I'm just wantin' y' t' be sure of th' reason you're goin' over there. I don't want y' to git hurt no more."

"You don't have anything to worry about. I'm fine. He's fine. We're fine." She grabs the keys and heads out the door calling over her shoulder, "I'll be back after while."

She gets in Tucker's truck and heads toward Preacher's. *He's just helping me get off these pills. That's all that's going on.* But her conscience whispers in her ear: *you enjoy looking at his eyes and feeling like he can see into your soul; when he greets you with a hug, you try to hold on for just a second longer; you've fantasized what it would be like to be in bed with him.* "Shut up and leave me alone!" April yells out loud. Like an obedient dog, her conscience shrinks away, but not before whispering, *"You know I'm right."*

When she arrives at Preacher's, he's in the front yard. The sleeves of his flannel shirt are rolled up and the top few buttons are unfastened. He smiles and waves as she pulls into the driveway. "Good morning," he says as she gets out.

Smiling, she says, "Good morning. What are you up to this morning?"

"Picking up sticks and limbs that have fallen over the winter, trying to do my part to hurry up spring's arrival."

As he gives her a hug, April peaks at the tattoos on his chest. When he releases her, she says, "And then it won't be long until we're complaining about having to mow the grass."

Preacher laughs. "You're right. We can't ever seem to be satisfied. We want cool weather during the summer and warm weather during winter." He puts his hands on her arms and holds her at arm's length. Studying her face, he says, "No dark circles under your eyes. Your color's good. Any cramping or cold sweats?"

"I woke up around four this morning with the sweats. I took half a pill like you told me to, and I was fine."

"Good. That's the way you have to do it. Only a slow taper is successful in getting people off opiates. If it's too fast, the withdrawal is so severe they'll go right back to using. Let's go inside."

As they turn toward his trailer, April slips her arm under Preacher's and walks by his side. Once they're inside, she says, "It still amazes me that you know so much about drugs and how to help people get off drugs."

"You've got to remember that you've only known me a short time. For a lot of my life I lived the way of the world. There's not much that I haven't done, April. Not that I'm proud of it."

"But you seem so perfect."

Preacher frowns. "I don't like that."

"Like what?"

"That you think I'm perfect, or that I'm professing to be perfect. I'm far from perfect. There's been only one perfect person and that's Jesus Christ."

"So now you feel like you've been given a second chance?"

Preacher laughs. "A second chance? I'd say I'm on my twelfth or fourteenth chance. God specializes in second chances. And that's why I'm trying so hard to live right. I figure I owe Him."

"I just don't see how He could do that for me. The things I've done have been – "

"So bad." Preacher finishes her sentence. "That's how we all feel, like no one has ever done things as bad we have done. I want you to listen closely to what I'm about to tell you. I don't know if you've ever heard the legend of The Sin Eater or not."

"Never heard of it."

"You ought to check it out. That's what God is. He is the original Sin Eater."

April stares at Preacher but doesn't see him. Her memory is playing a highlight reel of all her mistakes: the scars she still carries on her legs from when she used to self-mutilate; the actions between her and her brothers, driven by a child's natural curiosity, that ultimately resulted in March running away from home; her getting intentionally drunk that led to her being gang raped; that night in a pickup truck when she defended herself from being raped and she – . She blinks rapidly and Preacher's face comes back into focus. With her eyes wide she says, "I have to tell you something. It's something I've never told."

An expression of concern comes over Preacher's face. "What is it?"

"I killed someone."

Chapter Thirty-five

"You what?!" Preacher stares at April in disbelief.

"I killed someone. At least I think I did." April feels her heart thundering against her chest.

"Wait a minute." Preacher shakes his head. "That's not something that you 'might' have done. Either you did or you didn't."

April looks at him. "Have you ever had difficulty deciding if something you dreamed really happened or if it was truly just a dream?"

"Well, I guess so. But at least I finally figured out the truth. When is this supposed to have happened, this killing, or this dream, or whatever it was?"

April continues to face Preacher, but her focus is on a distant time in the past. "You know, I've kept it blocked out for so many years, I think I had completely forgotten about it. But sitting here with you and talking about mistakes from our past . . . somehow it just bubbled to the surface." She shakes her head. "Wow, more and more details are flooding in."

Preacher stands up. "Let me get us both a drink of water, then you can tell me the story."

April doesn't answer as he steps away. Her heart has slowed some. She licks her dried lips. As Preacher approaches her with a glass of water, she says, "Can I trust you to keep this strictly between us? I'm sorry. I shouldn't have asked that. I know I can trust you, but still, I don't ever want this told to anyone."

Preacher sits across from her and studies her face. "Then why do you want to tell me?"

"I just have this overwhelming urge to let it out. Maybe it's like a confession. I know you're not a Catholic, and this isn't a confessional type setting, but you are a preacher. Don't people tell you things to get them off their chest?"

In a quiet tone, Preacher answers, "Sure they do. It's something I didn't expect when I decided to devote my life to sharing God with others. I'm not always comfortable in that role, but it seems to bring people some kind of comfort. So I accept it." He shifts in his chair. "But there's something else I need to tell you about me that's just as important to be kept secret. I'll turn your question around. Can I trust you?"

April frowns at this unexpected turn. "Secret? Well sure you can."

Preacher says, "I'm a law officer."

"You're a what?"

"A law officer. I do undercover work."

April laughs nervously. "You've got to be kidding me. You? A policeman?"

"It's true. How do you think I've gotten the hydrocodone to help you wean yourself off? And even though I only used my personal money to buy them for you, it was still wrong."

April hesitates. "I guess I didn't give it any thought. I just figured you . . . " Her voice trails off when she has no explanation.

"Yeah. Well I work undercover in drug cases, trying to catch the dealers."

"Then it's my turn to turn a question around. Why did you tell me your secret?"

"Because if you tell me about a crime you've committed, I can't pretend I don't know about it. I may have to tell one of my superiors."

Preacher's statement pushes April back in her chair. Her shoulders slump. She feels as if she's standing on the edge of a cliff swaying back and forth. She sits quietly looking at her folded hands in her lap as she considers whether to jump or not. *It's all about choices.* The mantra she heard daily at Spirit Lake rings in her ears.

She opens her mouth to speak, then closes it. She does this two more times before she finally says, "There's really nothing to tell. It was just a dream, a nightmare really. I just got caught up in the emotions when I remembered it. It's nothing. I think I need to be heading back home."

Preacher reaches across and puts his hand on her knee. "April, running from demons and secrets is what gives them power over us. Facing them and revealing them is what sets us free. I want to help if I can, but maybe you need to talk to someone else. A counselor maybe?"

At Preacher's touch April feels a surge of electricity run through her. She starts to put her hand on top of his when Tucker's frowning face flashes in front of her. The only thing she hears him say is something about a counselor. At that, she stands up and says, "I really need to get back home." She walks to the front door, then turns around. "I almost forgot. What about more pills? What's the plan for me now?"

Preacher looks at her for a few seconds before answering. "You should be ready to taper completely off. I'm going to give you fourteen pills. You'll take three today, two a day for the next three days, then one a day for the next five days. After that, you won't get any more pills from me." He goes back to his bedroom and returns with an envelope. Handing them to April, he says, "Here you go."

April takes the envelope and stuffs it in her pocket. "I really appreciate what you've done to help me get clean. I don't know how I'll ever repay you."

Preacher points at her abdomen. "You take care of yourself and that baby. That'll be repayment enough for me."

April gives a weak smile. "I'll do my best." She starts to move toward him but waits to see if he makes a move toward her.

He opens his arms. "Give me a hug and be on your way."

April eagerly embraces him, squeezing tightly. She sniffs the smell of the outdoors in the folds of his flannel shirt. Keeping her head on his chest, she says, "Even though you've finished helping me with this problem, can I still come over and visit sometime?"

"Absolutely," Preacher replies.

April releases him and steps through the door.

"Don't forget my secret," Preacher says as she walks toward Tucker's truck.

She turns around. "My lips are sealed."

Driving back to Tucker's, April replays every second of her visit with Preacher, especially him putting his hand on her knee and their final embrace.

As she approaches the McDaniel place, she thinks about what happened the last time she was there. The deplorable conditions the Trevathan children live in stirs anger in her. She stops in front of the house, taking in the roof with a hole in it and the dilapidated porch. "That is ridiculous! Someone needs to do something about this." By the time she drives the short distance to Tucker's she has become agitated about it.

As soon as she walks through the front door, April says, "We've got to do something."

Smiley and Tucker look away from the TV, where they've been glued to The Price is Right, and look at April.

"What in th' world has yore tail twisted up?" Tucker asks. "Y' look like you're ready to fight somebody."

Pointing in the direction of the McDaniel place, April says, "Something has to be done about that house. There's no excuse for people living in a place like that, especially Benjamin and his brother and sister. I'm going to call Social Services and demand they do something about it."

"You sure that's best?" Smiley asks.

"What do you mean?" April replies. "Of course it is. They'll come out and do an investigation or something and fix things."

"Maybe. Maybe not," Smiley says.

Uncertainty suddenly dampens April's anger and she looks from Smiley to Tucker.

"Or," Tucker says, "th' way they fix things might not be what you're hopin' fer. They might take them kids an' put 'em in three different foster homes. Is that what y' want?"

April shakes her head. "No, no. All those kids have is each other. If they got split up, it would traumatize them."

"So you better think this through before you make that phone call," Smiley says.

"But we can't just stand by and do nothing when we know what's going on," April says, her feeling of desperation coloring each of her words.

"Me an' Smiley's talked 'bout it more than once. What we think we need t' do is pay a visit t' whoever owns th' McDaniel place an' tell them we're gonna make trouble fer 'em unless they make some repairs to th' house."

"That's a great idea!" April says excitedly.

"Trouble is," Smiley says, "we don't know who owns the place."

"That one's easy," April says. "I'll go to the Register of Deeds office at the court house and look it up. All of those kinds of things are public records."

"I don't know nothin' 'bout that kind o' stuff," Tucker says. "You sure y' can find that out?"

"Absolutely. As a matter of fact, I'll go there right now." She turns to head back out the door. "It won't take me long. I'll be back in a bit."

Chapter Thirty-six

Cassie Armour closes her locker and discovers Blake Barker standing on the other side of the door leaning on his elbow against a nearby locker.

"You heading to lunch?" Blake asks.

Cassie immediately feels a rush of excitement. Blake is the cutest and most popular boy in school. "Yeah," she answers.

"Me, too. I'll go with you."

Cassie heads toward the cafeteria, and Blake falls in step with her. They meet Benjamin Trevathan going in the opposite direction. Cassie tries to catch one of his furtive glances so she can acknowledge him, but their eyes never meet. As they pass each other, she says, "Hi, Ben."

Benjamin continues plodding down the hallway without replying.

"Is that the weirdest kid on the planet, or what?" Blake asks.

"There's nothing wrong with him," Cassie says defensively. She feels herself bristling at Blake's attitude but doesn't want to spoil the moment of walking with him.

"Really?" Blake says. "You couldn't prove it by the way he acts and talks."

"He's just a little different," Cassie counters. "But he means well."

As they enter the cafeteria a plethora of sounds envelopes them: students talking and laughing, tinkling of silverware, the banging of plastic trays and plates, announcements coming through overhead speakers.

Cassie expects Blake to veer off and join his football buddies at their usual table. So she's surprised when he says, "Want to eat lunch together?"

Cassie is certain her face is blushing, which is only worsened by her sense of embarrassment. She tries to recover by saying lightheartedly, "Sure. It's not like you're asking me out on a date."

Blake smiles. "Well, at least not yet."

Cassie feels her ears ringing and is afraid she may actually faint. She turns her back to him and gets in the lunch line, while also trying to take slow, deliberate breaths and calm herself. *I need to pinch myself because this must be a dream. Blake Barker wants to eat lunch with me! Unbelievable!*

After making their food selections, Cassie says, "You pick a table. It doesn't matter to me."

Blake scans the room and then strides confidently to an empty table.

Cassie sits in the chair across from him.

"You don't want to sit beside me?" Blake asks.

"It's not that. I just like to look at people when I talk to them."

"Oh. That makes sense."

Blake eagerly attacks his plate of food, but Cassie hesitates. *What if I get choked? Or what if a piece of food gets stuck on my teeth and I don't know it? What if I spill something?*

Blake looks at her. "Aren't you hungry?"

"Not especially," Cassie answers, less than truthfully.

"I'm not one of those who complains about the food in our cafeteria. I think it's pretty decent. At least it gives me the protein and the carbohydrates I need to lift weights after school."

"Why do you lift weights after school?"

"It's part of our football conditioning program. Do you like football?"

"I love it," Cassie lies.

Blake gives a faint smile. "So what does the center on a football team do?"

This time Cassie is certain her face is red, and there's no place to hide. "Well . . . he's the one who . . . you know . . . he's responsible for . . . "

Blake laughs. "You don't know anything about football, do you?"

Cassie gives up her charade. "Not at all. My dad watches it every weekend, but I've never figured out what's going on in the game."

"You've never been to one of our school games either, have you?"

"Guilty again. But my family only moved to Dresden in January."

"I didn't think I'd ever noticed you before. New girls always get attention here."

"I hate being the new girl," Cassie says.

"Really? How come?"

"Because none of the girls ever like the new girl. They think she's going to steal their boyfriends. It makes it hard to make friends with girls."

Blake sits up straight and puffs his chest out. Smiling, he says, "You can be my friend."

"Quit teasing. I'm serious."

"Hey! And I'm not serious?"

Cassie returns his smile.

"Who knows?" Blake continues. "We might become more than just friends."

"Friends sounds good right now," Cassie answers.

"At least I'm better than that Stutter Kid. You know, you don't have to keep lockering beside him. You can share a locker with me, if you want."

Cassie nearly bites her tongue off. She's just about to attack Blake for calling Benjamin a name. But when he invites her to share a locker with him, her mind reels, and she puts a brake on her tongue. "You sure you want to do that?" she finally says.

"Of course I am. You're the best looking girl in school. Why wouldn't I want you sharing my locker with me?"

At the edges of her conscience Cassie detects Blake's narcissism and her own feelings of guilt at abandoning Benjamin. But she quickly sweeps them into a corner and lets herself be carried away with the excitement of the moment. *It doesn't mean Ben and I can't still be friends,* she reasons with herself. "Thanks for asking," she says. "That would be nice."

Cassie notices two girls approaching their table. When she looks at them, she recognizes them as Courtney Wallace and Stefanie Vickery, members of the cheerleading squad.

"Hi, Blake," Courtney says. "Can we sit down?"

Cassie is unsure of their intention and hopes Blake will dismiss them. She's disappointed when Blake says, "No problem. Have a seat while I go take my and Cassie's trays to the counter."

With Courtney and Stefanie sitting on opposite sides of the square table, Cassie finds it impossible to focus on both of them like she would prefer doing. She feels herself getting braced for some kind of verbal attack, even though both of the girls are smiling.

"You start," Courtney says to Stefanie.

"Start what?" Cassie asks.

Stefanie flips her hair off her shoulder and says to Cassie, "We've never really gotten to know you very well since you've been a student here. And we apologize for that. But you have an excellent reputation. It seems everyone who knows you likes you."

This approach catches Cassie off guard and makes her even more wary, not trusting their motives. She decides not to say anything until she's certain what's going on.

"You know," Courtney says, "cheerleading tryouts are coming up in a few weeks. We're always looking for good candidates to add to the squad. We wanted to encourage you to try out. We think you'd be a great addition."

Cassie stares at Courtney, then turns and stares at Stefanie. She suddenly has the sensation that she's Alice in Wonderland and has tumbled into a world that is upside down and makes no sense. But yet, this invitation represents one of the very things she's always longed for – acceptance by a group of her peers, especially girls.

At this very moment she'd be hard pressed to say which has been more exciting, this invitation or the one given by Blake. Her heart soars as if on a magic carpet ride.

"I don't know what to say," Cassie says. "I've never done anything like that before. And I don't know if my parents would approve or not."

"Courtney and I will help you," Stefanie says. "As a matter of fact, the older girls on the squad always work some with those who are wanting to try out. And we'd give you extra help, if you want it."

"Are you interested?" Courtney asks.

"Yes, definitely. I really appreciate you asking me because I know I never would have volunteered to try out."

"There's just one thing you need to think about," Stefanie says. "The cheerleaders in our school are all looked up to as role models. We're some of the most popular people in school, and so we're really careful about protecting our reputation."

Cassie's a bit uncertain where this trail is leading. "My reputation is important to me, too."

Stefanie and Courtney exchange a look.

"What?" Cassie asks. "What's the problem?"

"Cassie," Stefanie says, "everyone in school knows you're really good friends with that new kid that's fat and stutters a lot."

Cassie feels a flash of heat pass through her.

"We think it would be best if you didn't spend so much time talking with him," Courtney says. "It just doesn't look good."

Just then, Blake returns to the table. "You three finished? We need to go get your stuff out of your locker, Cassie, and take it to mine."

Cassie feels as if her heart is being stretched like the corners of a tent, pulled in multiple and opposite directions. Her thoughts and feelings are all jumbled up. The callous and demeaning attitude of both the cheerleaders and Blake toward Benjamin infuriates her and goes against her sense of justice. But her long-suffering pain of always being on the outside looking in to social cliques is reaching desperately toward the hope offered her by these people.

She reaches absently toward Blake's offered hand and lets him help her out of her chair. He takes her elbow and turns her toward the cafeteria exit.

"See you guys later," Blake says to Stefanie and Courtney.

Cassie finds it easier to let Blake usher her out of the cafeteria than to struggle to find the right thing to do.

Chapter Thirty-seven

"Who is Herbert Walker?" April asks her question before she gets completely inside Tucker's house. She closes the door behind her.

Tucker and Smiley look at each other.

"The only Herbert Walker I knew," Smiley says, "lived up around Palmersville."

"Yep," Tucker agrees. "He was Tiny Walker's brother that worked fer th' county highway department. Wasn't their Ma named Beatrice?"

"You're right," Smiley says. "Everybody called her Aunt Bea, like on The Andy Griffith Show."

"An' she had twin sisters name Amelia and Cecilia, but ever'body called 'em A an' C, like th' letters in th' alphabet. They was called th' ABC sisters."

"I'd forgotten all about that," Smiley says. "I remember Tiny the most. He was Herbert's younger brother. Last I heard he was living outside of Dresden on the Boydsville Road."

"I always felt sorry fer Tiny. People made fun o' him just 'cause he was small."

"What do you think caused that?" Smiley asks.

April looks back and forth at them with an expression of disbelief. She holds up a hand like she's stopping traffic. "People, what was wrong with Tiny Walker or remembering the alphabet girls is not what we're concerned about. We're trying to figure out who owns the McDaniel place. Where does Herbert Walker live?"

"Is he th' one whose name's on th' deed to th' McDaniel place?" Tucker asks.

"Yes," April answers.

"I believe he died a few years ago," Smiley says.

"Seems like I remember hearin' 'bout that," Tucker agrees.

"Did he have a wife or any children?" April asks. "Maybe the property passed on to them."

"He had several children dropped all over Weakley County," Smiley says. "But as far as I know, he was never married."

April rolls her eyes. "Sounds like a fine, upstanding citizen. Unless there was a will stating such, none of those children would automatically get the house."

"What if there wasn't no family?" Tucker asks. "Where does that leave th' McDaniel place?"

"I'm not sure. But we don't need to get ahead of ourselves. I'm sure there's more than one Herbert Walker."

"Oh he's th' one all right," Tucker says. "I'm rememberin' now that he come out here an' looked at th' McDaniel place just before it sold on th' Court House steps fer back taxes."

April cocks her head to one side and looks at Tucker. "Why didn't you buy the place, since it was right beside you?"

Tucker shakes her head. "Too many memories of Miss Ella. I just couldn't've stood havin' other people livin' there, doin' things to it that Ella wouldn't've liked."

"Miss Ella," Smiley says respectfully. "Now there was as fine a woman as you'd ever meet. God rest her soul."

"Hold it right there," April says. "We're not going to start traveling down that memory lane or we'll all end up crying and sad. Let's remember what we're doing here."

Smiley says, "I'll tell you the best thing we could do is drive out to Tiny's house and ask him about the McDaniel place."

April claps her hands. "Okay then, let's hop to it. Come on."

Without protest, Tucker and Smiley stand up and follow April out the door. They pile into Tucker's truck and head toward the other side of town.

"Exactly where on the Boydsville road does Tiny live?" April asks.

"I think he lives where the Simmons used to live, out past where that kid was killed in a car wreck a few years ago."

"That was a sad thing," Tucker says. "Young people dyin' is th' worst. Wasn't his name Thomas, or Thompson, or something like that?"

"Seems like his Mama worked at the dry cleaners," Smiley says.

"I wouldn't know nothin' 'bout that. I ain't never took nothin' t' th' dry cleaners. Never saw no sense in it."

"Oh my gosh," April says, "you two are driving me crazy. Now I know what a student I met at UT who had come from Michigan was talking about. They said that we southerners can't just give a simple one line answer when it comes to people. We have to talk about everyone they were kin to, where they lived, and how they died. Just point out Tiny's house before I drive past it."

"Well my lord!" Tucker says. "We're just havin' a conversation."

"That's it yonder," Smiley says. "Just past that big red barn."

April stares in disbelief as she pulls into the gravel driveway. Tiny's house looks to be in as bad a state of disrepair as the McDaniel house. "Do ya'll think anyone still lives here?"

"Ain't but one way t' find out," Tucker says.

They all exit the truck and head toward the house.

April takes one look at the steps and says, "You all stay right here. I don't trust those steps. I'll get up there and knock on the door."

Neither Tucker nor Smiley object.

April bypasses the stairs and climbs directly onto the porch. Moving carefully, she eases her way to the front door and knocks.

Nothing happens.

"Y' ain't knocking hard enough," Tucker says. "He's prob'ly hard of hearin'. Give it a good whack."

April hits the door with the heel of her fist.

A few seconds later the door opens in small jerks as the bottom of it scrapes across the uneven floor inside. Once it opens a couple of feet a white-haired man in thick glasses, who is not even five feet tall, steps into the space. He is leaning on a wooden walking cane. "Who is it?" he says in a child's voice.

"I'm April Tucker. That's my grandmother Tucker and Smiley Carter. Are you Tiny Walker?"

"Well I sure ain't Goliath!" Tiny snaps. He lifts his glasses off his nose and squints toward Tucker and Smiley. "That you, Smiley Carter?"

"Yes sir, it is," Smiley replies.

"I knew your Daddy. He was the most honest man I ever knew. I hated that he died when you was away fighting in the war. Terrible thing. And you lost your boy to the war, didn't you?"

Hearing these two things that she never knew about Smiley, April turns and faces him.

"Life is full of trouble for all of us," Smiley says. "The Good Lord never promised us that life would be easy."

"Don't believe in Him," Tiny says flatly as he taps the floor with his cane. "What kind of God would put a grown man in a body like mine?"

Though April has run into people at college who didn't believe in the existence of God, she's curious to see how Tucker and Smiley respond to an atheist.

"Y' got a right t' think however y' want to," Tucker says. "But just 'cause y' believe somethin' t' be true don't mean it is."

"It's when you come to the end of life, Tiny," Smiley says, "that you'll be looking for someone's hand to lead you to the other side. Even if you don't believe in Him, God will be there."

"So you say," Tiny replies. He puts his glasses back on and looks up at April. "What did you say your name is?"

"April Tucker."

"Who's your mother?"

"My mother was Maisy Tucker," April answers.

"Mmmhmmm. Maisy. Everybody knows Maisy, at least all the men do."

"Now listen here!" Tucker puts her foot on the first step of the porch. "You better keep yore tongue under control or I'll do it fer y'."

Tiny looks toward her. "I'm only speaking the truth. If it stings, that's not my fault. What brings ya'll out here anyway?"

April looks at him and says, "We're trying to find out who owns the McDaniel place that's beside Tucker. The deed book at the Court House has your brother, Herbert's, name on it."

"Ha! Now there's you an SOB if there ever was one. I'd piss on his grave if I could get to it."

This trip out here has already been more challenging than April expected. Now this damning description of Herbert by his own brother leads her to wonder if they'll learn anything of value from Tiny.

"He was always buying junk houses," Tiny continues, "those that were being sold for back taxes. He'd let people rent them without him fixing them up. He never repaired any of them." Tapping the floor again, he says, "Just like this house. When people quit being willing to pay rent for them, he just let them go. He made enough money to make a profit, which was all he was interested in. There's several houses around like this one and probably like that one out by you. All ready to cave in on themselves."

"Who's kept the taxes paid on them?" April asks.

"Nobody," Tiny replies.

"Then why haven't they been sold at the Court House like they were before?"

Tiny points up. "Who's going to want to buy a place like this? The County's tried to auction them off, but nobody shows up."

April folds her arms across her chest and chews on her bottom lip. Turning to Tucker and Smiley, she says, "I think we found out all we needed to know, don't ya'll?"

"I'd say so," Smiley says.

April looks back at Tiny. "Thank you for your time. Sorry we bothered you."

"That's all right," Tiny replies. He backs back into his house and shoves the door shut.

April jumps off the porch to rejoin Tucker and Smiley.

"Now what's yore plan?" Tucker asks.

"We're going to hire Shady Green to patch that hole in the roof and fix the hole in the porch and kitchen floor. Even if it's not our house and no one is going to fix it, we're neighbors and that's what neighbors are supposed to do for each other."

Chapter Thirty-eight

Benjamin rests his forehead on the back of the empty school bus seat in front of him. Each time the bus hits a bump, his head bounces against the metal frame underneath the thin padding. The pain feels good. As a matter of fact, he feels like banging his head against it, or against the window, or against anything. Today has been the most agonizing day of his life.

When he earlier saw Cassie walking with Blake Barker down the hallway at school, he was curious about what it meant. He's seen other boys and girls pair off and become a couple, to the exclusion of their friends. But he didn't think Cassie and Blake were a couple because she never talked to him about Blake. She's never mentioned any boys that she was interested in or that it bothered her that she didn't have a boyfriend.

He'd thought that he and Cassie were like a couple. Maybe not in the ways most high school couples were, but in the ways that they talked to each other and were nice to each other. He listened in on conversations at school about students having sex with each other. He couldn't imagine doing anything like that with Cassie, though he was curious about what her body looked like. He liked the roundness and fullness of her figure. But sex? No way!

When he'd gotten to his locker to put his books away before going home for the afternoon, he noticed that Cassie's locker door was ajar. He started to close it for her, but peaked inside first. When he couldn't see anything inside the dark space, he opened the door wide. All he could do was stare. It was completely empty.

At first he puzzled over its emptiness, wondering if someone had stolen Cassie's things and if he needed to report it to the principal's office. Then he remembered Cassie walking with Blake. He looked down the crowded hallway and saw the two of them walking and holding hands. At that moment, Benjamin felt as if his heart had been thrown down a deep, empty well, the sound of it echoing as it bounced and careened its way to the dark bottom.

The school bus hits a particularly rough spot, bouncing Benjamin's head into the air. He slams it down onto the back of the seat in front of him. The resulting impact causes him to see stars, and the light dims for a moment.

He knew when he got on the bus and Cassie never showed up to sit in her usual seat that things in his world had shifted and would never be the same again. The one friend he had in the world was gone. Maybe all the taunts that Mark O'Riley had directed at him were correct. Maybe Cassie just felt sorry for him, that was all.

It made things worse when Mark showed up to make a rare appearance on the bus. Apparently his car was being worked on. He reminded Benjamin of a vampire: white skin and dark clothing. It even looked like he had black lipstick on.

From behind him comes Mark's voice. "What's the matter, Stutter Boy? Are you sad? Is your little heart broken? I saw your girlfriend and that Blake Barker guy walking down the hallway together. They sure looked awfully cozy, holding hands and all."

Benjamin grips his books in his lap. He tries to focus on the principal's advice to stay out of trouble.

"Poor baby," Mark says. "Are we crying?"

Benjamin feels his face getting hot and his hands are sweating. Pressure is building in his chest like that of a coming storm. Tears drip off the end of his nose. Something hits him in the back of the head and bounces off. There is laughter from the back of the bus.

Suddenly, Benjamin stands and whirls around to face Mark O'Riley. "I'm going to k-k-k-kill you!" He charges down the aisle toward a surprised Mark.

There are screams from everyone on the back of the bus.

Just before Benjamin gets to Mark, Mark produces a large knife from the inside of his boot. "Come ahead," Mark says with a wicked grin.

The image of the flashing blade registers on Benjamin's brain, but not deeply enough to cause him to pause and consider his next move. He continues his charge, but just as he's about to grab for Mark, his wide hips hit the edge of one of the seats causing him to lose his balance. He stumbles, and his shoulder hits the seat in front of Mark, dropping him to his knees. His open palms strike the floor of the bus, preventing him from falling on his face.

The brakes of the bus squeal as the driver makes an emergency stop in the middle of the road.

Mark quickly puts away his knife, then stomps on Benjamin's left hand with the heel of his boot.

Benjamin's adrenalin blunts the effects of the blow. He struggles to his feet just as the bus driver grabs him from behind.

"That's enough," the driver says.

"He's crazy!" Mark cries out. "He threatened to kill me. And he might have done it if he hadn't been so fat and clumsy and fallen down."

"Benjamin," the driver says, "you're coming to the front of the bus. Mark, you can tell your story to the principal tomorrow after I turn in my report in the morning."

Benjamin lets himself be turned around by the driver and follows him to the front, stopping to pick up his books along the way.

The driver has some children move to other seats and motions Benjamin to sit down. "Couldn't you have just waited another five minutes? We're nearly to your house. Just five minutes and none of this would have happened. I'm sorry Benjamin, but I've got to report this to the principal."

Benjamin keeps his head down and nods. As the bus starts back up, Benjamin looks at his left hand and sees that two of his fingers are turned at odd angles. The whole hand is beginning to swell and turn colors.

A few minutes later, the bus stops in front of their house and Benjamin, Alexander, and Maria pile out.

"Were you really going to kill him?" Alexander asks Benjamin.

"M-M-M-Maybe."

Pointing at Benjamin's hand, Maria says, "What happened to your hand? What's wrong with your fingers?"

Benjamin holds up his puffy hand.

"Damn," Alexander says. "They look broken."

Benjamin winces as the pain overwhelms his body's natural analgesic. "D-D-D-Don't tell Mama," he says.

Just then a car pulls up in front of their house. A woman is driving. From the passenger side, B.J. steps out. "Thanks for the ride," he says to the driver. "I'll be seeing you." He closes the door and looks at the children. "Your Daddy's home. What about some hugs?"

"Bennie's hand is hurt," Maria says as she walks toward B.J.

"Somebody's always got something wrong with them around here," B.J. says. "What about me? My back is all messed up, but do you hear me complaining about it? I still get out here and work."

"I think it's broke," Alexander says.

"What's broke?" B.J. asks.

"Show him, Bennie," Alexander answers.

Benjamin holds up his enlarged hand.

"Aw that ain't nothing," B.J. says. "I've done worse things than that to my hand. Once got it caught in a car door. My old man just put some ice on it, then made me go out and chop wood later. How'd it happen, anyway?"

"Bennie tried to kill somebody on the bus," Maria says.

B.J. stares at her, then at Benjamin. "What's she talking about?"

Benjamin has long since learned to try and keep his answers to B.J. at one word, thus hopefully avoiding any stuttering and invoking B.J.'s wrath. However, all the upheaval of emotions in the last fifteen minutes prevents him from succeeding. "N-N-N-Nothing." As soon as he stutters, he knows what's going to happen. He feels himself drawing up inside.

"Are you ever going to grow up, you stupid shit?! I get so sick of hearing you stuttering like a two-year-old. There's nothing wrong with your hand. But your tongue needs to be cut out and sewn back in right. That's the only reason I can figure out for your stuttering."

"He don't mean to, Daddy," Alexander pleads for Benjamin.

B.J. looks at Alexander. "Did I ask you for your opinion? No, I didn't! So keep your mouth shut and mind your own business. You three stay outside for a while while I go check on your Mama."

"I'm hungry," Maria says softly.

"You can come in and get everybody a pop-tart," B.J. says.

Maria follows B.J. and returns quickly with the shiny aluminum packages. She gives one package to Benjamin and the other to Alexander.

Alexander opens his and gives one pop-tart to his sister and starts eating the other.

Benjamin takes his package, walks to the large maple tree in the front yard and sits down under it, leaning back against the trunk. He gingerly places his injured hand in his lap.

Alexander sits down beside him. "Does it hurt?" he asks.

"It's b-b-b-beginning to," Benjamin answers.

"Want me to go get some ice for it?"

"N-N-N-No. B.J. will g-g-g-get mad if you g-g-g-go in now. He and M-M-M-Mama are together."

All three of them have learned that when B.J. comes home after an absence that the first thing he wants to do is spend time with their mother in the bedroom, no matter how sick she might be. And he doesn't want any of them in the house while he's with her, no matter how inclement the weather might be. Fortunately, this is a nice spring day.

Holding her hands behind her back, Maria steps in front of Benjamin.

He lifts his gaze to look at her.

"I got something for you," she says. In the tentative manner of a child who is unsure if the present she's chosen for someone will be as special to the recipient as it is to her, Maria brings her hands from behind her. In each hand is a bright, yellow buttercup. "These are for you," she says. When Benjamin doesn't immediately react, she slips the green stems between his broken fingers. "They'll make it all better."

Using his good hand, Benjamin lifts his hand as if it were a platter. Holding the flowers underneath his nose, he sniffs them. He looks Maria in the eye. "Th-Th-Th-Thank you. Th-Th-Th-They're

pretty and smell good, t-t-t-too. My hand f-f-f-feels better already,"
Benjamin lies.

Maria smiles and sits down on the other side of him.

They sit quietly waiting for permission from B.J. to enter the
house. When twilight falls and the chill of the night strikes their
skin, Benjamin decides to wait no longer. "Let's go in," he instructs.

"But won't we get in trouble?" Alexander asks.

"There's n-n-n-no lights on. He must h-h-h-have gone to sleep."
Benjamin leads the way into the darkened house.

They stand just inside the doorway holding their breath for any
sounds from within. When not even the sound of an Elvis movie can
be heard, they exhale.

"T-T-T-Time for bed," Benjamin whispers.

Without a reply, his younger siblings tiptoe to their bedroom and
close the door behind them.

Benjamin's feet feel as if they are wearing lead boots.
Exhaustion permeates his body. His hand is throbbing with every
beat of his heart. The couch, his womb of comfort, beckons him, but
it seems to him as if it is a mile away, an impossible distance to
traverse. With an act of will he forces himself to move, finally
arriving at his special place. Using his good hand, he retrieves his
treasure box and opens it.

One by one he takes out his prized possessions, comforted by
their unchanging form and their predictability. Tracing their lines,
he rolls them gently on the table, then on his face. Eventually all
twelve are lined up like they are at a car show. Their headlights stare
at him.

After a few moments Cassie's face floats in front of him. The
cars blur as tears fill his eyes.

Benjamin reaches for his journal and writes.

Why is it him and not me?

Was there something I couldn't see

That would have been plain to anyone else?

I don't know what we are anymore.

I only know that my heart has been torn

And I feel worse than I have ever felt.

I wish I was a different me.

One that could talk plainly and understand clearly.

One that wasn't short, fat, and ugly.

Would that matter to you?

Would it make you feel differently?

I hope tomorrow never comes

Because I don't want to see you with him and not with me.

Benjamin closes his journal and places it back in the box. He carefully returns his Matchbox car collection, too. But before closing the lid, he adds something new – two buttercups.

Chapter Thirty-nine

The next morning, Benjamin is awakened by loud clattering sounds outside the house. He gets up and peaks out the front window. There is a man unloading boards from the back of a pickup truck and dropping them onto the ground. The driver's door opens and Tucker's granddaughter, April, steps out. She's dressed in work boots, faded and stained jeans, and a rumpled flannel shirt. Leather work gloves adorn each of her hands. She points to the truck and then to the stack of lumber on the ground, giving some kind of instructions to the man with her.

"What the hell is all that noise?" B.J. walks out of his bedroom fastening and zipping up his jeans. He looks out the window. "What the – " He moves to the door, opens it, and walks barefoot onto the porch. "What's going on here?"

Benjamin follows him, and stands a little behind him and to one side.

Taking off her gloves, April strides purposefully toward them. "We're going to repair that hole in the roof of your house, this dilapidated porch, and fix that hole in the kitchen, too."

"Who gave you permission to do that?" B.J. asks.

"No one did. Why? Do you prefer to keep the hole?"

"I don't like people sticking their nose into my business."

"Well you know what? If you took care of your business, no one would have to do it for you. You let your family live in this shack and don't do one thing to try and make it better."

"What's going on?" Joyce says from the doorway. She pulls a thin sweater over her shoulders.

"It's those meddlesome neighbors from up the road trying to tell us how to take care of our business," B.J. says.

"What are ya'll doing?" Joyce asks April.

"We're going to patch the hole in your roof and fix this porch," April answers.

"But B.J. says the landlord is going to fix it as soon as the weather clears up," Joyce says as she looks at her husband.

"Landlord?!" April exclaims. "There is no landlord. The county owns this place. You all are basically squatters."

Joyce frowns as B.J.'s face reddens. "Who do you pay the rent to?" she asks him.

"None of your business!" B.J. yells as he whirls around to face her.

Maria and Alexander appear at Joyce's side. Maria rubs the sleep out of her eyes.

Shady Green has left his job of unloading the lumber from the truck and joins April. A hammer hangs loosely in his hand.

B.J. brushes past Benjamin and shoves Joyce and the little ones out of his way as he goes inside. "Get out of my way!" In a moment he returns wearing a jacket and his boots. He steps off the porch and heads toward April.

Shady clinches the handle of the hammer.

April braces herself.

"You people do what you want," B.J. says as he storms past her. "I'm going to work." He walks to the edge of the yard and heads towards town.

Joyce ushers Alexander and Maria back inside.

April lets out her pent-up breath. "Whew," she says to Shady, "I wasn't sure what was going to happen there."

"Me ee'er," Shady says. "'ut ah was 'eady wiff my 'ammer." He hefts the hammer over his head.

April laughs and punches him on the arm. "There'll never be another Shady Green. I'm glad you were ready to help."

Shady carries several of the boards to the porch and drops them in front of Benjamin. "I aim isss Shay-ee Gree."

"I'm B-B-B-Benjamin."

"Ooo 'ig 'oy. Ah ooo shrong?"

"I'm not b-b-b-big. I'm f-f-f-fat. I'm kind of strong."

April walks up while they're talking. "You understand him?" she says to Benjamin while pointing at Shady.

"Sure," Benjamin says.

Shaking her head, April says, "Nobody understands Shady, especially when they first meet him. How is it that you can?"

Benjamin shrugs.

"Oz eez so smar," Shady says with a snaggled-tooth grin.

Benjamin smiles, too. "Y-Y-Y-Yes, I am smart."

April laughs. "You two are a real pair." Suddenly she notices Benjamin's hand. "Oh my god, Benjamin! What happened to your hand?"

Benjamin cradles his hand protectively against his chest. "I h-h-h-hurt it. B-B-B-But it's okay."

April steps closer to him.

"P-P-P-Personal space," Benjamin says as he takes a step backwards.

April stops. "Huh?"

"Teacher says, 'P-P-P-Personal space.'"

"Okay then. I'm standing still. Listen to me, Benjamin. Your hand is not okay. You're fingers are broken and maybe some bones in your hand. When did this happen?" She leans in to look at it more closely but doesn't try to touch it.

"Yesterday on the b-b-b-bus," Benjamin answers her.

"Did you show your mom or dad?"

He shakes his head.

"Oh good grief! Well come on. I'm taking you to the hospital."

Benjamin looks over his shoulder at the front door of the house. "I-I-I-I have to feed them b-b-b-breakfast."

"Feed who?" April asks.

"Alexander and M-M-M-Maria."

"Your mother can take care of them." She reaches for his good hand and takes hold of it. "Come on. They'll be fine. Shady, you help him in the truck while I tell his mother what's going on."

"'ess 'am," Shady replies. "'ollow me," he says to Benjamin.

Benjamin steps off the porch and follows Shady.

April steps inside the house. Even though she's seen it before, she is still shocked by the deplorable conditions inside. She hears men's voices coming from Joyce and B.J.'s bedroom. She looks around but doesn't see the children.

Frowning, she walks to the bedroom and pushes open the door that is ajar. Joyce is lying in bed with an oxygen cannula in her nostrils. The voices are coming from the TV set. April stares at it for a moment and recognizes a young Elvis Presley. April starts to point out the stupidity of smoking around oxygen but decides not to waste her breath. "I'm taking Benjamin to the hospital," she announces. "You've got to feed Alexander and Maria their breakfast and get them ready for the school bus."

Joyce keeps her eyes locked on the television. "Okay," she says.

"Okay? Okay?! That's all you've got to say? What kind of mother are you? Don't you even want to know why I'm taking him to the hospital? Do you care?"

Joyce has a coughing spasm. "I've got the cancer. I'm doing the best I can."

"I'll tell you what you need. You need someone to take a stick to you. But all that would do is relieve the frustration of the one beating you. It wouldn't change you one bit. I've seen people like you, only interested in themselves and what is wrong with them. I'm leaving before I lose my temper. Get up and do like I said. Get those kids ready for school." April stomps through the house toward the front door. Before she exits, she turns around and yells, "And don't send them to school hungry!"

She jumps off the porch and jogs to the truck. "Shady, you go ahead and work on the porch. I'll be back as soon as I can." She jumps in the cab. The truck fishtails out of the front yard and onto the road to town.

Up ahead April sees B.J. walking down the side of the road. With an exercise of extreme will power she resists the urge to hit him with the side mirror of the truck as she speeds past him.

"Did he do that to you?" she asks Benjamin.

"N-N-N-No."

"You can tell me if he did. You can trust me. We will do something to make it stop, if he's been hurting you or your brother and sister." Even as she says this April wonders what she will do if the answer is yes. Tucker and Smiley's comments about what could happen if she reports things to Children's Services has tempered her urge to follow that route.

"The b-b-b-bus and Mr. Goth." Benjamin says it like it's the title of a book.

April steals a quick look at him. "What do you mean?"

Benjamin holds up his swollen and discolored hand.

"You mean it happened on the bus?"

"Uh-huh."

"Is Mr. Goth the name of your bus driver? He did this to you?"

"B-B-B-Black. Black shoes. Black p-p-p-pants. B-B-B-Black shirt. Black hair. B-B-B-Black lips."

April does a rolling stop through the four-way stops around the Court House, then takes Highway 22 toward Martin and Volunteer General Hospital. She puzzles over the meaning of Benjamin's words, wondering if he's describing the bus driver or someone on the bus. Or does the description have anything to do with his hand. *Maybe he's mentally handicapped, or something.*

She decides to go in a different direction. "How long have you stuttered?"

"Always," Benjamin answers.

"Have you had speech therapy?"

"S-S-S-Sometimes."

"You know, I had problems speaking when I was growing up."

Benjamin turns and looks at her.

"I know. Hard to believe, isn't it? Especially since I don't have any trouble now. But I didn't speak until I was six years old."

"Why n-n-n-not?"

"That's not a simple question to answer. And I'm not sure I even know all the reasons."

"How d-d-d-did you start t-t-t-talking?"

"Music," April answers. "Music was the key that unlocked my tongue. My grandmother helped me."

"T-T-T-Tucker?" Benjamin asks.

"No, it was my other grandmother. She died several years ago. Did you know there have been very successful singers who were stutterers?"

"Uh-uh."

"It's true. Mel Tillis, a country music star, has a terrible time with stuttering, but when he sings, he never stutters."

"I like m-m-m-music."

"Would you like for me to see if I could help you? We could make it fun. I love music and play an instrument called an Autoharp. I could even teach you to play it, too, if you wanted to."

Benjamin glances all around the cab as he considers April's offer.

April turns on the truck's blinker and pulls into the parking lot of the hospital. "You don't have to decide anything right now. You can think about it."

Chapter Forty

After seeing the doctor, Benjamin exits the hospital as April holds the door for him. "Does it hurt very bad?" she asks.

"S-S-S-Some," Benjamin says.

"I've got this prescription for pain medicine. We'll get it filled when we get to Dresden. Which pharmacy do you all use?"

"I d-d-d-don't take medicine."

April opens the passenger door of Tucker's truck and helps Benjamin inside. When she gets in the driver's side, she says, "But when you've been to the doctor in the past, where did you get your medicine?"

"N-N-N-No doctors. B.J. won't let us."

April starts to swear but realizes it would be useless, plus Benjamin might think she's mad at him about it. She reaches over, opens the glove compartment, and rifles through the contents. "There's got to be one in here somewhere," she mumbles. "Ah-ha!" she finally says as she extracts a permanent marker. "I want to be the first one to sign your cast."

Benjamin looks down at his arm as it hangs in a sling. "S-S-S-Sign it?"

"Yeah, you know, sign my name to it. It's what everyone does to someone's cast. All your friends will want to do it."

Benjamin turns his head to look out the door window. "M-M-M-Mama likes Elvis."

April frowns. "Yeah, I figured as much since she was watching one of his movies this morning. I'm going to slide the sling back just a little so I can have plenty of room to write."

Benjamin keeps his head turned away but cuts his eyes to watch her. One of his legs, ever the conduit for his anxiety, bobs up and down.

The aroma of the permanent marker fills the cab as she begins writing. Without looking at him, she says, "Who are your friends at school?"

"No f-f-f-friends. I'm odd and d-d-d-don't fit in."

April bites her bottom lip as she remembers her own childhood experiences of not feeling like she fit in, a problem she's continued to battle into adulthood. She writes some more, then sits up and says, "There you go! Take a look."

Benjamin looks at what she has written and reads it aloud. "F-F-F-For Bad Boy B-B-B-Benjamin. Your f-f-f-friend April."

April smiles. "Do you like it?"

"Y-Y-Y-You think I'm bad?"

"Oh my gosh, no. That's not what I mean. I mean like you are someone who is cool and no one better mess with because you're such a bad dude. It's a good thing."

Benjamin smiles briefly. He runs his finger over the words "your friend April." He looks at her.

"Yes," April says, "you and me are friends. We're neighbors aren't we? Well, neighbors are supposed to be friends. You want to be my friend, don't you?"

Benjamin nods.

"Good. Now let's head home."

On the drive April lets Benjamin nap. Occasionally she looks at him. *Yep, I'll bet he doesn't fit in. Kids have probably always made fun of him, his looks, his weight, and especially his stuttering. Then he has to come home to a completely dysfunctional situation. As limited as Tucker was with her parenting of us, she was always there for us and was consistent in how she treated us. I could always count on Tucker. But does Benjamin have anyone he can count on?*

As a tear, carrying her own emotional pain, rolls down her cheek, she feels completely overwhelmed with sympathy for Benjamin. "Things are going to be better for you now that I'm living beside you," she says softly. "I'm not going to let the world drive you into the ground and crush you. I promise, I will make a difference in your life, or my name isn't April Tucker."

Benjamin opens his eyes and looks at her. "Huh?"

"Nothing. I was just talking to myself. I do that sometimes. You'll just have to ignore me." She negotiates her way around the Dresden Square. "I guess I'm going to have to get your insurance card from your mother and then bring this prescription back to one of the drug stores to get it filled. I mean, you don't have your card with you, do you?"

"I d-d-d-don't know anything about that."

"Never mind. Don't worry about it."

A few minutes later, April pulls into the front yard of the McDaniel place. When Benjamin starts to open his door, she says, "No. You stay here. I'm going to get your insurance card, then take you up to Tucker's."

Benjamin looks at his house and says, "Tucker's?"

"Yes. I want to show you my Autoharp." *And I want to make sure you actually get to rest instead of having to be nursemaid to your mother and parent to your brother and sister.*

"B-B-B-But Mama may n-n-n-need some help."

"I'll see if she's okay. If she needs something, I'll take care of it. Just sit tight." April gets out of the truck and makes her way to the house.

Shady Green finishes nailing a board and stands up as she approaches. "Ah 'us abou got the 'orch 'ixed up."

"I can see you have," April says. "You're doing a great job." Once inside the house, she goes directly to Joyce's bedroom. Without knocking, she opens the door and steps inside.

Joyce is propped in bed watching Elvis gyrate on her TV screen. She doesn't acknowledge the interruption.

"Oh good grief," April says as she walks over and turns off the TV.

"Turn that back on," Joyce says.

"Is this your life?" April asks. "Being in love with a dead man? Watching him over and over? The operative word here would be obsession, don't you think?"

"You don't understand," Joyce says as she reaches for her pack of cigarettes.

"I know. You have cancer. But you don't care enough about it to quit smoking. Maybe you want to have cancer so you can continue neglecting your children." She moves to the light switch and turns on the overhead light. Only two of the five bulbs in the fixture are burning. "Look, I came here to get Benjamin's insurance card. I need to get his pain medicine filled."

Putting her hand on her throat, Joyce says, "B.J. won't like that."

"Once again, you're focused on the wrong thing, woman. The question you should be asking is, 'What's wrong with Benjamin?' But instead, you're just thinking of yourself and any complication it

265

might be for you." April feels her disgust shifting and turning into anger. "Where's his card?"

Joyce points a bony finger toward her bedside table. "It's there in my billfold."

April steps to the table. Multiple prescription bottles are resting on it. As she reaches for the billfold, she glances at some of the labels. When she picks up the billfold, she also palms the bottle of hydrocodone.

April rifles through the cards in the billfold until she finds one with Benjamin's name on it. Extracting it, she says, "This is what I need."

"Could you get me something to drink?" Joyce says weakly.

April is about to tell her no when she remembers her promise to Benjamin. "I'll get you some water," she says to Joyce. On her way to the kitchen she stuffs the pill bottle in her pocket. She hears Shady Green bang a ladder against the edge of the house then begin walking on the roof. A part of her is afraid that he could fall through the decaying roof and fall on top of her, injuring them both. "Be careful, Shady," she yells as loudly as she can, then moves quickly to get the water and takes it back to Joyce.

April hands the glass to Joyce and starts to leave, but she pauses and says, "By the way, your son broke bones in his hand and his fingers."

"Bennie's a quick healer," Joyce says. "He'll be fine in no time."

Let it go. Don't say anything. Just go. April leaves the house and gets in the truck. "You okay?" she asks.

"Is M-M-M-Mama okay?" Benjamin asks.

"She seems fine to me. She's watching an Elvis movie. I got her a drink of water." As he's talking, April is backing the truck

266

away from the house. Putting the truck in drive, she drives the few hundred yards to Tucker's.

April and Benjamin walk into the house. When she sees no one, April calls out, "Tucker? Smiley? Anybody home?" Her questions are met with silence. "They must be at the barn. Go ahead and have a seat on the couch," she says to Benjamin. "Are you hungry or thirsty or both?"

Benjamin looks at the spotless, relatively new couch and hesitates.

April notices. "Go ahead," she urges him, "make yourself comfortable. I'm going to fix you a sandwich and something to drink, then I'll run to town to get your prescription filled."

Benjamin eases himself onto the couch. He rubs his hand over the textured material.

April works on fixing the food while still keeping an eye on Benjamin. Once it's ready, she carries the plate of food and drink to him. Setting the drink on the end table, she says, "I hope you like ham and cheese."

Benjamin takes a big bite of the sandwich and chews hungrily.

"I'll take that as a yes," April says with a smile. "I'm going to leave you here, okay? The bathroom is right down that hallway. Make yourself at home."

"M-M-M-Maybe I should g-g-g-go with you."

"No. You need to rest and relax. I won't be gone long." April turns and walks out of the house.

Benjamin eats a couple more bites of his sandwiches and washes them down with the glass of iced tea. He scans the room while absorbing the silence of the house. His eyes stop on a wall covered with photographs. Carrying his sandwich with him, he walks over to it to exam the photographs more closely. All the photographs are of people. He touches a recent photograph of April and decides the other pictures of a young, blonde-haired girl are of April while growing up. Benjamin has seen pictures of himself, but only those taken by school photographers, none of which were ever bought or displayed by his mother.

He walks slowly along the wall looking at pictures of a wedding, featuring a large, bearded man, and pictures of someone who is racially mixed. He looks down the hallway, then back toward the living room. Taking small steps, he moves slowly down the hallway. He passes a bedroom, then the bathroom, until finally he arrives at a bedroom at the end of the hallway.

Standing at the threshold, he leans his head in to look around. The walls are a pale yellow and the sun is streaming through the windows. There are a pair of jeans and a shirt draped across a small chair that is sitting in front of a mirror with light bulbs all around its edge. Brilliant colored posters adorn the walls. Benjamin feels the room pulling him in. His body sways as he weighs his urge to step inside against his fear of getting into trouble. He takes a bite of his sandwich.

Lifting his foot high, he takes an exaggerated step into the room. He works his way around the room, inspecting the posters. Some of them are of musicians holding guitars. Others have catchy phrases on them surrounded by flowers and birds and butterflies. Arriving at the chair in front of the lighted mirror, he touches the shirt.

"Stop right there! An' don't move an' inch!" a voice shouts at him from the doorway of the bedroom.

Benjamin drops what's left of his sandwich and spins around. Standing in the doorway, Tucker is pointing a shotgun at him.

Chapter Forty-one

Cassie stands at Blake's locker, having retrieved her books for first period class. She looks down the hallway toward Benjamin's locker. She knows the bus he rides to school has already arrived, deposited its cargo, and left. But Benjamin hasn't shown up at his locker, a morning ritual with him. Cassie looks up at the clock hanging from the ceiling, gauging how much time is left before the bell rings to start class.

Blake appears from around the corner. "I got everything smoothed out with Coach for missing early practice this morning. I'll have to run some extra wind sprints but it's worth it to drive you to school this morning." He flashes a smile at her.

"Uh-huh," Cassie says absent mindedly while continuing to look down the hallway.

Blake follows her line of sight. "Hey, did you hear the latest about Stutter Boy?"

Cassie snaps her head around and fixes Blake with a fiery stare. "He is a person, a person with a name. His name is Benjamin."

Blake holds up his hands. "Whoa, no harm meant. Whatever you say. It's Benjamin."

Suddenly the jarring ring of the bell drowns out what Blake says next.

They begin hurrying toward their classroom. "What about Benjamin?" Cassie asks.

Blake answers her as they walk through the doorway of the classroom. "He tried to kill Mark O'Riley yesterday."

Cassie stops in her tracks. A girl who was following closely behind her runs into her. They both stumble and their books and papers scatter across the floor.

As they hurriedly gather up their things, the teacher, Ms. Shoulders, says, "That's quite a dramatic entrance, truly audience grabbing. But this is not drama class and I'm not interested in starting my class that way. If you wouldn't cut the time so close, you could have avoided this gaffe in your behavior. Now please take your seats."

Cassie quickly moves to her desk, certain that her face is as red as a fire engine. She opens her book and bends over it, as if intently studying it. But she neither sees the words nor cares about them. Blake's comment about Benjamin trying to kill Mark has sent her into a tailspin. Her mind races to imagine where such an encounter would have taken place. How did he try to kill him? What happened? And where is Benjamin now?

Not for the first time since she decided to share a locker with Blake, a wave of guilt washes over her. *I know Benjamin feels like I abandoned him.* The twin voices of the proverbial good angel and bad angel plague her with opposite views and pieces of advice. She wrestled with them all night last night, getting very little sleep.

However, this new development is making it harder for her to hear the voice that has told her there's nothing wrong in cleaning out her locker and joining Blake. What keeps pressing against her is, where is Benjamin now? Was he arrested? Is he in juvenile detention somewhere? Did Mark hurt him, putting him in the hospital?

Suddenly her fear and guilt-ridden mind seizes upon a terrifying thought: Has Benjamin run away? She almost jumps up and runs out of the classroom but doesn't want to draw any extra attention to herself. So she forces herself to wait until the end of class. When the bell rings she practically races out of the room into the crowded hallway.

Out of nowhere someone grabs her arm and spins her around. She finds herself face to face with Mark O'Riley. His dark features and clothing immediately put her in mind of a vampire.

He gives her a sinister grin. "Did you hear about your retarded friend?"

The shock of this encounter momentarily seizes up Cassie, and she says nothing.

"He really is psycho," Mark says. "You better stay away from him. And this jock you've decided to let paw you like you're his pet is only two notches above him." He puts his face within inches of hers. "I'm the only one for you. The sooner you accept that, the better off everyone will be."

Finally a surge of adrenalin releases Cassie from her temporary paralysis. She draws her fist back and punches him in the face with all her might.

The surprise and force of her blow makes Mark stagger backward.

Before he can regain his balance, Cassie turns around and runs toward the office. Once inside, she gasps to the secretary, "I need to see Mr. Clelland now."

"Let me see if he's busy." The secretary disappears briefly, then returns. "Go on in," she says to Cassie.

As soon as Cassie enters the principal's office, she says, "Where is Benjamin Trevathan? Is he okay?"

Mr. Clelland raises his eyebrows. "It's Cassie, isn't it?"

"Yes sir."

"Why don't you have a seat?" He motions toward a chair.

Her upbringing won't allow her to disobey someone in authority, so Cassie sits down.

"Would you mind telling me what your relationship is with Benjamin?"

The question makes Cassie feel like the principal has picked her up and pinned her to a bulletin board with a tack. She's never tried to put into words what she and Benjamin are to each other. "Well," she says slowly, "he and I ride the same bus, you see. And he and I started to school here at about the same time. We were both new kids in school."

Cassie stops.

Mr. Clelland says, "Go on."

Cassie squirms in her chair. "Won't you just tell me if Benjamin is okay?"

"So you and Benjamin ride the same bus and are both new to our school. Is that it?"

Cassie looks down. "I've tried to be nice to him. He's always been picked on by others. I feel sorry for him."

"I see," Mr. Clelland says. "The last time you were in here it was over an incident on the bus involving you and him and Mark O'Riley. Benjamin was trying to defend you. He was afraid you were going to get hurt. What do you think that says about how Benjamin feels about you?"

"I'm not sure," Cassie hesitates. "I guess he thinks we're friends."

"Are you?"

Cassie thinks about Blake and about Courtney and Stefanie's invitation to try out for cheerleader. She decides to walk the razor's edge with her answer, "I try to be friendly with everyone. I don't think there's anything wrong with that."

Mr. Clelland looks at her for a moment, then says, "I see. Did you ride the bus home yesterday afternoon?"

"No sir."

He considers her again. Finally he says, "Well I don't know where Benjamin is. He didn't come to school today. There was another incident on the bus between him and Mark. According to both Mark and the bus driver, Benjamin threatened to kill Mark and attacked him."

"Mark's a trouble maker," Cassie says.

"I won't disagree with that. But Benjamin is a troubled kid. He's not your average kid. He has special needs."

Cassie feels herself wanting to wriggle free from being pinned to the bulletin board and jump to Benjamin's defense. Instead, she weighs her options and their consequences. "I don't like to see anyone picked on."

"Cassie," Mr. Clelland says, "you would never have come bursting in here if you didn't care about Benjamin. I'm not certain what that means, but you need to be really careful with him. It would be very easy for him to misinterpret your words and actions, to read more into them than is really there."

Cassie cocks her head to one side. "Are you telling me that I shouldn't be friends, I mean act friendly toward him?"

"I'm not telling you what to do. You're a bright student. You figure it out."

Chapter Forty-two

April walks in the house carrying Benjamin's medicine and discovers him lying on the couch with a wash cloth on his forehead. Tucker is sitting on the edge of the couch beside him. "What in the world happened?!" April exclaims.

"Lord, am I glad you're back," Tucker says.

Benjamin starts to sit up, but Tucker puts her hand on his chest. "Just stay still," she tells him.

"What's wrong with him?" April asks.

"It was just a misunderstandin'. I come t' th' house from th' barn, an' when I walked in I felt like somebody was in th' house. Then I heard th' floor squeakin' toward th' end of th' hallway, so I got m' shotgun."

"Oh my gosh, Tucker. You didn't."

"Well how was I t' know it was Benjamin? I thought somebody had broke in. It wouldn't be th' first time it happened, you know."

"So what did you do?"

"I eased down th' hallway an' found him in yore bedroom. His back was to me. I pointed m' gun at him an' told him not t' move. When he spun 'round an' saw me with a gun, he passed out an' hit his head on yore table."

April kneels down beside Benjamin.

He slides the wash cloth down until it covers his eyes.

"Ben," April says, "are you all right? I'm so sorry this happened."

Benjamin doesn't respond.

"What happened to the boy's arm?" Smiley asks from the kitchen.

"An' what was he doin' in here?" Tucker asks. Pointing at the sack from the drug store, she asks, "What's that for? Where've y' been? I thought you an' Shady Green was goin' t' work on that house down there today."

April stands up. "All right, let me fill you in. I went and picked up Shady and some lumber from the Lumber Barn. When we got to their house and began unloading the wood, Benjamin's dad came outside and starting mouthing off like an ass. Benjamin came out, too. That's when I noticed that his hand was swollen like it had been stung by a yellow jacket and two of his fingers were bent unnaturally. I found out it happened to him yesterday."

"Yesterday?!" Tucker exclaims.

"Exactly. But had anyone done anything about it? Did his mother even know he was hurt?"

"I'm going to guess the answer to both those questions is no," Smiley says.

"Right again," April says. "I decided to take him to the hospital emergency room. That's where he got the cast. They gave him a prescription for pain medicine and that's what's in this bag. The reason he was in our house is because I wanted him to be able to rest and relax. Down at his house he's the mother and father to both the kids and his mom. I fixed him a sandwich and something to drink and told him to make himself at home while I ran to town to get his medicine."

She looks down at Benjamin who has lifted one corner of the washcloth so that he can see her. When he notices her looking at him, he drops the corner back into place. April lifts the cloth off his head. "Let me see, Benjamin."

There is a red knot just above his right eyebrow. There's also some darker bruising across his forehead.

"Will you bring him some water?" April asks Smiley.

Smiley fills a glass and brings it to her.

"Do you feel like sitting up?" she asks Benjamin.

Without the use of both arms and hands, Benjamin struggles but finally rights himself into a sitting position.

"Is your head hurting?" she asks.

"M-M-M-Mama says I h-h-h-have a soft heart and h-h-h-hard head."

Opening the bottle of pills, April hands him one. "Why don't you take one of these? It'll help."

Benjamin complies without protest.

"Somebody ought t' go tell his mom that he's all right," Tucker suggests.

April scoffs at the idea. "Do you really think she cares?"

"April! That ain't no way t' talk about th' boy's mother in front of him."

"Why not? It's the truth, and he knows it. Weren't you always truthful when you talked to me, August, and March about our mother, Maisy?"

"That ain't quite th' same thing."

"That's exactly the same thing," April counters. "Every child deserves to know the truth, for someone to be honest with him and not perpetuate the lies."

"I ain't gonna argue with y'."

"Tucker, you did the right thing. My brothers and I love you and appreciate you for that, even if it wasn't what we wanted to hear."

The two of them stare at each other. Tears well up in Tucker's eyes. She swipes at them and says, "You do what y' thinks best. He's yore project."

"I told Benjamin about my problems with speaking and how music was the key that unlocked my tongue. Then I mentioned Mel Tillis to him and said that maybe I could help him with music like Ella did with me."

"That's a right friendly gesture," Smiley says. "It always amazed me to listen to Mel Tillis sing and then see him interviewed on TV He was a bad stutterer."

Benjamin's head has been on a pivot keeping up with all the conversation swirling around him. "As b-b-b-bad as m-m-m-me?" he asks.

"Every bit as bad," April answers.

"Y' know," Tucker admits, "y' might be on t' somethin'. It could work."

"I'm going to get out my Autoharp. Smiley, you go get your banjo and let's introduce Benjamin to our kind of music."

She hurries down the hallway to her bedroom and Smiley disappears into his. They return to the living room carrying their instrument cases. April sits down beside Benjamin while Smiley brings in a chair from the kitchen to sit in.

As April unsnaps the fasteners on her case, Benjamin smiles and says, "I have a t-t-t-treasure box, t-t-t-too."

April looks at him. "Treasure box?"

"It's what I k-k-k-keep my M-M-M-Matchbox cars in."

"Oh, right." She opens the lid and lifts the Autoharp from its padded bed. Setting the case on the floor, she lays the Autoharp on her lap.

Benjamin stares wide-eyed.

Suddenly, Smiley gives his banjo a loud strum.

Benjamin nearly jumps off the couch.

"Sorry, Ben," Smiley says. "Didn't mean to scare you. This old banjo has got a pretty loud voice."

April presses some keys and strums her Autoharp.

The sweet, mellow sound turns Benjamin's head in her direction, and he smiles. "Pretty," he says.

April runs through several chords in the key of G, deftly pressing the keys and strumming with her finger picks.

Smiley listens and strums softly along with her, pausing occasionally and turning a tuning peg. He tilts his head so his ear is facing more toward the head of his banjo. Finally satisfied with his tuning job, he looks at April and grins. "You ready?"

April's eyes sparkle. "I'm ready if you are."

"What about a little John Hardy?"

"Let 'er rip. I'll be right behind you."

The fingers of Smiley's right hand start picking so fast that they are a blur and his left hand dances up and down the neck of his banjo.

April strums with a rhythm to match his.

They both glance down at what they are doing occasionally, but mostly smile back at each other.

Both of Benjamin's feet start tapping in rhythm with the song. Then he starts slapping his thigh with his good hand. His smile reaches from ear to ear.

Tucker joins him by clapping her hands in time to the music.

After a few minutes, Smiley does a quick turn around of the last phrase of the song, and he and April end the song on the same stroke.

"Whoo-eeee!" Smiley says.

"Yee-haw!" Benjamin exclaims.

Smiley, April, and Tucker laugh at their young guest's enthusiasm and unbridled joy.

"I've been missing you," Smiley says to April. "I don't hardly ever get my banjo out anymore."

"Well that's going to change," April says. "We're going to start practicing regular. Maybe even learn some new songs."

"Lordy," Tucker says, "that means I'll have t' git me some earplugs."

"You know you love it," April laughs. "Hey, let's play something and you sing, Tucker."

"I ain't in no mood t' sing."

April frowns at her and gives a slight nod toward Benjamin.

Tucker looks at her, then at Benjamin. "Oh, right," she says. "I changed m' mind. I do feel like singin' one. What about 'Ol' Dan Tucker'?"

"Kick it off, Smiley," April urges her playing partner.

Smiley does a short introduction, then nods at Tucker who sings:

Old Dan Tucker was a fine old man

He washed his face in a frying pan

He combed his hair with a wagon wheel

And died of a toothache in his heel

Get out the way old Dan Tucker

You're too late to git your supper

Supper's gone and dinner cookin'

Old Dan Tucker's just a-standin' there lookin'.

Looking at April, Tucker says, "Come on, April. Sing with me."

April joins her, singing a high harmony.

Old Dan Tucker's a-comin' to town

Riding a billy-goat and leading a hound

The hound dog barked and billy-goat jumped

Throwed Dan Tucker right straddlin' a stump.

Get out the way old Dan Tucker

You're too late to git your supper

Supper's gone and dinner cookin'

Old Dan Tucker's just a-standin' there lookin'.

Without a prompting, Smiley joins in the next verse, singing bass.

I come to town the other night

To hear a noise and see the fight

The watchman feet was a-running around

Crying "Old Dan Tucker's come to Town."

Get out the way old Dan Tucker

You're too late to git your supper

Supper's gone and dinner cookin'

Old Dan Tucker's just a-standin' there lookin'.

"Okay, Benjamin," April calls to him, "help us sing the chorus one more time."

April and Smiley continue strumming, marking time, waiting for Benjamin to start. He looks uncertainly at April, and she nods at him and mouths the words of the first line.

Benjamin sings:

G-G-G-Get out the way old D-D-D-Dan T-T-T-Tucker

April tries to make her strumming match Benjamin's irregular cadence while at the same time Smiley plays the song as it is supposed to be sung. The result of them trying to take the song in opposite directions has the effect of a wagon wheel falling off a wagon. The song lurches along until they both finally stop playing.

When they stop, Benjamin drops his head and his shoulders droop. "I-I-I-I knew it w-w-w-wouldn't work."

"Are you kidding me?" April says quickly. "That's your first time to even try. You haven't practiced any."

"April's right," Tucker agrees. "Ain't nobody good at nothin' 'til they've took th' time t' practice a whole lot. I don't care whether it's singin', playin' an instrument, or drivin' a tractor. It all takes practice. You'll see. April's gonna work with you an' help y' learn."

Just then there is a knock on the door.

Tucker rises from her recliner and walks to the door. Opening it, she finds Alexander and Maria standing there holding hands.

"We can't find Benjamin," Alexander says.

Maria says, "And we're hungry."

Chapter Forty-three

In mid-May, the day after getting his cast removed, Benjamin stands in his front yard watching Alexander and Maria playing some sort of imaginary game. Even though he's watching them, his mind is focused on the fact that there is no food in the house again. B.J. hasn't been around in nearly a month, and Benjamin wonders if this time he isn't coming back.

The window to his mother's bedroom is open. As spring's warm, late afternoon breeze blows in, Elvis's voice flows out. He is singing "Let Us Pray." Benjamin mouths the words along with him. On the phrase "when strangers reach out for your hand" he thinks about April.

Even though he's not making any progress with his singing, he enjoys practicing and being with her. Her long blond hair always puts him in mind of the story of Rapunzel. He imagines April letting her hair down for him to climb and escape his repetitive, colorless life. When she touches his hand to show him how to play her Autoharp, it feels like electricity running through him. There are even times that he has sexual thoughts about her. He feels himself blushing at the memory.

"Bennie!" Maria's call turns his attention to her.

"What?" he answers.

"Come play hide-and-seek with us. You be 'it' and we'll hide."

"Okay. What are th-th-th-the rules? Wh-Wh-Wh-Where can you hide?"

"You count to fifty by ones," Alexander says. "We have to stay in the yard and no going in the house."

"What is home b-b-b-base?"

"The maple tree," Maria answers. She's dancing up and down, eager to start the game.

Benjamin closes his eyes and starts counting aloud.

Maria squeals and yells, "No peeking!"

When Benjamin gets to the number fifty, he opens his eyes and hollers, "Ready or n-n-n-not here I c-c-c-come." He knows where Maria will be hiding because she always hides in the same place. But he doesn't go directly to the cedar tree in the back yard, for part of the fun in the game is thinking you can't be found.

He wanders aimlessly, saying aloud, "Where is M-M-M-Maria? I can't f-f-f-find her." After a few minutes, he lets his route meander toward the cedar tree. He hears her giggle from the other side of the tree. When he is close he says, "I see M-M-M-Maria behind the cedar t-t-t-tree."

Maria squeals again and runs toward the maple tree in the front yard.

Benjamin chugs along after her but doesn't intend to tag her, even if he could catch her. He calls out, "I'm g-g-g-going to get you."

Maria's high-pitched squeal and laughter is his reward.

As he comes around the corner of the house, Maria is standing with her hand on the tree. "Home free! Home free!" she says.

Benjamin arrives at the tree and tries to catch his breath. "Y-Y-Y-You're too fast for m-m-m-me. Now come with m-m-m-me and help me f-f-f-find Alexander."

"I know where he is," Maria says as she grabs his hand and pulls.

Benjamin allows her to lead him around the house and toward an old tool shed. The entire structure leans so far to one side that no one understands why it hasn't collapsed. The door hangs askew on one hinge.

Maria puts her finger on her lips signaling Benjamin to be quiet.

Following her lead, Benjamin tiptoes with her toward the back of the shed.

At the edge of the building, Maria stops and points toward the back. She silently mouths, "He's back there."

Benjamin steps past her and then jumps to where he can see the back of the building. "I see – " His words are cut off because no one is there.

Maria joins him and says, "I saw him go behind here."

They stand there a moment, scanning what parts of the back yard they can see.

Maria whispers, "Maybe he went inside the shed."

"We're not s-s-s-supposed to g-g-g-go in there."

"I know. But he might have."

They walk to the front of the shed. Standing back from the doorway, they try to see inside the black interior.

"It's scary looking," Maria says. As she is saying it, she is pushing Benjamin toward the doorway, wanting him to catch Alexander, hoping to get scared, but not wanting the imaginary boogey man to get her.

Benjamin gets to the doorway and leans his head inside. He opens his eyes wide as they try to adjust to the inky blackness. The musty smell of the dirt floor fills his nostrils. Gradually, shadowy shapes begin to reveal themselves. What little light that comes in through the doorway occasionally glints back at Benjamin, but exactly what it is reflecting off of Benjamin cannot discern. He holds his breath and listens.

Maria squeezes Benjamin's hand, steps from behind him, and peers inside the shed.

There is a scraping sound from the back of the shed.

"What was that?" Maria whispers.

"Is th-th-th-that you, Alexander?" Benjamin says in a loud whisper.

Suddenly there is a sound of metal objects banging into each other.

Maria screams.

Something slams into Benjamin, and he loses his balance, stumbling backward and pulling Maria with him into the fading sunlight.

"You have to tag me before I tag home!" Alexander yells as he runs past them.

"It's him! It's him!" Maria says excitedly. "Tag him!"

By the time Benjamin regains his balance and jogs after Alexander, Alexander is already streaking around the front corner of the house.

Benjamin and Maria hear Alexander with his sing-song call, "Ollie, Ollie oxen free!"

When they join their brother underneath the maple tree, Maria says, "Weren't you scared to hide in the shed?"

"Heck no," Alexander boasts. "I knew you wouldn't come in there looking for me."

"Against the r-r-r-rules," Benjamin say.

"Uh-uh," Alexander counters. "We didn't say anything about a rule against going in the shed."

"M-M-M-Mama's rule."

"That's right," Maria agrees. "Mama says we're not to go in that old shed. Says it's dangerous."

Before Alexander can give a counter argument, headlights strike them. The three of them turn to look at a vehicle pulling into their yard. The headlights are too bright for them to tell who is in it.

It slows to a stop and the passenger door opens. A staggering figure appears in the flood of headlights. The vehicle backs out of the yard and heads back in the direction it came from. In the pale light of dusk the children recognize B.J. swaying back and forth.

"It's Daddy," Maria says quietly.

"Daddy!" Alexander yells. He runs toward his father and grabs him around his thighs. For the second time this evening, Alexander's enthusiasm results in someone losing their balance. However, this time it's due to B.J.'s inebriated condition.

B.J. falls to the ground. With slurred speech, he swears and starts swinging at an imaginary opponent. One of his fists catches Alexander on the shoulder, knocking him to the ground.

"Alexander," Maria cries. Without hesitation she runs to the aid of her brother.

Benjamin tries to grab and stop her, but he's not quick enough.

Maria goes to her knees beside Alexander. "Are you okay?" she asks.

B.J. makes his way to his feet. He sees the children on the ground and kicks at them. His boot strikes Maria in the side. She screams in pain and falls on top of Alexander.

Like a raging bull, Benjamin runs toward B.J. He hits him in the stomach with his shoulder. B.J. is driven back a step but he puts his hand on top of Benjamin's head, jerks his knee up, and smashes Benjamin's nose. Blood streams down over Benjamin's mouth. He spits against the warm flood and swings his arm and fists like a windmill. One of his haymakers connects against B.J.'s jaw, knocking his stepfather to his knees.

"You've done it now, you little shit," B.J. says in an ominous tone.

Both Alexander and Maria jump up and grab their father's hands as he is standing up. "Stop it!" they cry together.

B.J. grips Maria's hand and, picking her up off the ground, slings her to the side. She hits the ground without making a sound.

B.J. then jerks his hand away from Alexander and slaps him hard enough that it drives him to the ground.

Benjamin kicks B.J. in the knee and hits him in the side.

"Come on, fat boy retard," B.J. retorts. "You've had this coming for a long time." He slams his fist against the side of Benjamin's face.

A burst of stars fills Benjamin's field of vision. B.J.'s next blow hits Benjamin in his soft abdomen. He doubles over as all the air explodes out of him. A vicious upper cut splits Benjamin's cheek open and snaps his head backwards. Like a tree that is being felled by a lumber man, Benjamin sways slowly for a moment, then falls directly on his face. Everything goes black.

When Benjamin regains consciousness, he feels someone tugging on him and hears indistinct voices. Night has fallen. He tastes dirt in his mouth mixed with the metallic taste of blood. The voices begin to come into focus. It is Alexander and Maria.

"Bennie, get up," Alexander says.

"Please, Bennie," Maria pleads, "you've got to be okay."

Benjamin gets up on his all-fours and starts to stand, but sharp pains throughout his body cause him to choose a sitting position. "Where is he?" he asks.

"He went inside," Alexander answers. "I think he's asleep."

Benjamin touches his burning cheek and winces. "How l-l-l-long have I laid here?"

"A long time," Maria answers. "I thought you were dead." She begins to weep.

"Are y-y-y-you all okay?"

"My head hurts," Maria says.

"I'm okay," Alexander boasts. "But you're hurt bad."

Benjamin feels the weight of the front of his blood-soaked shirt against his chest. "W-W-W-We need to go inside and g-g-g-get cleaned up."

"I'm afraid to go inside," Maria pleads.

"It's not safe," Alexander says.

Benjamin considers their comments and their options.

"What are we going to do?" Alexander asks.

"We're g-g-g-going to Tucker's."

Chapter Forty-four

"G'night, April," Tucker says as she turns out the light in April's bedroom.

"Goodnight, Tucker," April replies. "I love you."

"An' I love you."

Tucker heads down the hallway, crosses through the living room and heads toward her bedroom. Just then there is a knock on the front door. Tucker stops and listens, thinking she must be mistaken. Again, there is a distinct knock on the door.

Tucker turns on the kitchen light and the porch light, then opens the front door. Standing under the glare of her porch light is Benjamin, covered in blood, with Alexander and Maria at his side. "Oh my lord!" Tucker exclaims. "What's happened?!"

"Daddy hurt Bennie," Maria says quietly.

"W-W-W-We n-n-n-need to s-s-s-stay here tonight," Benjamin says.

"Quick," Tucker says, "git inside here. Smiley! April!" she yells. "Git in here quick."

The children shuffle in through the door.

"Come sit here in th' kitchen where I can see about y'," Tucker says. She turns a stove eye on high, fills a pot with water and sets it on the stove to heat.

April comes into the kitchen. Her swollen belly is peeking out from under her t-shirt. She sees the backs of the children and says, "What in the world are you all doing up here this late at night?"

When they turn around and April sees Benjamin's bloodied face and shirt, she screams.

"What's all this commotion?" Smiley says as he steps into the kitchen. When he sees the ghoulish spectacle, he says, "Lord Jesus, what has happened?"

"Their ol' man done this to 'em," Tucker explains as she kneels down in front of Benjamin. "Sit in th' chair an' let me see."

Benjamin obeys and winces when he sits.

"Point t' where you're hurtin'."

Benjamin points at his nose, then his cheek, then his stomach.

"Did B.J. use a knife?" April asks. "Did he cut you?"

Benjamin shakes his head.

"All that blood must have come from his nose," Smiley says.

"But yore cheek is laid open, Benjamin," Tucker says. "How'd that happen?"

Benjamin shrugs his shoulders.

"Take his shirt off'n him," Tucker instructs, motioning to April.

April takes hold of the bottom of his shirt. "Lift your arms over your head, Benjamin, so I can get this off you."

Benjamin starts to lift his arms, but grunts in pain and drops them back down.

"Git some scissors an' cut it off," Tucker says. She grabs a dish towel and soaks it with the warm water.

As April looks for the scissors in a drawer, Benjamin says, "H-H-H-He h-h-h-hurt them, t-t-t-too."

Tucker gives a sound like a growl.

Smiley eases Alexander and Maria to some chairs. He pulls up another chair and says, "What did he do to you?"

Maria begins to cry and put her hand on her side. "He kicked me and threw me through the air. My side hurts."

"He hurt my face and my shoulder," Alexander says.

"Okay," Smiley says, "I'm going to fix an ice pack for both of you. That will help."

The sound of April snipping through Benjamin's shirt fills the silence.

Once the shirt is off him, Tucker says, "Throw it in th' trash." She dabs at him with the damp towel. She wipes the blood off his chin and his mouth. "I ain't gonna touch yore nose 'cause it'll hurt like hell."

She turns her attention to the gash in Benjamin's cheek. "April, git me some alkyhol, some ointment, and some o' them buttiefly closures."

April immediately heads toward the bathroom to get the supplies.

Tucker dabs at the blood around the wound. Fresh blood oozes in response to her pressure. "That there's a bad cut," she mutters. Again something like the sound of a growl comes from her.

Smiley says to Alexander and Maria, "Now take this and hold against where it hurts. It'll make the swelling go down, and it'll help the pain."

Alexander gingerly touches his face with the ice pack while Maria holds hers against the side that B.J. kicked.

"Something's got to be done about this," Smiley whispers to Tucker.

"Don't you worry," Tucker whispers back through clenched teeth. "Somethin's gonna be done."

April returns and hands the alcohol to Tucker.

"Now Benjamin," Tucker says, "this is gonna sting like th' dickens, so grit yore teeth." She holds the towel underneath his cut, then tips the bottle and pours alcohol into the wound.

The only indication he gives that he feels anything is by closing his eyes.

"You're one tough kid," Tucker says. Then, whispering loud enough for everyone to hear, she says, "Ol' Smiley over there would've howled an' carried on, if I done th' same thing t' him."

Benjamin grins.

"What are you talking about, silly woman?" Smiley asks.

Tucker ignores him as she dabs ointment on Benjamin's cheek. "Now, April, you need t' push th' sides of this cut t'gether so I can put this closure on."

April sucks a breath through her teeth as she cringes at her assignment. "I'm sorry if this hurts," she says as she pushes the gash closed.

Tucker deftly applies the butterfly closures along the length of the cut. "Now, that looks better."

Benjamin begins shivering.

"Go git th' boy one o' yore shirts," Tucker says to Smiley. "Ever'body come in t' th' livin' room where it's more comfortable."

Once everyone is seated and Smiley helps Benjamin put on his shirt, Tucker says, "Now then, April, you call th' sheriff's office an' tell 'em t' come right up here t' th' house." She steps over to the corner behind her recliner and lifts her axe handle from its resting place. "While you do that, I'm gonna pay a visit down t' th' McDaniel place."

"No!" Benjamin says forcefully. "H-H-H-He'll hurt you."

"Don't you worry," Tucker says, "he don't stand a chance."

"Tucker," Smiley says.

She looks at him and they stare at each other for a moment.

"Just don't be foolish," Smiley concludes.

"What's that sayin'?" Tucker asks. "Ain't no fool like a old fool?" She wheels around, grabs her truck keys off the hook, and goes out the front door.

Pitching her axe handle onto the seat beside her, Tucker gets in her truck and heads down the road. Before pulling into the yard, she turns out her headlights, cuts the engine and coasts in silently. She grabs her weapon and gets out of the truck, easing the door shut.

Moving a silently as a cat, she gets to the front door. She lifts her leg and kicks it. The door explodes inward. Hinges and splinters of wood fly through the air.

A small cry of fear comes from the main bedroom. A soft light clicks on and light spills from the room into the living room.

Tucker strides directly to the bedroom and shoves the door open. Its doorknob bangs against the wall.

Joyce is sitting up in bed with a look of terror etched on her face. B.J. lies beside her, face down on top of the covers. "Don't hurt me," Joyce says.

"Then git outta that bed," Tucker says.

"But I got the cancer," Joyce says feebly.

"Then stay in bed an' take yore medicine like this sorry piece of trash you live with."

Joyce quickly slides out of the bed and takes a position in a far corner of the room.

Tucker pokes B.J. with the axe handle. "Wake up," she says.

"He's passed out," Joyce says from her corner. "You won't be able to wake him."

"Whatever you say," Tucker says. She pulls one edge of the bed sheet out from under the mattress and throws it over B.J. Then she walks to the other side of the bed and pulls the other edge of the sheet out. She makes a cocoon of the sheet, wrapping B.J. inside. "Now then," she says to the still form, "what I wish was that you was awake so's you'd know exactly what happened t' you an' who did it. But I can't have ever'thing th' way I want it, I guess."

In the distance Tucker hears approaching sirens.

"I got just enough time t' finish this up." She turns and looks at Joyce. "Now y' watch what I'm doin', 'cause you should've done this yoreself a long time ago. This man ain't nothin' but a piece of trash. He don't deserve t' live, but it ain't my place t' kill him, though I'd like t'. Fer what he done t'night, I expect he's goin' t' jail fer a while. But that ain't enough punishment. He deserves t' git what he give." Tucker turns around, raises her axe handle and strikes B.J.'s shrouded form around his ankles. Again and again she strikes him, working her way up his body.

As she finishes and turns around, two sheriff's cars come racing by with their lights flashing and sirens blaring. "I'm done here," she says to Joyce.

Tucker gets in her truck, wipes the sweat from her face, and proceeds back home.

By the time she gets there, the deputies are already inside. One of them is on one knee in front of the children shining a flashlight on Benjamin's face.

Benjamin closes his eyes against the glare.

The deputy stands and faces Tucker. "Hello, Tucker. What's happened here?"

Tucker goes to her recliner and sits down heavily. "These kids' Pa beat 'em. They live down at th' McDaniel place. His name is B.J. Trevathan. He's still down there."

A female deputy says, "I'm going to take the kids outside and ask them some questions. Come on, kids."

The three children clutch each other with the desperation of those who believe they cannot trust anyone except each other. Benjamin points at April. "C-C-C-Can she go t-t-t-too?"

The female deputy and the other one look at each other. The man shrugs. The female deputy says, "I guess so."

They all go outside and follow the deputy to her cruiser. "Let's sit inside where it's warm."

When she finishes her interviews with the children, she ushers them back inside. "Can we talk?" she says to her male counterpart.

The two deputies go outside.

"What's going on now?" April asks.

"They're just comparing the children's story to the one that Tucker told," Smiley says. "They want to be sure they've got the story straight."

Maria yawns. "I'm getting sleepy," she says.

"Where are we going to sleep?" Alexander asks.

"You're sleepin' right here," Tucker says emphatically. "We'll make y' some pallets here in th' floor so's you can be t'gether. An' I'm gonna sleep right here in this chair t' make sure nothin' else happens to y' t'night."

The deputies re-enter the house. "You're sure this B.J. is still in his house?"

A tiny smile darts across Tucker's features. "I'm fer certain," she says.

"Can these kids stay here with you tonight?"

"You just try an' take 'em. We've done decided this is where they're stayin'."

"Tomorrow the Department of Children's Services will be out here. We've got to report all this, and they'll have to do their own investigation. We're going to go down there and arrest the perpetrator and take him in."

Chapter Forty-five

The next day, Tucker sits in her recliner listening to the social worker from the Department of Children's Services.

"We're going to let the children continue to live with their mother."

"Why can't they stay with me?" Tucker asks.

"Because you're not the mother. You're not even related to them. It's always best if families can stay together, as long as it's a healthy situation."

"Y' think that woman can provide a healthy situation? That oldest boy, Benjamin, has t' see after her an' his younger brother an' sister. It ain't right."

"I'll agree with you that it's less than ideal, but – "

"Less than ideal?!" Tucker interrupts. "That's a peculiar way t' describe what's been happenin' down there."

"So would you like us to take this woman's children away from her just because she's not a perfect parent?"

Tucker pauses at the question as she suddenly remembers efforts to take her grandchildren away from her when they were young just because she didn't have running water. Slowly, she shakes her head. "I reckon not. I just want them kids to be took care of."

"And so do we. That's why we're going to have someone start coming to her house on a regular basis to help her with some parenting skills and homemaker skills. We'll also working with the kids. We hope that this will help them improve."

"What about that man? Is he coming back, too?"

"He's not allowed to have any contact with any of them. I suspect he's going to serve some jail time over this. When he gets out, we'll find out what his plans are. He may end up leaving the area. But he'll still be prevented from seeing any of them until he's had extensive counseling."

"Th' kind of counselin' he needs is prob'bly against th' law. But I sure wouldn't mind givin' it to him."

The social worker has no comeback to Tucker's assertions. She stands up. "I guess I'll be leaving now. I appreciate your time."

As Tucker is seeing the social worker out of her house, another sedan is pulling up. The driver gets out and dons a Stetson hat. He touches the brim of his hat as he and the social worker pass each other. When he gets to the front porch, he says, "Good day, Tucker."

"Good day to you, too, Sheriff Harris," Tucker replies. Though she has a pretty good idea why he is here, she decides to let him spell it out. "What brings y' out t' these neck of th' woods?"

"I'm here for sort of the same reason that Elizabeth has been here." He nods toward the departing social worker. "Except that she's investigating what was done by B.J. Trevathan, while I'm here to find out what happened to Mr. Trevathan."

"Happened to? What do y' mean? Did y' see what he done t' them kids? Man like that is lower than a snake."

"I'm not going to disagree," the Sheriff says. "You might say I'm just doing what I'm supposed to do whenever there's been an alleged crime." He and Tucker exchange stares. "Did you see Mr. Trevathan last night?"

"Last night? Last night I was busy seein' t' those kids that he bloodied. They come up here scared fer their lives an' hurt bad. I had m' hands full tendin' t' them. We called yore office soon after they got here."

"My deputies said you weren't here when they arrived."

Tucker folds her arms across her chest. "I wasn't inside th' house at the exact moment they arrived, but I was soon after."

"Where were you when they got here?"

"I'd stepped out t' git somethin' out o' m' truck. Why all these questions? What're y' huntin' fer?"

"Mr. Trevathan received several injuries last night."

"Maybe yore deputies roughed him up."

"That's not what happened," the Sheriff snaps defensively. "He was in that shape when they found him in bed."

"What kind o' shape."

"They said he was beaten and bruised from head to toe."

Tucker grins openly.

"I don't suppose you would know anything about those wounds," the Sheriff says.

"Only that they're deserved," Tucker replies. "What about his wife? What did she say happened?"

"She said he came home like that."

"She oughta know." *Good fer you, Joyce!*

Sheriff Harris pushes his hat to the back of his head. "Maybe, but if that's the shape he came home in, how was he able to do so much damage to his children?"

Tucker shrugs. "That's somethin' that people smarter than me'll have t' figure out."

"You know what I think?"

"I don't care what y' think, but I don't guess that'll keep y' from tellin' me, so go ahead."

"I think that after those kids showed up at your house you went down there to administer what you viewed as deserving justice. You took that famous axe handle of yours and laid into him. You had just about enough time to do that between the time the call came into our office and when you showed up back at your house."

"Sounds like a pretty good theory," Tucker says. "Got any evidence t' back it up?"

"Not a shred. The matter's closed as far as I'm concerned. I told Mr. Trevathan that I'd look into his allegations, and I have. So I'll be on my way."

Just then, April steps outside. "Oh," she says, "I didn't know what you were doing out here. Hi, Sheriff."

"Hello, April. How's the pregnancy coming along? You know, I've always thought pregnant women were the most beautiful things on earth."

April puts her hands on her bulging belly. "The little fella is really growing. Thankfully I'm past the morning sickness stage."

"So it's going to be a little boy?" the sheriff asks.

"Yep. I'm pretty excited."

"Good for you. I've never told you this, but I think you are one courageous young woman. You are a survivor who has an incredible story to share with other girls."

"Thank you for saying that," April replies with a smile.

Tucker looks at the Sheriff and then at April, then back at the Sheriff.

Touching the brim of his hat, he says, "I'll be on my way. Ya'll have a good day."

The two women watch him pull away from the house. Tucker turns to face April. "He's a married man, y' know."

April frowns. "Of course I do. Why did you say that?"

"He seemed t' be takin' special note of y', an' you seemed t' like it."

"What's wrong with that?" April asks.

"I just don't want no one doin' nothin' that'll cause someone t' git hurt. That's all."

"Tucker! You think there's something going on between me and the Sheriff? My gosh! You must think I'm some kind of a fool. There's nothing going on between us. He was just being nice, and I liked it. You know, not everyone around town is that nice to me. I see women looking at me and whispering, wagging their gossiping tongues. That doesn't bother me. I've been talked about before. It's just that it gets old after a while. So quit jumping to conclusions. I really don't appreciate it." She turns and goes back inside the house, slamming the door behind her.

Tucker looks at the closed door. She considers following April inside and continuing the conversation but decides not to. *I ain't gonna be around ferever t' watch over her. She's got t' learn some things on her own.*

She lets out a big sigh then turns to look at the McDaniel house. Benjamin, Alexander, and Maria are outside in the yard, while Joyce is standing on the porch. It's the first time Tucker has seen the mother outside of the house. "I wonder," Tucker muses aloud. "Maybe I can do fer her what Ella McDade done fer me years ago. Ever'body needs a friend of some kind."

The sound of her own front door opening draws Tucker's attention.

Smiley Carter joins her on the porch. "What in the world has got April so upset? She came in the house fuming like a steam engine. All the way back to her room she was mumbling to herself. Then she slammed the door to her bedroom so hard I thought some of the pictures would fall off the wall."

"It's times like this," Tucker replies, "when I wish Ella was still here. She'd know exactly what was going on with April an' what t' say t' her. I know she's pregnant an' got all kinds of hormones ragin' through her. Then all this happens with them kids. She didn't like th' idea of them returnin' home. An now th' Sheriff showed up here a minute ago."

"The Sheriff? What was he doing out here?"

"He was just checkin' out a story that someone beat up on B.J."

"Someone?"

"He knows I done it, but he had two problems. One was that he didn't have no proof an' th' other was that he sort of thought B.J. deserved what he got. In his words, he came out here just t' follow procedure."

Smiley sucks on his teeth. "Mm-hmm."

"But then April come outside," Tucker continues, "an' he was talkin' all sweet t' her an' her eyes was lightin' up like it was Christmas or somethin'. It made me nervous. When the Sheriff left, I said somethin' t' April 'bout it. She got her feelin's hurt an' stormed off. I don't know whether that means I was right or if it means I was wrong."

"You'd think," Smiley says, "that as much trouble as she has had with men that she'd be more standoffish with them. But just the opposite seems to be true. It worries me how much time she spends over at Preacher's place."

As if she's been standing in the wings waiting for her cue, April walks out of the front door and past Tucker and Smiley.

"Where y' goin'?" Tucker asks.

"I'm going to see Preacher," April says. "That is, if you don't object." Without waiting for a reply, April gets in the pickup truck and drives off.

Chapter Forty-six

"I get so tired of being treated like I'm a child!" April hits the steering wheel with the palm of her hand. "Sure, I've made some mistakes in the past, but who hasn't? I've learned a lot and am not as naïve as I used to be. But me and the Sheriff?! How stupid is that?! I've only met him a few times. The only person who treats me with the respect I deserve is Preacher. I feel like he treats me as an equal, never talks down to me or makes me feel like a little kid. It's no wonder I want to visit him so often."

April's conscience awakens at that last statement. *That's not the only reason you visit him.*

"Yes it is," April answers.

You can fool everyone else, but you can't fool me. I know you.

"Yeah, whatever."

Why did you take that bottle of pills that you stole from Joyce Trevathan and give it to Preacher?

"Because I didn't want to be sucked back into my addiction. I knew what would happen if I took them. I'd be right back where I was."

Then why didn't you just flush them down the toilet?

April searches for a reply that will sound logical. "I guess I just didn't think about that. I sort of panicked when I realized what I'd done. I knew Preacher would know what to do with them.

You are such a liar. You took them to Preacher because you wanted to impress him. You wanted him to hold you in high esteem and brag on you. You wanted him to think you are special.

"That's not true!"

When her conscience has no response, April says, "Sure I enjoy being around Preacher. There's so much that I admire about him. What's wrong with that?"

You like how he smells when you are close to him. His eyes captivate you. When he embraces you, it gives you sexual pleasure.

In this fencing duel of parry and thrust between her conscience and herself, April feels she's been backed into a corner. This last thrust by her conscience has come dangerously close. She tries to rally by swinging wildly, "You're just saying that because that's what Tucker thinks. For god's sake, he's a preacher! He doesn't want anything to do with someone like me. He's just being nice." Tears sting her eyes.

Her conscience sees an opening and delivers its final blow. *You love him.*

"I do not!" April yells in the empty cab of the truck. She pulls into the lane that leads to Preacher's trailer and stops. She looks in her mirror and wipes away her tears. "This is stupid, arguing with myself. I know what's true and what's not true. That's all that matters."

She puts the truck in drive and makes her way to the trailer. When she steps out of the truck, the sound of a chain saw in the woods draws her attention. She follows the sound, stepping past white oak, beech, and sweet gum trees. The rich, smell of humus from the layers of leaves left behind over the decades fills her nostrils. The sound of the chain saw keeps getting louder, but she still can't see the operator.

A hundred yards into the woods she climbs a small hill. At the summit she looks down into a clearing. Stripped to his waist, Preacher leans over, chainsaw in hand, and slices through the trunk of a felled tree. A sheen of sweat covers his torso. April can see the muscles of his back, shoulders and arms rippling. She leans against a tree to watch.

Preacher stands the piece of wood on its ends, then picks up a sledge hammer and a wedge. He taps the wedge in a couple of inches. He steps back and swings the sledge hammer with so much force that when it hits the wedge it drives it all the way through the center of the wood down to the ground. The wood splits into two pieces.

Preacher turns around and picks up an axe. He splits the two large pieces into smaller pieces and carries them to a trailer hooked to a 4-wheeler. Placing his hand on the small of his back, he stretches himself backward.

April feels a thrill at the sight of his taut abdomen.

When he sits down on the edge of the trailer and takes a drink from a thermos, April walks toward the clearing.

The movement catches Preacher's eye. His head snaps around, while at the same time he grabs the handle of his axe. When he sees April, he relaxes and breaks into a smile. "Well hello. You look like one of those woodland fairies coming through the woods. How are you?"

April laughs. "I don't think I remember any fairy tales with fairies in them who were pregnant." She places both hands on the sides of her belly.

"You may be right. But just the same, I think you're getting prettier all the time. Being pregnant seems to suit you."

April feels her heart kick up a notch. She tries not to blush. "I find myself getting tired more easily and sleeping more. But other than that, it's been a good pregnancy. At least that's what everyone tells me." She finds it difficult to keep her eyes on Preacher's face. They keep drifting down to look at his bare chest and stomach. "You've really worked up a sweat," she says.

Preacher picks up his shirt and wipes his face and body. "This is the kind of wood that warms you twice."

"Twice?"

"Once when you cut and split it, and then again when you burn it in the winter."

April smiles. "Oh, I get it."

Slipping his shirt on but leaving it unbuttoned, Preacher says, "What brings you by here?"

"I just wanted to talk. I got mad at Tucker and felt like I needed to get some air. Talking to you always helps me sort things out. I always feel better after being here."

"I'm glad it helps. Why don't you tell me about it?"

"To be honest it's probably several things. We've had lots of drama over our way during the last 24 hours."

"What kind of drama?"

"You know that family that's living in the old McDaniel place beside us?"

"Yes."

"Well last night the father came home drunk and beat all three of the kids, especially the oldest one, Benjamin. They came to our house in the middle of the night. Benjamin was covered in blood." April notices Preacher's jaw muscles flexing as he grits his teeth upon hearing this news.

"Did you all call the sheriff's department?" Preacher asks.

"Yes. The deputies arrested the father and the kids stayed with us overnight. Then this morning a social worker came out and said the kids were going back to their mother, which made me mad. The Sheriff came out, too. Why, I don't know. But he was being nice to me and Tucker turned it into he and I flirting with each other. I know this all sounds crazy. But I blew up and left."

"Wow. You weren't kidding when you said there'd been lots of drama." Preacher stands up. "Let's walk back to my trailer and get us something to drink and eat. I'm just going to leave the 4-wheeler and trailer here until I come back and get a full load to take out."

The two walk slowly through the woods. The sunlight flickers through the leafy canopy, casting light and shadows on the ground.

April makes her hand accidently brush against his.

Preacher says, "I know you have a heart for kids and realizing that those three were going to be sent back home had to have been very hard for you to hear. You were already upset by the time Tucker said something to you about you and Sheriff Harris. Her comments were just the match that lit your fuse. I'm sure she's just concerned about you and wants to protect you."

"But I don't need protecting. That's my point. I'm an adult and can take care of myself."

Preacher waits until they've walked a few paces before he replies. "I've never been a parent, but I can imagine that if I were, I would be as protective of my children when they're in their twenties as I was when they were a small child. You've been Tucker's world for a long time. Maybe you need to cut her a little slack."

As they break out of the woods into the open, April says, "Maybe you're right. I can fly off the handle sometimes."

They are approaching the back of Preacher's trailer when a dark-haired, nice-looking woman comes around the corner from the front. "Oh there you are," she says. "And I see we have a guest. I wondered whose pickup that was."

Preacher walks to the woman and puts his arm around her waist. "April, this is Penny Wiseman. Penny, this is April. This is the young girl I've told you about."

April is so stunned she can neither move nor speak. She stands there with her mouth open.

Penny approaches her with an outstretched hand. "Nice to finally meet you, April. Are you hungry? I've just put the rolls in the oven, so we're just about ready to eat. We'd be glad for you to eat with us."

April shakes her hand woodenly. She sees the admiration in Preacher's eyes as he looks at Penny. She has difficulty getting a breath. "I didn't . . . I mean . . . I just . . . "

"Penny's from over in Lake County," Preacher says. "We knew each other ages ago and have just started seeing each other. Penny makes a mean skillet of fried chicken. Come on and join us."

Moving as if she is walking through a lake of molasses, April walks slowly toward her truck. "I think I better get back home. Tucker will be wondering about me."

"Are you okay, honey?" Penny asks. "You look kind of pale."

April feels emotions boiling in her chest like magma in a volcano. She wants to get away from here before the eruption. She stumbles into the truck and backs out of the driveway. By the time she gets to the intersection of the lane and the blacktop she is powerless to hold her feelings in. She screams at the top of her lungs as tears pour down her cheeks. She pounds the steering wheel, slaps herself and pulls her hair. She bites her arm hard enough to bring blood. "Please, God," she cries out. "Take my life! I can't take this anymore!"

Chapter Forty-seven

It is dusk when Benjamin, Alexander, and Maria decide to go inside their house. Benjamin hears a vehicle approaching and recognizes Tucker's truck. He waves as he sees April driving, but she doesn't return his wave or even look in his direction as she passes by. A frown pulls the corners of his mouth down as his eyebrows knit together. April always waves at him.

He stands gazing at the receding taillights of the truck.

"Come on, Bennie," Maria says, as she holds the front door open. "Mama fixed us supper."

Benjamin looks at his sister, curious to see if what she says is true. He can't remember the last time his mother fixed a meal. When he walks inside an acrid smell fills his nostrils. He notices that his brother and sister are holding their noses. Looking past them into the kitchen, he sees his mother setting a pot on the table.

"Something stinks," Alexander whispers.

Benjamin snorts and shakes his head vigorously in an effort to clear his sense of smell.

"Ya'll come on in and eat," Joyce calls weakly.

The trio move slowly toward the table. As they do so, the offensive odor grows stronger.

Joyce shuffles between the stove and table, carrying another pot. "It's been a little while since I've cooked. I'm a little out of practice. I think I may have scorched those green beans. Come on, let's all sit down together."

Each of them takes a chair and sits down.

Benjamin reaches for a pot and spoons some macaroni and cheese onto his plate, then puts a lesser amount on Alexander and Maria's plates. The next pot he grabs has the green beans in it. On top are several burned beans. Nonetheless, he gets himself some and shares with his brother and sister, too.

There is also a plate of pop-tarts on the table.

Pointing at it, Maria says, "Can I have one of those?"

Joyce picks one up and places it on Maria's plate. "I didn't have any bread to go with the meal, so I thought pop-tarts was the closest thing to it."

Benjamin takes a bite of macaroni and cheese but finds the noodles are undercooked and crunchy. He looks at the scowl on Alexander's face as he tries a bite of the beans. Both of them reach for a pop-tart.

"Listen," Joyce says, looking toward her bedroom.

The children listen but are uncertain what they should be listening for.

"Go turn up the TV, Bennie. Elvis is singing 'All I Needed Was The Rain.' That's one of my favorites."

Taking his pop-tart with him, Benjamin goes to the bedroom and turns the volume up.

He's about to exit the room when his mother says, "Just wait there until the song is over, then you can turn it back down."

So familiar is Benjamin with the songs that when Elvis is about to deliver the final lines, he walks to the set, arriving just as the song is finished. He reaches down and turns the volume back down.

When he returns to join the rest of the family, Joyce says, "Kids, I want you to know that I'm sorry about what happened last night. No, I'm sorry about a lot of things. I haven't been a good mother to you. It's this cancer that keeps me dragged down. But I'm going to do better. I promise. And B.J.'s not coming back. I'm done with him. We really don't need him. He's gone all the time anyway. It's just going to be us. But we're going to make it. Aren't we?"

Although Benjamin has heard similar assertions by his mother through the years, her attitude and tone seems different this time, more believable. A breath of hope finds its way into his heart. He smiles.

Later that night, after everyone is in bed, Benjamin takes out his treasure box. When he opens it, the first thing lying there is a well-worn envelope with his name handwritten on it. As he has been doing every night since he received it a few weeks ago, he opens it and takes out the folded letter inside.

Dear Benjamin,

This is a very difficult letter for me to write. You are such a kind and sweet person. You deserve nothing but the very best in life, and I hope you get it.

I know it hurt you when I moved my books out of the locker beside you and started sharing a locker with Blake. But he and I are dating now, and it's just what couples do. I didn't want to hurt your feelings. I'm not mad at you or anything like that.

And then I got selected to be a cheerleader. That's something I never thought I would want to do. But it gives me a chance to finally feel like I'm accepted by everyone. I know that shouldn't matter to me, but it does. I told you once that I've always been an outsider. This is now my chance to fit in. I'm excited and hope you will be happy for me.

- Cassie Armour

It always strikes Benjamin as strange that Cassie put her last name when she's the only Cassie that he knows. Does she think he won't remember her?

And it makes him sad that not one time does she use the word "friend" in her letter, either that they've been friends or are friends. He wonders if this is the way it is with everyone who gets a boyfriend or girlfriend; that they cut themselves off from all their friends.

He refolds the letter and returns it to its envelope.

Next he engages in his nightly ritual of taking out his Matchbox cars one at a time and lining them up on the table. He's asked himself why he enjoys this so much but never has an answer to his question. He wonders if he'll be doing this for the rest of his life or if someday his urge to do it will pass.

Lastly, he takes out his journal, turns to a blank page and writes:

The dragon that has terrorized the town has been clapped in chains and locked in an iron cage.

A female warrior was his undoing. He was no match for her rage.

Fear that used to hang like a dense fog over everyone has vanished.

No more heads always bent, constantly looking at the ground, afraid to look someone in the eye.

All of those old ways are now banished.

But will things <u>really</u> be different now? Is that possible?

And if they change, will they stay that way?

I want a different life. I want to be someone else.

Someone that other people like and want to be friends with.

I want a friend who will hear me when I cry.

314

Chapter Forty-eight

Two days later, on Saturday, Tucker comes in from working in her garden and fills a glass full of water.

"Sure wish I could help you with the hoeing," Smiley says. "I just feel so useless sometimes."

"Aw quit feelin' sorry fer yoreself," Tucker says. "Neither one o' us can do th' work we used t' do. We just have t' do th' best we can."

"How's everything looking?"

"Real good. That bushel o' beans I took down t' Joyce yesterday was some o' th' prettiest ones I ever seen."

"It's amazing to me that she didn't know what to do with them," Smiley says. "I thought everybody around here knew how to break beans."

"Th' look on her face told me she didn't know nothing 'bout it. When I showed her how t' do it, she tried that ol' line o' hers about havin' cancer. I told her that was th' last time I wanted t' hear 'bout that. That if she wanted t' die, to go on an' git with it. But if she wasn't, then she needed t' start bein' more alive."

Smiley laughs. "You'd be just the one to tell her, too. You're a sight, Tucker. That's what you are, a sight."

"I just tell it like I see it," Tucker replies. Her expression becomes somber. "Has April been up?"

"I've heard her in her room, but she hasn't been out here. I'm worried about her. She has to eat."

"Ever' since she come back from Preacher's she ain't been right. Somethin' had t' have happened over there."

"You want me to call him and ask what happened?" Smiley asks.

Tucker folds her arms across her chest. "No. What I'm of a mind t' do is go in there an' drag her pregnant butt in here an' tell 'er t' straighten up. What ever happened it don't matter 'cause she's got someone else t' be thinkin' 'bout."

As Tucker finishes, there is a knock at the door. She goes and opens the door to find Benjamin standing there. "Hey there, Ben. Come on in here. What's on yore mind?"

Benjamin steps inside the house. He looks around the room. "A-A-A-April?"

"She's back in her bedroom," Tucker says.

Benjamin starts ambling toward the hallway to April's room.

"Whoa there, Ben," Tucker says. "She might not be dressed."

Benjamin freezes. His eyes go wide, and his face turns red. He starts walking slowly backward.

Smiley puts his hand over his mouth to cover his grin.

"Just sit down, Ben," Tucker says. "I'll go tell her you're here."

"W-W-W-We're supposed to s-s-s-sing."

"Oh, that's right. It's time for yore lesson, ain't it? Have a seat. I'll be right back."

Tucker goes to April's door, knocks twice, and lets herself in.

April is lying underneath a tangle of bed covers. "Go away," comes her muffled voice.

"I ain't goin' nowhere," Tucker says. She sits down on the edge of the bed. "Y' gonna tell me what happened over at Preacher's? Or are y' just gonna let it fester in side o' y'?"

"I don't want to talk about it."

"That's up t' you. But you're gonna git out o' this bed. An' you're gonna eat an' start doin' right. Ben's here fer his lesson."

April groans. "I don't want to mess with him today. Tell him I don't feel good."

"Y' sound like a six-year-old tryin' t' git out o' goin' t' school. I didn't lie fer y' when y' was six, an' I ain't lyin' fer y' now. Besides, you're gonna tell me that this boy that ain't got a friend in th' world is too much trouble t' mess with? What does that say 'bout you?"

"I don't know," is April's faint reply from her cocoon of covers.

"It says you is one conceited woman that ain't interested in nobody but theirself. An' what 'bout yore baby? Do y' now wish you'd got rid of it?"

April flings the covers off and sits up. "Don't you say that!"

"Why not? That's how you're actin'. Y' think just 'cause y' got trouble of some kind, 'cause y' got hurt over at Preacher's, that ever'thing's supposed t' stop while you git over it? Well let me tell y' somethin'. That ain't how it works, not if you're my granddaughter.

"When I was pregnant with yore Mama, an' didn't have nobody I could call on t' help me, I thought 'bout endin' ever'thing. Her life an' mine, too. But I wasn't goin' t' give in like that. I wasn't goin' t' let him win."

"Let who win, Tucker?" April asks.

"Whoever or whatever it was that was in control o' all th' evil things that had happened t' me. Back then I think I called it fate, or the stars. But it don't matter what they was called, I was determined t' show them that if they thought they could whip me, they had another thing t' learn. I shook m' fist in their face an' said, 'T' hell with y'. I'm gonna show y' that I can come out o' this.'" She puts her hands on both sides of April's face. "Now I know that it was Satan who was tryin' t' do me in, t' convince me t' give up. An' he's tryin' t' do th' same thing with you. But as long as I am drawin' breath, I ain't gonna let y' give up." She gives April's head a tiny shake. "I ain't. Y' hear me?"

The two women stare into each other's eyes until their tears spill over the bottom lids and drip onto their cheeks.

April uses her thumb to wipe away one of Tucker's tears. She mouths the words "I love you."

"An' I love you, too," Tucker says aloud.

They embrace each other and Tucker gently rocks back and forth. "It's gonna be all right, April."

"He's seeing someone," April says.

"Who is?"

"Preacher. He's dating someone."

"Oh. Y' got yore heart stepped on, didn't y'?"

April nods. "I don't know what I was thinking."

"You was thinkin' that Preacher was a good man, a kind man, an' a nice lookin' man. All of that drawed y' to him. It's okay. It's sort of natural that it happened. It don't mean there's somethin' wrong with y' for havin' feelin's fer him, an' it don't mean that he was tryin' t' hurt y' by seein' this other woman."

"I know you're right," April says. "I need to quit feeling sorry for myself, don't I?"

"It wouldn't hurt none," Tucker agrees.

April releases Tucker from her embrace. "Tell Benjamin I'll be out in a minute. I just need to get dressed."

"I'll do it," Tucker says. As she walks back into the living room, she uses her sleeve to wipe her tear-dampened cheeks. "She'll be here in just a minute, Ben."

"See what I told you?" Smiley says to Benjamin. "When a woman's pregnant, sometimes the only person who can talk to them about their woes is another woman. Even if a man said the very same thing to them, all it would do is make them mad. I know that doesn't make any sense, but that's the way it is with a woman. You'll need to remember that whenever you get married."

Benjamin's knee starts bouncing.

"Now look what y' done," Tucker says to Smiley. "Y' got him all nervous talkin' 'bout gittin' married." She looks at Benjamin. "Would y' like a sausage an' biscuit while y' wait fer April?"

Benjamin's knee stops. "Y-Y-Y-Yes ma'am. I'm thirsty, t-t-t-too."

Tucker heads to the kitchen. "Coffee or juice?"

"J-J-J-Juice, please."

"Y' hear that boy, Smiley? He said 'please.' Y' know, it wouldn't hurt you t' say please ever' once in a while."

Smiley grins and winks at Benjamin. He calls to Tucker, "It pleases me to know that you are pleased when I say please."

"Oh just shut up, ol' man," Tucker replies.

Tucker returns with a sausage and biscuit left over from breakfast and a glass of juice. Benjamin devours the sausage and biscuit in three bites then gulps down the juice.

April walks into the living room as she is pulling her hair back into a ponytail. She has put on a touch of makeup and a hint of lipstick. Smiling, she says, "Hi, Benjamin."

Benjamin focuses on a spot just beyond April's shoulder. A biscuit crumb falls from the corner of his mouth.

"Eye contact, Benjamin," April says.

Benjamin blinks and looks her in the eye. "H-H-H-Hi, April."

"I'm going to fix me something to eat," April says, "and then we'll get busy."

"Smiley," Tucker says, "why don't y' come with me t' town t' buy some feed?"

"Good idea," Smiley says.

Chapter Forty-nine

After Tucker and Smiley leave, April says, "I'm going to eat something. Are you hungry?"

Nodding his head, Benjamin says, "Sure."

"Come on in here and let's see what we got." April goes through the cabinets and refrigerator, naming things off as she goes, "Peanut butter and jelly sandwich, Cheeze whiz and crackers, soup, cereal, baloney, ham, turkey, something brown that is leftover from some time, eggs and bacon. What do you think? I'm going to have cereal."

Benjamin's eyes dance at all the choices. "I-I-I-I'll eat cereal, t-t-t-too."

April gets a couple of bowls out of the cabinet. "Get the milk," she says to Benjamin. She puts three boxes of cereal and the bowls on the table. "Help yourself to whichever one you want."

Benjamin watches April pour herself a bowl of raisin bran, then he pours himself a bowl full of the same. She adds two spoons of sugar. Benjamin does the same. Bite for bite, he imitates April's movements.

April stops eating and looks at him. "You know that's irritating, don't you?"

Benjamin stops with his spoon sticking out of his mouth. There is a drop of milk hanging onto the bottom of his chin, unsure if it wants to run down his neck or freefall back into the bowl. The only thing that moves is Benjamin's eyes as they dart around the kitchen.

"Take your spoon out of your mouth," April tells him.

Benjamin follows her instruction.

"You mirroring every move I make is creepy, Benjamin. You just need to eat like you normally would. I'm not trying to hurt your feelings. I'm just trying to help you learn some of your behaviors that are socially awkward at times."

He chews and swallows his mouthful of cereal. "I d-d-d-don't always s-s-s-see things the way other people d-d-d-do. You know, Asperger's."

April nods. "I know. But listen, you can't just use that as an excuse not to try to improve. I have a bad habit of making excuses for my behavior, too. I can sometimes feel sorry for myself."

"You? Why?"

"There's lots you don't know about me. For instance, I was made fun of a lot when I was growing up."

"Uh-uh."

"Yes I was. People made fun of the way I looked, the clothes I wore, the way my hair looked, where I lived, who was raising me. Yes, all of that."

Benjamin shakes his head. "B-B-B-But you're beautiful."

April smiles. "Well thank you. I'm not sure that's true now that I'm getting as pregnant as a cow. But you are nice to say that."

"What did y-y-y-you do when people m-m-m-made fun of you?"

"Sometimes I cried. Sometimes I hit them in the mouth."

Benjamin grins. He slams his fist into his palm. "In the m-m-m-mouth."

"Yep. But Tucker helped me to understand that how people saw me said more about them than it did about me."

Benjamin frowns. "I d-d-d-don't understand."

"Think of it this way. What if two farmers go to a cattle sale and look at the very same Black Angus bull that is for sale. One of them says, 'That's the best looking bull I've seen in a long time. I've got to have him.' And the other farmer says, 'That's the scrawniest looking animal I ever saw. I wouldn't let him near my cows.' Now tell me, what do we learn about that bull by listening to what those men said about it?"

Benjamin ponders silently over the riddle. Finally he says, "I can't f-f-f-figure it out."

"Exactly," April says. "The truth is that you don't learn anything about the bull by listening to their comments. But you do learn something about those farmers, what they like and dislike in a bull. They're really telling you about themselves by the comments they make. And that's precisely the way it is when someone talks about you. What they say says more about them than it does about you. Interesting, isn't it?"

He slowly nods his head. "Just b-b-b-because someone says I'm s-s-s-stupid doesn't mean I'm s-s-s-stupid."

"Bingo."

"And just b-b-b-because they say I'm ugly doesn't m-m-m-mean I'm ugly."

"Bingo again. Now you're getting it."

Benjamin sits back in his chair.

April watches his face begin to brighten as if he were standing outside and a dawning sun struck his face.

He gets up and starts pacing back and forth.

April decides to leave him alone.

After a few moments, he returns to the table and looks at April. "I l-l-l-like you. I want t-t-t-to be strong like y-y-y-you."

"I like you, too, Benjamin. This is the thing, though, how I am now is not how I have always been. I had to work at it, had to listen to other people who I trusted telling me things I didn't always like to hear, had to quit making excuses and feeling sorry for myself. Even as recent as this morning, I was lying in bed feeling sorry for myself. But," she places a hand on her stomach, "this baby and you are at least two reasons I need to quit feeling that way. You both need me. And maybe I need you, too."

"You need m-m-m-me?"

"I need you to need me. Just like you need Alexander and Maria to need you. It makes you keep trying, doesn't it?"

Benjamin nods and says, "Yes. And Mama, too."

April purses her lips to one side. "I can see that, but just remember that it's not your job to take care of your mother. She's the parent. You're the child. Although I suspect those roles have been reversed for a long time. I think your mother's going to start trying harder to do better, especially if Tucker has anything to say about it. She's sort of taken her on as a project."

"I like T-T-T-Tucker."

"She's a good woman, just hard to get to know."

"But she's not your M-M-M-Mama."

"No, she's my grandmother."

"Where's y-y-y-your Mama?"

"She was murdered when I was a little girl."

Benjamin's eyes grow wide. "Who d-d-d-did it?"

"Turns out it was actually my father. I never knew him."

Benjamin grows quiet. He folds and refolds his hands several times. Finally, he looks at April and says, "I'm sorry."

"Thank you, Benjamin. That's a really kind thing to say."

His knee starts bouncing. "I th-th-th-think I want to k-k-k-kiss you."

April's head jerks back and she blinks rapidly. Thinking she must have misunderstood, she asks, "What did you say?"

"It f-f-f-feels like I'm supposed to k-k-k-kiss you."

April thinks about making him leave but holds that urge in check by telling herself he doesn't mean to be inappropriate. "Benjamin, people kiss each other when they really like each other."

"I l-l-l-like you. And y-y-y-you said you like me."

"Yes, but it's not the same. You're still in high school and I'm in my twenties. For us to kiss each other would be inappropriate. That's the word – inappropriate. We can still be friends but not the kind of friends who kiss each other."

"Are you m-m-m-mad at me because I s-s-s-said that?"

"No, of course not. I know you didn't mean anything by it. You were just acting on a feeling. Feelings . . . " she pauses, thinking of her own feelings about her and Preacher. "They're hard to figure out, aren't they?"

Benjamin nods.

She gets up and takes their bowls to the sink. Turning back around, she says, "Now let's make some music."

Benjamin goes to the living room while April goes to get her Autoharp. She returns, sits beside him on the couch, and strums some on her instrument. "I've been thinking about trying a different song. This is an old song called 'In the Pines.' It's really simple, both in tune and lyrics."

April sings and plays the song while Benjamin watches and listens intently. After she finishes, she says, "Now I'm going to sing it again, and I want you to just hum along with me. That's all. Just hum. Got it?"

Benjamin nods. "G-G-G-Got it."

As April sings she leans a little closer to Benjamin to see if he is indeed humming along and if he is humming on pitch. She's thrilled to hear him following along perfectly. At the end she says, "That's great, Benjamin! You were right on pitch with me. You've got a really good ear. I thought you did but it's been hard to be sure because of your stuttering."

Benjamin smiles broadly at being bragged on.

"Now we're going to do it again, but this time I want you to just sing the vowel sound oooo, like in the word 'who.' Let me show you what I mean."

Benjamin looks closely at April's mouth as she demonstrates what she wants him to do.

"Can you do that?" April asks.

"I th-th-th-think so," Benjamin replies.

"Okay then, here we go." April launches into the song and nods at him to join her.

Again she is delighted to hear his nice clear voice following along. She keeps playing but pauses singing. "Louder," she tells him, then returns to singing the lyrics.

Benjamin is emboldened by her encouragement and their voices fill the living room with their strong tones.

April is almost in tears when they finish. "Oh Benjamin, you have a wonderful voice! Did you hear yourself? You sounded great!"

Benjamin's eyes sparkle with delight. "W-W-W-We sounded good t-t-t-together, didn't we?"

"Yes we did. This is exactly the way my other grandmother helped me to start talking. I'd forgotten about the small steps she took with me like this one. Now that you've got the tune perfectly, all you have to do is just think about the song and sing it with me. Don't think about anything else. Just sing the song. Here we go." April plays the introduction and nods at Benjamin to come in.

Benjamin opens his mouth and sings, "In the pines, in the p-pines, where th-the sun never sh-sh-shines"

April sees him getting frustrated. "Just relax, Benjamin. You're doing fine."

He continues, "And sh-sh-sh-shivers when the c-c-c-cold – " He stops abruptly and shakes his head. "It's n-n-n-never going to work."

April stops playing. She tries to hide her own disappointment. "I was wrong. I shouldn't have asked you to try the lyrics. I got in too big of a hurry. We should have just kept doing it with you oooing. Let's do that."

For the next thirty minutes April plays one song after another and Benjamin follows her with his monosyllabic lyric. But when he leaves they are no closer to him overcoming his stuttering than when they began.

Chapter Fifty

Tucker opens up her preheated oven and carefully slides in two apple pies.

Sitting at the table peeling potatoes, Smiley watches her and says, "So that's one for March and one for August. What about the rest of us?"

"Th' rest of y' can do without," Tucker replies. "An' if them boys want two pies a piece, I'll fix 'em fer 'em."

Smiley laughs. "I know what you mean. They haven't been home since back in the winter and here it is the middle of June. They're going to be surprised when they see how big April is, aren't they?"

From the living room comes April's voice. "I heard that." She enters the kitchen. Putting her hands on her swollen abdomen, she says, "I can't believe I still have three months to go in this pregnancy. How much bigger am I going to get?"

Tucker stands with her hands on her hips. "You'll be surprised."

"It's truly one of the marvels of nature," Smiley says. "That a microscopic seed can become a full grown baby inside of a woman . . ." He shakes his head. "It's a marvel, that's what it is." He looks at April's belly. "Are you sure that little boy doesn't have a brother or sister hiding in there with him?"

"You mean like twins?" April says. "There better not be. That would be one surprise I don't want to have."

"Have y' decided on what t' name him?" Tucker asks.

April shakes her head. "I'm still thinking about it. I bought one of those book of names, and I think it only made me more confused. Unlike my mother who named us after the months we were born in, I think a name should be well thought out and should mean something." She looks out the front window. "What time is the east Tennessee contingent supposed to get here?"

"I'm expectin' them any time," Tucker replies. "Y' know, I been thinkin'. Why don't we have us a big ol' hootenanny this evenin'. We'll git Shady Green t' come an' also ask Joyce an' th' kids t' come."

April's face brightens. "That's a great idea!"

"We could do some homemade ice cream," Smiley says.

"Another great idea!" April exclaims.

Tucker turns around to get something out of the cabinet. With her back turned, she says, "Would y' want t' ask Preacher t' come, too?" When April doesn't answer immediately, she turns around. "He's a good man, April, an' he's been good t' us."

"I know," April says. "I think I'm over being hurt. This would be a good chance to find out. You call him and ask him. And have him bring his girlfriend, too. I'll walk down to the Trevathan's and ask them to come."

"Y' sure y' want him t' bring her?" Tucker asks.

"I think I'll be fine. I need to accept things the way they are and move on. Right?"

"Right," Tucker answers. "Y' can drive down there if y' want."

"Walking will be good for me."

April steps out of the house into the brilliant light of the noonday sun burning in the cloudless sky. A meadowlark sings in the distance while a bobwhite calls in search of a mate. The incessant buzzing of locusts, freshly hatched from their thirteen-year sleep, accompanies her from their perch in the oak trees that line the road down to where the Trevathan's live.

As she approaches the house, she sees Joyce hanging clothes on a clothesline. Her tanned arms and face are a stark contrast to the pale visage she presented the first time April met her. Her sunken cheeks have filled out. "Hey, Miss Trevathan," April calls as she gets closer.

Joyce turns and smiles. "Hi, April. I keep telling you that you can call me Joyce."

"I know. I keep forgetting. I like your hair pulled back like that."

Joyce puts her hand on her hair. "I just try to get it out of my face when I do housework. How are you and that baby getting along?"

"I'm feeling fine, just a little more tired than usual."

"I remember that feeling. Taking naps was my favorite pastime when I was pregnant."

"I know I've told you this," April says, "but the change in you is remarkable. You look so much healthier. And you have a beautiful smile."

"Well, it's all because of Tucker. I swear I believe that woman would turn me over her knee and give me a spanking if I didn't do what she told me. And she's probably strong enough to do it."

April laughs. "Trust me, she is. Tucker is a force to be reckoned with, that's for sure. At the same time she can be both that proverbial immovable object and that irresistible force, depending on what she wants to be. There are lots of stories that have been told about Tucker and her grit and determination. And they're probably all true."

"I'm convinced she saved my life," Joyce declares. "And I'm not talking just about helping me get rid of B.J. She saved me from myself. She jerked me out of my self-pity, stood me on my feet, and shoved me forward. And when she couldn't shove me, she dragged me. She wouldn't be denied." Joyce holds her arms out to her side. "Look at me. I haven't looked this healthy in years. I think she scared the cancer right out of me!"

They both laugh.

"Tucker might be the new cancer antidote," April says.

"It's the beatin'est thing," Joyce says, "how your mind can convince you about something, and you'll believe the lie. I just knew the cancer had never left me, even though doctors told me I was cancer free. Now I can see I was just using it as an excuse to avoid things."

"Avoid what things?" April asks.

"Like being a mother, taking care of the house, and especially admitting I needed to get out of my abusive marriage. I thought my weakness gave me an excuse. That was a lie. Tucker has shown me what a strong woman looks like and that I can be strong, too."

"April!" Maria has come outside and spotted her friend.

"Come here, girl!" April calls to her.

Maria runs into April's arms.

"Be careful, Maria," Joyce says, "April has a baby inside of her. You don't want to hurt either one of them."

Maria steps back.

"It's okay," April says. "She's not hurting me. How are you, Maria?"

"I've lost two teeth." She grins to show the gaps left behind.

"Wow, you have, haven't you?"

"Run along," Joyce says to Maria. "April and I are talking."

Maria skips across the yard to the tree swing.

"I want you to know," Joyce says, "how much I appreciate you spending time with Bennie. I don't know what you all are doing because he says it's a secret. But I can see a change in him. He's coming out of himself more. And he doesn't say and do odd things as often as he used to. I think when school starts back in August things are going to go better for him."

"You're very welcome. I think Benjamin is a remarkable boy. We're working on a secret project I guess you could say. Once we're successful we'll reveal it to everyone. You'll really be happy and surprised, too."

"I can't wait."

"Listen," April says, "the reason I came down here was to invite all of you to the house tonight after supper. We're going to be sitting around eating homemade ice cream and singing and playing music. My brothers and sister-in-law are coming in today and we're going to celebrate."

Joyce looks down. "We don't need to barge in on your family fun time. That's just for you all."

"Yes, but we want you all to come. We're inviting Preacher and his girlfriend, as well. So there will be others there who aren't family. Oh, and Shady Green will be there, too. We'll be disappointed if you don't come."

"I haven't seen Shady Green since he came to repair the house," Joyce says. "He's such a unique person. I'd love to see him again. You're really nice to ask us. We'll be there. The kids will think it's such a treat."

"Great! We'll see you this evening then," April says. She turns around and heads back home.

As she's walking up the road she hears a vehicle approaching from behind. She scoots over and walks on the grassy shoulder of the road. She hears the vehicle slowing as it gets closer.

Suddenly a man's voice calls out, "Excuse me ma'am. I'm looking for a house that has a cantankerous old woman, a grinning black man, and a smart-mouth pregnant girl living in it. Can you help me?"

April whirls around and shrieks. "March! August! Debbie!"

Chapter Fifty-one

August, March, and Debbie get out of the car, leaving it parked in the middle of the road.

Looking at April, August exclaims, "Oh my goodness, look at you! I can't believe how big the baby is getting." He and April embrace.

"I've missed you," April says.

"And I've so missed you," August replies.

They let go of each other and April looks to Debbie who says, "April, you look so amazing." They share a hug.

"You're sweet," April says. "I've missed our late night talks."

"I know what you mean. Talking with a man is not the same thing. They just don't get it sometimes."

The two of them share a laugh.

Holding his arms open, March says, "Come here, Baby Sister."

"Oh March!" April exclaims and rushes into his arms.

March bear hugs her and lifts her off the ground.

April squeals with delight.

After he sets her down, March puts his hand on her stomach. "What's this? Have you swallowed a cantaloupe?"

"I think it's more like a watermelon," April says. She stands still while March's hands feel the shape of her stomach then move to her face where his fingertips inspect every inch.

"You look different," he says.

"Different? How?" April asks.

"You're more serious. But you're also more settled. Something inside you has shifted."

April grasps his hands. "And if you guess my age and weight, you can get a job working in a carnival."

They all laugh.

"Come on," August says. "Let's go."

The four of them pile into the car and travel the few remaining yards to Tucker's house. As soon as they pull to a stop, the front door opens and Tucker hurries toward them, followed by Smiley.

August reaches her first. They throw their arms around each other and kiss each other's cheeks.

"You're not eatin' enough," Tucker says. "Y' git skinnier ever' time I see y'."

August laughs. "I'm just a lean, mean, fighting machine."

"No y' ain't. You're skinny. Y' need t' spend a month or so here. I'd put th' meat back on yore bones."

"Just look what a good job of that she does with me," Smiley says as he pats his ample waistline.

"Hmpf!" Tucker grunts. "I keep waitin' fer his toes t' turn up like a horse that's foundered."

Everyone howls with laughter.

August walks up to Smiley. "Don't let them hurt your feelings, Dad. I still love you if no one else does."

Smiley puts his arm around August's shoulders. "That's a good boy. You all hear that? At least there's one loyal person in this crowd."

March holds Debbie's elbow as she walks forward.

"There's m' little baby, March," Tucker says. She touches his face.

He leans down and kisses her on the forehead. He "looks" at her face with his fingers. "You haven't changed a bit," he says. "As beautiful as ever."

"Oh hush," Tucker says. "Come here, Debbie, an' let me give y' a hug. You're th' one that's as beautiful as ever. I think married life agrees with both of y'."

"I won't disagree with that," Debbie says as they embrace.

"Ya'll come on in," Tucker says.

Everyone makes their way inside and finds a seat in the living room.

March sniffs the air. "Don't tell me you've got an apple pie baking."

"I got two of them in th' oven," Tucker says.

"He's got a bloodhound's nose for food," Debbie says. "I can't keep anything hid from him."

"A growing boy's got to eat," March says.

"Well you're definitely growing," April says. "Not that I have any room to talk."

"Tell us about your pregnancy," Debbie says. "How's everything going?"

"My doctor tells me that I'm doing great. I had morning sickness for a while, but that didn't last long. Other than getting tired in the afternoon and having some cravings for food, I have no complaints."

"Th' girl wants chili all th' time," Tucker says. "Even fer breakfast."

They all make a face.

"I can eat just about anything, anytime," March says, "but chili for breakfast? I don't think I could choke that down."

"You're having a boy, right?" August says.

"Yes," April answers.

"Tell us what you're going to name him," he urges.

"I haven't decided. I have several ideas but nothing definite. I'm for sure not going to name him September."

March and August laugh.

"When I tell people how I got my name," August says, "they think I'm making it up. And when I convince them I'm not, they don't know whether to laugh or to feel sorry for me."

"I guess it could have been worse," March says. "Maisy could have named us after the day of the week we were born on."

"Or the zodiac sign we were born under," April says. "Hi, my name is Aries." She laughs.

"Yore Mama," Tucker says and shakes her head.

"Guess what we're going to do tonight?" April asks.

"What?" August replies.

"We're going to have a hootenanny like we used to have in Ella's front yard."

"Oh how exciting!" Debbie says. "March has told me stories about the music you all used to play and sing."

"Is Shady Green coming?" March asks.

"Yes he is," Smiley says.

March claps his hands together. He says to Debbie, "Wait until you see and meet this fellow. There's never been another one like him."

"Speaking of Ella's yard," August says, "it looked like there are people living in the old McDaniel place, even though it looks like a heavy breeze might blow it over."

"That family blew in there on th' wings of a January wind, cold an' hungry," Tucker says.

"And lost and pitiful," April adds, shaking her head.

"But April became their guardian angel," Smiley says.

"I wouldn't say that," April says.

"Well I would," Smiley counters. "Those three kids look at you like you're an angel. And between you and Tucker you all delivered them from that abusive coward that lived with them."

"Whoa there," March says. "That sounds like there's a story to be told about that."

Smiley, Tucker, and April exchange looks.

"What was that?" August says. "You all looked at each other like there's some kind of secret."

"Let's just say this," April says, "Tucker still knows how to use her axe handle."

March slaps his thigh. "Man, I wish I could have seen that! Actually I wish I could see anything. But I especially wish I could have seen Tucker administer some justice."

Everyone smiles at March's self-deprecating attitude.

"The oldest boy, Benjamin," April says, "has Asperger's disorder, which, as I understand it, is a mild form of autism. He's a bad stutterer, too. I've been trying to help him to overcome his stuttering by using music like Ella did with me."

"What an awesome thing to do," Debbie says. "How's it going?"

"It's going nowhere," April says. "He's got a musical ear and a good voice, but as soon as he tries to say some lyrics it gets all gummed up. He's trying, and I'm working to be patient, but I'm afraid I'm not going to be able to help him."

"His Mama tells me you're helpin' him a lot," Tucker says. "She says th' boy's not nearly as backward an' odd as he was. She's tickled with how things is goin'."

"It's just not going like I hoped it would," April says. "Anyway, we've invited all of them to come to our hootenanny tonight."

"An' Preacher's comin', too," Tucker adds.

"Did you get hold of him?" April asks.

"Yep. He was tickled t' be asked."

April looks at her.

"Yes. She's comin', too."

"She who?" March asks.

"Preacher's dating somebody from over in Lake County," Tucker explains.

"I love that Preacher man," March says.

"I think everybody does," Smiley says. "He's quite an unusual man, a man that hasn't let his past define him."

There's a lull in the conversation.

"What I want to know is," March finally says, "what's for supper?"

"We went and got some barbeque from Trollinger's," Smiley says. "I know you can't get good bar-b-que over in Knoxville. So we thought you'd like a taste of west Tennessee bar-b-que."

"They sell barbeque in Knoxville," August says, "but it's not any good. Trollingers, man that's the best!"

"How 'bout some hushpuppies t' go with it?" Tucker asks.

"Ya'll excuse me," March says, "I think I'm going to faint. Trollinger's barbeque and Tucker's hush puppies? I think I've died and gone to heaven."

"And what about homemade ice cream afterwards?" April asks.

March falls over onto Debbie's lap.

Smiling, Debbie says, "I think that was the final straw. You pushed him over the edge with the promise of homemade ice cream."

A ripple of laughter runs through the family.

Debbie bends down and whispers in March's ear.

March sits up and says, "We've got a little bit of news to share with everyone."

Multiple responses of "What?" come from his audience.

Debbie takes his hand.

March turns his head toward her. "We're going to have a baby."

There is a split second of shocked silence before an explosion of shouts and squeals erupts.

April rushes to Debbie and hugs her. "That is wonderful! We'll both be new mothers! How far along are you? When are you due? How have you been feeling? Have you had any morning sickness? Oh I'm so excited!"

"Slow down, April," Tucker says gently. "Let 'er answer one question before y' ask 'er six more."

"I know, I know," April says. "I'm just so excited. Tell us the details," she says to Debbie.

"I'm just about two months along," Debbie says. "I've been feeling fine, though the funny thing is that March has had some morning sickness."

"You are such a wimp!" August calls out, laughing at his brother.

"Oh shut up," March says. "I can't help it. You didn't have to tell that," he says to Debbie.

Everyone laughs.

"The baby could be born on Christmas Day or maybe on New Year's Day," Debbie says.

"Now that'd be pretty special," Tucker says, "t' have yore baby born on yore anniversary."

Debbie's face glows. "I know," she says.

"It's time to pray," Smiley says as he kneels down on one knee and bows his head.

Everyone bows their heads and reaches for the hand of the one beside them until they're all connected.

"Our great God and Father in heaven," Smiley intones, "You are a most merciful God and a most gracious God. Your guiding hand has been upon each person in this room, leading us through our own personal 'valley of the shadow of death.' And here we are, whole and healthy and eternally grateful to you. Now you've seen fit to bless March and Debbie with the gift of a child. Our prayer is that you would carry that child in the hollow of your protective hand, letting it grow into a healthy baby, a baby that will be blessed to have these two caring people as its parents. Continue to watch over April and her growing baby as we eagerly await its arrival. Thank You sweet Jesus. In His name, let everyone say – "

Everyone in the room joins Smiley in saying, "Amen."

Debbie wipes away her tears as March reaches for his handkerchief and blows his nose.

April's face is shining with tears.

August keeps his head bowed as guilty feelings prick his heart.

"Can't nobody pray a prettier prayer than Smiley," Tucker says, wiping away her tears. She stands up. "But I've got work t' do. You kids bring in yore stuff and git settled in. Smiley, you an' April round up th' homemade ice cream maker. I gotta check on m' pies an' git ever'thing else t'gether. This is goin' t' be a evenin' of joyful celebration."

Chapter Fifty-two

After supper everyone pitches in to clean off the table.

"I'll tell you what I would love to have when we start singing and playing," April says.

"What's that?" March asks.

"What if we built a fire outside and sat around it? Wouldn't that be cool?"

"Oooo, I love how that sounds!" Debbie says.

"Good idea!" Tucker agrees. "I'll go out an' gather up some wood. August, you come help me. Our neighbors is gonna be showin' up soon. Smiley, you go grab our lawn chairs fer ever'body."

Smiley stands and salutes. "I never had a sergeant in the Army who barked orders any better than Tucker."

"Well I feel sorry fer yore sergeant if you was as lazy back then as you are now," Tucker retorts.

"You kids are my witnesses," Smiley says, "to the verbal abuse I have to take from this woman. One of these days I'm going to move out. The only reason I stay here is to see after her."

The three children and Debbie exchange smiles and winks.

"Just go on an' do like I said," Tucker says as she walks out the door.

The long shadows cast by the evening sun shining through the trees might make one believe the trees were a hundred feet tall. A cloud bank in the west appears as if it is on fire with various shades of red and orange.

Pointing to the fiery sky, August says, "Looks like fair weather ahead."

Tucker looks in the direction he's pointing. "Sure is. Y' still remember th' things y' learned growin' up on a farm, don't y'?"

"You know what they say, Tucker – 'You can take a boy out of the country, but you can't take the country out of a boy.'"

They walk to the wood pile.

"That sure makes me happy," Tucker says. "I worry 'bout you children livin' in th' big city an' bein' corrupted by it."

"You have something in particular in mind when you say that?" August asks.

Tucker pauses and looks at him for a moment. "Nothin' specific. I'm just talkin' in general. There's lots of meanness an' trouble in them big cities. Here, hold yore arms out."

August obeys and Tucker starts laying sticks on his arms. When the stack is up to his chest, she says, "Enough?"

"A couple more," August replies.

Tucker eases two more pieces on top. "I'll git some kindlin' t'gether."

As they walk back into the front yard, lightning bugs are flickering in the trees in their summer mating ritual and a chuck-will's-widow is starting its frenetic night song.

"Move out here, out from under th' trees," Tucker tells August, and he dumps his load onto the ground.

Out of the shadows, some figures appear and move closer to the pair as August arranges the kindling.

"Well lookee here!" Tucker exclaims. "It's th' Trevathans. Come on up here. We're just 'bout t' start us a fire out here. You kids ever sat 'round a campfire?"

The four Trevathans gather around Tucker while at the same time watching August getting prepared to start the fire. "They never have," Joyce says. "I haven't done it since I was a little girl. I can't tell you how excited the kids are about tonight. They've never seen people play and sing music."

Suddenly from the dark woods comes the high-pitched yipping sound of a coyote.

Alexander and Maria grab their mother's legs just as a small scream escapes her. "What was that?!" she cries.

August stands up laughing. He yells toward the woods, "Shady Green, come out of there you old polecat! Quit scaring these kids to death!"

There is rustling of leaves in the distance and a figure slowly emerges into sight carrying a guitar case. When he joins them, Shady says, "Ow ooo oh it wass me?"

"Because you used to scare me like that all the time when I was a kid," August answers.

"An' 'cause yore coyote always sounds like it's got a cold," Tucker adds.

"You got a match, Tucker?" August asks. She hands him a box of kitchen matches, and he kneels back down to light the fire.

Tiny yellow flames quickly devour the dried pine needles and dead leaves underneath the wood. Soon they begin licking the pieces of kindling. A cracking and popping sound soon follows.

"That's th' sound y' want t' hear," Tucker says. "It means things is heatin' up an' on their way."

The growing fire casts yellow light on the faces of everyone.

Shady Green takes off his cap an' bows toward Joyce and the children. "Ow-eee."

"Hello, Sh-Sh-Sh-Shady," Benjamin says.

"Ow ooo?"

"I'm g-g-g-good." Benjamin points at August and says, "Who's that?"

"That there is April's brother, August," Tucker explains.

August offers his hand to Benjamin who only looks at it.

"Shake his hand, Benjamin," Joyce says.

Benjamin grabs August's hand, vigorously pumps it twice, then lets go.

"I'm pleased to meet you," August says. "I've heard a lot about all of you." He shakes hands with the others.

The sound of aluminum chairs banging against each other gets everyone's attention. Smiley Carter is carrying and dragging lawn chairs in both hands.

August jogs to him. "Let me help, Pop."

April and Debbie come out of the front door carrying a card table, paper plates, Styrofoam cups, and plastic spoons. March stands in the doorway holding the ancient, wooden ice cream freezer. "If someone will give me a hand," he says, "I'll join the party."

"Joyce, that's m' other grandson, March," Tucker says. "He's blind. If you'll just go help him, he'll tell y' what t' do so he can follow y'."

347

As Joyce walks to the house, the sound of an approaching motorcycle can be heard.

"I hear Preacher and his chariot," Smiley says.

In a moment, the solitary headlight turns its attention to Tucker's driveway and helps Preacher steer his way into the yard. He and the rider behind him alight from his Harley. After they remove their helmets, they ease their way to the fire. Looking at everyone, Preacher says, "I don't believe you all have met Penny Wiseman."

Everyone speaks to her, except April.

Holding out a rectangular object wrapped in aluminum foil, Penny says, "I made a pound cake this afternoon. I thought everyone might enjoy a bite or two."

"That's mighty nice of y'," Tucker says as she takes the cake from her. "Oh my, an' it's still warm."

April watches Preacher and Penny as she sets up the card table.

As Tucker sets the cake on the table, she says in a low voice, "Y' need t' speak to 'er. It don't cost nothin' t' be nice t' people."

"Okay, okay. I will." April walks over to Preacher and Penny. "I'm really glad you all could come. And thanks for that cake. It'll taste really good with the homemade ice cream we've got."

"Oh my," Preacher says, "homemade ice cream. You all will have to hold me back. I think I could eat my weight in homemade ice cream."

"I heard that, Preacher," March says, as he sets down the ice cream freezer. "I don't want to have to hurt you, but I will if I have to fight you over this ice cream."

Preacher laughs. "Seeing as it's you, March, I guess I'll share some."

Soon everyone is sitting in a circle around the fire holding a cup of ice cream.

"I like this, Mama," Maria says.

"Me, too," Alexander agrees.

"It m-m-m-makes my h-h-h-head h-h-h-hurt," Benjamin says.

"You have to slow down," April says to him. "You've got what's called a brain freeze."

"I'll tell you all what's good," Smiley says. "Crumble up some of that pound cake on top of your ice cream and stir it up. It'll make your eyes roll up in the back of your head."

Everyone laughs, but no one looks up from their ice cream, intent on finding the bottom of their cup.

Tucker gets up and stirs the fire. Orange sparks rise up on the thermal of heat and disappear into the starry sky above. She adds a couple of sticks of wood. "Now then, ya'll git busy an' give us some music."

"I've got to run get my Autoharp," April says.

"Bring me my banjo, please," Smiley calls to her.

In a moment, she returns with the two cases as Shady Green strums and tunes his guitar. The three of them strum and listen to each other, bringing their instruments in tune with each other. They all look up at the same time, satisfied with their tuning.

"What about Foggy Mountain Breakdown?" April says.

"Foggy Mountain it is," Smiley says. In movements practiced over a lifetime, the fingers of his right hand are a blur as they pluck his banjo strings while his left hand and fingers find their way up and down the fret board.

April and Shady Green strum rhythm in perfect time with Smiley's tempo.

Before the song is over, everyone is clapping in time to the music. When it's finished, Joyce says, "Oh my goodness, you all are terrific!"

"Yes you are!" Penny agrees.

"Give 'em some John Hardy," Tucker says.

Without hesitation the trio of players begin playing. After a few measures, Tucker stands up and starts dancing.

A chorus of hollers and catcalls erupts from the delighted audience.

August jumps up and grabs Debbie's hand. "Are you too pregnant to dance?" he says above the music.

"Not at all!" a happy Debbie says.

Maria pulls on her mother's arm. "Dance with me, Mama."

Caught up in the moment of unabashed joy, Joyce lets herself be pulled out of her chair and dances with her daughter.

When the song is over, the dancers collapse into their chairs.

"We better slow this train down," Smiley says, "or somebody's liable to have a heart attack. April, sing us a Hank Williams tune. What about 'Your Cheatin' Heart'?"

April hesitates for only a second before she says, "Sure."

Halfway through the song, a new musical sound is heard. Heads quickly turn to discover Preacher playing a harmonica.

When it's time for another verse, April nods at him and says, "You play it."

The mournful whine of the harmonica fills the night.

When the song is over, the last notes hang in the air and echo softly in the woods. Respecting the quiet magic of the moment, no one says anything for a few seconds.

"I never knew you could play the harmonica, Preacher," an astonished April says.

"Prison time gives you opportunity to learn lots of things," Preacher replies.

"Well you play a fine mouth organ," Smiley says. "Really fine."

"Thank you," Preacher replies.

"Bennie," Alexander says, "why don't you sing a song?"

April quickly sees Benjamin's reticence and starts to say something to rescue him.

"Sing them an Elvis song, Bennie," Joyce urges him.

Before April can say anything, Benjamin stands up and strikes a pose as if he were Elvis. Without a stutter, he says, "Thank you. Thank you very much." Then he breaks into singing Viva Las Vegas at the top of his lungs. His voice is a perfect imitation of Elvis's, and he doesn't bobble a single lyric.

When he finishes singing his a cappella version of the song, everyone sits in stunned silence with their mouths open.

Chapter Fifty-three

"What in the world was that?!" April exclaims. "Seriously! Somebody pinch me because I must be in the middle of a dream. Benjamin, what did you just do?"

"Has he never sung Elvis for you?" Joyce asks innocently.

"Done what?" April replies. "'Sung Elvis.' What do you mean?"

"It's the beatingest thing," Joyce explains. "Whenever he sings a song like Elvis, he never stutters."

April stares at Benjamin with her eyes bugged out. "Why have you not told me about this?"

Benjamin's knee is bouncing. "B-B-B-Because you n-n-n-never asked."

"He sounds exactly like a young Elvis. And I mean exactly." August says.

"That's the craziest thing," Smiley says. "Why can he not stutter when singing like Elvis, but only when he sings like Elvis?"

April shakes her head in an attempt to clear her confusion. "Benjamin," she says, "look at me."

Benjamin's leg stops bouncing, and he looks directly at her.

"Is that the only Elvis song you sing like that?" she asks him.

"He knows all of Elvis's songs," Alexander interjects.

"Do you know 'Love Me Tender'?" she asks Benjamin.

Benjamin nods.

April gently strums her Autoharp. "Go ahead," she says to Benjamin. "Sing it."

From his lawn chair Benjamin stares at the fire and sings the song flawlessly.

Not far into the song Smiley, Shady, and Preacher join April in playing the accompaniment.

After the song is over, Preacher says, "What a voice. What a gift."

"I heard it with m' own ears an' I still don't believe it," Tucker says.

"Are y-y-y-you m-m-m-mad at m-m-m-me?" Benjamin asks April.

"Oh my gosh, no," April says. "I'm just so shocked. I never imagined you could do that. If I had known this, we would have been working in an entirely different direction. I'm excited for you. You sound amazing."

Benjamin flashes a broad grin.

"That's my Bennie," Joyce says proudly.

March holds up his empty cup and says, "Will somebody get a poor blind man another cup of ice cream?"

Debbie strikes him playfully on the arm. "Oh stop that!"

Everyone laughs.

Preacher walks over and takes his cup. "I'll get you some. I'm ready for round two as well."

"Go watch him," March says to Debbie. "Make sure he doesn't give himself more than me."

"Ouch!" April says as she leans back in her chair and grabs her abdomen.

"You okay?" Tucker says with concern.

"I think this baby wants to hear some more music so he can go back to sleep. He's kicking me."

"Maybe he just wants some more ice cream," Tucker says. "Here, give me yore cup an' I'll git y' some."

Everyone else decides to get seconds of ice cream also and lines up behind her.

When Benjamin comes back with his cup and sits beside April, she says, "I'll tell you what I'm going to do. I'm going to buy you a cd player and a packaged CD set of Elvis's greatest hits. Then we're going to use it when we work together. Ella always told me that it was all about finding the right key to unlock a problem. I just had no idea that your key would be Elvis Presley."

Benjamin eats a spoonful of ice cream and asks, "Wh-Wh-Wh-What's a CD?"

"It has music on it like records and albums used to have. But these are a lot smaller and can hold lots of music. You can even carry them around with you if you have a portable player."

Benjamin stares at her while he takes another bite. "C-C-C-Can you and I d-d-d-dance while S-S-S-Smiley and them play a s-s-s-song?"

"Bennie," Joyce says, "April is pregnant and may not feel like dancing."

He looks at April. "Inap-p-p-propriate?"

"No," April says. "You haven't said anything inappropriate. Asking a girl to dance is okay." She looks at Joyce and mouths, "Does he know how to dance?"

Joyce responds by shaking her head.

"All right everyone," April announces, "Benjamin and I are going to dance, providing our instrumentalists can do a slow number. I'm certainly not up to doing any clogging."

Smiley sets down his cup of ice cream and picks up his banjo. "Preacher, do you know 'Long Black Veil'?"

"Do I ever. Anyone who's spent time in prison knows that song. I may have to sing a line or two. I just hope it doesn't make me cry."

They begin playing the slow ballad and April joins Benjamin. They stand there looking at each other. When he doesn't make a move, April holds out one hand and says, "Take my hand in yours and put your other right here on my side."

Benjamin does as instructed and April rests her other hand on his shoulder.

"Watch my feet and do what I do," April says. She begins taking slow steps side to side.

Benjamin follows her lead but stays a half beat behind.

"How do they look?" March asks Debbie.

"It's very sweet," Debbie answers. "He's very childlike and clearly thinks the world of your sister." She takes his hand and pulls on him. "How about you and me dancing, too?"

March stands up and pulls her close to him. "Just don't dance me into the fire," he says with a smile.

Maria and Alexander stand up and begin imitating the dancing couples.

Joyce watches the scene and wipes a tear from her cheek.

Penny stands behind Preacher, resting her hands on his shoulders, and gently sways to the music.

Once the song is finished and everyone returns to their chairs, Tucker says, "This evenin' has been one of them memory makers, th' kind y' don't never want t' ferget. I'm so glad ever'one came."

Joyce clears her throat, trying to find her voice. "I don't remember anyone ever treating us so kindly. I don't know that I can put into words how much this has meant to me, to us."

"Joyce, let me tell y' a story 'bout a woman," Tucker says. "This woman grew up feelin' like life done kicked 'er in th' teeth an' held 'er face in th' dirt with a boot on 'er neck. You know what I mean? She growed up angry. She didn't like people an' didn't care what they said 'bout 'er. This woman didn't want t' have nothin' to do with people. She was gruff with 'em if they spoke to 'er. She never gave nobody nothin' an' never took nothin' from nobody. Ain't no other way t' say it except that she was mean."

Everyone else is listening intently to Tucker's story of self-disclosure.

"Then one day a woman come into 'er life. A woman that was as kind as any woman that ever walked this earth. She wasn't put off by th' mean woman's prickly exterior and ignored 'er when she done mean things to 'er. She even give th' mean woman gifts." Tucker's voice catches in her throat. She coughs to clear the emotion. "This kind, good woman treated th' mean woman with so much kindness that it melted 'er heart an' changed 'er."

Tucker turns her head from looking into the fire and looks at Joyce. There is a sheen on Tucker's cheeks from her tears. "Joyce, that mean woman was me."

Smiley reaches for his bandana in his back pocket, wipes his tears, and blows his nose.

April lets out a sob.

"That's not possible," Joyce says. "You've been nothing but kind to me and the kids."

"That's 'cause someone showed me kindness an' I learned what it felt like. So when you tell me it's hard t' express how much my kindness means t' you, I understand exactly what y' mean."

That night, before he goes to bed, Benjamin opens his treasure box but only takes out one thing – his journal. He writes:

Tonight I danced with an angel.

Around the edges of fire we moved

Nervously

Carefully

Softly.

Her hair shimmered in the light like strands of gold,

Bright

Brilliant

Beautiful.

The angel carries a life within her, a life within a life.

Tiny

Precious

And blessed.

How special it would be to have an angel as your mother!

Me and the angel were surrounded by an audience of family and friends

They were amazed at us.

The audience was led by a queen

Large

Powerful

Fierce.

When she moves the earth trembles.

When she speaks even the trees take notice and listen.

Many are afraid of her.

But not me.

I believe she would hear me when I cried

And that the angel would wipe my tears away.

Tonight was the most special night of my life.

Chapter Fifty-four

"Well, school's getting ready to start in a couple of weeks," April says to Benjamin. "How do you feel about starting back?"

"I-I-I-I'm ready," Benjamin replies.

"Remember, Benjamin, before you say something, you need to hear yourself in your head saying it as if you were Elvis. Try again."

Benjamin pauses, then says, "I'm ready."

"There, you see? I can't believe how much progress you've made in the last five or six weeks. It reminds me of how fast things changed for me when I started talking when I was little." She sits back and gasps while putting her hand on top of her swollen abdomen.

"The baby again?" Benjamin asks.

"Yes."

Benjamin watches her abdomen. "I see it m-m-m-moving!" he says excitedly. He takes a breath and says, "Moving."

April looks down and sees her clothes moving. "Do you want to put your hand on him and feel?"

Benjamin looks at her wide-eyed. "Really?"

"Sure. It's the coolest thing when you realize there is a human being inside there who is pushing and stretching, getting ready to come into the world."

When Benjamin hesitates, she takes his hand and lays it on the place where the baby is moving. She sits very still.

Benjamin's mouth pops open. "I f-f-f-feel it!" He looks at April's face. "Does it hurt?"

"Not all the time. Sometimes it's uncomfortable and then occasionally it does hurt. It's like he kicks me in the ribs. If he's as active when he gets here as he is now, I'm going to have my hands full."

"September twenty-fifth, right?" Benjamin asks.

"That's the due date the doctor picked, but that's just a pretty close guess. He could come before then or after then. Didn't your mother ever let you feel Alexander or Maria moving when she was pregnant?"

Benjamin takes his hand off of her and sits back on the couch. "I n-n-n-never knew she was pregnant."

April frowns. "But didn't you notice she was getting big? Or didn't she ever mention being pregnant?"

He shakes his head. "I don't think she w-w-w-wanted to be pregnant, so she pretended she w-w-w-wasn't."

"So you mean she would just come home one day with a baby?"

Benjamin nods.

"That's weird. You know, I've always wondered why your mom didn't leave B.J. and take you kids with her. It doesn't seem like she ever really loved him?"

Shrugging, Benjamin says, "Cancer, I guess."

"Oh yeah, I forget about that part of her story."

"You used to like P-P-P-Preacher, didn't you?" Benjamin asks abruptly.

April looks at him surprised. "What do you mean? I still like him. He's a really good man."

"No," Benjamin says, shaking his head. "I mean you liked him like you w-w-w-wanted to k-k-k-kiss him."

In spite of her efforts to act innocent, April feels her face reddening from this arrow of truth that Benjamin has shot into her heart. She toys momentarily with the idea of lying to Benjamin but decides to tell the truth. "Yes. You're right."

"Did it hurt your f-f-f-feelings when he started seeing that w-w-w-woman?"

April squirms in her seat. "It upset me, yes. But how did you know?"

"I-I-I-I." He pauses and takes a breath. "I may do and say things that make people uncomfortable, but I'm not stupid. I could just t-t-t-tell. I know how it feels."

For the second time in the last few minutes April is surprised by Benjamin's comments. "You had someone hurt your feelings like that?"

Benjamin nods.

"When?"

"Back in the spring."

"Why didn't you tell me? No, wait. I know the answer. Because I didn't ask, right?"

Benjamin nods again.

"Do you want to tell me about it?"

"Her name is Cassie Armour," Benjamin says. "She lives further d-d-d-down the road. I met her on the bus." Patting his chest, he says, "She made me smile in here."

April's heart is pricked by the tenderness of the gesture and words. "You were friends? I mean, like real friends, like the kind that kiss?

This time Benjamin blushes. "We n-n-n-never d-d-d-did anything like that. She was just nice to me and even stood up for me when people picked on me."

"Wow, I'd like to meet this girl. She sounds pretty special."

Benjamin smiles. "She even bloodied the nose of Mark O'Riley, a bully who rode the bus, too."

April tries to conjure up an image of what kind of girl would like Benjamin and take up for him, even punch a boy in the nose for him. The resulting image turns out to be not very flattering. Curiosity prompts her question, "What does Cassie look like?"

Benjamin doesn't hesitate. "Almost as beautiful as you, except she's not p-p-pregnant."

April laughs. "Well I'm glad to hear she's not pregnant. Tell me what happened between you."

"She decided she wanted to be popular b-b-b-but couldn't do that as long as she was nice to me."

April's opinion of Cassie immediately plummets. "Are you sure that's what happened?"

He nods. "A star f-football player asked her to be with him and some cheerleaders asked her t-to try out for cheerleader. She g-got what she wanted, I g-guess." He hangs his head and his shoulders droop.

"Well I'll tell you what," April says, "she chose the wrong path."

Looking up at her, Benjamin says, "Wrong path?"

"You know that Robert Frost poem 'The Road Not Taken'? About the two paths that diverged, and he had to choose one of the paths?"

He shakes his head.

"What? I thought everyone in high school read that poem. Let me see if I can remember it. We had to memorize it when I was in school.

Two roads diverged in a yellow wood,

And sorry I could not travel both

And be one traveler, long I stood

And looked down one as far as I could

To where it bent in the undergrowth;

Then took the other, as just as fair,

And having perhaps the better claim,

Because it was grassy and wanted wear;

Though as for that the passing there

Had worn them really about the same,

And both that morning equally lay

In leaves no step had trodden black.

Oh, I kept the first for another day!

Yet knowing how way leads on to way,

I doubted if I should ever come back.

I shall be telling this with a sigh

Somewhere ages and ages hence:

Two roads diverged in a wood, and I—

I took the one less traveled by,

And that has made all the difference.

Benjamin stares at her intently as she finishes reciting the poem.

"I surprised myself," April says. "I didn't know if I would even remember all of it much less recite it. But do you see the point he makes?"

"I think so. So Cassie chose the p-path of p-popularity, and I don't live on that p-path."

"That's definitely one way to say it. But there will come a day, and maybe already has, that she will think about that time when she stood looking at two paths. And she'll have regret about the path she took and regret about how she treated you."

They sit quietly for a few minutes. Then Benjamin says, "I write poems."

"Benjamin Trevathan, that better not be true. You better not have been writing poems and not told me about it."

He grins. "I have."

"That is the third time this afternoon that you've surprised me. You're just a wonderment."

"Would you like to see them?"

"Of course I would!"

Benjamin stands up. "I'll be right back." He exits the house before April can say anything.

Ten minutes later Benjamin re-enters the house huffing and puffing and clutching his treasure box in both hands.

"Good lord, Benjamin," April says, "don't have a stroke. Get you a drink of water and catch your breath."

He gets a glass out of the cabinet and fills it from the kitchen sink. After gulping it down and wiping his mouth on his sleeve, he joins April on the couch.

April recognizes the box from the time that he took her to his house to show her his Matchbox cars.

He opens it almost reverently.

She sees a worn envelope with two dried flowers sitting on top of it. She starts to ask about the items but decides this is Benjamin's show, and she'll wait for him.

Benjamin holds up the two flowers. "From Maria." After he sets them carefully on the floor, he holds up the envelope. "From Cassie."

April has to bite her tongue to keep from asking to open it and see what is inside.

Underneath the envelopes the Matchbox cars are lying helter-skelter, no doubt from the bumpy journey they just took from Benjamin's house to hers. He pours the cars out onto the floor and takes out the last item – a notebook. Handing it to her, he says,

"This is it. You have to start from the front and g-g-go toward the back. They've b-been written over the y-years. Some aren't so good, but that's when I w-w-was a kid."

April isn't listening to him. She has opened the notebook and is immediately fully engaged in reading. As she slowly turns the pages she feels herself being drawn into the mind and heart of this multifaceted, complex boy. Each poem resonates with honesty. The simple way that he expresses both complex and traumatic feelings and events takes her breath. When she reads about Cassie, the words blur as tears fill her eyes. She feels her heart echoing her feelings from when it was crushed by Preacher. And when she reads his poem about the night they danced around the fire, she begins sobbing. Tears splatter on the pages, causing some of the ink to smudge.

She closes the notebook and stares at the back of it, trying to decide what to say. "Benjamin, I don't know what to say." She holds up the notebook. "This is one of the most touching and moving things I have ever read." She puts the heel of her hand on her chest. "It touches me right here. What does your mother think about them?"

"Y-You're the only p-person who's ever r-r-read them."

April sobs again. "Oh my gosh, Benjamin. I am so honored that you let me read them. I will always treasure this moment."

Benjamin leans down and picks up his red Camaro off the floor. He hands it to her. "I want you to have this."

April holds up her hand. "But that's your favorite one. I can't take that from you."

"That's why I w-w-want you to have it. I won't ever f-forget you."

April takes the car and closes her hand around it. "I want to do something, but I want to explain it first so that you don't

366

misunderstand. I want to kiss you on your cheek. It's a kiss that means you are a special friend, that I admire you, and that I thank you for this gift. But it's not like – "

"Like we're b-boyfriend and g-g-girlfriend," Benjamin interjects.

"That's right. You understand?"

Benjamin nods and closes his eyes.

April leans forward and gently kisses his cheek.

Chapter Fifty-five

"The bus is here!" Benjamin calls to his brother and sister.

Alexander comes bursting out of his room with the strings of his tennis shoes trailing along on the floor. Just before he runs past Benjamin, Benjamin grabs him.

Kneeling, Benjamin says, "Let me t-tie your shoes."

"Hurry," Alexander says. "It's the first day of school. We don't need to be late."

When Benjamin finishes tying the shoes, he says, "Tell the b-bus driver that Maria and I will b-be there in a second."

"Okay," Alexander replies, and he runs to catch the school bus.

"I'm coming!" Maria exclaims as she exits her room. Her mother follows her, trying to pull her ponytail tight.

When they reach Benjamin, Joyce says, "Let me get this barrette fixed, then you'll be ready." She snaps it in place. "You look pretty," she says to Maria. Shifting her gaze to Benjamin, she says, "And you look handsome."

Benjamin takes Maria's hand. "Let's g-go. The bus won't wait f-forever." As the two of them leave the porch he says, "Bye Mama."

"Bye!" Joyce calls to the retreating figures. "Have a good day!"

Benjamin lets Maria get on first. He looks at the bus driver. "Who are y-y-you?"

"I'm the new bus driver."

"B-But you're a woman."

"I can't deny that. Is that a problem for you?"

This unexpected change has thrown Benjamin off, as do most unexpected changes. He hears April's voice in his head, *"Everything is not always going to go the way you want it to. You have to learn to adapt to change."* He looks at the bus driver and says, "N-N-No ma'am. Not a problem. Nice to m-meet you."

As he walks down the aisle, Benjamin notices that very few faces have changed. There are a couple of new kids who must be starting kindergarten. He's relieved to see that Mark O'Riley isn't on the bus. Benjamin's regular seat is unoccupied, so he sits there. He looks out the window as the bus resumes its rounds.

Without looking at the road he can tell from the landscape exactly where they are. When the bus slows close to where Cassie lives, he looks up and is surprised when it stops in front of her house. She stopped riding the bus last year when she and Blake started seeing each other. *Maybe she's moved and someone else lives here now,* he thinks to himself.

The front door of the house opens and a girl with bright, blonde hair steps out. She keeps her head down as she approaches the bus, preventing Benjamin or anyone else from seeing her face.

The door of the bus opens to let her in and she climbs the steps. When she looks up, Benjamin is shocked to see that it is Cassie, except that she's much thinner and that blonde hair is something new.

She walks down the aisle and stops at the seat in front of him. To the young girl sitting there. Cassie growls, "This is my seat. Get up and move."

The girl looks up, terrified at the tone and facial expression of this upper classman. She gathers her things quickly, slides out and moves to another seat.

Cassie flops onto the seat, sits with her back against the side of the bus and her legs stretched out on the seat. She doesn't acknowledge Benjamin's presence by speaking or by looking at him.

He sits in stunned silence staring at her as the bus begins rolling. *Another unexpected change*, he says to himself.

After a few minutes Cassie's head snaps in his direction. "What are you staring at?!"

The effect of her words and the intensity of their delivery wouldn't have been any stronger if she'd slapped him in the face. Benjamin's head jerks back and his eyes grow wide. He quickly looks away from her.

Several more minutes pass without any words passing between them. At last, Cassie says, "I'm sorry, Benjamin. I shouldn't have snapped at you. This is just not the way I envisioned starting my junior year of high school. I thought I would have a car and a boyfriend and would be popular at school. Ask me how that plan worked out."

Benjamin glances at her then looks away. "How d-did that plan work out?"

"Not too good!"

Once again Benjamin flinches at the venom in her tone.

"I thought I knew what I wanted," Cassie continues. "And I thought I was finally on my way to achieving it."

"What happened t-to your hair?" Benjamin asks.

Cassie grabs two handfuls of her hair. "Right! Look at this! I even thought that changing the way I looked was the answer. All that achieved was making me looking like an idiot."

Benjamin tries to piece together the bits of information Cassie is sharing with him, but he makes no sense of the puzzle. "I don't understand."

"Well let me start with Blake. To put it plainly, it turns out all he was interested in was having sex with me, to cut another notch on his belt of someone he's had sex with. It was just a game with him. He lied to me and played me like a character in a video game. My mistake was in being so gullible. I believed everything he said. I thought he really did love me, and that I was in love with him. Or at least I thought I was. He didn't try anything at first, but the more times we went out he kept pushing and pushing the limits. The last time we went out he got so angry with me I thought he was actually going to rape me. That's the last time I've seen or spoken to him."

Benjamin feels his face getting hot. He squeezes his fists and clenches his jaws. Suddenly he pounds his fist into his palm. "I'll t-take care of him."

Cassie looks at him with alarm. "No! No you won't. It's all over and done with. I don't need you to do anything. The last time you tried taking up for me we all got in trouble." She grabs his arm and shakes it. "Do you hear me? I said you are not to do anything. Okay?"

Benjamin takes a deep breath and lets it out. Nodding, he says, "Okay. What about your ch-cheerleader friends? Didn't that work out?"

"It went okay for a while until my dad saw me in one of the cheerleading outfits. He flipped out. He said there was no way he was going to allow me to put my body on public display in something like that. We had a big fight about it. But eventually I had to drop out."

"Were you s-sad?"

"Sort of. It was like I lost out on a dream I had. There were several really sweet girls on the squad that I had fun with. But I also learned that some of them were really two-faced, like Courtney and Stefanie. I think they and Blake were just playing some kind of sick game together and I was the pawn. I'm better off without friends like that."

"G-Good friends are hard to f-find," Benjamin says.

She stares at him. "Oh my God, Benjamin! What has happened?"

Benjamin blinks rapidly. "What d-do you mean?"

"I just realized you're not stuttering like you always have."

Benjamin flashes a broad smile. "I've been working on it. S-Someone's been helping me."

"It's wonderful! Unbelievable, really. Who's been helping you?"

"One of our n-neighbors. Her n-name is April. She's a good friend."

"I'm so excited and happy for you. April must be a pretty special person. Everyone at school is going to be so surprised." She continues to look at him. "You look different."

"D-Different how?"

"I'm trying to figure it out. For one thing, your clothes. Are those new?"

"Uh-huh. April's grandmother, Tucker, b-bought some for all of us."

"They look really nice." She continues to study him. "Your eye contact, that's what else is different. You are looking me in the eye more."

"I've been practicing," Benjamin explains.

"You just look more confident, Benjamin," April says. "That really sums it up. You look like you feel better about yourself."

"There's been lots of ch-changes at home. Mama doesn't have c-cancer. And my step-dad is in jail."

"In jail! What for?"

Benjamin relates the details of the night of B.J.'s assault on him and Alexander and Maria.

When he finishes, Cassie has her hand over her mouth. "Oh Benjamin, how awful and how scary. That could have turned out so much worse. I'm glad all of you are okay."

The bus slows to a stop in front of the high school. Benjamin, Cassie, and the other high school students get off. Before they reach the front door, someone steps in the path of Benjamin and Cassie.

Benjamin looks up to see Mark O'Riley, dressed in black and wearing sunglasses. "Back off," Mark says to Benjamin. "I've got something to say to Cassie."

Benjamin looks at him, then at Cassie.

"I've got nothing to say to you, Mark," Cassie says.

"I'm here to help," Mark replies. "I heard what that jerk Blake Barker tried to do to you. You deserve better. Just say the word and I'll take care of him." As he is speaking, he lifts his shirt to reveal the handle of a pistol protruding from the waistband of his jeans.

Chapter Fifty-six

Cassie slaps Mark's hand that is holding up his shirt. The deadly pistol is once again hidden. "What do you think you're doing?" Cassie says in a hoarse whisper. "Do you realize how much trouble you'll get into for bringing that to school? I don't know if you're crazy or just plain stupid."

Mark steps closer to Cassie. "I told you one time," he says in a low voice, "that we were meant to be together. The sooner you accept that, the better we'll both be. Anyone who thinks they are going to get in the way of that happening doesn't realize how much danger they're in."

Benjamin studies Cassie's face closely, looking for any signs of fear or panic. She appears relatively unperturbed by what for him was a jolting image of the pistol in Mark's waistband.

"Listen to me," Cassie says, her voice rising. "You and I are never going to be together. Not today, not tomorrow, not in the next millennium. The sooner you get that through your head, the better off you'll be."

Mark's hand shoots out, and he grabs Cassie's arm.

In the next instant Benjamin strikes a hammer blow to Mark's side with his fist.

Air is forced out of Mark's lungs. Releasing Cassie, he clutches his side and bends over.

"It's the first day of school and my favorite trio is gathered together, I see." Mr. Clelland's voice booms.

The group turns to see him exiting the building and walking swiftly toward them.

Mark stands up and sprints toward the parking lot.

Benjamin and Cassie face Mr. Clelland.

"I see the three of you were renewing your friendship," Mr. Clelland says. "I wonder where Mr. O'Riley is heading in such a hurry." When Benjamin and Cassie don't answer, he says, "What, no reply? I doubt you all were making plans to meet around a campfire and hold hands and sing Kumbaya together. So tell me what that was all about."

Benjamin starts to answer him when Cassie says, "It wasn't anything. I haven't seen Mark or Benjamin all summer, so we were just talking about what happened while school was out."

"Sort of a prelude to your essay 'What I did over summer vacation'? That's what you're telling me? Please don't insult me." He shifts his gaze to Benjamin. "Is what Cassie said, true?"

Benjamin is reminded of watching a cat holding a mouse under its paw, letting it go, then pouncing on it again. He feels the weight of knowing that Cassie wants him to back her story, though he doesn't know why she lied. But there is also the pressure of the truth that is in his throat, begging to be told. He fights the urge to follow Mark's example and simply run away. Biting his bottom lip, he decides to say nothing.

Mr. Clelland puts his hands on his hips. "You two are really something, you know it? As unlikely a pair as I've ever seen in all my years of teaching. I heard about you and Blake breaking up, Cassie. I hope it wasn't too painful for you."

Benjamin watches Cassie frown. Anger tinges her voice when she says, "How do you know that?"

"We live in a small town. Not much goes on without people finding out. Anyway, let me tell you that you didn't lose anything by getting rid of Blake. You deserve better."

This surprises Benjamin. He thought that everyone held a positive view of Blake, seeing as how popular he is.

"I just wish you hadn't quit the cheerleading squad," the principal adds.

"Thank you, sir," Cassie says. "My dad and I sort of had a difference of opinion on that subject. And in my house, my dad's opinion rules."

"Nothing wrong with that," he says with a smile. The jarring ringing of the school bell interjects itself into the conversation. Mr. Clelland steps to the front door and holds it open. "Okay, what say we get this new year started?"

Familiar smells and sounds greet Benjamin as he steps inside the school building. Voices, footsteps, and banging doors of metal lockers fill the air. Freshmen girls, eager to impress and catch the attention of the older boys, have overindulged in their use of perfume, creating a concoction that causes Benjamin to sneeze.

A girl calls out Cassie's name.

Cassie waves excitedly. "Hey, wait for me."

Benjamin watches as Cassie blends into a crowd of girls.

Chapter Fifty-seven

"Why did she l-l-lie?" Benjamin looks pensively at April.

"Did you ask Cassie?" April asks.

"No."

"Why not?"

"I didn't see her again. She didn't ride the b-b-bus home."

April sees the hurt and confusion in Benjamin's eyes. "I don't know why she lied, Benjamin. Maybe she didn't want to cause more trouble. Sounds like this Mark guy is whacko. April might be afraid that if she told on him, and he got in trouble, that he would do something to her. The truth though, is you need to be careful."

"B-But it's Cassie he wants. Why do you think I n-need to be careful?"

"You're right when you say he wants Cassie. That is exactly the reason he's not going to hurt her. But this is at least the second time you've hurt him and embarrassed him. A guy with an ego like Mark's won't tolerate being embarrassed without finding a way to exact revenge."

April watches Benjamin turn over in his mind the things she's said. After a few moments, when he doesn't say anything, she says. "Come on, let's sing a song."

Ignoring her question, Benjamin says, "W-Will I ever have g-girlfriend?"

April detects a hopeless tone in his voice. She feels as if someone has pinched her heart, and she reflexively puts her hand on her chest. She looks at his unblinking eyes. A dozen answers to his question line up side by side each saying, "Choose me! Choose me!" But they are all variations of a lie, a lie meant to spare Benjamin's feelings. And though hurting his feelings is the last thing in the world April wants to do, she reaches past the lineup of lies and pulls out the truth. "Benjamin, I have never met anyone like you. People use an expression sometimes that goes like this, 'When God made you he broke the mold.'"

Benjamin cocks his head to one side and frowns a bit.

"It's a compliment," April explains. "It means there's not another person quite like you. Benjamin, you have a genuine heart. When you act, it's in response to your truth. It's not to impress or manipulate. Do you realize how unusual that is?"

"Is that good or bad?" Benjamin asks.

"It's rare," April answers. "As a matter of fact I only know one other person who has that trait."

"Who's that?"

"My grandmother, Tucker."

"I like her. At f-first she scared me, b-but not anymore."

April laughs. "Yes, she can be pretty scary. And very few people look past the outside of her, the scary part of her, to see the beautiful person she really is. She really does have a heart of gold, just like you do." She pauses as a new truth dawns on her. "Maybe that's why I've wanted to help you. Because you are so much like her, and nobody helped her when she was growing up."

"Soooo." Benjamin stretches out the word as if it were a rubber band around his wrist. He holds it for a second, knowing that when he releases it, it's going to hurt. "So you're saying I'm like T-Tucker. She n-never got married, so I'm n-n-never going to find s-s-s-someone who wants t-to m-m-marry m-m-me."

Grabbing his hands, April says, "Now wait. That's not exactly what I'm saying. You see, Tucker never married because she never wanted to." She releases his hands and sits back. "I'm not doing a very good job of explaining myself."

She sits back up to give it another try. "You asked if you are ever going to have a girlfriend. I think that one day you will, but it will have to be someone who is as special and rare as you are. And you may have to look for a long time to find her."

Benjamin nods slowly. "I think I understand. I have to be p-patient, don't I?"

"Absolutely. It's a lesson that I have had to learn the hard way. There's two reasons to be in a relationship with someone: because you have to and because you want to. The first reason means you're desperate. And if you're desperate, you'll end up making a poor choice. The second reason is the one that will lead to a lasting relationship."

Benjamin listens very closely to her. "You d-don't think C-Cassie is the one for me, do you?"

April shakes her head. "No, I don't. But I also don't think you're the one for her. Remember, it has to go both ways. You need to just enjoy being sixteen and continue working on making friends with people. Your time will come, Benjamin. I'm certain of it."

At home that night, Benjamin writes in his journal:

The way of love is such a mystery to me.

I look inside my heart and try to see

If what I feel can possibly be

Something that can grow from me into we.

Questions, questions, questions

Will I someday find that person who will see in me what I see in them?

Will I feel like I'm looking in a mirror?

Or will that person be the missing pieces of me that will make me complete?

Is it really possible to find someone who will

smile with me,

sing with me,

cry with me?

Chapter Fifty-eight

The next day April and Tucker are sitting in the waiting room of the doctor's office.

April says, "The way I answered Benjamin I almost felt like I was pouring water on a campfire. I know it wasn't what he wanted to hear."

"I remember Ella sayin' t' me one time, 'The truth will set y' free, but first it'll make y' miserable,'" Tucker replies. "Them's true words, April. Ben trusts y'. That's 'cause he knows you're honest with him. I know it was hard fer y' t' tell him all that, but anything else would've hurt him worse in th' long run." She pauses and puts her hand on April's leg. "I'm real proud of ever'thing you've done fer that boy. You've made a real difference in his life."

"I'm just paying back, or maybe I'm paying forward, for all the help I received when I was growing up. I was such a mess. If it hadn't been for you and Ella and the people at Spirit Lake, there's no telling where I would have ended up. I'm not saying I've got my life all together, but I'm a lot further along than I was just six months ago."

"Lord, you was a mess," Tucker says with a smile.

"Well you don't have to agree with me," April says with feigned seriousness.

"April?" A woman in scrubs is holding a door open.

"Hi, Jeannie," April says. "You ready for me?" To Tucker she says, "She's one of the nurses."

Jeannie says, "We're ready."

"Come on," April says to Tucker. After making the obligatory stop on the scales, April follows Jeannie to an exam room.

Once inside, the nurse takes April's vitals. When finished, she says, "A.A. will be in in a bit."

"Is that th' midwife's name?" Tucker asks.

"Yes."

"What kind of name is A.A.?"

"It's the initials of her first and last name, Amy Anita. She said she's always been called A.A. You're going to like her."

"It don't matter whether I like 'er or you like 'er. What matters is whether she knows what she's doin'."

"I've talked to several other people who've used A.A.," April says, "and they all say she is wonderful in the delivery room. None of them have had any complications or problems."

"Well there better not be. This here's my first great-grand-youngun. I don't want nothin' t' happen."

There's a quick rap on the exam room door and the door opens. A petite woman with red hair and a stethoscope around her neck breezes in. Smiling, she says, "Hi, April."

"Hi, A.A. A.A., this is my grandmother, Tucker."

The midwife puts her hands on her hips and says, "So we finally meet. I must admit that I was beginning to wonder if you were real or not. All of April's stories about you sounded almost mythical." She sticks her hand out. "I'm honored to meet you."

Tucker's large hand swallows A.A.'s as she shakes it. "April here has had some pretty good things t' say 'bout you, too. How many babies have y' delivered?"

A.A. laughs. "I used to keep up with the number, but once I got past two hundred I quit. It didn't seem so important anymore."

"That's a rightly good number," Tucker says. "I had me a midwife when I give birth t' April's Mama. She didn't have no education, but delivered babies 'round here fer probably fifty 'r sixty years."

"Wow," A.A. says, "that's impressive. It's people like her who were the forerunners and trailblazers for people like me. I would have loved to have met her. What was her name?"

"We all called 'er Mama Mattie."

"Believe it or not I've actually had other people tell me about her."

"Excuse me, people," April says, waving her hand. "I think this appointment is for me and my baby, not for you two to detail the history of midwifery in northwest Tennessee."

"You'll have t' excuse 'er, Miss A.A.," Tucker says. "She sometimes acts like she's th' first person what ever carried a baby."

A.A. cackles like a hen laying an egg. "Oh you're a good one," she says to Tucker. "I need to keep you around." Taking her stethoscope from around her neck, she says, "But I guess I need to take a listen, if for no other reason than to satisfy this young woman."

April lays back on the exam table. The white paper crackles. A.A. puts her stethoscope on her abdomen. April says, "You and Tucker need to put together a comedy routine. You're hilarious." Before the compliment has time to be taken seriously, she adds, "Not really."

The midwife has suddenly shifted from being socially engaging and relaxed, to all business. Her face is impossible to read as she moves the stethoscope to different places and listens closely. She pulls the stethoscope out of her ears and places her hands on April' abdomen and pushes. "How have you been feeling? Any spotting or cramping?"

"Other than feeling tired, I've felt all right. He hasn't been moving around as much, but I figured that's because there's not much room to move around."

A.A. gives no indication she's heard April's comment as she continues her examination. "What's the baby's name?"

"Now if'n y' git that out of 'er, I'll give y' a dollar," Tucker says. "She won't tell none o' us what it is."

"Mm-hmm," A.A. replies.

"I'm pretty sure what I'm going to name him," April say, "but I'm going to let it be a surprise." She looks up at A.A.'s face. "What's wrong?"

Ignoring the question, A.A. makes practiced moves with her hands, pressing and pushing on April's abdomen. When she stops and washes her hands, April says, "Something's wrong, isn't it?"

A.A. leans back against the sink as she dries her hands with paper towels. "Your baby is turned the wrong way."

"The wrong way? Is he going to be okay?"

Tucker stands up, walks to April's side, and takes her hand. "Y' mean th' baby's breeched?"

"Yes. But that doesn't mean he'll stay that way. It's possible he may get turned before you deliver."

"What if he doesn't? What does it mean? Will everything still be okay?"

Tucker pats her hand, then helps her sit up. "Y' just let Miss A.A. take care o' things. Lot's o' baby's git birthed when they's breeched. Ain't that right Miss A.A.?"

A.A. looks at Tucker then at April. "A breech birth is not the easiest to handle, but there are options."

"What does that mean?" April asks.

"It might be that we decide to do a cesarean. But that's not something we have to decide until it's time to deliver. There's nothing for you to worry about or to do. We'll just see what Mother Nature does and make our decision then."

Chapter Fifty-nine

Two weeks later when Benjamin arrives at April's house to practice, he hands her a piece of paper.

"What's this?" she asks as she scans it. "Oh, the Annual Talent Contest," she says before Benjamin can answer her. "Do they still do that? I remember it when I was in high school." She looks up at Benjamin with a questioning expression.

"I w-want to sing in it," Benjamin says.

Pointing at the paper, April says, "In this? The school talent contest?"

Benjamin nods. "Yes. F-First prize is one hundred dollars. My Mom's b-birthday is October second. I've n-n-never bought her a birthday present. I want to this year."

April glances back at the paper. "September twenty-fifth is the date of the contest? That's a coincidence. It's the same date as when my baby's due."

Benjamin grins. "I know. I wasn't going to be in the c-contest until I saw that d-date. I th-think it's an omen. Is that the right word?"

Looking back at him, April says, "An omen?"

"Me being in the contest on the same d-day as when your b-baby is born is sure to bring me good luck."

"Look, Benjamin, first of all there's no way to know for certain that the baby will be born on that date. It could come earlier or later."

He shakes his head. "Uh-uh. I had a dream and the baby was born on the twenty-fifth."

April starts to disagree with him but decides not to. "Okay. But the other thing is that luck has nothing to do with winning a talent contest, Benjamin. You have to be good."

"You d-don't think I'm good?"

"What are you thinking about doing in the contest?"

"An Elvis song."

April closes her eyes, bends her head down some, and rubs between the middle of her eyes with the tip of her middle finger. She envisions Benjamin impersonating Elvis in front of the school student body and all of them laughing and mocking him. "Oh Benjamin," she says without opening her eyes.

"What the m-matter?" Benjamin asks. "You told me I sound j-j-just like Elvis. Was that not the t-truth?"

April looks up at him and realizes that her lack of enthusiasm about his idea has eroded his recently found self-confidence. As she often is with Benjamin, she finds herself on a tightrope trying to balance being honest with him and being encouraging to him. "Yes, it was the truth. You really do sound like him. I'm just concerned with how your audience will react. I know how cruel kids can be. I don't want you to be hurt."

"If they th-think I'm Elvis, they won't make f-fun of me."

"If they think you're Elvis? What do you mean?"

"I think that as soon as I walk out in front of everyone that s-some of them will start laughing and m-making fun of me. But if I sing with the voice and the heart of Elvis, I think it will silence them. I think they'll be s-s-surprised. You always tell me to just let the m-music flow through me. Not t-to worry about anything but the song. I think I can do it."

April drops her protests as she feels herself being drawn in by Benjamin's confident and passionate words. She smiles. "You

387

know what? If you're willing to put yourself out there like that, to climb out on the edge of a cliff, then by gosh you just might pull it off. And if you do, 'surprised' won't be the word to describe everyone's reaction. 'Dumbfounded' will be more like it. There are only four weeks until the contest. We've got to get busy and choose the song you'll sing. Then I'll order one of those accompaniment CD's that you can use to practice and use at the contest, too. I think we need to just focus on the vocal performance and not try to get into the costume and movements like Elvis. It'll be more dramatic if it's just your voice that wows them. The more I talk about it, the more excited I get. This could be one of the most memorable talent contests Dresden High School has ever had."

Chapter Sixty

"It's awfully nice of you to fix supper for all of us," Joyce says.

"This here's a pre-celebration meal," Tucker says. "We're all celebrating Ben there winnin' th' school talent contest t'morrow. I been hearin' him practicin' with April. I'm tellin' y' them kids at school won't know what t' think when he starts singin'. I can't wait t' see it."

"You're going to be there?" Joyce asks.

"Heck yeah. Me an' Smiley is goin' with April, ain't we?"

"You bet," Smiley replies. "It'll be a sight to behold. Young Benjamin has blossomed into such a fine young man and has a voice to match. All those kids who've made fun of you, Benjamin, are going to be picking their jaws up off the bleachers when they witness the miracle you've become."

Benjamin grins.

"Of course our plans'll change if April decides t' have 'er baby t'morrow," Tucker says.

"Ha!" April says. Looking down, she explains, "I don't think this boy is ever going to come out."

Joyce gives her a sympathetic look. "Those last few weeks are the most miserable. All three of my kids came late. Don't you worry, when it's time for him to be born, he'll pop right out."

"Can me and Alexander be at the talent contest, too?" Maria asks.

"Yeah," Alexander says, "we want to cheer for Bennie."

"Y-You've got school," Benjamin answers them. "They won't let you out f-for something like this." Pointing to his heart, he adds, "You'll be with me r-right here."

"Bennie's right," Joyce concurs. "You'll get to see his prize when he brings it home."

"Everyone needs to slow down just a bit," April says. "This is not about winning. It's about being brave enough to stand up and perform in front of your peers. They are the toughest audience to impress. And even if Benjamin does a flawless job of singing his song, the judges could simply not be fans of Elvis and frown on his performance."

"Not like Elvis?!" Joyce has a horrified expression. "How could anyone not like the King? That's plumb un-American."

"April makes a good point," Tucker says. "It's a pretty good victory fer Ben t' be participating in th' contest. Somethin' like that would've seemed impossible just six months ago."

Everyone turns their attention to Benjamin. He tries to return their gaze, but the cumulative weight of them proves too much, and he looks at the floor. "When we m-moved to Dresden," he says, "I figured it w-would be like every other time we moved, and we'd be here for a little while then we'd m-move again. The first t-time I walked in th-the McDaniel house I told myself there's only one step lower than this and that is t-t-to be h-homeless." He points at April. "That's when you showed up. You were like the Greek goddess Athena we read about in English. When I read that Athena was the patron g-goddess of heroic endeavors, I said to myself, 'I have m-met Athena, and she is real.'"

Listening with rapt attention to Benjamin, his audience looks at April's blushing face then back at him.

"You convinced me I could b-be b-better than I was. You refused to l-l-let me give up." He then points at Tucker. "And you are a f-female Hercules or maybe even Z-Z-Zeus. You aren't afraid of anything." Spreading his arms to include everyone in the room, he says, "I finally feel a feeling that I had decided I would never feel. I feel like I have a home and a family." Benjamin's voice catches in his throat.

Sniffles can be heard from every quarter.

Tears stream down Joyce's face.

Tucker lifts her glasses and wipes her eyes with her finger and thumb.

Benjamin coughs to clear his emotionally choked voice. "I f-f-f-feel safe with you people."

Overwhelmed, Smiley gushes, "Oh my lord, boy, you are too much! You're absolutely going to make my heart burst. Come on, let's all hold hands."

Everyone reaches for the person beside them and they lock hands.

Satisfied, Smiley closes his eyes and lifts his face toward the ceiling. "Sweet, blessed, Lord, what have we done to deserve Your sending this precious family into our midst? They blew in like a tumbleweed, lost and without a home. Because of Your bountiful grace and mercy toward us we were able to share with them what little we had. But what they shared with us was more lasting than the mere food and clothing and shelter we shared with them. It was the imprint of their souls on our lives, an imprint that will stay with me until I breathe my last and Your angel takes me by the hand to lead me to the other side. To witness their blossoming, once they were delivered from the mouth of that evil lion, has been like beholding a miracle." He raises his hands over his head and everyone else, refusing to let go of their partner's hand, lifts theirs as well. "And now, sweet Jesus, we ask You to bless Ben tomorrow. Fill his chest with courage and his voice with strength. Help everyone at that school see the miracle, too. And one last thing, Lord, April would sure like to hurry and have her baby. So if it's all the same to You, let him get here sooner rather than later. Amen."

Chapter Sixty-one

Sometime after midnight, April awakens with a start. The first thing she notices is that her sheets and gown are wet. As her sleepy brain puzzles over the why of that, she feels a gripping pain in her lower back and across her abdomen. Realization dawns quickly. "Tucker!" she cries out.

The walls shudder and the floor vibrates as Tucker comes thundering down the hallway. "I'm comin' Baby Girl!" She flips on the light switch as she enters April's bedroom. "What's th' matter?"

April pulls back her covers to reveal the soaked sheets. "My water broke."

"Are y' havin' contractions?"

"Yes. I just had one."

"Okay. Ever'thing's gonna be fine. It's all right on schedule."

"Is everything all right?" Smiley calls from his bedroom.

"This girl's fixin' t' have a baby," Tucker answers. "If you'd've prayed last week fer the baby t' be born, we wouldn't've had t' wait so long." She turns her attention to April. "Sit on the edge o' th' bed while I get a towel t' dry you off an' a dry gown t' put on. You watch th' clock an' time when yore next contraction is so's we can know how far apart they are."

Leaving April to struggle herself to a sitting position, Tucker goes to the bathroom, grabs a towel, and then goes to April's dresser to get a gown. She returns to April's side and says, "Let's git this wet thing off'n y'."

April allows herself to be undressed without protest.

Tucker pats her dry and then puts the clean gown on her.

Suddenly April grips Tucker's arm and sucks in a quick breath.

Tucker stops and looks at her. "Another contraction?"

April holds her breath and nods.

"'member what Miss A.A. said. Keep breathin'. Them contractions is already close together. Seven minutes or so?"

Between quick breaths, April says, "Yes."

"That's it then. We ain't waitin'. We're goin' t' head t' th' hospital now."

"Call A.A.," April says. "Her number is by the phone in the living room."

"Will do," Tucker replies. "Stand up an' head toward th' front door. I'll git yore jacket."

Smiley is in the living room as April enters. "This is a momentous occasion, sweet April. All the pain you feel now will disappear like a summer dew under the bright sun. You'll hardly remember it. God bless you." He kisses her on top of the head.

As he's doing so Tucker is calling A.A. She hangs up and says, "She says she'll meet us there."

"Wait," April says. "What about Benjamin? Today's the day of the contest. He's counting on us to be there. What's he going to do?"

"I'll go down there before they go to school," Smiley says. "I'll explain it to him. I think he'll take it in stride. He's come a long, long way."

"But I want to hear him sing," April says.

Tucker folds her arms across her chest. "Well all right then. We'll just sit around here an' wait. Then we'll take y' to th' school an' y' can have th' baby right there in front of all them kids. They might even award you first prize."

"You're right," April says. "Let's go on to the hospital."

Chapter Sixty-two

Benjamin sways in his seat as the bus takes the curves on their crooked road, heading toward school. A mixture of emotions churns within him. Finding Smiley Carter at their front door this morning was a surprise. When he shared the news about April being in labor, Benjamin felt fearful for her. He'd had a dream during the night that April went to the hospital to have a baby but Mark O'Riley showed up and killed her.

Realizing that April wasn't going to be with him at the talent contest raised his anxiety considerably. He had counted on her giving him some final pointers and helping calm his nerves. Now he was on his own.

His right leg bounces up and down. *"Take long, slow breaths,"* he hears April saying to him. *"It's the key to helping you calm yourself."*

He takes a long breath as he counts slowly to seven. He holds the breath for a second then releases it on a slow count of seven. Twice more he performs the exercise.

The bus pulls to the front of the school and slows to a stop.

Benjamin grabs his backpack that contains his accompaniment CD's and heads to the school building.

Even though he sat through his first two classes, he would find it impossible to say what topics were discussed. All he could think about was the talent contest and April.

Just before time for the bell to ring ending second period, an announcement comes through the P.A. "All those who are participating in the talent contest today, please report now to the gym."

When Benjamin starts walking out of the classroom, his teacher says, "Benjamin, where are you going?"

395

"T-To the gym," he answers.

"You mean you're participating in the talent contest?" the teacher asks with a look of incredulity on her face.

"Yes," Benjamin says and continues out the door.

He's not sure what he expected to see when he got to the gym but it was certainly more than the dozen or so students who were gathered there. One of them notices Benjamin approaching and whispers something to the person beside them. They both look at Benjamin and cover their mouths to stifle a laugh.

After a couple minutes, Mr. Taylor, the band director, joins the students. He hands out pieces of paper. "Everyone needs to fill out this form with your name, what your talent is, and the name of the song you will be using or performing. If you are performing as a duo or more, put all your names on one form. All these will be placed in a box and drawn out randomly to decide the order in which you will perform."

The students quickly fill out the necessary form and place it in the box.

As Mr. Taylor starts drawing out the entries one at a time to announce the order of performance, Benjamin pays little to no attention to anyone else or what kind of act they will be. He just wants to know when he'll perform.

Mr. Taylor pulls out form after form from the box, until he finally pulls one out and says, "Benjamin Trevathan, you will be the last performer. The contest starts in fifteen minutes. You all may go wait in the office. A student will come get you when it's your turn. Good luck to all of you."

Once the contest begins and the other performers gradually leave the office as they are called, Benjamin is surprised that his nervousness steadily declines. *"Just focus on singing the song,"* he hears April admonish him. *"Not just the song on the paper, but the song in your heart. That's the one that people will respond to."*

Suddenly the door opens. "It's your turn," the student says.

Chapter Sixty-three

Tucker stands beside April's bed as she breathes rapidly, letting her squeeze her hand.

A.A., the midwife, is looking at a video monitor as she takes an ultrasound of the baby. "That's what I thought," she says.

Through gritted teeth April says, "What's wrong?"

"Two weeks ago your baby got turned in the right direction, but right now he's back in the breech position."

April's contraction eases its grip on her and she lies back on her pillow.

Tucker wipes the sweat from April's face. "That's why this is takin' so long, ain't it?" she asks A.A..

"What are we going to do?" April asks.

"What I'm concerned about is that the baby's heart rate is dropping. I was hoping you could go ahead and deliver, but I'm now thinking we need to do a cesarean."

April sits back up as another contraction hits her. As it increases in intensity, she breathes harder. Suddenly she cries out. "Something just happened!"

"What do you mean?" A.A. asks.

"I feel like something just gave way or ripped. Something deep inside."

A.A. looks at her nurse. "Call Dr. Franklin and tell him to meet us in the O.R. stat. Get someone in here to help me roll her into the O.R."

The nurse hurries out of the birthing room.

Tucker grabs A.A.'s arm. "What's goin' on?"

"I think her uterus has ruptured. We've got to do surgery or we could lose them both."

A man in scrubs comes in and unlocks the wheels on April's bed.

"Tucker, I'm scared," April says.

Tucker looks at April's face as it pales and at the serious, no nonsense expression on A.A.'s face as April is being rolled out of the room. "Don't you worry none. You're in good hands. God's going t' take care of all of you."

The nurse meets them in the hallway. "Dr. Franklin is on his way."

A.A. looks at the monitors rolling beside them. "Blood pressure is dropping. Get me two units of blood," she says as her voice rises in both pitch and volume.

They turn a corner where a short hallway leads to a double door with a "No Admittance" sign.

Without stopping, A.A. says to Tucker, "This is as far as you can go. We'll keep you updated as best we can."

With her eyes brimming with tears, Tucker says, "Please, please, y' have t' save m' April an' her baby."

The midwife disappears through the door without answering.

As the doors close, Tucker feels as if they are squeezing her heart. She bends double at the sharp pain. Slowly she stands straight. She looks up at the ceiling and yells, "Lord, please don't take my baby!"

Chapter Sixty-four

As Benjamin walks into the gymnasium there is a low murmur of voices following the last contestant. But as more of the students notice who is walking to the middle of the floor, some are pointing and talking behind their hands to their neighbor. A few people laugh, which acts as an accelerant and quickly more people begin to laugh. Someone calls out, "Stutterboy!" which produces raucous laughter.

Mr. Clelland strides to the middle of the floor and quiets the entire assembly with his icy stare. He takes the microphone off its stand and says, "Ladies and gentlemen, you are expected to be respectful to all the contestants. If you choose not to be, then you and I will have to have a conversation in my office. Am I understood?"

The silence in the cavernous gym is deafening in reply. Only an occasional squeak from the wooden bleachers can be heard.

Satisfied with his results, Mr. Clelland puts the microphone back in place. He smiles at Benjamin and says, "Good luck."

Benjamin nods at the person operating the sound system, signaling for him to start the accompaniment CD. The music flows out of the speakers and washes across the audience. Benjamin scans the audience and spies Cassie sitting at one end of the gym on the bottom of the bleachers with a group of her friends. She smiles at him and gives a small wave of her hand.

Benjamin steps closer to the mic and starts singing, "In the Ghetto."

As the last echoing notes of the song fade, everyone sits in stunned silence. Many are wide-eyed with amazement while others stare with their mouths open. After several seconds one person can be heard clapping slowly.

Benjamin turns to see Cassie standing, clapping, and looking at him with admiration.

Cassie's cue seems to be what everyone is waiting for. Practically in unison, the entire audience stands and begins applauding. The applause grows louder and louder, whistles are heard, and several shouts of "Yeah!" "Awesome!" "Good job!" can be heard.

As the cheers begin to die down three loud "pops" come from the end of the gym where Cassie is sitting. Then there are screams and a commotion on the bleachers.

Benjamin looks and sees Mark O'Riley holding Cassie in front of him with a gun to her head.

Students are streaming off the risers, stumbling and falling, stepping on each other in their panic to get away.

Pushing Cassie along in front of him, Mark walks toward Benjamin. "You think you're really something don't you!" he yells. "Well you're not. You're a fat, ugly, retarded idiot. And you see her?" He nods at Cassie. "You'll never have her. If I can't have her, no one's going to have her."

Cassie's face is a mask of terror.

Benjamin starts walking toward them.

"Stop right there!" Mark says. He presses the barrel of the pistol against Cassie's temple. "I'll kill her right now."

Benjamin never slows his pace.

When he's twenty feet away from them, Mark points the gun at Benjamin. "So you want it? Is that what you want me to do? I'll shoot you. Stop right there or I'll shoot you."

Benjamin is now ten feet from him.

Suddenly Mark fires at him.

More screams erupt from the students who have yet to leave.

Benjamin feels a searing pain in his right shoulder. He looks down at it and sees a small hole in his shirt. He feels the warmth of his blood as it runs down his arm and drips off his fingers. Looking back at Cassie and Mark, he continues toward them.

When Benjamin is five feet from them, Mark fires two more times.

This time Benjamin feels like he's been hit in the chest with a baseball bat. He lunges forward, knocking Cassie out of Mark's grasp, and grabs the lapels of Mark's black jacket. He drags him to the floor and falls on top of him.

Chapter Sixty-five

Following the hearse, Tucker turns into Sunset Cemetery and drives slowly past the ancient cedar trees that have guarded the entrance for over a hundred years. Aging grave markers, both large and small, give way to more modern ones as they proceed to the newer sections of the cemetery.

In hoarse tones, Smiley says, "It just doesn't seem possible."

Tucker does not reply. There is nothing to add.

The hearse comes to a stop in front of the green funeral tent. A mound of fresh earth is covered by green outdoor carpet.

As Tucker stops, she looks in her rearview mirror to see the ambulance coming to a stop behind her. She says, "Come on. Let's go."

Wiping his eyes with his bandanna, Smiley exits the truck. He and Tucker walk back to the ambulance as two attendants are opening its back door.

Tucker looks inside and sees April in a wheelchair holding her baby. "Are you two okay?" she asks.

April's pale cheeks are streaked red from her stinging tears. She nods. "He didn't even wake up," she says, looking at her baby.

One of the attendants fastens a ramp in place as the other moves to the back of the wheelchair. They work in tandem to help ease April out of the ambulance.

April places her hand on one of them. "Walter, I really appreciate you all doing this for me. It's the only way the doctor would allow me to attend the service."

The young man smiles at her. "No problem. Anything for an old classmate."

"Just be sure th' bill fer this gits sent t' me," Tucker says.

"Yes ma'am," the other man says.

One of the doors of the hearse opens and Preacher steps out. He turns back to help Joyce, Alexander and Maria out. The funeral director steps out from under the tent and escorts them to their places. Tucker, Smiley, April, and her baby, join them.

As they are sitting down, Cassie appears at the edge of the tent, flanked by her mom and dad who have their arms linked behind her back. The Kleenex in her hand has black smudges on it from her tear-smeared eye makeup.

Everyone looks up to see the casket being carried solemnly by Mr. Clelland, the band director, two coaches from the high school, and Blake Barker.

Cassie stifles a cry and buries her face in her mother's chest.

Once the casket is in place the pall bearers remove the flowers from the lapels of their jackets and place them on top of the casket. They then move to the edge of the tent.

Preacher takes this as his cue and stands up and faces everyone. He opens his Bible and reads, "Greater love has no man than this: to lay down one's life for one's friends." Closing the Bible, he says, "Those are the words of Christ. His measure of the depth of a person's love is this, to lay down your life for a friend. Many of us have friends, but would we really be willing to give our life for them? I'm afraid I might not measure up. I might be too selfish. But not Benjamin Trevathan. No sir, not him. If I'm any judge of a person's character, I'd say that Benjamin never thought of putting himself first, of being selfish. That makes him a rare find. Those who took the time to know him, I mean to really know him, like some of you did, you know exactly what I'm talking about. Have you ever met anyone like Benjamin?"

Preacher pauses for effect as he looks at those gathered. "He's the unlikeliest of heroes. When we conjure up an image of a hero, he is likely to be tall, muscular, and good looking. Quite honestly, Benjamin was none of those. At least not on the outside. On the inside, however, he stood head and shoulders above all of us when it came to character and purity of motive. And he may not have had muscles that rippled or six-pack abs, but he possessed a strength that helped him weather the storms of taunts and ridicule that would have destroyed a lesser boy. But most of all Benjamin was beautiful. He was beautiful because of his childlike innocence and the purity of his heart. Let's rejoice that we were blessed to have known such a person."

Smiley gives a resounding, "Amen!"

Preacher looks at Joyce. "But we are left with the question, why? Why did this have to happen? Where is God in all of this? If Benjamin was so special, why did God allow this to happen? We want answers. But not just any answers. We want answers that make sense to us, answers that allow us to say to ourselves, 'Oh now I see. That makes sense. That's okay.'

"I've been there. I've asked those questions on more than one occasion. After wrestling with them through many sleepless nights here's what I've decided: I don't have to know the *why* of a thing. The truth is, if I could understand everything that happened on this old earth, I would have the mind of God. And let me assure you I don't.

"So I say to all of you, we are going to be sad because of the loss of a friend, or a brother, or a son. However, let's also remember with fondness this young man's life. Let it be an inspiration to all of us and hopefully to our entire community. The world needs more Benjamins."

Preacher pauses and looks at April. "April would like to say a few words."

Everyone turns and looks at her. Holding her son to her chest, she leans forward and slowly stands up.

"April," Tucker says, reaching for her. "You don't need to be standing."

"I will stand to do this," April says. She stands facing the casket. "I never met anyone like Benjamin. And when I decided to help him with his stuttering, I could never have imagined how much I would grow to admire him. He's one of the most courageous people I've known."

A tiny whimpering sound comes from the bundle in her arms. April kisses her son and says, "Shhhh, go back to sleep."

April turns slowly to face everyone. "For months now all I've heard is, 'What are you going to name your baby?' And for months I didn't say because I wasn't sure. About a month ago I finally knew for certain what I would name him. But I wanted to keep it a secret until he was born. I wish now that I hadn't. My son's name is Amazing Benjamin Tucker."

April's announcement produces smiles and tears from all those gathered under and around the tent. She turns and sits back down in the wheelchair. "You hear that?" she whispers to her son. "You are Amazing Benjamin Tucker."

THE END

Acknowledgements

A big thank you to Tina, Bonnie, and Katy for their work in helping me edit my manuscript.

All of you Tucker fans are absolutely the best! Thank you for loving my characters and books and asking for more.

About the Author

David Johnson has worked in the helping professions for over thirty-five years. He is a licensed marriage and family therapist with a master's degree in social work and over a decade of experience as a minister.

David maintains an active blog at www.thefrontwindow.wordpress.com and is on Facebook https://www.facebook.com/david.johnson.author. When he's not writing, he is likely making music as the conductor of the David Johnson Chorus.

Printed in Great Britain
by Amazon